Readers love Mason Thomas

"Please just trust me when I say this writing is a joy with which to spend your precious reading hours. The dialogue, the descriptions, the unexpected twists and turns, and revelations. Every story should be so lucky as to be told like this."
—Prism Book Alliance

"*Lord Mouse* was a welcome surprise and I found myself appreciating nearly every minute of the book."
—Joyfully Jay

"This was one hell of a story that kept me glued to the page with excitement and want."
—Boy meets Boy Reviews

"The characters were intriguing and engaging. The plot was awesome as it draws the reader deeper into the mysteries throughout. Twists and turns and many close calls...left me on the edge of my seat. Great read."
—Just Love: Queer Book Reviews

"This book was fantastic! It's the type of book that makes you want to pick up a sword and join the battle."
--It's About the Book

By Mason Thomas

The Witchstone Amulet

LORDS OF DAVENIA
Lord Mouse
The Shadow Mark
Mouse: Scoundrel at Large
Three Tales

This is a work of fiction. Names, characters, places, and incidents either are the product of author imagination or are used fictitiously, and any resemblance to actual persons, living or dead, business establishments, events, or locales is entirely coincidental.

The Witchstone Amulet
© 2019 Mason Thomas
ISBN: 979-8-9856701-3-4

Original Cover Art © 2019 Tiferet Design
Cover Redesign: © 2023 Tim Barber DissectDesigns.com
Cover content is for illustrative purposes only and any person depicted on the cover is a model.

All rights reserved. This book is licensed to the original purchaser only. Duplication or distribution via any means is illegal and a violation of international copyright law, subject to criminal prosecution and upon conviction, fines, and/or imprisonment. Any eBook format cannot be legally loaned or given to others. No part of this book may be reproduced or transmitted in any form or by any means, electronic or mechanical, including photocopying, recording, or by any information storage and retrieval system, without the written permission of the author, except where permitted by law. To request permission and all other inquiries, contact Mason Thomas at masonthomas999@gmai.com.

Printed in the United States of America

For my dad
The first great storyteller in my life

THE WITCHSTONE AMULET

MASON THOMAS

1

HUNTER WORE his black eye like a tiara at the ball.

He paraded around O'Malley's Pub, looping through the thickening crowd to make sure everyone saw it, an absurd grin on his face. The elbow that had caused it had come out of nowhere while he was crouched over in a ruck. Probably intentional, but he didn't care. It was his first visible in-match injury since joining the squad, and he was going to revel in it.

And it was destined to be spectacular. Purple already swooped under his eye the length of his cheekbone. The skin was tender, and his eye was swelling shut. Tomorrow he'd look like Quasimodo and only be able see out one eye. But he sure as shit wasn't going to let that stop him tonight.

Team members whooped and hollered as he passed, lifting their glasses to him. A few clapped him on the shoulder. "Hey Pickles," someone called out. "You use that face to stop a train?" Everyone laughed—and Hunter laughed along with them, his grin spreading wider. It made the side of his face sting, but he didn't care.

He'd crossed some invisible line. He was no longer just someone on the team—he was a squadmate now. He was one of them.

O'Malley's was in full swing. Families and friends had filtered in, along with a spattering of spectators, and filled the pub to the point of splitting like an overinflated ball. Far too crowded for his liking, but he was feeling good and had poured enough drink in him to make it tolerable. He'd duck outside for a minute if it got too much. Classic rock pounded out of the speakers, and the crowd yelled over the music. The two squads—the Lions and the Griffons—seized the main room like prisoners that had taken over the cellblock. A few hours ago, they had tried to bludgeon each other on the pitch; now they hung drunkenly on each other as if they'd been comrades for years.

The rugby widows, wives and girlfriends who were forgotten for the time being, stayed to the sidelines in little pods, clear of all the postcarnage bonding. They shook their heads and laughed at the nonsense. Their time would come later.

Hunter worked his way past a cluster from the Griffons, who shouted out bawdy songs from the corners complete with crude choreography. Another group toward the back had their shirtsleeves and pant legs pulled back to compare scars and tattoos. A barback scurried among the chaos, loading empty pints onto a tray, while the frantic bartenders scrambled to fill more.

Billy the Hobbit squirmed his way past Hunter, holding his beer over the heads of the crowd. Like all good scrum halves, he was the smallest on the squad, barely five and a half feet tall. Fast, tough, and built solid. And fucking adorable.

He looked up at Hunter with his bright green eyes as he shouldered his way by. "Zulu dance in about twenty minutes. We're going to have to clear a path somehow."

The traditional naked run for first-time scorers was supposed to be done out on the pitch, but city ordinances wouldn't allow it anymore, so it got moved inside the host bar. In some ways it was worse—people tended to slap asses as they ran by or splash beer on them. "Good luck with that," Hunter said.

"No shit, right? Nice shiner, by the way, Pickles," Billy added with a smile as he wedged deeper into the crowd.

Hunter raised his glass. "Thanks, Bilbo."

He circled back around to his spot at the end of the bar. It was out of the traffic flow and afforded him a little more breathing room. Resting one asscheek on a stool as if unwilling to commit to standing or sitting, he leaned an elbow against the sticky wooden surface. He drained the last of his beer, thumped the glass onto the bar, and lifted his chin to the bartender to get him another.

"That one's on me," someone called from behind.

Hunter rotated about on the stool. A tank of a man with a closely cropped beard gently guided nearby people aside to make room for him. He was a forward from the opposing team. A lock. Number four. He sidled up to the bar and leaned in, lifting his own empty glass to the bartender. He dropped a twenty on the counter and set the empty glass on top of it.

"You win the day for the best trophy," he said. His voice was deep, like a radio broadcaster's, and it resonated over the beat of the music.

Hunter smirked and touched the puffy skin beneath his eye. "Most would call it an improvement."

"Doubt that. Starting to hurt yet?"

"Not really," he said.

"Liar," the man laughed.

The bartender set the two full pints of amber on the counter between them. Hunter picked his up and held it into the air a moment. "This will help," he replied. "Thanks."

"No problem," the man said with a broad grin. He had perfect teeth and, despite his size, a very boyish look when he smiled. "Least I can do for the man of the match."

"Not official yet."

"It will be. You played like a fucking beast today."

Hunter felt his face redden. Shit, was he fucking

blushing? The man was rugged and beautiful, and that rich voice of his was making his palms sweat. And he was standing very close to Hunter. If he didn't know better, Hunter would have sworn he was flirting.

"You're Hunter, right?"

"That's me."

"Name's Darren." He held out his hand and Hunter took it in his own. Darren's grip was strong. "You're a damn good player."

Not sure how to react, he settled on a noncommittal shrug. "Nah. Just a fat bloke good at getting into people's way."

"Fat?" Darren's eyes dropped a moment to Hunter's torso, and his brow lifted. "That's rich. I could learn a lot from you. How long have you been playing?"

Hunter pulled his gaze away from Darren's brown eyes. "Most of my life. My dad was from Cardiff. Forced a ball in my hand the moment I could stand on my own."

"Explains a lot. All the best players here either got a young start because their dad played, or they're transports themselves."

Hunter smiled. "Tried football for a while. Mostly because I was pissed at the old fucker and wanted nothing to do with anything that reminded me of him. But the slow pace about killed me. My dad wasn't right about a lot of things, but he was right about rugby. I joined a club after college to get back into it."

"The Dragons, right?"

Hunter's stomach flipped. So… he knew about that, did he?

"Yep," he replied in slightly forced casual tone. "Played with them for more than four years." Hunter could hear the nervousness in his own voice.

Darren's expression changed, lost some of its cheerfulness. "I'm sorry," he said. "Shit, I guess I sounded like a crazy stalker just then. Some of my squad was just talking about you earlier, is all, and…."

Hunter made a low chuckle in his throat, but there was little humor in it. "No doubt."

"No, it wasn't like that, really. Maybe a stereotypical comment or two from the assholes, but most were just curious about it. Really." Darren paused, looking down into his beer. He took a gulp from the pint and used his thumb and forefinger to wipe droplets from his full lips. "So, what was it like? You know, playing on an all-gay team?"

Hunter smiled at him.

"Fun," he replied with a shrug. "Sometimes *really* fun," he added with a lift of his eyes to the ceiling. "Still friends with most of them. But… the skill set, you know? Some had only picked up a rugby ball for the first time when they joined the squad. And there were different levels of commitment. Not that there's anything wrong with that, but sometimes it felt more social than competitive. After a while I guess I just needed more."

"So, from that to the toughest fuckers in Chicago. Maybe even in the Midwest." Darren shook his head. "Quite the leap."

Hunter shrugged.

"Don't even try to act modest." Darren grinned at him. "I tried out for the Lions last year. Didn't make it past the first round."

"I promised to make everyone scones each time we met for practice."

"You're ridiculous." Darren gave Hunter a playful shove on the shoulder.

"You've not tried my poppy seed scones. They've opened many doors."

Darren took a drink but kept his eye on Hunter over the top of the glass. "Been watching you with them tonight. Your team. You can tell they accept you."

"Wasn't always like that."

His skill had gotten him on the squad, but for a long time he did little other than wear the uniform. No one was openly hostile to him—namely because Coach Titan made it clear he would have none of it—but for a long time, there was this impassible chasm between him and others. Few circles were tighter than a team of rugby players, and he always knew it would take time to prove himself. But being the only out gay player made it all the more difficult to bridge the gap.

"Well, you'd never know it today," Darren said. "I envy that. What you have is more rare than I think you realize." Hunter could hear a vein of regret in his voice.

Hunter happened to look out past Darren's shoulder. Across the bar, someone leaned against the far wall, watching him. The figure's stony face was shadowed beneath the hood of a brown woolen coat. No… not a coat. It was more of cape—which was an odd choice to wear out to a bar. But candlelight from a nearby high-top table glinted off eyes that stared at Hunter with a singular intensity. The man was smallish—like a scrum half, however Hunter had never seen him on any squad.

The hard stare sent shivers chasing down Hunter's shoulders and back.

Darren must have noticed his attention shift. He straightened, pulling his elbow off the bar. "Well, I just wanted to come by and, you know, say hey."

"No, I'm glad you did," Hunter said quickly. He reached out and touched Darren's forearm. Darren stiffened, and his eyes darted around. Hunter, reminded of where they were, slipped his hand back. "Your squad doesn't know?"

"Some suspect, I think, but no." His expression turned pensive. Hunter regretted bringing it up. "Maybe it would have been easier if they'd known from the beginning, like you. I don't know. But at the time I wasn't ready for that."

"Sure, I get that." Hunter looked out across the bar again. The hooded guy had moved, but his gaze was still locked in his direction. Weird. He looked at Hunter like he either wanted to fuck him or kill him.

An obsessed rugby fan? They were out there, he knew.

Something about the gladiatorial nature of the game seemed to attract a certain brand of fanaticism. Other guys on the squad had picked up the occasional stalker, but he'd been lucky so far.

Hunter turned his attention back to Darren. "It's not too late, you know. May be bumpy for a while, but they'll come around."

"Not so sure about that." Darren shrugged. "Besides, it's none of their business, right?"

"Sure," Hunter replied, not knowing what else to say.

"Pickles!" Samson, the fly half, was suddenly at his right shoulder. "Quit flirtin' and help out. We need your bulk and ugly face to start clearing a way for the zulu." He raked his eyes over Darren briefly before looking back at Hunter, eyes narrowed in scorn. "Seriously, bro," he said, "this dude's clearly straight. Give it up."

Samson disappeared into the crowd again. Darren and Hunter looked at each other and chuckled.

"Looks like I'm going to be busy a while," Hunter said.

"Why do they call you Pickles?"

"Long story. Interested in coffee sometime? Can I give you my number?" He wasn't sure about going out with someone so deep in the closet. He lived his own life open and unapologetic. But Darren had a kind, boyish face that Hunter found magnetic, and he sure filled out that T-shirt well....

"Way ahead of ya." Darren looked sheepish as he slid a folded napkin across the bar counter. "I took the liberty. Give me a call?"

Hunter couldn't help but smile. He took the napkin, stood from the stool, and slipped it into the back pocket of his jeans. "I will." He straightened out his T-shirt and picked up his beer. "All right. Duty calls. Thanks again for the beer."

Darren smiled back at him. A warm, genuine smile. His cheeks were colored just above the line of his beard. Holy shit, he did have the sweetest little smile. If they were anywhere else, Hunter would have leaned over and kissed those full lips of his—and he was just about drunk enough to do it anyway.

"Anytime," Darren said. "Make sure you take care of the eye later. You should probably ice it."

"And ruin all this beautiful color? No fucking way!"

Hunter started to push his way back into the crowd, then stopped. What the fuck, he told himself. How often was he going to be man of the match? He made an impish grin back over his shoulder.

"Planning on sticking around?"

Darren's smile widened. "I've got nothing going on."

"Keep your docket clear," Hunter said. "This shouldn't take too long."

Before he launched into the churning crowd once more, he glanced around for the weird guy in the cape. Nothing. Hunter scanned the sea of heads. He didn't spot him anywhere.

Thank God. The guy gave him the creeps.

2

HUNTER FUMBLED with his key, trying to get the end of it lined up with the keyhole. He must have seemed drunk off his ass, but it was mostly nerves. This wasn't like him. All he could think about was what his apartment must look like. He certainly hadn't planned on entertaining.

"You all right there, chief?" Darren said with a low chuckle. He seemed more comfortable with this sort of thing. More comfortable than Hunter was, certainly.

"Sorry."

Wrong key, Hunter realized with a groan. He riffled through the ring again, lifting his hands into the light. He located the right key and breathed a sigh of relief as it slid into the lock. It turned around twice before the mechanism inside clicked and the bolt slid aside. He picked up his kit, shouldered open the door, and stumbled inside. Darren followed on his heels.

They both dropped their heavy kits onto the floor with a thump. Hunter reached for the light switch, but Darren snagged a thick arm around Hunter's waist before he could reach it and pulled him in closer with a rough jerk. Without warning, Darren's mouth was pressed against his. Hard. Too hard. His tongue thrust inside Hunter's mouth and was wildly exploring like a squid's tentacle searching for food under a rock.

A hand slid up under Hunter's T-shirt to explore the contours of Hunter's back. A few of Darren's fingers were bound with white first-aid tape, and the stiff edge scraped against Hunter's skin. Hunter would have marks there tomorrow. Which meant awkward questions in the locker room after practice. Darren's other hand dropped to cup Hunter's ass.

Hunter gently pulled himself off Darren's face and smiled at him. "Let me get the door. I, uh, don't want my cat to get out."

Darren pulled back. "You have a cat?" He looked around the room with part interest and part concern. Maybe he was allergic.

He didn't, but it was the only thing he could think of in the moment. The last thing he needed was one of the neighbors walking by his open door and seeing Darren trying to eat off his face like this was the start of a zombie apocalypse.

"She's shy," Hunter said, slipping out of his bear grip. He tugged the hem of his T-shirt back below the belt line. "You probably won't ever see her."

If this went anywhere, he'd have to fess up about not owning a cat or make up a new lie about what happened to it. His mind was already racing to come up with plausible scenarios. She ran away. Had to give it up. It died unexpectedly. Or he could actually get a cat. He'd always wanted a pet. He'd be home more now, at least....

He closed his eyes and sighed. What was he doing? He knew exactly what *this* was. After tonight, Darren would ghost him. He was too anxious about getting exposed to his teammates. Hunter would never see him again.

Did that bother him? He wasn't sure yet.

"I'm surprised you're single," Darren said. "To be honest."

Hunter shrugged as he closed the door. How was he supposed to respond to that? That the one-on-one thing really wasn't his thing? He was a pack animal by nature and knew how to negotiate a group, but seemed to fumble when faced with the dynamics of two. It always felt awkward. Pretend. He never knew what to talk about, so he talked about what he knew, and guys wanted to hear about a relationship with thirty other guys only so much. Most came to him with a preconceived idea of what it would be like to date a rugby player—and left disappointed. They expected him to be something he wasn't.

A few stuck around, willing to accept the time he doled out. But Hunter always caught himself choosing to spend more and more time with the squad until the guy stopped coming around.

"Ask anyone who knows me. They aren't surprised," he said, turning the deadbolt into place. The room fell into a thicker darkness without the light from the hallway. The only light now came from the orange streetlight outside the window.

"You always make jokes when you're nervous?"

"Who says I'm nervous? I'm the picture of self-possession."

"Right." Darren had drifted over to the collection of pictures that hung on the wall by the window. Amber light from the street angled across the small collection of frames.

"Your mom?" he asked. He swayed a little as he leaned in, betraying that he was drunker than he was letting on. Hunter nodded, but Darren probably couldn't see it. "You two seem real close." Something about the way he said it sounded like an accusation.

"You could say that," Hunter said.

"No dad in any of these. You mentioned him back at the bar. Not close I take it?"

"He left when I was a kid. Haven't heard from him since."

"Shit. Sorry. Your mom is beautiful. I can see where you get your looks." He flashed a smile at Hunter. "She live here in Chicago?"

"She died last year."

"Fuck. Dude, I'm sorry. I keep putting my foot in it tonight, don't I?"

"It's all good." He tried to sound nonchalant, but suddenly Darren felt like an intruder. More reservations were worming into his brain. This wasn't going anywhere, so what was the point? A pint of ice cream on the couch with an old rerun would be better company right now.

"Big place. Live alone?" Darren seemed quick to change the subject. He stepped away from the pictures as if they were to blame for the sudden awkward silence that landed in the room.

"Not big on feeling confined."

"Ironic. For a guy that spends his time locked in a scrum."

Darren was right, he supposed. It was ironic. But there was something different about a scrum. He was surrounded by his squad, his pack. People he trusted. When the ref yelled "engage" and everyone started pushing, he was part of something larger, part of something powerful. "Can I get you something to drink? A beer?"

"Yeah, sure."

Hunter crossed the room toward the light switch on the opposite wall. He tripped over something in the middle of the floor and stumbled. What the hell had he left there?

He thumbed the switch and warm light flooded the room. Hunter froze. Darren's eyes shifted back and forth to take in the scene.

The apartment had been ransacked. Overturned furniture. The contents of every drawer dumped onto the floor. Someone had rummaged through the entirety of his belongings and left them in a pile in his living room.

"Dude… I think you've been robbed," Darren said.

He looked around in disbelief, the shock sinking deeper. *No, I always live like this*, Hunter thought dourly. His gut soured with the thought of someone rummaging through his space. He spun about, making a quick inventory of all the things of value that were probably gone, lost to the fuckers that had done this.

But his large TV still hung from the wall. The PlayStation was still underneath it in the cabinet. Even his laptop was sitting on the coffee table right where he'd left it.

If not the electronics, what were the thieves searching for? He had no cash in the apartment. No real valuables.

Had they broken into the wrong apartment?

Hunter circled around the debris.

"Careful," Darren said. He pointed to the floor by his feet. Wineglasses were scattered around, most of them broken or cracked. "You want me to call the police?"

Hunter nodded. "Yeah. That'd be great." His mouth was dry, and his body felt numb. He surveyed the chaos, searching for something that was missing, but his mind couldn't pinpoint anything that should be there that wasn't. Everything of value was still there, only tossed aside as if unimportant. It didn't make sense.

He stepped into the kitchen. Every cabinet door was spread wide, every drawer pulled out. And all the contents had been dumped unceremoniously onto the hardwood floor. Plates, utensils, cookware. Hunter took ginger steps through the debris and checked the back entrance—chained and locked.

How had the thieves even gotten in?

Darren, standing at the threshold of the kitchen, dug his phone from his back pocket and tapped at it with his forefinger.

Hunter drifted down the short hallway to his bedroom, his mind in a weird disconnected fog. The door to the bedroom was ajar. Distantly, he could hear Darren on his phone talking as Hunter swept the door aside with his arm and stepped inside. Every drawer of his dresser had been pulled out and the contents dumped onto the bed or the floor. Every garment he owned was ripped from its hanger and tossed from the closet.

His skin crawled with the idea that some unknown creep was in there. On the bed, casually dispersed among the clothes, was a tube of lube and a flesh-colored silicone cock he kept in his bedside drawer. His mouth tightened. He didn't know why, but knowing some thief had handled them felt humiliating. It made his insides twist.

They'd be thrown in the garbage now.

He circled around the room, again searching for something—anything—that was missing. The small television on the dresser was still there. His guitar rested on the stand in the corner. It sat askew on its stand—clearly the thief had picked it up to examine and put it down again.

He scanned the floor, kicking aside clothes to see what was beneath them.

He spotted the box sticking out from under the bed and his heart dropped into his stomach.

The small red-painted wooden box, decorated with scrolling symbols, had belonged to his mother. In her will, she had stipulated he was to cherish it and keep it and its contents safe. It was important, she'd said. She wouldn't say why. But it was more important than he could ever imagine.

It was the only thing of hers he still possessed.

The wooden box had a simple latch on the front and two iron hinges on the back. The box was on its side, open, with the red velvet lining hanging out. It was empty.

"The police are on their way," Darren called from the other room.

"Okay," he managed to call back.

Maybe it had just fallen out. Maybe it was on the floor somewhere, underneath all the layers of clothes. He'd find it, he told himself. It was still there.

He started to pull up clothes and toss them onto the bed, slowly at first, forcing himself to maintain calm. Each time he exposed a portion of the floor, expecting to find it—but nothing was there. He grew more frantic. He got down on his knees and dug under the bed. Still nothing.

His heart raced with near panic. He tried to tamp it down, not wanting to accept the truth that it was gone, but he was losing the battle.

The box had been kept in the closet up on the shelf. Maybe it was there. It could have possibly fallen from the box when the thief grabbed it. He stomped across the room to the closet door, kicking aside the debris.

He grabbed the knob and gave it a turn.

The door burst open, crashing into him as the man in black exploded from the closet. Hunter flailed as he stumbled backward. A shirt slipped under his heel on the hardwood floor, and he fell against the side of his bed. The man bolted from the room.

Hunter recognized him immediately. The strange little man from the bar. And in that split second, Hunter's attention zeroed in on the man's hand. Something was clenched inside his fingers.

His mother's broach.

Shouting to Darren, he scrambled to his feet. He dashed out into the hallway, pinballing against the wall, knocking picture frames to the floor, and gave chase. In the dining room, Darren sat on his ass, rubbing at his cheek, and the door to the apartment was wide open.

"Fuck," Hunter growled, and hit the stairwell at full speed. He leaped down the stairs, two or three at a time.

Before Hunter was even past the second floor, he heard the familiar squeak of the front entry door. The thief was already out of the building. The little fucker was fast.

Thick and bulky, Hunter wasn't built for speed. He was losing ground. Desperate, he leaped the whole length of stairs to the next landing below. His momentum crashed him into the wall. He righted himself quickly and renewed his pursuit.

As he blasted out of the front door, he looked left and right for a sign of the thief. He caught sight of him slipping into the gangway between two buildings about half a block down. Hunter leaped into a sprint again, pumping his arms to get his sizable bulk moving faster. As Hunter entered the gangway, the thief was at the alley and veered left. Hunter was gaining some—but he wouldn't be able to maintain this pace long. Already, his legs were tightening.

Only one yellow streetlamp lit the narrow alleyway. The rest was shrouded in the night. Hunter could just make out the dark form sprinting in the distance. His footfalls echoed off the brick of the buildings.

As Hunter reached the alley behind his building, the thief made a sharp right and disappeared down another narrow alleyway.

Hunter had him. It was a dead end, ending behind a large condo building. The thief was cornered. Hunter drove himself harder, ignoring the stabbing pain in his side. As he rounded the corner, the thief was running at full speed directly toward the garage doors that lined the length of the first floor.

What was he doing?

The thief pulled something out from under his strange hooded cape. It was too dark, and Hunter was too far away for him to tell what it was. The man cocked back his arm and chucked it at the wide garage door. Hunter's first thought was that it was his mother's broach, that he was getting rid of any evidence. But no…. Hunter could see something dark and round sail through the air. It struck the garage door in the center.

The air around the impact seemed to ripple outward like water, a dark and disturbing undulating wave. Lightless energy crackled around him, and the hair on his arms lifted and his skin prickled. Then a wall of force nearly brought him to a halt. He staggered to keep his feet, and when he looked again, a perfectly round section of the door was no longer there. It was simply gone.

Hunter squeezed his eyes shut in disbelief. When he opened them again, the hole was still there. The center of it was moving, swirling, like a maelstrom of storm clouds.

The thief made one quick glance behind him, picked up speed, and ran straight for it.

Hunter couldn't believe what he was witnessing—surely this was a strange optical illusion. The thief showed no sign of slowing down as he ran for the black swirling hole. When Hunter thought he was going to run directly into the garage door, the thief sprang, lifting one leg up like a track runner clearing a hurdle.

And he was gone.

Stunned in disbelief, Hunter lost some of his speed. How was that even possible?

Then he realized the black circle was starting to shrink.

No. Whatever was happening, the thief wasn't going to get away from him that easily. He broke into a sprint again, kicking his legs as hard and fast as they would carry him, ignoring the burning in his lungs and the sharp pain in his side.

By the time he reached the garage door, the circle had shrunk by half. It was barely wider than his shoulders. He dove for it, arms straight out in front of him.

He expected to hit the solid door, but instead felt extreme cold as his arms entered the blackness. When his head and body followed, he was consumed by a nothingness so complete he felt as if the world had disintegrated around him. His skin burned with sudden intense cold. He tried to pull air into his lungs, but there was nothing there. He panicked—tried to flail about, fight toward *something*, but he no longer had control of his body.

Then, his consciousness abandoned him.

3

HUNTER ROSE out of a dark fog to realize his face hurt. Specifically his cheek. Something hard and sharp bit into the skin. He pried his eyes open and peeled himself up.

Harsh sunlight stabbed through the slits, forcing his lids closed again.

Daylight? Some part of his muddled brain was troubled by that. It should be dark, but he wasn't certain why.

His first thought was he was at a match, that he'd had the wind knocked out of him after a hard tackle. Wouldn't be the first time he'd had his noggin rattled. But no, he didn't hear any of the sounds he expected—the referee's whistle, shouts from the crowd. He only heard the wind and the squawk of a strange bird some distance away.

He lifted his torso off the stony surface underneath him. Tiny rocks jabbed into the meat of his palm. He forced open his eyes again, squinting. Beneath him were old flagstone tiles, weathered and cracked. Sprigs of stringy grass sprouted from the seams between them. Overhead, a dome of unblemished azure.

The side of his face stung. He gingerly touched around

his eye. It was puffy. Tender. And his eye wouldn't open fully. The black eye.

Fragments of his memory started to reassemble, like he was taping a ripped photo back together. The match was over. He was drinking at the bar after. He'd then left the bar with… with….

Fuck, what was his name? They'd cabbed back to his apartment. And….

The break-in. The guy hiding in his closet. The chase down the alley. It was all piecing back together.

That had been nighttime. Ten o'clock at least. Now he could feel the sun warming his face above him, which put it at around noonish. How did he end up here, some twelve, fourteen hours later?

His head throbbed behind his eyes. He'd had a bit to drink, certainly, but not enough to experience a blackout. Had someone tampered with his drink? He felt rough all over—sore and stiff, like he'd been tackled hard by a cement truck, and felt oddly disconnected somehow. But not hungover.

As he pushed himself up and eased onto his knees, he dried his eyes with his T-shirt sleeve. His forearm brushed against his cheek and dislodged a tiny stone embedded there.

He was in the remains of an old stone building. Very old.

All that stood was a portion of a wall and the crook of one of its four corners. The rest had been reduced to a rocky foundation no higher than the grass around it. Whatever this place had once been, it had been abandoned for centuries.

The ancient building lay in the middle of a wide field that seemed to stretch for eternity in all directions. An ocean of yellow grasses surrounded him. The tasseled tops flowed as if an invisible giant raked his fingers across the top. With the sun overhead, figuring out one compass direction from another was futile. The land rose up into rolling yellow-green hills one direction. A heavy band of brown streaked across the horizon in another. A forest?

He knew of no place like this around Chicago. Ireland,

maybe. But not the Midwest.

What the hell was happening?

More memories percolated out of the fog in his head. The hole in the wall that the thief had jumped through. How he'd followed immediately behind him.

A sickly tightness bloomed in the pit of his gut, a wave of unease that threatened to inflate and consume him. This was all very wrong.

He clenched his fists and shoved the impulse to panic back down. *No*, he told himself. Something would explain all this. It had to.

He needed information. With a groan, he rose up. Every muscle complained and resisted him. He brushed off the dirt and pebbles from his jeans and T-shirt and shook more loose from his dark hair. His legs were wobbly, and it took a moment to trust he was stable enough before he swept the inner boundary of the ancient building. Tucked in the lee of the standing corner, he found the remains of small campfire. He lowered next to it, elbows on his thighs. Someone had spread out the coals. Hunter floated his hand over the small mound of charcoal chunks and gray ash. Cold.

His thief?

That didn't make any sense. He was less than a minute behind him.

He grunted and shook his head. Ridiculous. That bizarre hole in the wall hadn't brought him here—the idea of that was idiotic. Something else had. It didn't matter that the last thing he remembered was jumping through it. Somehow, the thief must have knocked him out, brought him to this place, and then abandoned him....

The sour ball of anxiety swelled more. That didn't add up either. And he knew it.

He needed answers. And he wasn't going to get them here.

With a hand cupped over his brow, he circled about and scanned the entire horizon. He couldn't just wander aimlessly across an unfamiliar countryside. He needed a direction. Some sign or indication that civilization was out there.

He spotted a thin tendril of gray in the distance, nearly indiscernible against the unspoiled azure of the afternoon sky. Smoke. He'd almost missed it. It originated somewhere beyond the next hill—how far, he couldn't tell. But that didn't matter. Smoke like that wasn't natural. It meant people. And if he could see it, that meant he was within walking distance.

So he started walking.

THE ROLLING countryside had an eerie, postapocalyptic isolation about it, as if no one else existed. He encountered no roads, no other buildings. Not a single jet stream cut across the sky. That in and of itself was disconcerting.

Again, he tamped down the compulsion to panic that, if left unchecked, he knew would overpower him. First, figure out what was going on, he told himself. Then decide if it was worth panicking over.

The afternoon slogged on as he marched in the direction of the twisting gray thread, which turned out to be farther than he originally estimated. Each time he crested a rise in the terrain, he expected to see the source, but it was always beyond the next one, and then the next. An unobstructed sun pressed down on him. Sweat cascaded down the center of his back, soaking through the fabric of his T-shirt, and his crotch and thighs were starting to chafe under his jeans. His mouth felt like he'd rinsed it out with sand.

It was the wrong temperature for a day in March, but he pushed that unsettling detail from his mind too. He pulled the T-shirt off over his head, wiped his brow with it, balled up in his hand, and then tugged it through a belt loop. At least he could work on getting his summer color back.

Around midafternoon, from the top of a high hill, he saw something different along the horizon. A tree line. The smoke rose from the canopy.

He was closer.

He quickened his pace, ignoring the raw chafing of his thighs. Yellow grasses gave way to red rock and bracken. Thorny branches scratched and poked at his skin as he negotiated his way through. The thicket transformed into a forest of twisting and misshapen trees.

He slowed, despite his burning need for answers. The terrain seemed in pain. Tortured. Each tree trunk reached out of the stony ground in a distorted mockery of what a tree should look like. Limbs writhed in frozen agony, the leaves more brown than green. He felt unwelcome here. Like an intruder. He was tempted to turn around and head back to the open fields. At least there it was warm and beautiful.

But something rose above the moan of the wind. Voices.

Some instinct told him to crouch low and hold very still with his breath locked in his lungs. The sound came from up ahead. Very close.

4

THE SOUNDS were guttural and savage, like someone clearing their throat and trying to form words at the same time. If it was a language, it was one he'd never heard before. He imagined it was how bears might sound if they could talk.

He crept forward, trying to avoid the fallen twigs littering the ground, but still each step made him cringe. He might as well stomp for all the good his attempt at stealth was doing. The wind shifted, and he could smell the smoke and hear the crackling of a fire too—but he saw nothing through the trees ahead of him.

He soon discovered why. As he inched closer, the ground ended at an abrupt rocky ledge. Hunter crawled on hands and knees to the edge and peered down over a steep drop-off.

The three ghastly misshapen creatures grunted and growled with each other around the roaring campfire. One paced about the small clearing casually swinging a crude club the size of Hunter's leg as if itching to bash something in, while the other two sat on the ground looking like lumpy clay sculptures only half formed. They resembled something human, but only in the sense they had two legs and two arms and walked erect. Their skin was a sickly gray-green and covered in scars, their limbs bulky with muscles that would make gym grunters weep with envy. Their heads were almost comically large and covered in coarse black hair. They had grotesque pointed ears, laden with rows of iron hoops from lobe to tip. Drool-covered tusks shot out from their lower jaws.

He couldn't breathe. His heart thumped like thunder and the world around him tilted dizzily. *Holy shit, I'm having a psychotic breakdown.* It was the only explanation. Creatures like this simply didn't exist. Which meant he had to be lost in some wild hallucination.

But did people actually having a psychotic break ever think that's what was happening to them?

Burlap sacks and wooden crates circled the periphery of the camp to form a makeshift border. One of the crates near the natural stone wall directly beneath Hunter was cracked open and the contents were spilled out onto the ground, a pile of medieval-looking weapons. Maces, flails, swords.

The creatures hadn't heard him approach. Thankfully. The last thing he needed was to gain their attention. With their battle scars and weapons assortment, friendly certainly wasn't a word he'd use to describe them. They fit in this ugly and unforgiving landscape as they grumbled and snarked at each other like bored Girl Scouts.

The question was could he sneak away now without being heard. He wasn't so sure. It was a wonder they couldn't already hear his pounding heart. And were there more of them? Would he haplessly stumble upon another group of them traipsing through this forest?

One of the seated creatures lifted to his feet. Hunter pushed himself lower to the ground, worried he'd been spotted, but the creature only stomped over to a woodpile to fetch more logs. But movement snagged his eye. Positioned behind where the creature was seated was a man, hogtied and gagged, squirming to get himself free.

The thief.

He thrashed against the ropes that bound his hands and ankles. The creatures gave him no notice, as if they'd forgotten he was there. Hunter's jaw clenched and his insides hardened. The little fucker had probably tried to steal from them too. Served him right. For a moment he was tempted to back away and let these creatures deal with him. But something in his gut made him stay put.

The conversation between the creatures seemed to turn. Their disagreement intensified. They barked at each other louder, and the creature swinging the club stopped his pacing, spat on the ground, and snarled something to his comrades. Even though Hunter couldn't understand the words, the animosity behind them was clear, and it sent chills racing over Hunter's skin. The creature looked over at the thief. He thrust the club to the ground with an air of decisiveness and pulled a long knife from his belt.

That needed no translation.

The thief must have understood what was about to happen. His struggles against his bindings intensified to frantic. The creature's mouth broke into a yellow grin as it stomped toward him. The other two made low throaty chuckles and watched.

Hunter's jaw clenched. That man was his only hope of finding answers. And Hunter wanted his mom's broach back.

During a match, Hunter was always driven by instinct. Get to the ball, then improvise. Do what was needed to defend the line. Figure out what to do next later. It was a strategy that always served him well.

But on the pitch, he understood the rules. He knew how things were supposed to work. Here, he had no idea how any of this was even possible, and he didn't know anything about the creatures or what they were capable of.

He leaped down off the ledge.

He landed hard but silent into a crouch, feeling the impact in his ankles. The creatures didn't appear to notice him—but the thief did. His eyes shifted from the creature standing over him for a second, narrowed, then widened again with sudden recognition.

That's right, Hunter thought. *It's me.*

Hunter reached for the first weapon that caught his eye. A spiny mace. He adjusted his grip on the leather-bound handle, surprised at the weight of it, then sprang for the one still seated on the ground.

He cocked his arm back, the head of the mace behind his head, and put the full strength of his shoulder into the two-handed swing. The back of his brain questioned what he was even doing, but he was already committed. Would the beastly thing even notice? It looked like it could sustain the direct hit of a semitruck. All Hunter could hope to do was stun the thing. And then the full attention of the other would shift to him.

Then what?

The mace struck the massive head behind the ear.

Some years back, he'd broken someone's nose during a match, felt the cartilage shatter under his elbow. When the mace made contact, he expected to feel something similar. It was nothing like that. It was extravagantly worse.

First came a terrible crack, like the sound a tree makes when it begins to fall. The force of the impact rattled the handle, and the vibrations stung his hands. The creature's skull caved in on one side, and the gray-green skin tore apart like tissue paper while the side of the face was wiped away. Blood exploded outward, the hot liquid splattering Hunter's face and chest. The body rolled forward like a wave cresting onto the shore before it collapsed face-first into the firepit.

Hunter stumbled back, stunned at the impact. His stomach heaved, but he choked it down.

The other two looked down at their dead companion, their grunts freezing in their throats, then made a painfully slow turn toward Hunter. Their eyes narrowed, and their lips pulled back into a yellow snarl.

Hunter realized this was a poorly conceived plan.

The closest one lunged at Hunter, a ham-sized fist careening toward his head. Hunter leaped clear of the swing, but a second swing followed. He sprang to the side, ducking his head, but this time wasn't quite fast enough. The fist grazed the top of his head and sent him reeling. He hit the ground on his shoulder, air rushing from his lungs. He rolled and skidded to a hard stop. Had the punch landed better, he'd be dead, head crushed.

His head throbbed, and the world spun as he tried to recover. Doubts he entertained that none of this was real were fractured. The pain sure felt real enough. And falling unconscious seemed a genuine possibility as well. He shook his head to clear the fog and tried to stand but could only manage to get himself onto his knees. From the corner of his eye, he saw the second beast closing in, too, the thick knife lifted in its meaty grip. He grunted something unintelligible to his companion.

Yep, this was a very bad idea.

The first creature made a swipe for him, thick fingers splayed wide to grab him. The plan was obvious: hold him while the other one skewered him.

If he didn't act fast, he'd be dead.

Hunter didn't know hand-to-hand combat. But he did know how to tackle. He dropped the mace, ignored his spinning vision and urge to vomit, and launched himself directly at it.

Head low, he sprang into the beast's tackling radius and dipped underhand, reaching for him. He aimed carefully. A knee to the face would put a quick end to his plan. His shoulder locked against the thigh just below the waistline, and he thrust his legs.

The beast grunted in surprise as Hunter put his back into a lift. He coiled his arm around the back of its thick leg for control, slimy sweat from between the thighs coating his skin, and he hoisted the beast off the ground. It was bigger than any player he'd been up against, but it was a solid hit and he had fear as a motivator.

The beast's legs flew up, and the torso dropped. Hunter drove through on the lift with all the strength he could rally. Once the creature was horizontal, legs in the air, Hunter shifted his weigh and dump-tackled the beast directly on its head.

As luck would have it, he landed directly on the mace Hunter had dropped.

The creature made a piteous groan and flopped heavily onto its side. Blood seeped from a jagged gash on its forehead, and one of its tusks was bent at a painful angle. He'd live, but for the moment, he was out of the fight.

Hunter turned about as the last beast roared and launched at him. Knife clutched in its ham-like fist, it swiped at his midsection. Hunter clumsily sprang backward, arms flailing. The knife slashed the air an inch from his side.

Head still spinning, Hunter shuffled his feet and kept himself out of range. The lumbering beast drooled and snarled as it herded him around the campfire. It made quick little pseudo-lunges at him intended to keep him off his guard. Hunter sustained the safe distance, his arms spread out, ready for the next attempt. His only hope was to find a way to escape.

Could he outrun it?

He doubted it.

But the thing was craftier than Hunter gave him credit for. Without realizing it, Hunter was corralled right into a trap. The beast made a series of sharp lunges that backed Hunter up against the natural stone wall behind him.

The beast's eyes narrowed at Hunter, and the drooling lips retreated into a sneer. It knew it had won. Hunter had nowhere to go. It lowered into a crouch, its stance wide in case Hunter tried the same trick he'd done with his friend.

Its arm pulled back.

Hunter braced himself. His only hope was to try to block or redirect the swing. But he had no idea how to do such a thing, and was pretty sure that its strength could overpower any attempt he made anyway. His heart beat wildly, and his hands shook as he waited for the attack to come.

As the creature leaned in to start its assault, it stopped. The massive body froze in place as if someone hit a pause button. Its ugly sneer melted away as its face contorted and its eyes rolled back. Then it dropped to its knees and collapsed to the side. The thief stood behind it with a bloody knife clutched in his hand.

5

ADJUSTING THE knife, the thief stepped over the slain creature and strolled casually over to the one still on the ground.

The remaining creature rolled over, a veil of crimson over its monstrous face. It saw the thief's approach and scrambled to lift itself from the ground. But the thief was on it too quickly.

Hunter's stomach heaved, and involuntarily, he turned his head from what was coming. But that did not protect him from the sound of the knife entering flesh and an almost gentle sigh that came from the creature as it died. He braced his hand against the natural wall to prevent himself from falling over. His head swam, and his knees were ready to buckle.

"Fucking hell!" He dropped his head low as he tried to get his breathing under control. Bile reached up to burn the back of his throat.

"You're welcome," the thief said.

Hunter shot him an acidic glare over his shoulder. "Excuse me?"

The thief wiped the blade clean on the body and tucked

it into his belt as he walked off. The hooded cape from last night was gone, giving Hunter his first real look at him. He was about the size of Billy the Hobbit, the squad's scrum half, a full head shorter than Hunter, and like Billy, he had a tight, muscular frame. But his hair was coal-black, and he had eyes to match. He wore a brown leather vest buckled over his chest, with a sleeveless linen shirt beneath it, exposing arms that would make an Olympic gymnast put on a sweater in shame. He had loose brown pants buckled just below the knees, and high black boots.

Using the heel of his boot, the thief rolled one of the beasts over onto its back. Thick arms flopped out at its sides. The beast's mouth was open in death, and its tongue protruded out like a rotting tenderloin. The thief removed a pouch from its wide belt, loosened the drawstrings, and dumped the contents into his hand.

A few crude-looking coins spilled out first. Then what looked like a collection of teeth. Lastly, the broach he'd stolen dropped into his palm.

Hunter sprang from the wall. "I'll be taking that back now."

He grabbed for the thief's wrist. Strength alone would be enough to overpower this little shit. His arm was deflected with surprising ease, and a fraction of a second later, a sharp pain materialized under his chin. He glanced down to find the point of the knife at his throat.

The thief glared up at Hunter, his hand steady as iron and ready to thrust.

"That's mine," Hunter growled.

"I just saved your life. I'd say we're square." His voice was rich and oddly melodious. Hunter couldn't place the accent. It seemed a strange amalgamation of dialects. British maybe. Eastern Europe too. The thief lowered the knife from the Hunter's throat and tucked it away again in his belt as if Hunter posed no threat to him.

"Bullshit," Hunter replied. He touched the skin under his

chin with two fingers and looked at it. No blood. The knifepoint hadn't broken the surface. "These things would have slit your throat if not for me."

"I had it under control," the thief said.

"You were flopping about like a fish."

"The amulet stays with me." His voice had a tenor of finality. He turned his back on Hunter dismissively and tucked the broach into a leather pouch at his belt.

Hunter stared at the thief as he circled about the campsite, pulling lids off crates and opening sacks. The cold arrogance of this guy made Hunter's blood seethe. Hunter weighed his options with a tight jaw. Should he try again? But he'd anticipated Hunter's first attempt with ease and reacted faster than Hunter would have thought possible.

Hunter looked around at the carnage. "Where am I?"

The thief tugged things out of a sack and tossed them onto the ground. "You shouldn't even be here."

"You broke into my place, thief!"

"And if you had gone to his dwelling like you were supposed to, I would have been long gone."

Was Darren in on this somehow? He'd wanted them to head out to his place in the suburbs. Hunter's apartment was closer. "With my mother's broach."

"You would never have noticed it was gone. For years, probably."

"Because you were so careful how you ransacked my apartment."

"That amulet is important. It has a greater purpose than sitting in a box in your bedchamber."

Amulet. A dim memory from his youth blossomed in his mind. His mother had called it that too.

"What the fuck are you talking about?" He stomped closer, fists clenched. He was losing his patience and was ready to start pounding on him, regardless of that knife he carried. He'd take his chances. In the past, most people had the good sense to look concerned or step back when Hunter was like this, but the thief didn't even seem to notice. "Start answering my questions, thief."

"You wouldn't believe me if I told you."

"Try me."

The thief, looking almost bored, paused his search to look at Hunter. "Fine. We needed the relic returned. It has powers that—"

"Powers?"

"Yes, powers."

Hunter's brow tightened. "As in magic?"

"Call it what you will."

He was right. Hunter didn't believe him. "Look, I may not be in line for any Nobel Prizes, but if you think I'm going to fall for—"

"Look around you," the thief snapped, his patience with Hunter clearly thinning. He kicked the head of one of the creatures. "Do you have these in your world?"

Hunter was stunned into silence for a heartbeat. "My world?"

The thief stared at Hunter with a slow shake of his head. "Zefora's hammer, you *are* dense. You obviously saw the portal hole yourself because you jumped through it. And you ended up here." The thief leaned in and raised eyebrows at him, as if waiting for Hunter to connect the dots. "If you are not going to believe your own senses, I cannot help you."

The cold weight of conviction landed in his gut. His logic fought against it, trying to cling to any shred of rationality, anything that might explain this in some other way. But he had nothing. He opened his mouth and somehow managed to force words from his constricted throat. "How do I get home?"

The thief turned and put his attention on the contents of a crate. "You don't."

"Excuse me?"

"There is no way home for you." His voice tempered, lost some of its edge. "Two portal stones. That is all I had. One to get me there; one to get me back."

"Then find another one of those stones."

The thief closed his eyes as if mining for patience. "Not that easy. Even if I could find another portal stone, it wouldn't matter. It's too late for you."

Too late? What did that mean?

Hunter's hands began to shake. The thief's casual indifference to how Hunter's entire life was now in shambles made his vision blur with rage. He could no longer restrain himself. He sprang for the guy's neck—but again, the thief was faster than Hunter. He twisted aside with ease, and this time the sharp edge of the blade was pressed against the side of Hunter's neck.

"Try that again and I will not stay my hand," the thief said quietly.

Hunter shoved the thief's hand away and stepped back, his insides roiling.

"I have no desire to kill you," the thief added. "But I will not hesitate if you interfere in my mission."

"What *mission*?"

The thief ignored him. He returned to his search of the campsite, and piece by piece threw items he found into a canvas sack. He acted as if Hunter was not even there.

After a few minutes, he tossed the sack at Hunter, who caught it against his chest.

"We don't want to be in this region when it gets dark," the thief said. "Let's move. I'll explain what I can as we walk."

"What makes you think I'm going anywhere with you, thief?" Hunter growled.

"Because if you stay here, you will die." He picked up a leather pack and hung the strap over his shoulder. "And the name is Dax. Not thief."

6

"GRAB THE mace," Dax said. He glanced down at the creature with the smashed-in skull. "Seems like a weapon you can handle. And you won't slice your finger off trying a sword." Adjusting the position of the pack, he marched off into the trees.

"Hold on a minute," Hunter called out to him.

Dax ignored him.

"I'm supposed to trust you? Just like that?"

"You have a better option?" Dax replied. "And put that tunic on. Your pallid skin will be easily spotted."

Tunic? His T-shirt?

"How about you give me some answers?"

But Dax was vanishing into the trees, silent as a deer. In moments, he'd be gone. Hunter pursed his lips. He didn't have any other options. And as much as it chafed him, if he was ever going to get his mom's broach back, he had no choice but to stick with him. Hunter pulled on his T-shirt and with a grunt of irritation, snatched the mace from the ground. He grabbed the sack with his other hand and jogged to catch up before he lost him. He fell in behind Dax as he wove through the trees.

Dax threw an annoyed look over his shoulder. "Move quieter."

Hunter never wanted to punch someone more. "What are you talking about?"

"You'll attract more of them."

How was he supposed to move any quieter?

Dax released an exasperated sigh as he shook his head. He made no noise as he walked, as if his boots hovered over the ground.

Hunter thought about jumping him from behind. He could tackle him, throw him to the ground—that was something he was better at, certainly. He'd then wrestle the amulet back. But the fucker was quick. And seemed to anticipate any move Hunter made. Hunter had no doubt that Dax would stab him in the neck just to take it back again.

He had to be smart. Wait for his chance.

"Look, about what you said back there. How can there be more than one world?" His head was whirling, unable to focus, and his brain pushed back on the idea each time he attempted to consider it. Despite everything he'd experienced, he simply wouldn't allow himself to believe. There had to be another explanation. "And what did you mean I wasn't supposed to be at home? And what is so important about that broach?"

Dax kept on as if he hadn't heard.

"You can't ignore my questions all day," Hunter pressed.

Dax spun about. "No. But I can stab you in the leg and leave you behind for the wolves."

Wolves? At least he'd be killed by something he recognized.

"Stop talking," Dax added with a pointed look. "I will explain what I can when I feel it's safe. Right now, it's not." He spun about again with an audible huff and resumed his march.

Clenching his jaw, Hunter took a few breaths to fight down a retort, then followed. He tried to emulate Dax's movement, even stepping directly where Dax did, but the effort was pointless. It didn't matter where he put his foot, there was dry twig underneath it. He gave up even trying.

The land sank down to a lively creek. Dax waded through the water in his high leather boots, undeterred. His movement barely made a ripple. Not wanting to soak his gym shoes, Hunter attempted instead a leap from rock to rock. Halfway across, a stone rolled under him and slipped him into the creek with a splash. Cold water flooded the shoes and socks in an instant to bite at his toes. Jeans soaked from the knees down, he slogged the rest of the way to the opposite bank.

Dax was already up the incline on the other side. Hunter hurried to catch up. Every time he stepped, his saturated shoes now made high-pitched squishy noises as water squeezed out. Dax, ahead of him, shook his head.

Dax stopped. He held out his palm toward Hunter and lowered down to one knee. He brushed aside leaves to expose the black soil and investigated the ground with his fingers. Hunter squeaked closer and leaned in to look over Dax's shoulder. A large indentation was pressed into the soft loam of the forest.

"Eight hours old," Dax said. "Maybe ten."

The track had been half buried in leaves. How had Dax even spotted it? "Same ugly bastards as back there?"

"Yes." Dax rose back to his feet. He scanned the trees around them, eyes narrow. "Could be from one of the same ones we killed. No way to know for certain."

"What were they?" Hunter asked, keeping his voice low.

"They call themselves the kug'ra. Which means 'manslayer' in their tongue."

"Charming," Hunter replied dryly.

"They may be daft and ugly, but do not be fooled. They are brutal and pitiless against our kind."

"Our kind?"

"Human. And they are faithful to their overlords, the

Henerans."

"Henerans?" Hunter was beginning to wonder of Dax was making these words up on the fly. Or maybe this was all part of Hunter's own psychotic break.

"Something we'd be wise to avoid. Which we won't if you keep blathering on." He glanced down at Hunter's wet shoes. "And making unnecessary noise. This is their territory, and we are trespassing. That alone is enough to have us killed."

"Why'd they have you tied up, then?"

"They were debating about the best way to torture me when you showed up." He rose back to his full height and dusted off his hands on his pants. "Somehow, I was known to them. They wanted information."

"You could understand them?"

"Some," Dax replied. "They believed I was a spy."

In the distance, a noise cut through the silence of the forest. A horn. Three blasts.

The sound was unnerving. Hunter felt the direness of it in the bottom of his gut. He glanced at Dax, who scanned the trees around them with a tight frown. His dark eyes betrayed his unease. The entire forest seemed to hold its breath.

"No more talk," Dax told him. "Stay quiet."

This time, Hunter only nodded. He adjusted the sack higher onto his shoulder and followed in Dax's wake. He had a million questions still sticking to his tongue, but he reluctantly agreed that for now they'd have to stay there.

They traveled on in silence for the remainder of the afternoon and into the evening. As the sun sank toward the horizon, the trees gradually thinned, and then segued into a band of saplings and brush. Beyond that, another great ocean of yellow grasses similar to what he'd left behind that morning.

Dax made an unexpected change in direction and plunged into a thicket of scrub and hunkered low. Hunter pushed in after him, wondering if Dax had spotted something around them. Inside was a shielded little den of foliage. Dax, calm and unconcerned, slipped the pack from his shoulder and sat cross-legged on the ground. He rummaged through the pack, pulled out a small bundle wrapped in burlap, and set the package on the ground between them.

Hunter lowered to one knee as Dax unwrapped it. A hunk of bread, a wedge of spotted cheese, and some strange pieces of fruit that looked like blue apples.

Hunter's stomach twisted at the sight. He hadn't realized how hungry he was until he food was right in front of him. How long had it been since he'd eaten?

Dax tore the bread in half and dropped the other half back on the burlap. Elbows on his knees, he tore off bits of his share and popped them into his mouth. "Sit down," he said, as if granting Hunter permission to remain in his presence. His voice was curt and low and barely above a whisper. "Eat. We have a long way yet to go."

Hunter reluctantly took a seat on the ground across from him. It felt strange—oddly congenial—sitting across from the man who'd robbed his apartment and was now offering up his food. A part of him wondered where the food had come from, if it came from those kug'ra. He wasn't sure he would trust eating any of it. He decided it was better to not know. He grabbed the bread, then tried to not shove the entire piece into his mouth all at once. He tore off a piece. It was dry and rubbery and made his jaw pop as he chewed, but it tasted wonderful. Maybe the best bread he'd ever had. But that might have been the hunger talking.

Dax next pulled a water skin from the pack, removed the cork stopper with his teeth, and tipped it against his lips. He drank for what seemed forever, then he wiped his mouth with the back of his hand and tossed the skin over.

The skin wasn't filled with water at all, but a weak honey beer. While Hunter drained the last of it, he looked up through the foliage. The sun was low, close to the horizon now, drowning the landscape in warm gold. An evening wind formed gentle eddies across the surface of the field. It was the same sun, he realized. The one he'd experienced his entire life. And the same sky. Whatever this place was, it had parallels with what he knew. It would be so easy to shove the other stuff aside and pretend he was still back home. Back in his own world.

His world. His heart felt the stabbing loss of it like an arrow to the chest. Everything he knew, everything he loved, gone.

How could this have happened to him?

He tossed the flaccid water skin aside and leaned in. "What did you mean by it's too late for me?"

Dax, about to bite into the fruit, closed his mouth, and his eyes shifted up. Hunter could tell he was perfectly content with the dense silence between them. Hunter had broken it, and he could feel Dax's irritation.

Hunter didn't care. He wanted answers. Any danger they were in was now secondary to that.

Dax held his eyes on Hunter. He seemed to weigh whether to even respond. In time, he lifted his chin and said, "What season was it before you jumped through the portal?"

A cold wave walked down Hunter's spine. It was not the response he expected, but it was a detail that had nagged at his gut all day.

"Winter, yes?" Dax said when Hunter didn't respond.

"Early spring."

"Here, it is clearly summer."

"What does that have to do with anything?"

"Everything," Dax replied. "Your world and this world are not aligned."

"Aligned? What are you talking about?"

Dax took a bite of the blue apple and wiped the juices from his lower lip with a forefinger and thumb. "Think. Why would the seasons be different? Time runs different here."

"Ridiculous," Hunter grunted. "Time is time."

Dax shrugged and took another bite of the fruit.

A wave of unease blossomed in the pit of his stomach. Dax's matter-of-fact posture seemed to bear a cold veracity that Hunter couldn't ignore. "Okay, then. How different?"

"Impossible to say. But I'd assume a month has already passed in your world."

Hunter's chest went hollow. A month? His brain was whirling, and his head throbbed behind his eyes. He pinched the bridge of his nose and tried to steady his breathing. "That can't be."

Again, Dax lifted his shoulder. A sign he didn't care if Hunter believed him or not.

Hunter tried to image what was happening back home. Were they still searching for him? Was he presumed dead? He imagined Darren talking to the police when they arrived at his apartment. *He ran after the thief, officer. I don't know what happened to him after that.* Hunter's mouth filled with saliva, heralding that his stomach might empty.

"I need one of those stones."

Dax's eyes shifted up to lock on to Hunter's. "A portal stone?" He made a sound that might have been a chuckle. "Those cost us nearly all of our resources. Even if you managed to acquire one, which is improbable at best, it would take years."

Which meant Hunter would have been missing from his world for decades.

His eyes dropped to his hands. Everyone he knew would be old, perhaps even dead. The world would have changed beyond recognition. How would he ever explain his absence? How would he ever be able to pick up the threads of his life again?

His vision was closing in around him. He couldn't take it in, and his brain was shutting down. He was stranded here, in this insane forgery of his world. One by one, things lost to him forever paraded through his mind. Regrets chewed at his insides. Inane things. Shows that were still on his DVR that he hadn't watched. An upcoming match he would have missed.

None of that mattered—but it cluttered up his brain.

The team. All the work he'd done to gain their acceptance. And now....

Something in him pushed back against the rising despair. No. He had to believe that there was a way back. There was a way around this. There must be.

If people could travel between worlds, there must be a way to travel through time too.

In the silence between them, a question occurred to him, a part of this that still didn't makes sense. "I entered the portal right after you. Why didn't we show up together?"

"I was warned the gateway could be… unstable. The exit point must have shifted between the time I went through and you followed. Dumped you in one location, and me in another. It's how the kug'ra grabbed me, actually," he added. "Landed right near their camp. The *only* way they'd ever manage to capture me alive."

Something unreadable passed behind Dax's eyes. He looked as if he was about to say something more, but he stopped, head tilting and eyes lifting. Hunter opened his mouth but before he could form any words, Dax extended his palm to silence him.

Hunter strained to listen too. Carried on the whisper of the wind, he heard something, distant and faint. Voices.

Dax lifted slowly to peer out from their haven of thick brush. He grunted and dropped again. "I knew your ungainly clomping through the forest would lead them right to us. They know we're here."

Hunter swallowed back a robust protest, deciding it wasn't the time to have thin skin. "More kug'ra?"

"Worse. Henerans."

7

HUNTER CRANED his neck to peek out across the field. Against a backdrop of a fiery evening sky, a small group of the same kind of bulbous creatures from back at the campsite lumbered through the grass. Four in all, still some distance away. Kug'ra. They were spread out in a line and beat at the grass with their clubs, occasionally calling out to each other in their grunting language. But there was another figure with them.

"Stay down," Dax hissed.

Hunter ignored him for a moment. The figure drifted behind the four kug'ra like a grim shepherd, dressed in black leather and with a cape that caught the wind and flowed behind him like waves of oil. He looked small in comparison to the others, frail almost, but Hunter still put him above six feet. He glided through the grass as if floating, his shape lissome and delicate. His complexion was ghostly pale, like fresh plaster, and black hair ran in a slick sheet down either side of his gaunt face.

A curl of horns extended out of his temples. Horns like a ram.

Hunter lowered his voice to a whisper. "Tell me that is part of a helmet."

Dax didn't respond. He was closely monitoring the movement of the four kug'ra with narrow eyes.

"What is that?" Hunter pressed. "Some kind of demon?"

"That is a Heneran. A powerful one at that," Dax said low in his throat. Hunter didn't want to ask how he knew that or what it meant. The eyes of the Heneran turned to gaze directly at them. "Get. Down," Dax repeated.

This time Hunter obeyed.

Dax, crouched on one knee, frowned and scratched his chin in thought. "Our work back there clearly attracted the attention of someone important, and your inept blundering through the woods likely led them right to us."

"What do we do?"

"You've done enough. I'll handle them. Did you see the far tree line? Straight east."

Hunter nodded.

"Stay low, and head for there. Once in the trees, wait for me."

"What are you going to do?"

"Save our asses," Dax said, and then he slunk off silently out of their hiding spot. A second later, he vanished. No movement. No sound. It was as if the land had consumed him.

Hunter opened his mouth to call out "Wait a minute," but caught himself. It was too late. Dax was gone, and anything said above a whisper risked him being heard.

Fuck. Hunter's heart spiked with a fresh surge of adrenaline. What was he supposed to do if he ran into trouble? And how would Dax find him again anyway once he made it to the trees? And if Dax got himself killed or captured, what then?

He risked another look out. The search party was spreading outward, and a couple kug'ra were angling his way. He had to move or they'd stumble right into him. Dax had left his pack behind; Hunter slipped his arm and head under the strap, grabbed the sack he'd been carrying and the mace, and scurried out awkwardly from the seclusion of the brush. Every movement seemed to announce his location. Even his breathing seemed too loud.

How had Dax done this so effortlessly?

Trying to minimize the shifting of the grass stalks around him—and silently grumbling curses at Dax—he shuffled along the ground as fast as he dared. Dax had probably abandoned him. Let the search party find Hunter, and then Dax could make a clean escape. With his mom's amulet.

Behind him, he could hear the grunting and the swoosh as their clubs swiped through the grass.

Hunter kept crawling—and with the two unwieldy packs and a mace to contend with, it was a slow and inelegant progress. He had no idea how close he even was to the tree line. Or if he was even still heading the right direction. He could be crawling in circles as far as he knew.

The sound of rustling grass was alarmingly close. One of the kug'ra had drifted closer and was maybe ten yards from him. It grunted out something, and from the other side of Hunter, a second kug'ra responded. Hunter was stuck between them.

If he moved, they'd hear him. If he stayed put, they could stumble right into him. He set down the sack and let the strap from the leather pack slip off his shoulder, then brought his feet under him in a squat. He tightened both hands around the handle of the mace and was ready to spring if it got close enough.

The sun was at the horizon and the light was failing quickly. The sky was still indigo, but on the ground, packaged within the clumps of tall grass, night had snuck up on him. He scanned the direction of the noises for movement, but everything around him was now choked in shadow. The sounds seemed close enough for him to see something— anything. But nothing. Beyond his tiny sphere was only thickening darkness.

His thighs burned from the low, constricted squat. But he was afraid to change his position now. Any move might make a sound or shift the tops of the stalks around him.

Something darker than the shadows swooped through the grass two yards away from him. The kug'ra was nearly on top of him. He adjusted his grip on the mace's handle.

A high-pitched squawk erupted in front of him, and a dark shape bulleted directly over his head. A large wing batted Hunter in the face as the bird soared up into the air, making angry squawking protests as it lifted.

Hunter fell back onto his ass, and it took all his willpower not to cry out in surprise. He held his breath, waiting for the reaction from the kug'ra. In front of him, he heard snorting laughter. It had surprised them too.

Then it started moving closer.

Through the tassels that waved in the evening breeze , he saw the head of the closest one. It was looking to the right, at its companion, still chuckling deep in its throat. A turn of its head and it was over. All it had to do was look down and it would see Hunter on his ass. In no position to attack.

Every muscle tensed, ready to act. He tightened his knuckles around the wood. His heart was in his throat.

A sound blasted from across the field. A horn. The kug'ra started, and it spun toward the sound and constricted in surprise. It pulled back its upper lip in a snarl. Long yellow teeth glowed in the fading light. It and the nearest companion grumbled and snarled a quick exchange, and the two of them bolted through the grass in the direction of the horn.

Hunter collapsed to the ground and rolled onto his side. Eyes closed, he waited for his panting breath to diminish. Once his breathing was under control, his heart no longer threatening to rupture, he rose and peered over the top of the grass. The kug'ra were on the move, galloping across the field—toward what, Hunter couldn't see.

The Heneran glided in their wake. His palm was extended outward, and a blue glow seemed to race from him across the surface of the grass, shards of light darting over the tassels like manic fireflies. The shards whirled and zigzagged. Searching.

Searching for Dax.

Hunter watched the chasing lights with dread in his gut. Dax was out there somewhere, not only hiding, but leading the search away from *him*. Was he equipped to hide from something like *that*?

Dax had been true to his word. He was risking his life to lead them away from him instead of taking the opportunity to ditch him and make it to safety himself.

Every muscle compelled him to run toward them. Every instinct told him to fight. Maybe he could sneak in behind and take one or two of the kug'ra out. He'd been trained to run toward the action. On the rugby pitch, that was his one job— get where the ball was and stop others from reaching it.

But this wasn't a rugby pitch. And this wasn't his world.

It was the jets of light skimming over the tops of the grass that convinced him to resist the impulse to follow. He had no way to fight against something like *that*. And who knew what else that demon-looking thing could do? The search continued—which implied they hadn't located Dax yet—so he was, for the moment, not captured. If Hunter tried something, he might only manage to make things worse. He had no choice but to trust that Dax knew what he was doing.

Yet as he collected the gear and scrambled off eastward at a low crouch, his insides were twisting with guilt for running away.

Hunter spotted more of the kug'ra, a separate search party inspecting the area closer to the tree line. Keeping his head low, he tracked their movement, studying the pattern. They seemed less vigilant. Almost bored. This was a perfunctory search—they didn't expect him and Dax to be this far. Hunter stayed at a crouch and drifted the opposite direction to avoid them, then circled back into the low brush that bordered the grassland. The sun was well below the horizon now, and the last vestiges of the day faded from the sky. He pushed on blindly through the scrub until he was deeper into the cover of older forest.

It was too dark to continue, so he settled onto the soft forest loam and leaned against a large tree to wait.

Wait for what? he wondered.

Was there really a chance that Dax would escape that? And even if he did, how would he ever find him here in the dark?

A gust of wind sliced through the trees and bit at Hunter's skin. Now that the sun was gone, the temperature was dropping rapidly. He knotted his arms in front of him. Cold was something he was accustomed to. He'd played plenty of matches on a frigid March day. But he wasn't running around right now, pumped with adrenaline, and it was going to get worse before it got better.

A pale light pressed between the tree trunks to the east. Two moons. Thick crescents, their light reaching under the canopy and giving the forest floor a ghostly sheen. One was familiar. The moon he knew—though the face of it was slightly different. The second was smaller and higher in the sky.

What had Dax said? His home and this world were variants of each other. The same, yet not the same. The stars too were different, he realized. He saw no constellations that looked even remotely familiar to him.

The face of the moon—his moon—tugged on his heart. Something about that one familiarity, that one shining equivalence between there and here, made all the other differences stand out in stark relief. He missed his home.

A memory came to life in his mind, a distant recollection of how the sight of the moon always seemed to sadden his mother. He asked her about it once. "I can never see it the same way I once did," she told him.

He hadn't understood what she meant then. He was beginning to now.

The night sounds pressed in around him with fervor. Bugs, birds, frogs—other critters Hunter could not identify—sang out in a cacophonous chorus. A woodpecker repeatedly tapped out exactly four beats against a tree, providing the percussion to the ensemble. But fatigue had settled deep into his bones. The long day of action and anxiety had amassed in his system and finally taken its toll. Head against the tree, his eyes drooped, but the sharp wind and a persistent rustle of leaves not far from him kept jarring him awake—fear that the kug'ra were now sweeping through the trees. Or perhaps, hopefully, it was Dax's return.

But from the movement of the two moons, rising higher into the night sky, hours had drifted by. And Dax had still not returned.

Captured? Or had he abandoned him? Either seemed likely.

So what now?

The sounds around him eerily cut out. They simply ended, as if someone threw a switch. The forest around him fell into an uneasy silence.

Hunter waited, very still. Something was happening. Some inner sense warned him of danger. He lifted to his feet.

A light emerged from the darkness a short distance away. Hunter blinked at it. The trees obscured the source, and the light stabbed between the trunks, pure and intense, like a headlight. But it possessed a warmth too.

He wondered at first if someone was approaching, another of the Heneran maybe, and this was more of the power Hunter had witnessed emitting from its fingers. But the light was steady, unwavering. And strangely, nothing about it felt alarming or threatening. More the opposite—it piqued a curiosity in him. He needed to know the source of it.

He drifted left to glimpse the source, but it remained just beyond his sight. He stepped closer and angled right. Same thing. Every time he moved for a better vantage, the source of the light was still obscured. He saw no movement, heard no sounds. But the light remained, pure and welcoming.

He considered ignoring it, sitting back down and waiting for Dax to find him, but something about the light confounded him. He needed to know what was producing it. It nagged at him until he started moving toward it. Beyond the next tree he'd see it, he told himself. And if Dax was going to find him somehow, it didn't really matter if he was here or over there. He rounded the nearest thick trunk, but the source remained outside his view. He kept going. Passing the next tree. And the next. And the next. But always the source stayed just beyond his reach.

He picked up speed. Eventually he had to arrive at the source.

The terrain rose beneath his feet. Stone outcrops broke the surface of the forest floor, shining like ashen blisters on the landscape. He broke from the trees at the base of a rocky hillside. The light radiated from a small cave halfway up the hill, the warm entrancing light dusting the sides of the stony walls within. It beckoned him onward. He was so close now. He could feel it. The source was there, just within the entrance.

He jogged up the hillside, nearly giddy with excitement.

Hunter slowed as he reached the cave entrance, a feeling of unease coming over him. But he fought against it. He had no choice but to keep going now. He was almost there, and he had to know.

He stepped into the cave.

Something tangled around his knees, and Hunter dropped to the ground. He landed hard, air rushing from his lungs. With a grunt, he tried to roll over, but a weight was scrambling up to his torso. A hand pressed his face into the dirt.

"Shut your eyes, you fucking prat," Dax hollered into his ear.

"What are you doing?" Hunter mumbled as he tried to push himself up.

Dax shoved a knee into the center of his back. "Shut your

fucking eyes."

It was a relief he was there. Hunter hadn't thought Dax would ever find him, honestly. But irritation burned through his blood. Why had Dax tackled him to the ground like that? All he wanted to do was keep going into the cave. He complied with Dax's demands, begrudgingly, only because he was so insistent about it.

Something changed. It was like being jarred from a nightmare. What was he doing?

Where was he?

"Keep your eyes closed," Dax told him. Hunter felt a length of cloth tied around his head, covering his eyes. He felt dizzy, disoriented. His brain seemed to remember that it controlled his body, and his limbs spasmed all at once.

"The effects will fade," Dax said. He grabbed his arm and guided him to his feet. "But we have to move."

"What… what the fuck happened?" His memory seemed fuzzy, with pieces missing. He remembered moving toward… toward something he thought was beautiful.

Blind, Hunter stumbled along with Dax leading the way. His legs were shaky, ready to buckle, but Dax's surprising strength held him upright. The ground was sharply angled, and loose rocks rolled under Hunter's feet. The two of them skidded down the hill at all possible speed.

"All right," Dax said finally, slowing them to a stop. He let go of Hunter's arm. "I think we're safely out of its range."

Hunter pulled the blindfold off. Dax had dropped to the ground and was sitting with his elbows on his knees, his head low between them. His back rose and fell from heavy breaths.

"Zefora's mighty hammer," Dax said, "I can't leave you unattended for one fucking minute, can I?"

8

DAX PULLED out the hard bread from his pack, tore it in half, and dropped half on the ground between them while keeping the other half for himself. "This is the last of it."

Hunter picked it up and dusted off the dirt and a small leaf stuck to it. He turned it about in his hand, scowling at the depressing breakfast. The cheese was gone. So was the honey beer. He pinched off a spot of green that might have been a flake of herb and took a bite.

"Too dangerous to hunt," Dax added. "We'll have to wait until we are out of Heneran territory."

"How long will that be?" he asked.

"Depends how quickly you get up and we start moving. Midday at the earliest."

A dark energy radiated from Dax. Hunter suspected he was in a perpetual state of ire—but the dial seemed to be turned up to nine this morning as opposed to his default setting of six. And Hunter was fairly certain it was directed at him. Presumably about the cave incident the night before.

Hunter climbed to his feet, his body still stiff from sleeping on the cold ground, though it was debatable whether he'd actually slept at all. He probed the flesh around his eye socket with his fingertips. Tender still, but less puffy. He could at least fully open his eye.

"That light from last night," he began haltingly.

"The fey lantern," Dax corrected, slipping the pack on his shoulder. "Will o' the wisp."

"Yeah, that. Those don't exist in my world. There's no way I could have known about it. Or known it was dangerous." He wasn't sure why he felt the need to defend himself.

Dax glanced over with a cool, indifferent look. He considered Hunter a moment before his eyes shifted away. "Just as there are dangers in your world that you know to avoid, there are dangers here. I'll be more mindful of what you might not know. But more caution on your part would be appreciated. Assume everything can kill you."

Dax started walking, as usual not checking to see if Hunter followed. Hunter grabbed the mace leaning against a tree and slung it over his shoulder, lifted the burlap sack, and fell in behind him.

"Surprised you came back for me, to be honest."

"As am I," he replied in a low voice. "Be thankful I did."

"So, what would have happened if I'd entered that cave?"

"You don't want to know."

THEY HEADED east through wooded lands that rose and fell, rose and fell. The day warmed quickly as the sun climbed in an unblemished blue dome, and Hunter was grateful the journey was spent under the cover of the heavy canopy.

With no food in reserve, Dax reasoned there was no need to stop, and he kept them at a hard pace. He moved as if Hunter wasn't there, not speaking or acknowledging him except when Hunter stepped on something that snapped, or walked through a dry branch he hadn't seen. He would scowl back at Hunter, a silent reprimand to stay quiet. Hunter did his best to limit the noise, but there was simply no way he could compete with Dax's freakish talent of moving without a sound. And when Hunter tried to mimic his movement, he only succeeded in slipping farther and farther behind.

The morning lagged on, and Hunter felt increasingly isolated. And ignored. He knew it shouldn't have bothered him that the thief who robbed his apartment wasn't being conversational. But darkening unease gummed up his thoughts. His mind either rehashed the events of the last two days or tormented him with imaginings of what was happening in his world. The worst part was wondering if anyone had noticed he was missing yet.

He didn't give a shit about irritating Dax. The silence was maddening. "How did you manage to escape them?"

Dax glanced back over his shoulders with a predictable narrow gaze.

"Last night," Hunter pressed. "How did you escape?"

"Easy enough," Dax replied.

Hunter couldn't tell if this arrogance was an act or if he really believed himself to be that infallible. "I'm certain it was, but please, thrill me with the details."

Dax held his eyes on Hunter a moment as if attempting to read him. "They were searching for a larger force. No surprise. You left enough traces behind to appear like an army had marched through."

Hunter had enough of biting of his tongue. "I get it. I'm terrible at walking through the woods. Not a skill I've needed in the past."

Something new passed behind Dax's eyes. Surprise? Amusement? "That much is obvious. I dropped a few clues around to lead them away from you. Ones I knew the kug'ra wouldn't be able to resist. They may be formidable and strong, but they're easily manipulated. I circled back around them and searched for you."

"But what about those blue chasing lights?"

"I was well away by then. That fiend had no hope to find

me, even with his sorcery." His expression darkened. "Do not think to let down your guard. They are still searching. Even now. I'll not be satisfied until we quit these lands."

"If it's so dangerous here, why did your—what did you call it? Portal stone? Why'd it bring us here?"

"Because you forced me to use it far from where I entered your world."

Hunter grunted. Yes, this was all his fault.

Dax returned his attention forward to climb over a fallen tree, and the brief conversation came to a complete and abrupt end.

Afternoon supplanted the morning, and the terrain swept downward into a rugged valley, a deep furrow that sliced through the landscape like a wound, cut by a twisting river at its bottom. Hunter followed in Dax's wake as he navigated his way down, and in time, they stood at the water's edge. The river here was wedged into a narrow channel. It rushed by in a frenetic torrent, surging and dipping around boulders the size of small cars. It was clear they weren't going to cross here. Dax signaled Hunter with a tilt of his head, then turned to follow the river's path downstream.

They pressed through the thick growth that hugged the riverbank. Hunter heard the low rumbling of the waterfall long before it came into view. The river tripped over a series of rocky steps before the ground disappeared, and the water tumbled over the lip. From the bank, Hunter craned his neck to glimpse the dizzying white veil that landed foaming and misting in a quiet pool below. Beyond that, the river continued again on its journey.

Dax was quick to find a way down a series of tiered rocks. He hopped from one to the next with the nimbleness of a squirrel. Hunter followed more cautiously. His size, the awkward load of a pack, the mace, and slick mossy rock made his descent harrowing. He used tree trunks and branches as handholds as he slunk from tier to tier. As he descended, the steady roar of the falls grew louder.

Dax dropped his pack near the bank of the pool. "The Green River," he announced. "The border between the Heneran lands and Andreya."

"Andreya?"

"The domain of men. Once across, we can rest."

Hunter rested the mace on his shoulder and looked to the far bank. "Is there a bridge?"

"We swim," Dax replied. He sat down on a log and started to unlace his boots. "You *can* swim, yes?"

Hunter bit back a retort and instead narrowed his eyes at him. He wasn't going to open himself up to more of Dax's condescending barbs. Yes, he could swim. Somewhat.

Hunter was used to having to prove himself. It went along with the territory of being a gay rugby player. But he always did prove what he was capable of. Often it was hard won, and it took time, but he never doubted in his own abilities. So why did this guy manage to make him feel incompetent?

Dax made an unconvinced little shrug and began the long production of removing his gear, unfastening buckles and stripping off the layers. Hidden beneath it all was a tight, muscular frame, with proportions so perfect as to seem unnatural. Hunter caught himself transfixed. His eyes drank in the flawless contours of his chest, his hips, and his legs as each were unveiled. Standing naked on the bank, Dax glanced over—Hunter quickly averted his eyes, embarrassed and annoyed with himself for enjoying what he saw.

Dax tugged at his ball sac unconsciously as he strolled over. From the edge of his vision, Hunter could see his uncircumcised cock flop about joyfully, and he forced his attention to the trees. Dax grabbed the burlap sack from him, opened it, and stuffed his gear inside. He glanced over.

"Don't recommend crossing in that," Dax said, his eyes raking over Hunter from his shoes on up. "You'll regret it later. We've a long march ahead of us yet."

Hunter frowned and made a reluctant start of undressing

by pressing his toes at the heel to pull out his foot from his shoes. He wasn't sure he wanted Dax to see *him* naked.

Dax tossed the sack back, and it landed with a thump at Hunter's feet. "I'll take this one," he said as he scooped up the leather pack. It had the broach in it—of course he would. "Can I trust you to get my gear across?"

"I'll manage," Hunter replied dryly.

Dax hoisted his pack up onto his shoulder and splashed into the water. Hunter focused his attention on peeling off his own clothes instead of watching Dax's naked form disappear little by little beneath the surface. His eyes involuntarily shifted over in time to catch the water rise over the bulbous curve of Dax's buttocks.

Hunter forced his eyes shut and grunted. He hated everything about this place. It tore at his insides that he was trapped here. And he hated that right now he was dependent on Dax for his own survival—and that Dax knew it too. He hated that Dax had saved his life. Not once, but twice now.

On top of it all, he hated that Dax looked like *that*.

Hunter took the time to fold up his pants and T-shirt before adding them and his shoes to the sack. He kept his underwear on.

He wouldn't be able to swim across carrying both the sack and the mace, he realized. Too awkward. He'd need at least one arm free. And he sure as hell wasn't going to leave it behind. Gripping it by the handle, he stood on the shore, and after taking a few preparatory swings to gauge its weight, he launched the weapon across the pond. It sailed in a great arc over the water and landed with a thump on the opposite shore.

With the sack propped up on his shoulder, he stepped into the water and pulled in air through his clenched teeth. The water was freezing.

Dax was nearly halfway across the pond already. He held the leather pack balanced on his head with one hand, while his other hand dragged him through the water.

Cold slime squeezed between Hunter's toes as he

stepped out farther. The waterline stung as it worked its way up his legs. He choked down any complaints, knowing it would only result in more derision from Dax. Holding his breath, he pushed out into the deeper waters and, following Dax's example, balanced the sack on his head as he waded in.

He'd always felt awkward and clumsy in deep water. His thick body didn't have buoyancy. The thrashed his legs to lift himself while his one free arm struggled to pull his bulk along. The sack shifted on his head, and part of it rested in the water, but there was nothing to be done about it. It was taking all his strength and control to keep his face above the surface.

Dax pulled himself from the pond, dropped onto the bank in a patch of sunlight, and leaned back on his elbows. He scrutinized Hunter's progress with a hand shading his eyes. It looked like the corner of his mouth was lifted. The fucker was enjoying watching him struggle.

Eventually, Hunter reached shallower waters and got his legs underneath him. Attempting to hide his panting breath, he marched up onto the shore as water cascaded off his body, and he tossed the sack down next to Dax, whose eyes immediately moved to where sand and dirt clung to the large wet spot on the bottom. He made no sign of getting up, but instead seemed perfectly content to lie there naked in the sun.

"Shouldn't we be moving on?" Hunter asked.

"In time. Best to dry off."

Annoyed, Hunter strolled off to retrieve the mace from where it landed on the bank. He turned it about in his hand and inspected it more closely. It was an intriguing weapon. Heavy, but not as heavy as he would have expected. Five pounds, maybe. The knobbed ball of iron at the end was the size of grapefruit. He choked the handle with two hands like he would a baseball bat and swung it around a few times.

"Your stance is wrong."

Hunter spun about. Dax had silently snuck up to stand behind him, still naked. The man moved like a ninja. He watched Hunter with his arms crossed.

"Excuse me?"

"Your stance. If you want to maintain balance and stability in a fight, your feet need to be properly positioned."

Hunter let the mace hang down at his side. "And how is that?"

Dax came closer to stand next to him. Hunter tried not to think about his nudity, but it was like trying not to notice an argument. Dax, on the other hand, was perfectly comfortable. Hunter caught a glimpse of all the scars that marred his skin. Raised white lines crisscrossed his arms, shoulders, and chest. "Your feet were parallel," Dax said. "Like this. But you want one anchored behind you. And shift your weight onto it."

Hunter mimicked Dax's stance.

"Bend the knee. Yes. Like that," Dax said. "Angle your foot more. Now you can step into the attack. Or back away from an attack at you." He demonstrated the movement, stepping forward, stepping back. Hunter copied it.

Dax frowned at him. "It is clear you've had no weapons training."

"Yeah, in my world, this is obsolete tech. People have guns."

"Here, you will need to learn how to defend yourself. Like I told you, my world has dangers that are unlike anything you've encountered. The mace seems to suit you, but it is a clumsy weapon. Inelegant. I'd recommend a longsword, but I'm not certain you have the agility for it."

"I'm more coordinated than I look."

"We'll see. Practice those movements one hundred more times. Step in, pivot back. Step in, pivot back. Then I will show you more." Dax strolled back to his patch of sun, but froze.

The sound of a horn soared over the trees from the west. The same sound they'd heard the day before. It was distant, but it was answered by one considerably closer.

He looked at Hunter with a scowl, and his eyes alight with alarm. "Grab our gear and move."

9

THEY CRASHED through the dense underbrush, quickly putting distance between them and the river. Branches whipped against Hunter's near naked body, and stones jabbed into the tender skin of the bottom of his feet. Dax, fully nude except for the strap of his leather pack over his shoulder, trudged heedless through the thicket ahead of him, the soft white of his ass directing Hunter along like a lighthouse beacon.

"I thought you said we were safe?" Hunter grumbled.

"Not from arrows," Dax replied sourly. "Or sorcery. They are being more tenacious than I would have predicted."

They stumbled upon a trail shortly after. It was little more than a thin brown line that wove through the trees, but it was enough to allow them to double their pace, and Hunter's bare feet were thankful for the relief. The trail snaked up a rocky incline. Toward the top of the rise, Dax slowed to a stop.

"We should be well beyond their range now," he said as took the sack from Hunter. He pulled out pieces of his gear and dropped them on the path. "And they will not dare enter our borders." He sorted through the garments and began to pull them on. Hunter tugged his clothes on too, all the while chiding himself that he was disappointed Dax was covered once more.

"I'll hunt for something to eat," Dax added. "There's a flint kit in the sack you're carrying. You know how to use one, I trust?"

"Of course," Hunter said, as if it was ridiculous question. He had no idea how to start a fire without a lighter, but he didn't want to add any more to Dax's growing list of his incompetencies.

"Good." Dax tossed the sack over to Hunter. "Get started. I shouldn't be long," he said as he stepped into his pants and tightened the laces in front. "I'll—"

He stopped.

Sounds came from the forest around them. Movement. Dax sprang for his knife as shapes emerged from the foliage around them. Kug'ra. Five of them stepped from the trees to surround them. Instead of the clubs from before, each bore a long curved blade of iron in their meaty grip, and they grinned in triumph as they tightened their circle around them. Hunter brought up his mace and tried to look tough, but his hands betrayed him by quaking. He was still in his underwear.

A sixth figure glided out of the trees, like a ghost taking on solid form. Hunter recognized him as the same Heneran that pursued them the night before. The branches were undisturbed as he stepped closer. His dark eyes shifted from Dax to Hunter with an expression of cold hate and ruthlessness. Up close, he was even more chilling with his sheet of black hair and flawless alabaster skin. The rust-colored horns twisting from his temple were somehow both grotesque and beautiful. Hunter could not break his gaze.

A sharp pain sparked between Hunter's shoulder blades. While spellbound by the strange creature's appearance, one of the kug'ra had moved behind him and positioned the point of its blade into his back. It moved with surprising speed for a creature its size. The kug'ra kicked him behind the legs and Hunter dropped to his knees.

"Drop it," the Kug'ra growled, its mouth seeming to struggle to form the sounds. Hunter hesitated until the point pressed harder into his flesh. Clenching his jaw, he released his grip on the mace.

Another did the same to Dax, kicking him roughly to ground. Dax tossed the knife out in front of him. A third creature looped around and kicked the weapons out of their reach.

"Do you not have the courage to face us in person, fiend?" Dax hissed.

Hunter threw a questioning look at Dax. What was he talking about?

The Heneran's mouth lifted a fraction in a cold and haughty sneer as he fingered a strange crystalline pendant around his neck. It glowed with a deep blue from within. "My servants do not need my presence to slice your throat. Only my blessing."

"This is bold, even for one of you," Dax replied. His voice had a forced calm about it. His eyes were shifting, surveying the scene. Hunter could tell he was waiting for the opportunity to lunge for his knife. Hunter's heart pounded against his sternum. Dax was going to get them both slaughtered. "Sending your slaves into our lands? A violation of the treaty—"

"So sanctimonious," the Heneran purred. "Coming from the vermin that violated the treaty first. We are simply executing our right to dispense justice for the crime committed against us."

Hunter studied the Heneran more closely. There was a strange translucency about him, an unreal quality that he hadn't noticed at first. Somehow, Dax had spotted it straight away. This was some form of illusion. More magic.

The Heneran might not be real, but the sword poking into his back certainly was.

"Your *justice* has no jurisdiction here," Dax said.

"Yet, oddly, there are no patrols to prevent it."

Something changed on Dax's face, a realization that gave him pause.

"Splitting your company up will not save any of you," the Heneran continued. "We have several search parties in the area and will hunt down all of the agents involved. You will simply be the first to learn how we deal with spies. But we will find the others too."

Anger darkened Dax's eyes. "This is an invasion. You'll regret it."

"I will regret nothing." The Heneran wove his arms together like two intertwining snakes. "How you die today will depend very much on how you answer my questions. Why were you in our lands?"

Dax shrugged. "We took a wrong turn. Innocent mistake."

A kug'ra kicked Dax in the gut. With a heavy grunt, Dax collapsed onto his side and pulled himself into a ball. The Heneran swung his cold attention over to Hunter with a single raised brow.

Hunter held up his hands. "Don't look at me. I'm new here. I have no idea what's going on."

The self-assured smirk faltered. "Very well. If you prefer to toy with me and waste my time, I am compelled to demonstrate my determination."

With a subtle look and tilt of his head, the Heneran signaled something to his minions. A beast pinned Dax to the ground by stepping on him, while a second held the tip of the blade against his throat. The other three kug'ra converged around Hunter.

"One of you will talk," the Heneran said. "Eventually. You need proper motivation, is all. Let's start with the big one. Remove his hands."

Hunter's insides went hollow and cold. He flinched to pull himself away, but the beasts were on him. They forced him down onto his belly. He twisted and tried to pull away, but for all his strength, he was no match for theirs. A knee was shoved into the small of his back, pressing him to the dirt. He tried to pull air into his lungs, but the weight on him only allowed quick and insufficient gasps. Panic gripped him, adding desperation to his struggle, but he couldn't move. A kug'ra grabbed his flailing arm and forced it out and on the ground.

"No!" Hunter cried out. He tried to wiggle himself free, kicking his legs and shifting his arm. But their viselike hold on him would not give.

He looked up to the see the kug'ra step forward with the blade, ready to bring it down onto his arm.

"Wait," Dax called out. "Wait. I will talk."

Talk? About what? The Heneran was clearly convinced their presence was some kind of clandestine plot. Hunter knew he would never believe the actual truth.

The Heneran chuckled. "I know you will. That was never in question. But I tend to err on the side of caution. You may still require some encouragement to not waste any more of my time. Do it."

Frantic, Hunter fought harder, putting all his strength into the struggle to free himself. But he was pinned. Helpless.

He closed his eyes. His heart hammered, and his head was dizzy with disbelief. Bile chewed at the back of his throat. All he could do was wait for the moment to come. Wait for the pain.

10

THE KUG'RA standing over him chuckled in a deep and unsettling voice. The creature was going to enjoy this. But the sound cut off with a sudden gurgle. Warm liquid spattered onto his face.

Hunter opened his eyes in time to see the kug'ra hit the ground next to him, an arrow protruding from its throat. Lifeless eyes stared back at him.

The other beasts cried out in alarm, and Hunter felt the weight on him lessen. The restraining hands pressing on his arm withdrew. Seizing the opportunity, Hunter flung himself from the ground, pulling in a full breath of air.

The kug'ra were spinning about looking for the source of the attack. A hiss cut the air as another shaft rocketed from the trees and struck one directly in the eye. The kug'ra made a pathetic sigh, and it collapsed as if all its bones had vanished. Hunter dodged for the mace and scooped it from the ground. He sensed more than saw one of the kug'ra closing in behind him. Without slowing, he spun about, giving the mace a wide swing. It made contact against the kug'ra's sword arm, coming in with a downward slice. The arm was knocked aside, the sword thrown from its grip. Hunter clasped his other hand to the handle and with a savage cry he'd only spewed out in a scrum, swung it back around. The knobbed ball struck the creature just under the jaw and tore off the bottom half of its face.

The kug'ra staggered back, swaying but somehow keeping its feet. Fury like he'd never experienced pounded in Hunter's blood, and one thought blazed like a furnace in his head. These fuckers were going to chop off his hands.

He swung the mace again with two sets of white knuckles on the handle. The kug'ra's eyes widened just before the weapon struck its temple. Hunter felt the skull cave in, and the creature went down.

Panting, he spun about, looking for the next skull to bash in, but no others stood. Five large bloody corpses littered the forest floor. The Heneran, standing in the middle of it all, frowned down at the carnage. His eyes narrowed at Dax a moment before he touched the strange pendant on his chest and vanished.

Hunter's mind was slow to accept the danger was over. It took a moment for the rage to begin its gradual bleed out of him. It left behind a cold void in his gut and furious quaking in his hands.

Dax stepped over one of the bodies to approach Hunter.

"It's over," he said.

Hunter nodded and tried to get his breathing under control again.

"Your stance still wasn't right," Dax added.

Hunter shook his head and grunted out a humorless chuckle. "Well, I haven't had the time to practice it one hundred times yet, have I?" His chest throbbed like a steam engine. He tried to keep his voice steady but could hear his own heartbeat in his ears.

Dax's mouth twitched into something very near a grin. But it disappeared in an instant, and his voice dropped low. "Let me do the talking. Stay quiet."

A woman was the first to step from the trees. Her

complexion was dark, and her black hair was cut an inch from her scalp. She was dressed in leather armor the color of espresso and gripped a bow in her left hand. A quiver stuffed with arrows hung on her back. She strolled in with a casual air, inspecting the scene.

"Zinnuvial," Dax said. Hunter could hear a tinge of surprise in his voice. This was not who Dax expected.

The woman lifted her chin at him as she kicked one of the dead kug'ra over onto its back.

Three more emerged from the trees, all men. One was as large as Hunter—he may even have bested him by an inch or two—but he was lumpish and oily, and one side of his upper lip was lifted in what was likely a permanent snarl. The second was stout but strong. His head was shaved and half of the skull was inked in an elaborate scrolling tattoo. But Hunter's attention was drawn to last one to enter the battleground.

The man had a lithe frame like a marathon runner and skin the color of faded khaki. His cheek bones and nose were flushed pink as if this were his first time in the sun in a month. He wore black leather pants and a sleeveless vest and a longsword strapped to his back, but the resulting look was more absurd than menacing, as if he was trying to fit in with a tougher crowd. Hunter could tell immediately this was the guy in charge. Superiority clung to him like bad cologne. He walked stiff-backed and moved like someone who enjoyed his power.

"Dax," he said with a heavy exhale. He marched directly to him and pulled him into a tight embrace. One more intimate than Hunter would have expected. The man closed his eyes and rested his temple against the side of Dax's head. "I feared the worst."

Dax closed his arms around the man in return, but he seemed reluctant. Self-conscious. He patted the man twice on the back before he peeled himself away. Brief as it was, the embrace signaled their relationship extended beyond the professional. "I appreciate a dramatic arrival, Quinnar, but that was cutting it rather close."

"We came as quickly as we could."

The lumpish brute stumbled in Hunter's direction. "And who's this?" he grunted.

Hunter straightened his back in return and adjusted the mace in his grip. He'd almost lost a hand today. He was in no mood.

"Corrad, hold," Dax told him.

Corrad's face scrunched in irritation, but he came to a halt. His eyes held, steady and cold, on Hunter, and his fist opened and closed. Hunter didn't flinch. He was well practiced at squaring off with brutes like this.

Quinnar didn't seem to know what to do with his hands now that they were no longer around Dax. He planted them on his hips. "When you didn't return…."

"A miscalculation," Dax replied. "I adapted."

Zinnuvial was circling around the area, inspecting each of the slain kug'ra. Bracing her foot on a body, she ripped her arrows free. She flashed a bored look Hunter's direction as she dropped the shafts back into the quiver.

"And the amulet?" Quinnar asked.

Dax picked up the leather pack from where he dropped it and tossed it over to Quinnar, who stared back at Dax in disbelief. He flipped up the flap, reached in, and pulled out the broach.

"You certain this is it?" he asked.

Dax turned to face the trees. He seemed to be deliberately not looking in Hunter's direction. He nodded. "No question."

Zinnuvial sidled up next to Quinnar and looked over his shoulder at the amulet in his palm. "So… that's what all this fuss was about. Better be worth it."

Quinnar glanced at her, and his mouth lifted in a smile. "It will be." Then he dropped it back inside and hung the pack from own his shoulder. Hunter's stomach clenched in irritation. It had grated him when Dax possessed the broach.

Sitting in Quinnar's hands somehow made it worse.

"How did you locate me, Quinnar?" Dax asked. Something about the way he asked—or the way that Quinnar stalled before replying—told Hunter that Dax already knew the answer. And he wasn't happy.

"That's not important."

"Zefora's Hammer, you used it, didn't you?" Dax said, rolling his head back. "Drained the last of it, too, I suppose."

"It was the only way to ensure—"

"We talked about this. At length."

Quinnar made a dramatic wave of his arm at the dead kug'ra around them. "If we hadn't used the stone's power, you'd be dead right now."

"I knew the risks when I took the mission."

Quinnar sighed and pushed his shoulders back, broadcasting that he was in charge. "My position allows me the prerogative to decide how our resources are spent. And what—or whom—is worth the expense."

Dax ignored him and marched away.

Corrad continued to level his eyes on Hunter. "Quinnar? What are we doing with him?"

Quinnar looked over at Hunter and seemed to really notice him for the first time. His eyes narrowed, as if to gauge if he was a threat. "Who is this, Dax?"

Hunter, still standing in his underwear, felt self-conscious with everyone's eyes on him. "You could just ask me yourself," he said.

"His name's Hunter," Dax announced, with a wave of his hand in Hunter's direction. A deep part of Hunter's mind wondered how Dax could know that. He'd never told him. "I picked him up along the way."

Was he a stray puppy now?

Quinnar lifted his brow. "Picked him up? Where?"

Dax didn't answer.

"He's trying to tell you that I'm not from the neighborhood," Hunter said.

"Fuck," Quinnar said as he spun away. He dug his fingers through the hair above his forehead. "He's from… there? How did this happen?"

"He followed me through."

"Chased him through, technically," Hunter added.

Quinnar and Dax both shot him cold looks. "What do you know about him?" Quinnar asked.

"I know enough. I'll vouch for him."

"After two days?" Quinnar replied with his brow arched. He shook his head. "No. He knows nothing of what's happening here. Has no allegiancy to our cause. What if he's captured? How long would it take for him to turn on us to save himself?"

"He won't."

"You can't know that. He's a liability, Dax. A complication we don't need. We don't have the resources to nursemaid—"

"Suddenly, you're concerned with our resources," Dax replied coolly. "I'll handle it, Quinn."

"I could just kill him," Corrad said.

"You always this charming?" Hunter asked him.

Corrad glared back at him. "No. Sometimes I'm in an ill humor. Usually when people get in my way."

"No one is killing him, Corrad," Dax replied as if suddenly tired.

Corrad grimaced and looked disappointed.

"We'll discuss this later," Dax said with a note of finality. "Now, we need to move. That Heneran bragged there are several search parties already on *this side of the river*."

Quinnar looked dubious. "You think they'd be that brash?"

"Wake up, Quinn. Haven't you noticed anything peculiar? Where are the patrols?"

That seemed to get his attention. His eyes bulged a fraction. "She's pulled patrols from the border."

"Certainly appears that way. And that's not all." Dax

grabbed the sack Hunter was carrying, dug out several items, and tossed them on the ground at Quinnar's feet: a hooded lantern, a leather-bound journal, a tin box, iron stakes, and a small earthenware jug with a cork stopper.

"Just a sampling of the items I discovered in a kug'ra camp a day west of here," Dax continued. "Crates of it. Weapons too. None of this is kug'ra made. Or Heneran."

"Stolen?" Quinnar asked. "Or supplied?"

"An excellent question," Dax replied.

Zinnuvial stepped closer and leaned toward Quinnar's ear. "Someone's approaching."

Everyone tightened into alert until a woman jogged out from the trees to join them. She was small and dressed in green wool, her dark hair pulled back into a ponytail. She went straight to Quinnar. "Word coming in from the north. A band of kug'ra spotted, heading this way."

Quinnar glanced at Dax with a sour frown. "Patrols?"

She shook her head. "None reported."

"Are they readying an invasion?" Zinnuvial asked.

Dax bit his lower lip. "Or just freeing up their movement."

Quinnar nodded. "All right. We head to the camp, regroup, and decide our next course of action from there."

Everyone snapped into action. Practiced and efficient, the group headed into the trees.

Hunter fell in alongside Dax. "So…," he said. "You and Quinnar…."

Dax wouldn't look at him. "Don't start with me, Hunter. Or I *will* let Corrad kill you."

11

A HIGH-PITCHED call came from a nearby tree. Birdlike, but Hunter was fairly sure it didn't come from a bird. None that he'd heard before anyway. He scanned the canopy but saw no sign of who or what made the noise. Moments later, a response came from farther down the path. Their arrival had been noted.

Light streaming through the canopy told Hunter it was drifting toward evening. They'd been traveling through the forest without signs of slowing for hours now, a long steady line that wound through the dense understory of massive ferns and brush. He was positioned in the middle of the pack, sandwiched between the tall, dark-skinned Zinnuvial and the ogre Corrad. Dax had spent the entire time up toward the front with Quinnar, and the two of them talked quietly together while they led the hike. The pace they set was sharp, with no apparent interest in hiding their presence. No fear, it seemed, of Henerans or kug'ra or whatever other horrid surprises this world had out there.

Since the arrival of his friends, Dax hadn't said a word to him or even looked his direction.

His calves first noted the path begin a steady incline.

Slow at first, but then growing steeper. To his right, he spotted a lanky man in brown leather in the trees. He leaned one shoulder casually against a large tree and yawned as he watched the procession drift by. Most of the others ignored him, but Zinnuvial lifted her chin at him and the man responded with nod. The ground eventually leveled off again. At the top, the trees hung back as if reluctant to broach the bald crown of the hill. The wide clearing had a circle of canvas tents, like a mountain range in miniature. Packs and crates were stacked outside each one. Horses were tied at the tree line. In the center was a large firepit, set up as an outdoor kitchen, with iron kettles hanging over the coals from a horizontal rod.

A dozen people or so, all dressed in the same primitive garb, milled about the camp. They glanced up as the line filed into the clearing, then returned their attention to their tasks, unconcerned. Only one, a severe-looking woman with gray-streaked hair pulled back into a tight bun, stopped what she was doing. She straightened from the sawhorse table she was bent over as they emerged from the tree line. The edges of her mouth lifted at the sight of them.

"I'd hoped it was you returning," she said as she casually strolled over to meet them. She was relaxed and had a warmth about her that belied her harsh features. "Pleased to see you are safely back with us, Master Dacuro." She bowed to Dax.

From farther back, Hunter could hear Dax mutter a low "thank you." He scanned the camp as if suspicious.

"Immediate area is secure, Master Quinnar," she continued. "Appears the other kug'ra parties have lost interest or got nervous and made it back across the river. Scouts from the north, though, have returned with some intelligence you might find interesting." She gestured to the table with a wave of her hand.

Quinnar nodded. He rested a hand on Dax's shoulder a moment and split from the group, following a step behind the woman.

As the rest streamed into the camp, they dispersed, some heading for the central fire and the pot hanging over it, others disappearing into the tents. Zinnuvial drifted closer to Dax, whose eyes shifted in Hunter's direction for a brief second.

"Find him a tent," Dax told Zinnuvial.

She had a stiff coolness about her that Hunter couldn't read. "All have been assigned," she replied.

"Then reassign," Dax replied flatly. "And see that he is provided with… more appropriate gear." He marched off to join Quinnar at the table. Hunter opened his mouth to call out to him, but snapped his mouth closed again. Dax wouldn't answer him, and Hunter was too tired and too hungry at this point to fight it. He'd corner him later.

Zinnuvial regarded him coolly for moment. Her nose twitched as if she'd been assigned the most unpleasant of tasks. "Follow me."

They circled to the opposite side of the camp. He caught himself once again wringing fingers around his wrist as if to reassure himself everything was still attached and unharmed. His appearance drew surreptitious attention from the others. He could feel their unsettled eyes on him as they stopped what they were doing to watch him pass. His presence was causing a quiet stir that he could feel on his skin. "Remain here," Zinnuvial said. She marched over to a man dragging a long tree branch in from the surrounding woods with one hand while he gripped the handle of an ax with the other. After a quick exchange, he pointed to one of the tents with the blade of the ax. Zinnuvial shook her head, and based on how his expression darkened, he wasn't happy with what she told him. He was being evicted.

The man dropped the branch, lobbed the ax blade into the wood so it stuck, and trudged off toward the tent. After only a moment inside, he slipped out again with a sack slung over his shoulder and his eyebrows knotted. As he tossed the sack inside a different tent, he shot Hunter a cold look.

Hunter was already making friends.

Zinnuvial gestured toward the newly vacated tent with a sweep of arm. "Stay inside and out of sight."

"Why is that?"

"You are dressed funny and people don't know you. These folks get jumpy when a stranger's lingering about."

Hunter sighed and nodded. He ducked under the flap and went inside.

The peak at the center was high enough for him to stand erect, and the ceiling angled sharply down from there to short walls on either side. The inside was dark, except for one wall glowing yellow from the firepit outside, and it was as extravagant as a prison cell. The ground was covered by a woven mat, and two cots pressed against canvas walls on either side, folded blankets set on one end. He sat on the edge of a cot and let the mace drop with a thump by his feet. Elbows on knees, he propped his forehead onto his fingertips.

What now?

It had taken the rest of the afternoon for his nerves to settle, for the shakes to finally diminish from his hands. He'd survived—intact—and his brain was only now beginning to believe it.

For the first time in two days, here in his dark little cocoon, he realized he felt a modicum of safety. He was out of sight. Alone. And the camp was apparently well guarded. But was that feeling an illusion? He knew nothing about these people. They didn't have horns or gruesome teeth, but that didn't mean they weren't dangerous. He wasn't exactly made to feel welcome.

But the ordeal had left him with a lingering damage. His psyche was frayed and unraveling. The trauma might have been over, but it had settled somewhere in the depths of his gut, and like a prowler, waited silently in the sediment for the opportunity to strike at him again. The quiet isolation in the tent in some ways made it worse. He couldn't escape the images of what might have happened had Quinnar's rescue party arrived but one minute later. And it made Hunter's stomach lift into his throat.

He could hear activity beyond the canvas walls, albeit staid. Voices and the sounds of productivity reached into the tent. The talk among the people of the camp was sober, direct.

There was something odd about this group. They wore no uniforms or any identifying symbols on them. They were all rather "come as you are," and some seemed a bit ragtag. Yet there was definitely a hierarchal structure. Clear leaders, like Quinnar, and rank and file. They carried about as some form of military.

And why were they so suspicious of strangers?

The crunch of boots on the hard ground outside the tent stirred Hunter from his dark reverie. Someone was approaching. Dax, he hoped. Then maybe he could get some answers. But the fact that he heard the footfalls at all told him it wasn't likely him.

The tent flap pushed inward, and Zinnuvial poked her head in and then bent inside.

In one hand, she carried a wooden plate. Tendrils of steam rose up from it, and Hunter caught the smell of cooked meat. A bulging linen sack was in the other, which she tossed on the ground at his feet. "Some appropriate garments," she said as she handed him the plate. "Less conspicuously… strange… than your current attire. Can't speak for how well they'll fit. Not many around the camp your size."

Slices of roasted meat and cubes of something that looked like beets covered the plate. Heat emanated through the wood of the bowl to warm his palm, and the rich smell seemed to go up through his nose and straight to his stomach. No utensils. He set the plate on the cot next to him, and pinching a slice between his fingers and thumbs, he tore off a piece and dropped it into his mouth. He closed his eyes and relished the explosion of flavor on his tongue. He'd never tasted anything so good.

When he opened his eyes, Zinnuvial was heading out of the tent.

"Wait."

She paused at the opening, hand pushing on the flap, looking impatient. Her form was statuesque in a way that was martial and resilient, poised with a sense of power and grace. But she eyed him like one would an unfamiliar stray dog that wandered too close.

Was everyone here this guarded? "I have questions."

"I have other duties to attend to—"

"I know nothing of what's happening here."

Zinnuvial lifted a single dubious eyebrow. "What has Master Dax told you so far?"

"Literally nothing."

Zinnuvial's lips tightened. "I am not confident in how much I am authorized to say. If Master Dax has said nothing—"

Hunter set the bowl down next to him and stood. "Forget it. I'll hunt down Dax and ask him myself." He had to be one of these tents, right? Shouldn't be too hard to find him.

Zinnuvial let the hand holding the flap open lower, and she took a step closer. Her head almost reached the top of the tent ceiling. "That would not be advisable. You were instructed to remain here and out of sight. And he is occupied with others matters. Matters more pressing than you."

"Well, it doesn't hurt to ask, right?"

She held her eyes on him, blocking the way out of the tent.

Hunter crossed his arms. "Look, I'm not asking for secrets. Just what is this shit pile I landed in the middle of. Huge ugly creatures that want to cut off my hands—"

"Kug'ra."

"—creepy-ass people with demon horns that shoot lights out of their fingertips—"

"Henerans."

"How do these things even exist?"

She held her eyes on him and seemed confused by the question.

"Where I come from, there's nobody like that," he said. "Just people like us." He wagged his finger back and forth between them. "For fuck's sake, give me something."

"Very well," she replied softly, almost like a sigh. "Not much I can tell you about the Henerans, frankly. Master Dax is probably the most knowledgeable of their kind, but there isn't much known about them. They were the first to occupy these lands. Our kind settled here later when a catastrophe drove us from our original homeland. They tried to enslave us."

"Like they did with the kug'ra."

"Not exactly. They lifted the kug'ra up from mere beasts, so they feel the kug'ra owe them for their sentience, limited as it is. No, the Henerans intended to enslave us as punishment for defiling their land with our presence. We have been at war ever since."

"How long has that been?"

"More than a century," Zinnuvial said.

Hunter shook his head, unable to grasp how a war could have continued for so long. And the impact it would have had on all the people. "How do you fight against something with powers like that?"

"We have our own sorcerers. Fewer perhaps. But we have greater numbers in our army. Henerans are tribal, primitive." Her voice was saturated with disdain. "Disorganized as a whole. They may be powerful, conniving, but when it comes to the art of war, they are lacking and too arrogant to realize it."

"So, is that why this camp is here? Part of the war effort?"

Zinnuvial's lips pursed and she lifted her chin. Hunter could tell she was trying to decide how much to say. "This camp is not part of the war against the Henerans. We are… part of an independent organization. Attempting to mire the spread of tyranny."

Tyranny. Hunter bristled—it was a word too easily

inflated. "So, this is some kind of rebellion?"

She hesitated, her lower lip pinching. These questions were making her uncomfortable. "We are not in open rebellion. Not yet. But support for our cause grows daily." Her voice had a thread of solemnity.

The dynamics of the camp, its strange, pseudo-military structure, were starting to make more sense. "A resistance movement, then. Who are you resisting?"

She stared at him with her brow knitted in bemusement. "The crown, of course."

"The crown," he repeated quietly.

Which meant a kingdom. Or city-state. A primitive form of government at any rate. More indication the world here hadn't developed beyond medieval. He wondered how many modern conveniences he'd come to take for granted were absent from this world. Obvious things, like electronics, certainly. But things like health care, food safety, and a general awareness of basic human rights were notions he never had to live without. And what of the long list of classic preindustrial problems he might have to contend with here? War. Slavery. Superstition. Wanton and indiscriminate violence.

Add in an assortment of horrible creatures, and strange, inexplicable powers…. It made his insides constrict.

In his world, uprisings against monarchies weren't uncommon. But he knew enough history to know how those pushbacks usually worked out. These people would likely all end up with their heads in a basket.

"Some kind of succession fight? Your guy wants the job?"

Zinnuvial's cheeks darkened, and she stepped closer, fists clenched, until they were face-to-face. "This is about the future of the kingdom. Safeguarding it before it is lost forever."

How did fighting the crown save a kingdom if this wasn't a fight over who was in power?

Hunter forced any reaction from showing on his face. He

sat back down on the cot and looked up at her, arms folded. "Explains why everyone is so jumpy and suspicious."

Zinnuvial huffed and turned away. "You are an outsider. An unknown. People have had to learn to be cautious."

"What do you hope to achieve? Independence? A new government?" Curiosity was getting the better of him. He couldn't help but wonder what level of idealism he was facing here. Was this just a group of fanaticized youth, hell-bent on a fight, or did these people have a legitimate ax to grind?

And what did sending a guy into his world to steal a broach have to do with any of this?

She pulled in a long breath while she held her gaze on him, as if trying to untangle some puzzle. "You would not understand."

Hunter didn't buy that. People with a fight in their belly were always more than willing to rattle off all the injustices they'd suffered. It wasn't that she didn't trust him. She was reluctant to tell him for some other reason he couldn't tease out yet.

"I will tell you this," she continued. "Everyone here believes in our cause. But many are afraid. For themselves, perhaps. Or for their families. But fear makes them distrustful. And dangerous."

"So, you're saying to keep my distance."

"I'm saying the danger is greater than you realize," Zinnuvial told him. "The people here are risking all. They cannot trust their own neighbors, some even their own kin, for fear of being exposed as traitors. You are a stranger to us and your intentions here will be suspect."

"I'm no danger to your resistance."

"And you expect everyone will take your word on that," she replied dryly. "You will be closely watched, stranger. Should you think about stealing off during the night or doing something that arouses suspicions, no one will hesitate to put an arrow through your skull."

"Just like that?" Hunter said.

"Just like that."

"Including you?"

"Without hesitation. I agree with Corrad. Keeping you alive is a foolhardy risk."

The icy assurance with which she said it sent wild shivers over his shoulders and arms. The plate of food was forgotten next to him. "Then, why am I still alive?"

"Because Master Dax ordered that you not be harmed. Pray that Quinnar does not override that order."

Dax had saved his life a third time. This was getting embarrassing. "Look, I don't even belong here. I only want to find a way home."

Zinnuvial shook her head. "That will not be allowed. You already know too much."

So… he was stuck here with a band of violent and paranoid insurgents, unwelcome and distrusted, but also not permitted to leave. Great.

"What's going to happen tomorrow, Zinnuvial?"

She lifted one eyebrow and turned again to leave. "Wear the garments to bed. We will leave before the dawn."

Before Hunter could say another word, Zinnuvial ducked out of the tent.

THE CONVERSATION with Zinnuvial left a bitter film in Hunter's mouth, but he forced himself to clear the plate anyway and used the bread to sponge up the last of the meat juices swirling around. No telling when they'd decide to feed him again. Not knowing what else was in store for him, he needed to keep his strength up.

It seemed quieter outside. The firelight cast fewer shadows of people on the walls of his tent, and any voices he heard were hushed or distant. The camp was settling into a nighttime calm.

He thought about peeking his head out to scope out what was happening—maybe see if Dax was anywhere. But

Zinnuvial's warning left him disinclined to push any boundaries yet. His tent was surely being watched. He'd seen enough violence in two days to believe her when she said anyone in the camp would happily kill him in cold blood.

A yawn stretched his jaw to its limit, reminding him how exhausted he was. He might as well call it a night himself. There was nothing else he could do. The sleep would do him good—and he might actually get some, tired as he was.

He stripped off his clothes and kicked them aside. In in odd way, it felt like abandoning his home, as if removing them was somehow conceding to the madness of this world. But it felt good to be out of the filthy jeans, stiff with dirt and dried blood. A grim reminder of everything that had happened. He was tempted to keep on the underwear, if only to maintain a connection to home, but after days of wear, they were sweat-soaked and clung to him like a grimy second skin. He peeled them off slowly as if removing old wallpaper. Naked, he stood in the center of the tent for a time as the cool evening air licked his skin. What he wouldn't do for a hot shower. Or a toothbrush. With a sigh of surrender, he pulled the garments from the sack one at a time and angled them toward the illuminated wall to inspect them. A blousy beige shirt that hung more like a nightshirt, a pair of brown pants only long enough to reach his shins, a rust-colored vest, boots, and a long leather belt that had a ring at one end in place of a buckle.

He started with the pants, stepping into them and sliding them easily over the curve of his ass. They seemed a "one size fits all" design, with plenty of space in the legs to accommodate his thick thighs. They ended just below the knee and were tied off with drawstrings. The waistline had a drawstring, too, and leather laces over the crotch, which had to be loosened a bit. The shirt fit well enough, perhaps tight under the arms. He sat on the edge of the cot, tugged on the boots, and laced up the sides. They were snug, but not uncomfortable. Overall, Zinnuvial had guessed his size rather well.

What he couldn't figure out was how to fasten the damn belt.

It was simply a wide strap of leather with an iron ring at one end. No buckle or fastener to keep it around his waist. He fiddled with it for a time, looping and tugging, but couldn't work it out, at least not in a way that kept it snug around his waist. He was ready to give up and toss it on the bed when the sound of the tent flap opening pulled him around.

Dax stepped in. He carried a small lantern that tossed warm light and black shadows against the tent walls.

Hunter froze. He hadn't expected Dax to show up again. A part of him was relieved, and he hated himself for it.

"Have everything you need?" Dax asked. He let the tent flap fall closed behind him, but he stepped no farther inside.

Hunter shot him a look. "Other than what actually belongs to me? I'm good."

Dax ignored the comment. "The garments fit well."

Hunter grunted as he once again looped the leather around his middle and held both ends, trying to figure what to do next.

"Is there a problem?" Dax asked.

"No, I got it." He slipped the end through the ring and pulled it tight, then bit the inside of his cheek, thinking.

"Have you not worn a belt before?"

Hunter sniffed. "Plenty. But we've invented a thing called a buckle. Makes it a bit easier."

Dax's eyes narrowed at him. "Cinching a belt is not difficult."

Hunter let go of the loose end and the strap fell from his waist and hung at his side. His upper lip curled, he stared back at Dax.

"Come. Give it to me." Dax set down the lantern and closed the distance between them. Before Hunter could react, Dax took the belt from his hand and wrapped it around his middle with the ring in front.

Hunter tried to resist this sudden and awkward invasion

of his space with a step back, but Dax tugged on the ends and drew his waist close again. Hunter was tempted to punch him, now that he finally had the chance, but instead sighed and held out his arms, feeling ridiculous.

He could only imagine what their shadows on the tent wall looked like from the outside.

Dax guided the end of the belt through the ring; then slipped it under. The end was drawn down through the loop it made. Little by little, he tightened the slack by drawing more belt through the ring and adjusting the loop until the leather was snug around Hunter's waist.

It felt weird and oddly intimate, having Dax so close to him, helping him dress, and it made Hunter's insides squirm. The warm smell of Dax's leather armor wafted into his sinuses. Dax, biting his lip in concentration while he tugged and pulled on him, only made it worse.

"A ridiculous amount of effort to keep your pants up," he said.

"It will go faster after some practice."

Silence followed, which only accentuated how awkward this was. "So, seems you weren't that excited to see Quinnar when he showed up." He had to say something but had no idea why he chose that particular subject to bring up.

Dax's body stiffened a moment. He made one final rough tug and stepped back. The belt remained firm around his middle. "We'd be dead if not for him."

Hunter could tell the question irritated Dax, but the subject was broached, so he pressed on. "Only saying it wasn't the warmest reunion I've ever seen. Rough patch?"

Dax turned and strolled toward the exit. "I'm not discussing my relationship with Quinnar."

Hunter stared at his back as he swept aside the flap. Just like that, he was going to leave again. With no explanations or answers about anything that had happened. His frustration level flipped. Anger flared, sudden and hot.

"Anything you are willing to discuss with me?"

Dax didn't respond, but bent to pick the lantern up from the ground.

"Am I a prisoner here?"

"A prisoner?" Dax looked back over his shoulder at Hunter, puzzled.

"You know, someone not permitted to leave."

"No," Dax said. "But I don't recommend you wander off on your own."

"Will I wake up to find one of your friends in my tent with a knife at my throat?"

Dax shook his head. "You are under my protection."

What was that worth? Hunter wondered. He felt he needed more answers. But he wasn't even sure what the questions were anymore. They'd all blended together in a dark churning soup in his head. "Dax, I need to make sense of what's happened. For Christ sake, I almost lost my fucking hands today."

"Tomorrow. Get some sleep." He left the tent. Hunter watched the glow of his lantern slowly fade.

12

NEARING MIDDAY, at the top of a ridge, they broke the tree line.

The land sloped downward to a wide plain, which was a patchwork quilt of striped farmland and a meandering river, yellow from the late morning sun, stretched across the full length of it. At the center was a great sprawling city. Ancient from the look of it, a commotion of wood and stone, quarantined within a massive wall as if to protect the pristine lands around it from contamination. Thin vines of gray twisted up from rooftops, and even at this distance, Hunter could smell a sooty trace of the smoke on the wind.

The river severed the city into two sloppy halves. Along a slow bend, a castle sat majestically on the haunches of a natural stone ridge, a sparkling white structure that loomed over the rest of the city and caught the sunlight like mother of pearl. The contrast between it and the city at its feet was jarring, like a priceless jewel set in a rusted iron band.

"Something you don't see every day," Hunter muttered.

The guy marching in front of him, the bald man with the

tattoo on the side of his head, glanced back over his shoulder at him. "A sight to behold, yes? You are not the first to be awed by her. The most beautiful city in the world."

That wasn't precisely what he meant, but he let it go. It was the first time someone had bothered to speak to him the entire morning. "What is it called?"

The man gave him a confused look. "Andreya, of course. The capital city."

Hunter sighed. They were heading right into the hotbed of their insurgency. He still hadn't been given any indication what they were going to do with him. He wasn't dead—so that was a plus. Zinnuvial woke him at dawn and rushed along like someone late for the bus, and he and perhaps fifteen resistance members had filed out of the camp and spent the entire morning hiking through the dense forest. No one told him where they were going. No one actually said a word to him, just shooed him along with impatient grunts.

Dax told him he wasn't a prisoner. But Hunter couldn't think of anything else to call it.

He was put in the middle of the pack again, and for the most part ignored. It felt like the first day he entered the Lions' locker room as a new player. Everyone knew he was there, but they went about their business as if he didn't exist.

Dax remained up at the front with Quinnar, leading the charge, their heads bent toward each other in quiet conversation.

The looming questions were how disciplined were these insurgents? How strong was Dax's influence against them acting on their own? Zinnuvial certainly intimated they would act if they felt the need. And Dax's wishes didn't mean shit if Quinnar decided he wasn't worth the headache.

He was descending into the hive of a political mess he didn't understand, but if he was going to ever find a way home, he would find it down there, in that city. He had to believe that.

Corrad shoved Hunter from behind. "Keep it moving."

He clenched his fists and somehow managed to fight the

impulse to turn about and punch him in the face.

Beyond the city, the land surged upward to a line of rugged and uninviting hills. The tops were flattened as if sheared off, and erosion had chiseled deep gashes into the bald sides, painted in horizontal bands of rust and gold.

Hunter decided to capitalize on the opening the bald guy made. "What is that place?"

The man followed the line of Hunter's finger. "That there's the Crags." He chuckled. "Where you're like to end up, y'ask me. Mining witchstone."

"Witchstone?"

The man narrowed his eyes at him. "You dim or something?" And he turned his attention forward again. The conversation was over.

After a slow snaking path down from the ridge, they merged with a cobblestone road that angled toward the gates in the wall. The tightly placed stone was worn flat and smooth except for two parallel ruts that ran along its length, presumably from centuries of carts and wagons that followed this path. A testament to the age of this place.

Others were on the road as well. Most were on foot, packs on their backs or tugging along small handcarts, but a few rode horseback, wending through the travelers and barking at the people who stood in their way. An ox-drawn cart, fully loaded with something buried under a gray tarp, lumbered and creaked its way from the city, the wheels fixed within the ruts in the stone.

The road curved into a young copse of birch trees. The city and the hills beyond were no longer in sight.

A call came from up at the front of the line to halt. Everyone seemed to expect it. Without hesitation, they left the road and moved into the trees. Someone jogged from the front back to Hunter—he recognized her as the messenger from yesterday. She came right to him.

"Master Quinnar calls for you."

He could feel everyone's eyes on him, then. With a nod,

he moved to follow her up the line, but someone grabbed his arm and gave him a rough tug.

Corrad brought his face in close to Hunter's. "Those are my boots you're wearing. You remember that. I want them back."

Hunter groaned inwardly. Of course they belonged to this greasy fucker. His feet immediately began to itch. He leaned in until their foreheads almost touched, his eyes locked into Corrad's. "Feel free to take them off me," he snarled.

"I follow orders," Corrad replied as if that was in question. "Was told they'd come back to me today. Just saying they'd better."

"First chance I get," Hunter said as he yanked his arm free. "And your feet are a lot smaller than mine, by the way. That shouldn't come as surprise to anyone, right?"

He smirked as he turned and followed the messenger up the line.

She jogged ahead, while he walked at an intentional pace. He wasn't going to hustle at the snap of their fingers. Dax and Quinnar stood with folded arms as he walked up. They leaned into each other's ear and spoke in conspiratorial whispers that cut off when they saw his approach. Both looked annoyed. Zinnuvial was with them, leaning on her bow.

"You're to continue on to Andreya," Quinnar said. "Accompanied by Dax and Zinn. The rest of us will follow later in smaller groups."

"It's best if we not try to approach the gates all at once," Dax added directly to Hunter. "Could attract attention."

Hunter nodded.

"Once in the city, they will take you to a secret location. You will submit to being blindfolded—"

"I will not," Hunter said.

Quinnar stared back at Hunter, stunned into silence for a moment; then he flashed an angry glare at Dax. "I will not have him risk the security—"

"I will handle it," Dax replied coolly.

90

Hunter wove his arms together. "Forget it. I won't do it."

Dax held out a palm to Hunter to quiet him. To Quinnar he said, "I said I'll handle it. Our location won't be compromised."

Quinnar's expression remained stony, but he eventually gave in and managed a small acquiescent nod. "You best be right."

Dax gestured with a tilt of his head for Hunter to follow and headed back to the road. Zinnuvial, without comment, fell in pace alongside Hunter.

When they were out of earshot, Dax glanced his way. "It would behoove you to not antagonize him. He is quickly provoked, and I have only so much sway over him."

"It makes no fucking sense to blindfold me, Dax. I don't know the first thing about this city of yours."

"You will need to trust me," Dax replied. "In the future, let me speak."

Trust. Hunter wanted to scoff at that, but the truth was, Dax was right. He had no choice but to trust him. He was apparently the only one in this world who didn't want him dead.

The road emerged from the trees and rolled out over the broad green plain of the valley, the city walls once again in view. In time, the road merged with another wider and more established road, one brimming with travelers heading to and from the city—much of it on foot, but oxcarts and horse-drawn carriages threaded through the flow as well. Canopy tents, decorated with colorful flags and streamers, appeared on the shoulders, filled with vendors behind tables. Fruits and vegetables, bolts of cloth, candles. There was even a table covered in weapons of all sorts, which struck Hunter as disconcerting. It was a symbol of the overt violence of this world. By necessity, it appeared everyone was armed to some degree. The vendors shouted at the travelers passing by, promising better prices than they would find within the city.

Hunter's eye was drawn to a group that unloaded their

wagon on the side of the road. Their skin was a striking bluish-violet tone that reminded Hunter of glacier ice. They each had black hair and ears that rose to form gentle points. A few were arranging tent poles while others unfolded the canvas of their tent. A shirtless man pulled crates from the back of the wagon, arms and shoulders bulging. The sunlight striking the sweat on his torso made it look as if his skin was melting.

Hunter leaned closer to Zinnuvial, who marched at his side like a prison guard. "Who are they?"

Zinnuvial glanced over. "The Mazenti. Nomads from the east, here to sell their wares." Her tone was cool and impatient, as if it pained her to speak with him.

Hunter found it hard to pull his eyes from them. They were captivating, alluring.

"These were likely turned away," she added. "Fewer are allowed entry into the city of late."

"Why is that?"

"Many trade with the Henerans. So they are not trusted and treated with suspicion."

Farther along, they approached a brightly colored tent considerably smaller than the others. An old man sat behind a table covered in large chunks of clear crystal.

"Witchstone!" he called out to the three of them as they passed. "You won't find beauties like these in Andreya!"

Zinnuvial curled her lip at the old man. "Charlatan," she grumbled under her breath.

Hunter remembered seeing a similar chunk of the stone hanging around the neck of the Heneran. "What is witchstone?" he asked.

"Pay him no mind. Likely not real. Or if they are, they are depleted."

"But what are they?"

Zinnuvial glared at him like he was an idiot.

"I'm not from around here, remember?" Hunter said.

Hunter could tell Zinnuvial was having a difficult time wrapping her brain around that. "Fyrollite. It is the source of power for sorcery."

Magic power came from rocks?

"Not sold in any city market," she added. "That is for certain."

As they drew closer to the gate, the wind shifted, and the scent of rotting meat made his face scrunch. He glanced at Zinnuvial, ready to ask her where it was coming from—she was looking up toward the crenulated parapet of the wall. Her face hardened, and she turned her eyes away. Hunter followed her gaze. Blackened shapes hung from ropes at the top, and crows squawked and flapped about them, snatching off pieces of flesh in their beaks. Long wooden stakes stood like naked trees atop each crenellation, each with a black hair-covered orb affixed at the top.

He stared in horror, and his mind fought to reject what he was seeing. It couldn't be real.

"What the hell!" he breathed. "Fucking barbaric." What kind of civilization was this?

Zinnuvial shifted her eyes his way. "This practice is new. A warning to any entering the city."

"Are… are those friends of yours?"

Zinnuvial took several moments to respond. She held her eyes on the road in front of her as she walked. Her mouth was pressed into a firm line. "Some. But others were perhaps unfortunate enough to not have enough coin for the new taxes. Or said something in the wrong ear that might be construed as critical of the crown."

Hunter couldn't pull his eyes from the gruesome display. Dark stains ran down the stone from each body and Hunter couldn't help but wonder if they were still alive when they were strung from the wall.

"It is why we fight," she said.

Dax threw them a look over his shoulder. "Quiet." He glared directly at Hunter. "Don't speak."

The portcullis was drawn up only partway, as if they were preparing to drop it closed at a moment's notice. It was high enough to walk under, but the larger wagons entering or leaving the city were being forced to wait for it to be raised higher. Several wagons had been pulled off the road to be inspected. Bored guards leaned on the heavy shafts of their pikes on either side of the wide opening of the gate. They gave the three of them a once-over as they approached. They were dressed in a dense leather armor. The thick chest plate was dyed bloodred, and iron studs lined the shoulders. One of them grabbed a tablet resting on a stool and stepped closer.

"Residents of Andreya?"

"We are," Dax replied.

"Yes," Zinnuvial said.

The guard looked at Hunter, awaiting a response. On instinct, he opened his mouth to answer but then closed it again. His accent would give him away as a foreigner.

"I'll need you to answer," the guard told him.

"He's mute," Dax said. "A horse kicked him in the head."

The guard considered Hunter a moment with narrow eyes, but then seemed to accept the story. It didn't surprise Hunter at all. Most people assumed he was a moron when they met him.

The guard looked back down at his tablet and scribbled something. "Why did you leave the city?"

"Hunting," Dax said. "No luck."

The guard's mouth pressed into a line. His eyes took in the long bow in Zinnuvial's hand. "Very well," he said. "Move along then." He returned to his position, and the three of them were already forgotten.

The crowd beyond the gate was a churning mass of bodies, wooden vehicles, and various animals. Everyone was funneled into a narrow street that twisted along like a snake. There were no sidewalks. Carts, wagons, and people all occupied the same limited space. Buildings made of thick timber and fieldstones lined the street with no spaces between them. The second stories reached out over the road, pitching out the sky. Hunter felt like he was entering a canyon. The stench of the place burned his sinuses. Sweat, urine, animals, rotting garbage, and God knew what else was mixed in with it.

He'd spent a good portion of his adult life in a rugby locker room, which made him a bit of an authority on things that reeked. This was worse. A lot worse. This made his insides roil.

"Amazed we didn't get pulled away for questioning," Zinnuvial said once they were beyond the guards' earshot. "They grow more suspicious of those entering the city each day."

"It will only get worse," Dax replied. "Her grip is tightening. A day will come when all will be interrogated before being allowed to enter."

They ducked under a brick arch on the left and entered a less occupied side street that was barely wide enough for three people to walk side by side. The path swerved downhill between tightly packed buildings and stone walls. Behind Hunter, someone called out from a window above, and moments later a loud splash hit the cobbles. People jumped aside and swore up at the woman leaning from the opening.

"What day is it?" Dax asked Zinnuvial.

Her brow was furrowed as she tugged on her ear. Hunter could almost see the calculations happening in her head. "Lundus. The second."

Dax slowed to a stop and pursed his mouth. "Head back. We will meet you there shortly."

She raised a single brow at him. "If Master Quinnar asks where you are?"

"Looking for confirmation," Dax told her.

She nodded, accepting the cryptic answer, and at the next alley, she peeled off from them and disappeared.

Dax glanced his way for only a moment. Despite the hardness of his expression, Hunter thought he saw something else behind his eyes. Sadness? Regret? "Follow me."

They wound their way through the confusing network of

streets. Dax seemed to know where he was heading, but to Hunter, it felt erratic and random. For a while, the crowds had thinned, and the rank smell by the gate had mercifully thinned as well. Dax kept them to the narrower byways. He seemed to be avoiding the more populated areas. Hunter caught a glimpse of a large square crammed with brightly colored tents and throngs of people—a market, apparently.

The city was ancient. Hunter couldn't gauge how old, but he could feel the deep passage of time around him. Stone buildings were weathered and timeworn. The cobblestone streets had deep parallel ruts that ran their lengths, formed by thousands of carts being dragged up and down them for centuries.

Dax hooked his hand under Hunter's arm and tugged him into a shadowy alcove.

"What—" Hunter protested, but Dax slapped a hand over his mouth.

"Quiet," Dax hissed.

A group of four men stomped past, dressed identically in black leather and flowing black capes. Two of them dragged a balding middle-aged man behind them who kicked his legs and fought to gain his feet, but couldn't get his legs under him. His pants were torn at the knees, and Hunter could see the flesh underneath was scraped and bloodied.

"Wait, please," the man cried, but the men ignored him.

Dax pressed his body against Hunter, his hand still over Hunter's mouth. Hunter could feel Dax's breathing against him.

"I've done nothing wrong," the man continued. He tried to tug his arm free from the man's grip. The man in black's expression changed from indifference to sudden anger. He turned, tightened his hand into a fist, and slammed it into the older man's temple. Hunter lurched and gasped at the sound of bone cracking, which caused Dax to press harder against his mouth. The man fell limp and he was dragged out of sight.

Dax waited before he released Hunter and then stepped

out of the alcove.

"What the actual fuck," Hunter breathed.

Dax didn't reply, but stared down the direction they'd gone with a tightened jaw.

"Who in the hell were those thugs?" Hunter asked. His heart thumped with revulsion and anger. He'd witnessed plenty of brutality on the rugby pitch over the years—broken bones, gashes that bled so much it looked like a murder scene. He considered himself fairly hardened on the matter. But he found himself stunned with his hands shaking. He'd never seen anything so heartless and cruel.

"They call themselves the Black Brotherhood," Dax replied. "An unofficial patrol, we believe. Answering directly to the queen."

"What are they going to do with him?"

Dax didn't answer but let the silence linger between them. Then, he tilted his head for Hunter to follow. "Let's go."

Still shaken by the incident, Hunter followed Dax deeper into the city. They merged into broader, more trafficked thoroughfares. Here, crowds were heavier, but Hunter noted a steady influx of even more people filtering in, like water trickling into the bottom of a sinking ship. The mood of the swelling crowd was muted, almost docile. And everyone seemed to be flowing in the same direction, herded along as if by some unseen force.

Dax's smaller frame threaded the growing crowd easily while Hunter had a harder time forcing his bulk through to keep up. Only occasionally did Dax glance back to make sure Hunter was still behind him.

Over the clay tile rooftops, the grand alabaster towers of the castle loomed larger. They were nearing the center of the city.

They reached a bridge that spanned the river, and the crowd marched on over it. Dax and Hunter were caught up in the flow. White marble statues stood as sentries along each side. The figures, all dressed in extravagant armor and wielding oversized weapons, stared down at the crowd with pinched faces, disgusted by the rabble that crossed at their feet. The stone sparkled in the sun, utterly free of the city's grime. No crevice or crack was in any way soiled. The purity of it was astonishing—until Hunter spotted boys and girls, dressed in rags, straddling the balustrade and scrubbing away at the stone with brushes latched to both hands.

No one around him seemed to notice the beauty of the bridge—or the poor urchins that kept it in the condition it was in. They marched along, oblivious.

"Stay close," Dax said over his shoulder as he slid the hood of his cloak over his head.

On the other side of the bridge, the street twisted around official-looking buildings with more of the guards clad in red leather posted outside. They leered at any from the crowd who drifted too close. Hunter identified other structures as likely temples of some sort, but the symbols and iconography that adorned them were alien and strange. The religions here seemed to have no parallel to his own world.

After one final bend, the street opened into a massive square. At the far end was the wall of the castle.

The crowd spread out but still moved toward the far side of the square. Already a large throng of people had taken position beneath the balcony that reached out over the edge of the square.

"A lot of people," Hunter commented, more to himself.

Dax frowned underneath his hood. "Fewer than they once were."

"Why are we here, Dax?"

Dax looked over his shoulders, and Hunter could only just make out his eyes underneath the hood. "Same reason everyone else is here. To pay our respects to the king and queen."

The king and queen?

The cold edge in Dax's tone told Hunter that was not at all why they were here. Hunter's stomach clenched like a fist, sensing danger. Dax was up to something—and Hunter knew on instinct he wasn't going to like it.

Hunter scanned around him, looking for others who might be resistance members. Others with hoods drawn up over their heads. What the hell was going on?

They worked their way across the great square, past the colossal statue of a man on a horse on their left, and a shrine or monument surrounded by a circle of pillars to the right. The crowd below the balcony was swelling. When Dax and Hunter reached the outer boundary of it, Dax was undeterred and cut in deeper. Hunter took a deep breath and followed.

He hated tight spaces—and for him, tight crowds were the worst. They had an unpredictable energy about them, the way they shifted and shoved. There was nowhere to go if something went wrong. He forced himself in to keep up with Dax, bringing on some fiery complaints as he pushed in deeper, but most of the protests withered away when they saw his size. Bodies were pressed up against him on all sides. He couldn't escape it. His heart rate spiked, and sweat beaded on his forehead.

He'd been in enough crowds to know they all had their own unique temperament. And the mood of this was odd. It was stilted. Apprehensive. Unnatural in a way he couldn't explain. He spotted two more of the Black Brotherhood, one circling the perimeter of the crowd, the other slicing through it. Both scanned the faces around them with tight brows and hard gazes like panthers stalking prey. The people formed a wide corridor for them to move through when they spotted their approach, and parents clutched their children close to them as they passed.

Dax slowed and made a cursory glance Hunter's way, presumably to make sure Hunter had kept up. The look was quick, but it had an oily slickness to it. He was up to something. At Dax's shoulder, Hunter scrutinized him, studied his taut stance. He seemed alert—watchful. But cool.

Two jesters, dressed in riotous colors and absurdly large

hats, pranced and cavorted about the balcony. Chuckles spread through the crowd at their antics, but few seemed genuinely invested in the performance. Toward the end of their routine, they tossed weighted streamers into the crowd. People cheered as the brightly colored meteors of ribbon sailed into the air. Bodies lunged and collided where they arched down into the crowd.

One of the streamers came down near Hunter and Dax, and a scuffle broke out to snag it. Hunter caught a glimpse of the weighted end before it was snatched and clutched against the winner's chest—a portly little man with the face of a toddler. A small sack. The man loosened the drawstring and dug his fingers inside. He plucked out a shiny gold coin and held it up in the air between his finger and thumb for everyone to see.

"Many of these people are visitors to the city," Dax said. The harsh edge of his voice had softened, and Hunter caught a glum undertone he'd not heard before. "Some return out of loyalty. Perhaps hope. But *that* is the main reason they come. Handouts."

Once the jesters had thrown the last of their favors out, they bounced up and down with fervent waves to the crowd below, then disappeared through the doors at the back of the balcony. The crowd made a collective moan of disappointment.

Hunter sighed. They'd been traveling all day, and his feet were tired and blistered from Corrad's ill-shapen boots. He was no longer in the mood for this, and his temper was fraying.

"Patience," Dax said, obviously reading Hunter's body language. "Nearly time."

The sound of trumpets exploded from above. Three men in red midlength coats and tights had slipped out to replace the clowns, and they stood at the balustrade with their long instruments to their lips and blasted out a triumphant fanfare that left no doubt what was coming next. An expectant hush fell over the crowd as everyone lifted their heads toward the balcony.

A tautness was in the air, as if everyone held their breath. A subtle but noticeable tension. Like at a circus just before a dangerous trick was going to be attempted. The crowd wasn't eager to see the royal couple—it was something else. Something closer to nervousness.

The trumpeters finished, lowered their horns in practiced precision, and stepped back to the wall. A man in a long golden coat now emerged and strode to the balustrade. His hands were hidden into his wide sleeves. His arrival was greeted with polite applause from the crowd—not hostile or unwelcome, but not warm either. More indifferent. His gaunt face surveyed the masses with equal detachment.

"Lord Chancellor Abazel," Dax murmured to him.

Abazel made a few announcements about local policies that didn't mean anything to Hunter. The crowd muttered to each other about them, but they didn't stir any noticeable reaction either way. Then, "The king will have a few words today, and once His Royal Majesty has concluded his announcements, he has graciously decided to bestow favors up his faithful subjects."

This received a larger reaction from the gathering. People cheered and applauded. Like Dax had said, it was why they had come.

"I present His Majesty, King Ruzad, and Her Majesty, Queen Jenora." The chancellor made a small bow, spun on his heel, and left the balcony. The trumpeters lifted their instruments to their mouths again and broadcast the arrival of the royal couple.

The applause level rose, but Hunter felt it was a bit forced. People cheered, but it seemed almost polite and didn't carry any measurable enthusiasm.

Hunter felt Dax's eyes on him. He was watching him, waiting for something.

King Ruzad traveled out to the balcony first, smiling and

waving. He was a burly man, strong if round in the middle. He had a heavy black beard and eyebrows to match. A gold crown rested upon his head. His smile seemed warm, but his eyes didn't seem to see anyone. The action felt rehearsed.

Behind him, Queen Jenora strolled out on the balcony. She glided to the balustrade and pressed her palms to the stone. A sudden gust caught her silken red gown and the fabric billowed outward. Her hair was pulled up, braided and elegantly twisted atop her head, and a jeweled circlet surrounded it. She didn't wave and barely smiled. She eyed the audience with a cool scrutiny.

Hunter was dimly aware of this heart thumping wildly and the sickening pain in his gut. For a long time, he could only stare up at her.

"This… this isn't possible," he said.

He turned to Dax, who was watching him closely with narrow eyes. "Tell me."

Hunter shook his head. "No. Something's not right."

Dax grabbed Hunter's arm. "I need to hear you say it."

"That's my mother."

13

HUNTER WAS only dimly aware of Dax grabbing him under his arm and dragging him into motion. He allowed himself to be led back through the crowd, staggering along in a daze, looking over his shoulder again and again at the woman standing on the balcony. His mother. The king was speaking to the crowd, but Hunter couldn't make sense of the words. His mind whirled, and his heart ached at the sight of her.

They broke from the thinning outer perimeter. Dax released his arm. "Stay with me," he said. He pressed on without looking back, as always, expecting Hunter to follow. For a moment, Hunter was tempted to ignore him and push back into the crowd again for a closer look. It had to be a mistake. That couldn't be her. But he forced himself to pull away.

At the edge of square, the king's voice had faded to a dull drone, and as they rounded the temple, the sound was lost entirely. Hunter slowed one last time to glance back at the distant balcony. They were too distant now for him to make out any details other than her standing at his side with hands clasped at her waist. At this distance, he could almost pretend it wasn't her.

But it wasn't her, he told himself.

It couldn't be. The woman standing on that balcony couldn't have been thirty years old. His mother died at his side at fifty-eight. And his mother was warm, friendly, and more generous of herself than anyone he'd ever known. The woman on the balcony was aloof. Cold. Whoever she was, *that* wasn't his mother.

But the resemblance made his insides twist into knots.

There were only a few pictures of her when she was that young. None of her in her youth or childhood—at least none that he'd ever seen. One photo was his favorite, one he felt captured her the best. It was tattered and bent from years of being carried around in his pocket or backpack. His mother, seated on an old kitchen chair, was cradling a small bundle against her breast. Hunter's father stood behind her. Hands resting on her shoulders, he leaned around to one side and gazed down at her small bundle. They both were smiling. And even though Hunter's face wasn't visible in the picture, he always imagined that he was smiling too.

A family. For a time.

They crossed back over the now empty bridge and plunged back into the dense city. Dax led the way. The two of them didn't speak as they zigzagged through a network of narrow streets. Hunter's surroundings were an inconsequential blur. All he saw was the image of his mother standing on the balcony. He stumbled along trying to get his head around what he'd seen.

Seeing her again, young and alive, was more excruciating than he could have imagined. He thought he'd healed. Believed he'd moved on. But the wound was open again as if no time had passed. He felt his insides were split and bleeding. It was too cruel, and rage flared throughout his body.

"You knew," he said.

Dax slowed his pace. "I needed to be certain."

"You couldn't have warned me. Prepared me for what I was going to see."

Dax's head was half turned. He nodded. "I know."

Staring at Dax's back as he walked away from him, Hunter found the urge to tackle him to the street, pound him for what he'd just done. For one bright moment, he'd believed it was her. Believed he could be reunited with her. But in an instant, the hope evaporated, and a cold void swelled where his heart should be.

Instead, Hunter grabbed Dax's arm and yanked him to a halt. "That wasn't her. That wasn't my mother." His jaw was set, and he could feel the heat pulsing from his cheeks and forehead. His eyes twitched. Whatever this bullshit game was, it wasn't fair. And it was cruel.

"Can you be sure?"

"I was with her when she died." He'd watched as she took her final breath and the life left her. The moment was etched indelibly into his brain. He was there—and it was real. More real than anything he'd ever experienced. His mother had lost her fight and was gone.

He had no idea who *that* woman was, but when she came to the balustrade and rested her hands on its edge, he saw her hands. He saw her fingers curl against the stone. All her fingers.

His real mother was missing half her left hand.

"I don't know what kind of bullshit game you're playing at," Hunter growled. "But that wasn't her."

Dax met Hunter's eyes with a cool, unreadable expression. "I believe you. It wasn't her."

The response jarred Hunter a moment. "So… so, this was some test?"

Dax didn't respond, but his lips tightened. He was keeping something from him. Hunter clenched and unclenched his hands. "What the fuck is going on, Dax?"

"I'll explain when…." He paused. A man was approaching, pushing a wheelbarrow full of bricks.

"Fuck that. You dumped this on me and expect me to wait? No. Who was that up there?" Hunter's voice was rising. People were slowing to listen, and a man craned his neck around a fruit stall to catch a glimpse of what was happening.

Dax shoved him into the alcove of a building with surprising ease—but then, stupefied as he was, Hunter wasn't capable of putting up much of a fight. Dax leaned in and dropped his voice. "We don't know. All we know is she's an imposter."

"An imposter. There's someone pretending to be my mother from *thirty years ago?*"

"Thirty years from your perspective," Dax said. "Here it's only been months. Perhaps a year. We can't be certain."

"A matter of…?" In a flash, Hunter understood. "Hold on. Are you suggesting my mother is from *here?*"

Dax didn't reply, but held his cool and unblinking gaze on Hunter.

"Don't be stupid. My mother grew up in a small town in northern Wisconsin."

"That may be what she told you."

Hunter ran his fingers through his hair. "That doesn't make any sense. There has to be some mistake."

Dax shook his head. "There is no mistake."

Hunter shook his head. "Next you're going to tell me she was the fucking queen."

Dax glanced around to make sure no one was listening. "Too dangerous to have this conversation on the street." He stepped out of the alcove and marched on. "If you want more answers, you'll have to follow me."

FISTS CLENCHED, he followed close behind Dax, staring at his boot heels and the stones in the road. The streets around him fell away into an irrelevant haze, unnoticed. He was too angry. Too confused. The bustling cacophony of the city was nothing more than a distant hum.

It was all too much for his brain to process, and he felt himself shutting down. Pain spiked behind his right eye. It couldn't be true. His mother couldn't have come from here— it didn't make sense. But as he sifted through memories of life with her, looking for any shard of evidence that would prove Dax wrong, they only served to confirm it. Why had she never spoken of her childhood? She never mentioned anything about her time at school and never spoke of family. Hunter had never met a single grandparent or uncle or cousin from her side. And she had odd gaps in her knowledge of the world. It always mystified him how she could have gotten through life not knowing some of the most rudimentary details of how things worked.

He felt lied to. Betrayed. Felt he didn't even know who his mother really was now. How could she have kept this from him?

He rose out of his sulk after a time to find the neighborhood had taken a decidedly different turn. Filth lined the gutters, and cobbles were missing from the street. The buildings were neglected and dilapidated; the layers of dirty plaster that covered the bricks were cracked and crumpling. Most of them looked abandoned, but a few people leaned out on windowsills and watched them pass with narrow and suspicious gazes.

Dax made an unannounced shift and ducked into the narrow gangway between two buildings. The alley felt like a deep gully, the sky a narrow band of blue overhead. They pushed through an iron gate and descended a rough staircase of cut flagstone, sinking into deeper shadows. The air was cooler here and smelled ripe with piss. The stairs ended at a heavy plank door, and Dax thumped the side of his fist against the wood.

A small window popped open and a bulging eyeball pressed against the opening. The eye didn't react to Dax, but as it shifted to Hunter, it widened a fraction.

"'S all right, Uri. Open up."

"Not supposed to."

"He's with me."

"Not supposed to." The eye shifted back and forth a few more times. "Does Quinnar know? He said nothin' about this."

"He knows, Uri."

The eyeball disappeared, and the little door slammed shut again. A moment later, Hunter heard a metallic scrape of something being released. "He better not be cross with me."

"He won't be," Dax replied as he gripped the handle and pulled.

Dax gestured for Hunter to enter first. Hunter hesitated, unsure—but what choice did he have? He stepped across the threshold, ducking his head under the low doorframe, and entered the heavy dark within. At first he saw nothing but thick shadow, but by the way sound echoed, he could tell they were in a narrow corridor. He put his hand to the wall to steady himself and felt rough natural stone. Dax pulled the door closed behind him, and Hunter heard the clank-thud of the door being barred. The daylight was shut away, bringing a small amount of relief to the throbbing behind his eyes.

Uri stood to the side of the passageway, arms crossed, watching Hunter with suspicion. He was barely a teenager, lanky like a reed, with a thin face and an unkempt band of spiky black hair across the top of his head. His ears had a slight point at the top, and even in the low light of the passageway, Hunter could see the color of his skin was a pale blue, almost gray.

Dax pushed between them and rested a hand on Uri's shoulder as he moved past.

"Has Quinnar returned?"

Uri shook his head. "He sent word." He paused a moment, eyes on Hunter, clearly reluctant to say too much in front of him. "Checking on a supply shipment."

Dax nodded. "Have him find me when he arrives."

Uri sat down on a little stool by the door, but Hunter could still feel the boy's eyes on him as he followed Dax deeper into the hideout.

The passage was dug out from solid stone, shored up by heavy beams, and it angled downward for a time. An occasional hooded lantern dangled from a ceiling beam, casting only enough light to safely navigate the tunnel. The air grew thick and sooty and coated the inside of Hunter's throat as he breathed.

"Where are you taking me?" Hunter asked. The passage constricted, and he twisted his trunk to prevent his shoulders scraping against the rough wall. He was having a hard time pulling in a full breath, and his gut fought with him to turn heel and get out. This was worse than the crowd. He already hated it down here.

"Under the city," Dax replied. "Old salt mines. Unused for centuries."

The passage opened into a wide and moderately better lit chamber. Bookcases and tapestries lined the uneven walls, and a mismatch of worn woven rugs tried to hide the gray plank floors beneath—an attempt to give the room a cozier and inviting feel. But despite the furnishings, it couldn't escape the reality that it was still a dingy stone cavern.

Three men and a woman sat around a table playing at cards. They glanced up as Dax and Hunter entered, and their quiet conversation broke the moment they spotted Hunter. They remained frozen in place, and as Hunter followed Dax toward a passageway on the opposite side, he could feel their distrusting eyes bore into him.

Hunter followed Dax blindly through the grim passageways, paying little attention to their snaking route, his mind still wrestling with what he saw and what Dax had told him.

Dax unhooked a hanging lantern from the ceiling, then cracked open a door and peeked inside. With a tilt of his head, he gestured for Hunter to follow him, and he slipped inside. The room was small and filled with wooden crates stacked along one wall and a table and stool pushed into the corner.

Dax set the lantern down on the nearest crate and stood with his hand still grasping the latch of the door.

"Remain here."

Hunter's head was still in a fog and the stabbing pain behind his eye had intensified. Images of his mother on the balcony kept usurping his mind's eye. "You're dumping me here?"

"There are affairs to get in order. And I can't have you seen. Not yet. I will return when I can."

"When you can." Hunter made an incredulous grunt. "What is this place? Your hideout?"

"Our main cell," Dax replied. "We have others, but this is the most secure. Your presence here will cause a stir. Prepare for that."

He didn't know what to expect today—maybe he'd be taken to some smoky backroom. He certainly didn't expect this sprawling underground lair. "Zinnuvial made it sound as if your resistance wasn't that big yet."

"She will not be satisfied until we have a full army ready to move," Dax replied dryly. "But the queen's behavior has driven more to our cause as of late. More are seeing what we claim."

"That she is an imposter."

Dax nodded. "More and more she tips her hand, showing herself to be cruel, vindictive, and petty. People are realizing she is not as she once was." He moved out into the corridor, pulling the door shut behind him. "Talk to no one."

And before Hunter could ask another question, the door was latched shut.

Hunter thought he heard a quiet click a moment later. Dax had locked him inside.

14

A COLD lump had formed inside him, he realized. Somewhere deep, and it was growing. It was born of a hatred of this world, of swelling resentment. He resented the circumstances that brought him here. He resented feeling trapped and being treated like a criminal. He realized, too, that he was angry with his mother. She had kept a whole other life from him. Keep the broach safe, she'd told him. Without ever explaining why. Might have done some good if he'd understood why it was important. And now he was stuck here because of it—and he still didn't know the relevance of it.

Had she said something to him, he might have been prepared. But then, would he have believed her? Would he have simply dismissed it as a delusion, a hallucination brought on by the tumors that ultimately took her life?

A click brought his eyes open. Sitting on the table with his head against the wall, he must have dozed off. For how long, he had no idea.

The door opened, and Dax leaned into the room. He made a single curt nod at Hunter—a signal he was to follow, apparently—and he disappeared, leaving the door ajar. Hunter slid his ass off the table and left the room to join him.

They traversed more of the tunnels, passed some closed doors and a few darkened rooms. The size of this complex was staggering, and Hunter wondered about getting lost. He spotted warm light up ahead. It spilled into the passage from a doorway. He heard the low pulse of conversation drumming off the walls.

Dax spun about and stopped Hunter with his palm to his chest.

"Hold your tongue in there," he said, his voice a low warning. "Stay by the door. Do not speak." He punctuated each word like the crack of a gavel. "I'll not risk you are as clumsy in diplomacy as you appear to be with everything else."

Hunter's jaw clenched. "Not making any promises."

"The less they know of you, the better. Give them no reason to fear you." Dax lifted a warning eyebrow at him as he entered the room.

Hunter followed, but stepped no farther than the threshold. He leaned a shoulder against the jamb and folded his arms.

The people huddled around the long conference-style table were a strange and varied cross section of what Hunter imagined medieval life would be. Some were clearly working-class and looked as if they'd dropped their tools and left their workshop only minutes ago to join this party. Others, dressed in finer and more ostentatious garb, were certainly higher on the social ladder. They had rings on their fingers and carried themselves with a self-important air that apparently was a universal human trait no matter what universe you hailed from. A few were military. This resistance had brought all manner of people to the table. This wasn't the youthful ideological uprising Hunter had suspected it might be.

He could immediately sense these people were serious. And anxious. The room stank with tension, like a locker room before a match.

Most were seated but a few stood with backs to the wall, arms folded. Hunter couldn't get much farther in than the doorway. He swept his eyes across the faces. Two he knew—Quinnar and Zinnuvial—others were unknown to him. Quinnar, positioned at the far end of the table, sat with his fingers tented against his chin as he listened. His eyes shifted briefly to catch Dax's eye, but he made no other acknowledgment that they'd arrived.

"These new taxes are intended to break us," said a dark-haired woman to Quinnar's right. "Plain and simple."

"They are to help pay for the extravagant renovation of the royal apartments, I'm sure," someone replied from the far corner.

A man with a thick ruddy beard took heavy puffs from a wooden pipe and shook his head. White smoke blasted from the corner of his mouth like an old steam engine picking up speed. "Gold spent so she can live in greater luxury while her subjects starve."

"We are *not* her subjects, Master Azun," the dark-haired woman said. "And she is not our queen. Let's not forget that."

A hearty man wearing a brown vest and tight leather cap frowned and drummed his fingers on the table. "Our businesses are failing, crushed beneath these taxes and these absurd laws. People are suffering, many turned from their homes. Some starving. They cannot take much more."

"Which will only draw them to our cause,"

"Not if they are imprisoned," Azun said. "Or leave the city entirely."

"Or are too terrified to act. The Black Brotherhood is growing more bold each day," the dark-haired woman added.

"They were out in force today," Dax said from his corner of the room. "And out in the open. No more skulking about the shadows."

Azun lifted his chin. "Master Dax. The rumor was true then. Pleased to see you safely returned to us."

Many around the table turned their gaze to him. It was

clear many weren't even aware he'd entered the room. Some followed with a "hear, hear," while others bobbed their heads in agreement, but a few appeared almost uneasy to find him in the room.

Dax bowed his head to the room but said nothing more.

"Which," Quinnar interjected smoothly, drawing the attention back to him. He wove his fingers together and let them drop to the table's surface, giving time for all the eyes to settle on him. "Leads us to why I called you all here. I am happy to report that the mission was a success. But before we continue, we will need consensus from this council regarding our next steps. In my view, the path forward is rather clear."

"Clear?" challenged the dark-haired woman. She anchored her elbows on the table and leaned in. "Hardly. This mission of yours has depleted us of nearly all our resources. Risked our most skilled infiltrator. And for what? What did we actually achieve?"

"The means to expose her," Zinnuvial replied.

"Dependent on the minor detail that she puts it on," said a balding man standing against the wall. He had a narrow face and a pinched nose and wore a leather apron over his shabby blue tunic. "Which no one has adequately explained to me how we intend to orchestrate."

"That is why it is the next item on our agenda, Master Ronlin," Quinnar put in calmly.

"Well, we can forget using a member of the city council," the ruddy-bearded man put in. "Now that she is dismantling that body, there is no one in our organization that can get close enough to her to attempt it."

"A move intended to consolidate her power," Ronlin added.

"And isolate her from potential threats on the inside," Azun added. "She's no fool."

"This increases the challenge," Quinnar said. "But it is hardly impossible."

"Then, you have a plan in mind?" Ronlin asked.

"Several, in fact." Quinnar glanced up at Dax with a raised eyebrow. "Well?"

Dax wormed closer to the table. "Confirmed."

Quinnar frowned and nodded. "Friends, it is important to note that the mission rewarded us with more than just the amulet," Quinnar told the council. "But also with vital intelligence we require. We now have the definitive proof we needed. Proof that will bring more to our cause."

He reached down to his side, and when he brought his hand back to the table, he unclenched his fingers. The jeweled broach that Dax stole from Hunter's apartment tumbled onto the table.

Hunter's chest constricted. The room was knocked into a stunned silence as they stared at it. Some lowered their chins, while others fell against the backs of their chairs.

"Our beloved queen is indeed gone," Quinnar continued, pushing the item farther toward the center of the table. "Sent to that distant world. We now know, without a doubt, an imposter indeed bears her crown."

Hunter wanted to throw up. Or better yet, punch Quinnar in face. The heavy-handed theatrics felt like nothing more than political machinations, a way to wrangle these people under his control. And he was using Hunter's mother as a way to leverage it.

He felt eyes on him. He glanced over at Dax, who was watching him from the corner of his eyes. As soon as their eyes met, Dax looked away.

"With respect, Quinnar, how is this proof?" asked an older woman with braided white hair, tied with a green ribbon. She seemed kindly at first glance, but Hunter could see a strength in her eyes that said she was not someone he would want to cross. "Sorcerers might be able to confirm the amulet's authenticity, but that will hardly sway those still skeptical that Jenora was exiled to this other world. They will say it was stolen from the palace in an elaborate heist."

"We can confirm," Quinnar told her, "by witness

account, that she was in fact in that world. And has since died. When people hear—"

"A witness?" someone asked. "How is that possible?"

Several around the table nodded.

"This man?" the dark-haired woman exclaimed. "Is he your witness?"

The entire room turned to Hunter at once, and the air seemed to thicken around him. Eyes bore down on him like nails being driven into wood.

A man in a cloth cap with a bulbous red nose shifted against the arm of the chair as he studied Hunter with a furrowed brow and narrowed eyes. "Master Dax, isn't this the man you found wandering about in Heneran territory?"

A collective gasp circled around the table.

"I heard word of this as well. Master Dax? Is this true?"

"Friends," Quinnar said as he lifted his hands into the air, an attempt to draw the attention back to him. "That is not precisely—"

Ronlin pushed forward between two of the chairs and slapped a palm onto the table. "Why are we even discussing this with *him* in the room? Why is he even here?"

"I would add why was he even allowed into our base?" the dark-haired woman added.

"How did you allow this to happen?" someone else asked.

Quinnar rapped his knuckles on the table several times. "Good council, please. I approved of his being brought here. All will be made clear in time, but I believe he could prove be a valuable resource—"

"Too great a risk, Quinnar. He's a liability."

"A liability?" Dax asked, with a dangerous sort of calm.

"Master Dax, you know I respect you. But you ask too much this time. You cannot expect us all to trust him on your word alone. He could betray us."

Quinnar shook his head. "I assure you, he will be monitored at all times and not be allowed to leave."

Hunter leaned closer to Dax's ear. "Still claiming I'm not a prisoner?"

"Quiet," he snapped.

The balding man shook his head. "I'm quite uncomfortable with this, Quinnar. If he is a witness, as you claim, and can prove that the queen is false, who knows what wrath it will rain down on us here if they learn of it. He should be under lock and key in a safe location. Not here."

"He knows too much already," someone else chimed in. "If he were captured, he could not only reveal the location of this base but could now identify all of us as well. The entire council is in danger."

"There are already too many rumors of a mole among us. His presence will only serve to heighten them."

A number of them around the table pounded the surface.

Quinnar stood and slapped a palm to the table. "Good people of the council!" The voices around the table dropped to a grumble and then fell silent. "When have we become the warren of frightened rabbits that I see before me? You have all put your faith in me to guide this coalition, and I promise you I am not casually putting you in any direct danger." He waited a moment, raking his eyes over each of their faces to see if any were about to challenge him, but the room remained quiet. "I am not deaf to your concerns, but I promise, in time, more will be revealed. In the interim, have trust. There is no need for this panic."

A few around the table shared looks, but most looked down at their hands. The firm reprimand had, for the moment, shamed the group into silence. No one challenged him.

Quinnar nodded slowly, clearly satisfied with the result. "For now, he remains."

For now? Hunter's heart rate spiked, pounding a fresh surge of anger through his bloodstream. So he was allowed to stay here conditionally, hanging on the whim of this slick politician? A change in the wind and Hunter had no doubt he'd be tossed out onto the street in a city he knew nothing about.

Or worse.

"A break is in order, I think," Quinnar continued. "We'll reconvene later. I'll send word when I'm ready."

At first no one moved. The entire group seemed to pretend they hadn't heard the dismissal. Zinnuvial was the first to make toward the door—not in anger, but as an obedient soldier. Then, one by one, people lifted from their chairs and drifted away from the table, grumbling and whispering among themselves. The members of the resistance pushed past Hunter, some brushing against his shoulders as they exited, but Hunter made a point of not budging. He made them all move around him.

In time, all that remained was Dax and Quinnar on opposite sides of the table and Hunter standing by the door.

"Go rest," Quinnar said to Dax. It sounded more like a command than the voice of concern. He was irritated with Dax; that much was clear. He made a dramatic show of shuffling together the yellow documents on the table in front of him.

"I'm fine," Dax said.

Quinnar's face twisted into a look that said *suit yourself.* "Don't know how you talked me into this, Dax. I don't think you appreciate the headaches this is going to cause."

"They will come around," Dax said.

Quinnar gave Hunter a quick glance from the corner of his eye. "There are already too many whispers about him."

Hunter stepped closer to the table. "I didn't ask for any of this. Find a way to send me back home, then. That will solve everyone's problems."

Quinnar made a humorless noise his throat. "There is a far cheaper solution, frankly. And many will call for it."

Dax leaned his knuckles on the table. "You gave me your word, Quinn."

"And I intend to keep it," Quinnar responded with a sigh. "From my hand, he will not be harmed. But Keya's arrest has everyone shaken, Dax. No one feels safe, which has made

118

managing the council tenuous at best. They grow more restless by the day. A time may come when my protection of him will not matter."

"Their fear of him will subside," Dax replied. "Their distrust will fade."

"For his sake, I hope you're right."

"Why is my presence here causing such a freak out?" Hunter asked. "No one has ever joined your resistance before?"

Quinnar leaned back in his chair. "Only the most trusted of us are allowed down here. The most vetted of members. We've been very careful. We've had to be. And you've sidestepped a very basic rule. You can't blame them for being anxious." He drummed his fingers on the tabletop, his mouth pursed in thought. "The question remains what to do with you."

"You could start by giving me some answers. Like why you stole my mom's broach. And who that woman was up there on that balcony."

"Right now, the less you know the better," Quinnar replied.

"Bullshit. I deserve—"

"Deserve? We owe you nothing," Quinnar snapped, leaning in on one elbow. "I encourage you to remember that. You're alive. That is the best you can ask for currently. And be very careful about making demands upon me. Accept the generosity I'm willing to extend to you and cause me no trouble."

Hunter clenched his hands into white, shaking fists. Generosity? He was only here because they robbed his house. His only crime was chasing down the thief. Dax threw him a warning look. It was nearly not enough, but he managed to choke back a response.

"Get him food," Quinnar said to Dax while rubbing his eye with the heel of his hand. "Find him a place to sleep. And keep him out of the way. But be here when we resume. I need your insight. Hopefully in a day or two I can figure out what to do about him, but right now, we have bigger questions."

Dax nodded and departed, once again not bothering to check if Hunter followed him or not.

15

HUNTER STEPPED through the opening into the small room lit by a single lantern on a round table. Three low cots covered in brown blankets lined the walls, looking like freshly dug gravesites.

"Nothing with a door?" he asked. "Preferably one with a lock."

"Those are few," Dax replied from the corridor. "These are not residences, but merely temporary accommodations. A place to disappear, or sleep when needed."

"Appears I'm the first permanent resident, then." A familiar loose-weave sack was in the center of one of the beds closest to the door. Hunter reached in and pulled out his jeans. Someone had already claimed the cot for him. "And you had someone deliver my luggage. Let me know where I should leave the tip."

"This will not be permanent," Dax said.

No. Only until someone slits my throat, Hunter thought. He was a heavy sleeper—he was going to have to learn how to sleep with one eye open.

"This area was selected because it is more isolated than

the others," Dax continued. "You are less likely to have to share it with anyone."

Hunter nodded, not wanting to appear grateful. Although the prospect of a little privacy right now, especially when everyone seemed hell-bent on seeing him dead, was welcome.

"How does anyone know what time it is down here?"

"You'll hear chimes. From dusk to dawn is one sound. Dawn to dusk another. There is more to show you."

"Sure. I'm sure I'll have time to unpack later."

Dax took Hunter through more corridors. The place was a labyrinth. He pointed out strange symbols carved in the walls. They looked like they might be some form of alphabet, but Hunter wasn't sure.

"These will help you navigate the tunnels," Dax told him. "Do not wander too far until you've learned them, lest you lose your way."

"Don't suppose you have a map. Or a key."

Dax pointed out the basic necessities. The toilets, first of all—which Hunter could certainly have found on his own. Blindfolded. Scrunching his nose, he peeked his head into the dark little room that had a long bench along a wall with three ovoid holes cut into it. Mercifully, the room had a door, but he would need to remember to bring a lantern along. Dax showed him a storage closet, though Hunter had no idea what supplies he would need from it, and a room that had a trough in the middle. Water trickled down the rough back wall and collected in barrels. A place to clean up, obviously, but with the city directly above them, Hunter couldn't help but wonder about the water source.

Warm air carrying the sweet smell of cooked meat wafted past him. They were nearing a kitchen, and his stomach responded with a groan. He hadn't eaten anything since the morning.

The kitchen occupied a wide cavern and felt more like a hellish forge. The floor was wood, but the walls and ceiling remained natural rock. In the center, a round cookfire blazed red and fierce like something demonic. Pots hung from chains over the flames on one side, and a whole pig was skewered on a spit over the other, fat dripping down to hiss on the coals. A soot-covered iron hood caught the rising black smoke and led it away.

The air was sultry and hot, but the smell of cooked meat was intoxicating. Hunter's stomach felt suddenly vacant.

"I must return," Dax said. "Eat. Return to the bedchamber. I trust you are able to find your way back."

Hunter glanced up at the symbol etched into the wall. "I'll figure it out."

Dax nodded. "Once we are concluded, I will look for you there."

Sitting in a dark empty room. "And what am I to do in the meantime?"

"Stay out of the way," he said as he departed back down the corridor.

"Hey! Dax?" Hunter called after him.

Dax slowed and looked over his shoulder.

"Thanks for sticking your neck out for me," Hunter said. "I guess you didn't have to do that." The truth of it was, if hadn't been for Dax these last few days, Hunter would have met a horrible death several times over already. The least he could do was acknowledge that.

In the dim light of the corridor, Hunter couldn't quite make out the shift in Dax's expression, but something had changed. Something subtle. Dax nodded and continued on his way.

Surrounding the central firepit were a number of wooden sawhorse tables and benches. Hunter approached tentatively, not knowing the protocol, and took a seat on a bench.

A hard thump drew Hunter's attention across the room. The cavern was not unoccupied as he first thought. A man stood at a higher table against the wall. He slammed a cleaver down on a hunk of meat and scraped the pieces aside. At his side, a dog sat very still with its muzzle pointed up. The man flicked a chunk of meat off the table, and the dog snatched it out of the air and swallowed it without chewing. The man glanced over his shoulder and took notice of Hunter.

"You waitin' on something?" the man asked. He was older and looked haggard and frail, like he hadn't left the kitchen in days. His white beard had dark bits hanging from it.

"Was told to come here to eat," Hunter replied.

The man scowled. "My food's for the fighters. Not strays."

"Dax sent me here."

His lip curled in a snarl as he turned away. "Ain't no tavern, and I ain't no serving wench. You want supper, get your ass up and get it. Plates and such over there."

As Hunter pushed himself up, the man was already turning back to his butchering.

The only option appeared to be a large black kettle with a bubbling stew. He ferreted out a ladle and scooped out a portion onto a wooden plate with a high lip. Wedges of dark bread were in a basket nearby, and he dropped a chuck of it on top. Off to the side, he found a keg with a twisting wooden spigot. He grabbed a mug and held it under the spigot, expecting water, but amber liquid poured into the mug and frothed on the top. Beer. Warm—but still beer. At least this place had something familiar, something reminiscent of home. A cold comfort. But enough of it and it might make this place mildly endurable. He carried his meal back to the table.

Voices echoing from a corridor announced the arrival of others. They erupted into the kitchen, laughing and shoving each other about like boys making their way back from the playground. They spotted Hunter as they broke the threshold, and the laughter cooled. They scooped up their food from the kettle and moved to occupy the table farthest from him.

Hunter ignore them while he ate, though he felt their disapproving stares the entire time, as if his presence was souring their meal. They spoke in low conspiratorial voices peppered with deep-throated grunts and snorts. Hunter didn't need to understand what they were saying to know he was the topic of their conversation. Word of his arrival here had clearly spread, and the consensus was not in his favor.

He sopped up the remains of the stew with the bread and slid his empty plate aside. Warning tension knotted his shoulders and neck. He recognized the body language well enough to know what might come next. Should the group decide to wander over, he was ready.

Of course, he could push up from the table and return to that little cave of a room, sit in the dark and wait for Dax to fetch him. He could give these boys a bit of breathing room, a chance to get used to his presence. But after everything, he didn't feel like being charitable. He didn't ask to be here, and they were just going to have to deal with it. The last thing he wanted was to send a message that he was easily intimidated. Far tougher guys had tried, and he wasn't about to be scared off by a sour look. So he leaned in on his elbows and locked eyes with anyone who looked his way.

From the corner of his eye, he caught someone else enter. The newcomer hugged the wall and entered cautiously, like a mouse scoping out the room for a cat. Hunter recognized the spiky, unkempt hair immediately. Uri. The kid who manned the entrance to the hideout. Here, in light that was better than in the corridor where he first saw him, Hunter got a better look at him. His skin was a pale blue, almost gray, and his ears were tapered upward to a rounded point.

Not Mazenti, like he'd seen outside the city walls. Or at least not entirely. The skin didn't have the same vibrant blue color. The boy was mixed race, human and Mazenti.

He crossed over to the cookfire and ladled a plate of stew for himself. Bowl in hand, he scanned his seating options. His gaze touched on Hunter briefly before he veered away from him, choosing a table near the others. As soon as he lowered onto a bench, one of the men slammed the side of his fist on the tabletop. He looked up and sighed, as if irritated his meal had been interrupted.

"What do you think you're doing, skeg?" he hissed.

"You know the rules," said another. He shoveled a spoonful into his mouth and shook his head.

Uri slowly rose again. He stood there a moment, steaming bowl in hand, clearly unsure what to do. The only other table put him closer to Hunter. With no other option, he shuffled over and sat on the edge of the bench as far from Hunter as he could.

The men chuckled as they exchanged looks, titillated with the power they exerted. Their attention was no longer on Hunter but on the boy, and Hunter could see the gears turning as they continued to smirk in his direction. The group was looking for a reason to escalate this and cause Uri more grief, punish him for some imagined crime. They'd obviously decided Hunter wasn't a worthwhile target and centered on the boy. Uri felt it too. He shoveled the food in his mouth as if someone might take it away from him. He couldn't wait to be out of there.

Hunter leaned forward and stared at the four of them. One by one they noticed him, and Hunter made sure to lock eyes until they turned away. The wicked grins slipped from each face, the joy in their game quashed.

One of the men pushed his bowl away in disgust. "Lost my appetite."

Hunter chuckled loud enough for them to hear. The plate was empty. The others nodded in agreement. They stood as a unit and left, plates abandoned in the center of the table.

Uri's shoulders seemed to deflate once the men were gone. He grabbed the plate and started to lift from the bench, ready to retreat to a table farther away.

"What's a skeg?" Hunter asked him.

Uri froze, not quite standing, not sitting. His fingers tightened around the edge of the plate. "I'm not supposed to talk to you."

"Why's that?"

"People say you don't belong here."

Word sure traveled fast down here. "Can't say I disagree with them," Hunter said with a low grunt in the back of his throat. "But here I am."

The reply seemed to confuse him a moment. His eyes flared with annoyance as he looked back down at the food waiting for him on the plate. "Doesn't mean you're welcome. Or trusted."

The irony of that made him want to chuckle. "Seems you know something about that."

Uri's head snapped involuntarily toward the empty passageway where the others had withdrawn before he turned a hot gaze in Hunter's direction. In the torchlight, his eyes glinted like a campfire ember. He was irked, and he only wanted to eat his dinner in peace. Hunter's questions were as unwanted as the harassment he endured by the four other men. "They don't mean anything by it."

Hunter sighed. Uri didn't believe that any more than he did. "My mistake."

Uri started to move again, rising to his full height and lifting a leg over the bench.

"No," Hunter told him as he stood. "Stay and finish your meal. I'm done."

He set the plate in a wooden tub with others and left the kitchen.

16

HUNTER'S ONLY indication that he'd been asleep at all was a vague recollection of disturbing dreams.

He swung his feet off the cot and rubbed his eyes with the heel of his hand. The dark cave of the common bunkroom hadn't changed, except someone had taken occupancy of the cot closest to the door and was snorting like a grizzly with a head cold. It was likely what had woken him up.

As he sat, a tall figure stepped into the doorway. Zinnuvial.

"Good," she said. "You're awake. Follow me." She disappeared down the hall again.

Hunter reached down to pull on the boots, but they were gone. Corrad had apparently stuck to his promise that he would reclaim them first chance he had. Either that or they'd been stolen, which meant he'd have to deal with Corrad about that. He considered putting on his own shoes, but athletic shoes with neon trim defeated the purpose of trying to fit in. He opted to go without and strode barefoot down the corridor after her.

He caught up with her in the kitchen. She glanced down

at his naked feet. "Where are your boots?"

"Repossessed apparently," he said. "Where's Dax?" He'd not returned to talk to him like he'd said he would. Hunter stayed awake as long as he could, hoping to have a word with him, but Dax never showed up, and Hunter fell into a fitful sleep.

"Attending to more important matters. Eat, before we lose more of this day." Her annoyance that she was shackled with him was palpable.

It was hard to even imagine it as daytime. His head felt foggy and his body sluggish as if he'd been roused in the middle of the night after a bender. This perpetual gloom was fucking with his internal clock. And heightening his sense of feeling trapped.

The only thing over the cookfire was a cast-iron pot filled with a viscous gray slop that bubbled and hissed. Hunter ladled himself a bowlful and took a seat. She filled a mug from a keg, set it down in front of Hunter, and sat across from him at the table, then watched as he ate without comment. She didn't seem the type for small talk, so Hunter didn't bother trying to engage her. The gray slop didn't look like much, but it had flavor. And it filled him up.

As he scraped the last of it from the bowl, Zinnuvial rose from the bench and marched off again. Hunter deposited the bowl in the bin and hurried to catch up to her.

Zinnuvial grabbed a lantern that hung from a peg in the wall, and they delved into a series of unfinished tunnels of raw stone, part of the mine network not yet tamed by the resistance. The area was eerily isolated; the general hum of activity in the hideout had faded to nothing. He was putting a lot of faith in someone who easily admitted she would kill him if she had the chance.

The tunnel ended at a narrow set of wooden stairs. Zinnuvial climbed up and used the heel of her hand to punch up a trap door. Sunlight blasted down in a deluge of light. Hunter groaned and covered his eyes with his forearm as the pungent smell of a barn besieged his sinuses.

Half-blind, he climbed out after her, blinking and squinting. Even though it had been only a single day of being held in a dark hole, the sun on him felt like an emancipation.

He shaded his eyes with his palm and felt packed warm sand under his feet. It took a bit for his eyes to open more than a slit, and he stumbled awkwardly after Zinnuvial's long silhouette. They emerged from under an open-air horse stall that reminded Hunter of a crude carport and into the heat of direct sunlight.

Blinking, Hunter scanned around him. They were in an enclosed courtyard, surrounded by buildings that looked either neglected or abandoned. Much of the yellow plaster walls had crumbled away to expose the stone bricks underneath. Wooden balconies, warped and ruined, hung precariously from the upper floors. The only visible exit was an arched tunnel that ended with massive double doors and a wooden beam lying horizontally across its middle, resting in heavy iron brackets.

He and Zinnuvial were alone. The quiet of the place was disconcerting.

"What is this place?"

Zinnuvial threw up the lid of a large pine box. She glanced his way, her expression cool, before bending into it. "A stable yard. Formerly. We use it for training." She dug two wooden swords from the box and tossed one of them roughly in Hunter's direction. On reflex, he extended his arm and snatched it from the air.

Something flashed behind Zinnuvial's eyes. Surprise, perhaps. She had expected a different outcome.

She gripped the hilt of her practice weapon and let the lid drop with a thud, then drifted to the center of the courtyard, her movements graceful and efficient. Nothing wasted. She looked like a dancer moving to the center of the stage to take her position before the music began.

Feeling clottish and awkward, he inspected the fake

weapon as he strolled out to meet her. The length of the wooden blade was marred with chips and gouges.

"Is this really necessary?" he asked.

"According to Master Dax, it is." Her face gave away nothing. Even holding a wooden sword, she looked strong and fierce. Intimidating. "I am told you have had no training." She spoke plainly, but she managed to make it sound like an insult.

"None," he told her. This was not what he wanted to be doing today. Still reeling from yesterday, he couldn't decide what he did want to do—slink back to bed or march out of this place. How was any of this helping him find a way home? It was waste of his time. And hers.

"Very well," she said. Hunter could almost hear her inward groan. "We begin at the beginning."

He adjusted his grip on the hilt, which had been wrapped in soft brown leather. Holding a weapon again, even though it was fake, brought back in a sickening rush the memory of the mace striking the head of the kug'ra. His arm seemed to recall the impact, and he nearly tossed the thing to the sand.

Zinnuvial didn't wait for his permission or compliance. The exercises began in earnest whether he wanted it to or not.

She first ran him through basic drills, just as Dax had done. Defense stances mainly, focusing on the position of his arms and feet, and the alignment of his back. She was very particular about the direction his feet were pointing. They ran through a series of poses together, side by side. "Guards," she called them, ways to position the sword to defend himself from an attack. They stepped into each pose, one transitioning into the other. She would count them off one at a time. When they reached the wall, they would turn and do it again from the other direction.

She drove him hard, demanding precision. She circled him, barking out each command. With the slightest variance from her instruction, she would grab the blade to redirect it to the right angle or kick his foot for being positioned incorrectly.

"No, no, no," she snapped at him. "You are treating the

sword as separate from your hand. It is not. It is an extension of yourself."

And as soon as he believed he had the hang of it, she would add a new guard position and run him through the list again from the beginning.

Hunter breathed through his nose and kept his teeth tightly set. He had plenty to say back to her, but his ego kept the words locked behind his tongue. Without even being aware of it, he settled into training mode—a hardened and deep-rooted coach/player dynamic that was etched into his brain like acid on metal. He accepted her treatment. He almost welcomed it. It scratched something familiar in him.

The physicality, the repetition, the snarling commands, the sun and sweat on his skin. It was all something he knew. He caught himself digging in, fighting to get it right, and giving himself over to it.

He would have preferred a rugby ball to the wooden sword, but it was better than nothing.

After more than an hour, they took a break for water, taking turns ladling it out of a rain barrel. Hunter's heart rate was up, and his tunic was soaked through. He pulled off the tunic, swept it across his forehead, and tossed it aside. The activity had cleared his head and burned off some of the black energy that had built up in him. He felt more focused and alert than he'd been in days. It felt good to move again.

Zinnuvial stepped back out to the center of the yard. "Get into your stance and face me."

Hunter obeyed.

"I will call out the defensive guard, then step in. Use the guard to ward off my attack."

Hunter nodded and readied himself. His mind quickly tried to catalog all the varying poses she'd demonstrated to him. There were too many to remember. He hadn't had enough time to build them into his muscle memory yet.

"Full iron gate," she barked, and she came at him.

He expected her to come in slow, at least in the

beginning, to give him time to get used to this new drill, but she came at him at nearly full speed. A straight thrust aimed at his belly. His timing was off. The blades didn't connect. The tip of his sword dove into the sand, and hers came to a halt an inch from his rib cage.

"Too slow," she said as she drew back. "A mistake like that means death. Again. Full iron gate."

She hardly gave Hunter enough time to get into his proper stance before she stepped into her attack. This time, Hunter matched her speed—and deflected the attack.

She stepped back and returned to her starting position. "Full iron gate."

Over and over, she came at him with the same attack. But each time it varied slightly—by speed, or direction, or intensity—forcing Hunter to adapt and adjust his defense. But she didn't get past him a second time.

"Where's Dax this morning?" he asked as they stepped away from each other.

"Employed in more important matters."

"Is he around? Here in the hideout?"

Her eyes lifted to meet his as she slid into her stance. "No."

Hunter wasn't sure he believed her. He adjusted the angle of his feet and shifted his weight on his back leg. "What can you tell me about him?"

"I can tell you nothing."

"Nothing? I get the impression the two of you work pretty closely."

"It is not for me to speak of him. If you have questions, speak to him yourself. Full iron gate."

"He's not the forthcoming type. You could give me your perspective."

"I have no perspective I am willing to share."

"All right. What about yourself. Can you speak on that?"

She paused and held his gaze a moment. "You ask a great deal of questions. We are here to train."

She was dodging. But he had to start somewhere to break the ice. He didn't have a single soul in this world to talk to beside Dax.

"How long have you been fighting?" he asked as they pulled back to their starting positions once again.

"Since I could hold a sword. Half iron gate." She came in higher and at an odd angle, driving Hunter's left elbow up more, but he still guided the weapon aside.

"Who taught you?"

"My father. Half iron gate."

She came in with a different attack. Hunter's brain scrambled to remember the position. He gave in to instinct and executed a sloppy, half-cocked version of the guard, but he managed to meet her blade.

"Why so young? Were you expected to become a soldier?"

"You are relying on your strength to protect you," she said. "It will not. Reflexes. Cunning. Planning. Those are what you need to sharpen. Half iron gate."

He was ready for it this time.

"What brought you into the resistance?" he asked.

Her face darkened. "These are not questions you should be asking."

"Of you?"

"Of anyone here. You're prying—"

"I'm not prying. They're harmless enough questions."

"No question is harmless. Mother's guard."

A new one again. But the position stuck with him because of the odd name. He met her attack easily.

"I'm just trying to get to know you," he said. She had come in harder than before, and the impact made his hand sting.

She ignored him and came at him again. Faster this time. He could feel her holding back, but still her speed and precision were unsettling. He imagined there were few who could best her in combat.

"Since I'm here," he said, "shouldn't I know what this fight of yours is about?"

"The less you know, the better."

The same bullshit line Quinnar gave him. "Apparently, I'm here for a while. I should know what I'm facing."

"It will be hard enough to keep a knife out of your belly without you giving people a reason."

"Knowing why you fight makes me a threat?"

"Full iron gate," Zinnuvial said and came at him. "Your questions will make people suspicious."

"Then, you answer them."

Again, cold silence followed as she ran through the drill. She didn't trust him either. She was only here because she was ordered to train him. But she wasn't about to divulge any information that could threaten their cause.

"Why does everyone assume I'm some evil spy? A villain twirling my mustache, waiting for the opportunity to betray you all."

"Betrayal doesn't always come in the form of deceit and duplicity. Stupidity, ignorance, even weakness, can lead to treachery."

"Maybe I'm not any of those things," he shot back.

"Maybe you are all three."

"Maybe you could take a minute to get to know me first," he grumbled. "Then decide."

Her attacks were ramping up. She no longer called off the guard but came at him with random strikes. He met each of them. Sometimes clumsily, but his blade still deflected hers aside. He could sense her frustration building. She wanted him to make a mistake so she could criticize his technique.

His own pride kicked in. He wasn't going to give her the opportunity if he could help it.

This was what he did. He was an athlete. He trained. For strength, of course. But he also trained his reaction time. Trained his ability to read an opponent. And he was a fast learner. This was just a new twist on a game he'd played his entire life.

The speed intensified. She came at him harder. Two attacks in a row. Then three. His sword was moving faster now, driven by instinct and muscle memory. He gave in to it. Trusting it. A deep part of his brain took over and anticipated her attacks, subtly picking up on cues as to what was coming next, while a fragment of his conscious mind was amazed how quickly he'd adopted the positions and was ready for each attack.

But then she shifted her tactic. She came in and feigned an attack—then altered her approach. He recovered and managed to block an upward swing, but she returned immediately with a reverse that brought her blade against the side of his head.

It was intentional. She was too skilled for that to have been a mistake.

He pressed his fingers against the bone of the temple along the edge of his eye socket. The skin was still tender from the elbow he'd taken during the match. Had that really only been a few days ago? He hadn't seen a mirror since he'd been here and wondered absently if it was still bruised.

There'd be a fresh one there now regardless.

He looked directly into Zinnuvial's eyes—and glimpsed the anger behind them. She tried to hide it behind a stoic wall of indifference, as if Hunter didn't matter to her.

But it was there. Hunter had no idea what fueled it. His mere presence in the hideout? Her being forced to babysit him when there was important work to be done? His ability to at least somewhat hold his own the first day of training? Perhaps it was all of it.

She watched him, awaiting a response. Her eyes were slightly wider, her cheeks flushed. Perhaps she was as surprised as he was that she allowed herself to strike him. It was clear she expected a complaint from him, expected him to flare in anger, maybe shout at her or storm off. He didn't. Instead he returned to his starting position once more.

But she lowered her arm and tossed the fake weapon to the ground.

"Enough for one day." She walked off the practice field with a controlled gait. She flung open the trapdoor to the underground and froze. Hunter could see her shoulders rise and fall as she took on long breaths. She looked over her shoulder.

"You know nothing of us," she said. "Nothing of our plight. And yet you believe we should trust you. Simply because."

She disappeared below, leaving Hunter alone in the midday sun and warm sand.

His mind whirled. The turn in her had occurred so quickly, he fought to make sense of what happened. But his gut told him the truth.

He'd gone about it all wrong.

Zinnuvial was governed by loyalty. Loyalty to her pack—and the pack was always suspicious of the outsider. He'd tried to elbow his way in, looking for answers, but force never worked. He'd been the outsider long enough to know that.

And like it or not, he was an outsider. Again. He had to remember that.

He was seized by an unexpected memory—time in the scrum during their last match. Eight of them, grunting and calling out, driving hard and digging cleats into the ground. Him in the back, his head squeezed between the hips of the two locks, guiding and stabilizing the push forward. A scrum was as much a chess match as it was a show of raw power and strength. Eight fighting as single unit, one mind with one goal, and trust was everything.

His heart tightened. He hadn't really thought about it much, but he missed them. The tribe he'd worked so hard to infiltrate. His new family. But this training session seemed to hook into his connection to them and drag it all to the surface, and thinking about them—Bilbo, Samson, Torch, Captain

Cowboy, and all the rest—it made his insides ache. He missed that sense of belonging, the camaraderie. The strange language they had that no one else understood. It ate away at him like a slow-burning acid sitting in his gut.

His acceptance into the rugby squad had been hard fought. At the beginning, no one thought he was worthy. No one thought that a faggot could stand with them, keep up, and hold his own. Daily, he stood up to the underlying machismo culture that dominated the locker room. No one was overtly contemptuous—Coach Titan would never allow it. The ostracism was more subtle. More nuanced than something organized or planned.

It took months, but it did change. Slowly. With minuscule differences that were impossible to qualify and slipped by without notice. And one day, with a black eye as his ticket of entry, he was one of them. He had no awareness of the journey until it was over. Somehow he convinced them that he deserved a place among them, and he had no recollection of when or how the switch occurred.

Now it was gone. Probably forever. He was starting all over again. With a new pack.

A pack that wouldn't only reject him but would likely kill him. For whatever reason, Dax had decided he was worth keeping alive. But no one else here felt that way. Hunter needed to remember that. If he was going to survive this, he needed to be smarter.

He picked up the practice sword Zinnuvial had dropped, returned both to the pine box, and sat on the lid.

For a time, he stared at the massive doors and considered giving up. He could lift the beam from the brackets, push open the door, and be gone. It would be easy enough. Just slip out and be away from this madness. Disappear into this city. But then what? He knew nothing of this world, nothing of its dangers. How long before he was dead? He may be treated like a prisoner here, but in a strange and inexplicable way, he was protected.

He had no choice but to stay.

But he also had no desire to head back inside, back into the dour confinement of the hideout, back to grim little room he'd been assigned. If he was going to be alone, he'd rather experience it here, in the sun. So he sat there until the sun sank behind the building and the courtyard was draped in shadow.

Hunger finally compelled him to head back down. Feeling sullen and tired, he retraced the path through the tunnels. In the now quiet and empty kitchen, he loaded up a plate of food and ate it without tasting it, then he drifted back to the small room and his cot. A part of him wondered if Dax would be around, maybe waiting for him, but the room was vacant and dark. With a sigh, he stripped off the sweat-soaked clothes and left them on the foot of the bed. After traveling in them and training in them all day, they were starting to smell a bit ripe.

For a time, he could only stare at the dark stone ceiling. Tired as he was, sleep felt distant and unobtainable. Despite everything, he was still finding it hard to accept any of this was real. More so, accepting that this was once his mother's world was beyond comprehension.

How could his mother, a woman of such grace and generosity, come from a place teeming with such violence?

But then, was his own world any different? A memory of his past crawled up from the dusty basement of his mind. From their roach infested one-bedroom apartment on the fifth floor, he would often wake to the jarring pop of gunfire in the middle of night. It was their first home after his father had left. All she could afford, she said. When he crawled in bed with her, frightened, he remembered her murmuring to herself about how their Uptown neighborhood was a war zone.

Guns were uncivilized, she'd told him once. Dishonorable and cowardly. He hadn't understood what she'd meant by that. Until now.

Not long after, they moved from that apartment to a place farther west. It took her longer to get to work, but she said it was worth it. And Hunter would sleep through the night.

Strange that he would recall of all that now.

Violence was everywhere, he supposed. Regardless of the universe you were in.

With his hands behind his head, thinking of his own quiet apartment on his quiet tree-lined street, he eventually drifted off to sleep.

17

SOMETHING DREW Hunter out of a fragile sleep. He wasn't alone.

He pried open his eyes and lifted his head. Yellow light from the corridor spilled in through the open doorway and brushed over a figure that sat on a cot, back to the wall. Hunter blinked and used the heel of his palm to wipe the wet from the corner of his eyes that blurred his vision. It took a moment for him to recognize the small stature and curve of his bare shoulder and arm.

"This is more than a little creepy," Hunter said.

Dax lifted his head, jarred from some thought. "It's quiet here. I was using the time to think." There was uneasiness in his tone, a sense that something weighed on him. Or maybe he was only tired. His presence here wasn't happenstance; that much was obvious. In this sprawling old labyrinth of tunnels, certainly there were plenty of other places he could hide for some quiet reflection time. He was here for a reason.

Hunter rolled to his side and propped his torso up on one elbow. "What time is it?"

"Late," Dax said and fell quiet again. He turned toward

the open doorway, but Hunter got the sense he wasn't looking at anything.

Hunter was loath to admit it even to himself, but he was relieved to see him. After facing borderline hostility the entire day, Dax was the closest he had to a friendly face. He swung his bare legs off the cot, placing his feet on the cold floor. He remembered then he was naked, having stripped off the ripe, sweat-soaked clothes before turning in. Feeling exposed, he slid the thin blanket he had over his lap.

"Your boyfriend know you're here?" he asked.

Dax rose and moved to the cot nearest to Hunter's and sat on the edge, facing him. Even in the dark, Dax's presence seemed to press in on him. His body was in silhouette from the light in the corridor. Hunter couldn't read his face, but he thought he saw Dax's lips tighten. "Do not antagonize Quinnar. It will bode ill for you."

Me? Antagonize him?

"Can't make any promises," Hunter grumbled.

"He can be short tempered and intolerant of those who push him—"

"Same here."

"—and he can make things quite difficult for you."

"My life sucks pretty hard right now, so…."

"He will make it worse."

Hunter made a noncommittal shrug. He wasn't about to grovel to Quinnar or allow him to intimidate him. He didn't do anything to deserve any of this, and he would walk straight out of the place if came to that, regardless of the consequences. He knew a way out now if need be.

"Is that why you're here?" Hunter asked. "To warn me about him?"

Dax leaned in, elbows on his knees. He took a deep breath and exhaled slowly—and Hunter caught the acerbic burn of something potent on his breath.

Dax had been drinking. From the smell, possibly a lot. "In part." His stoic veneer had been stripped back, but in the

142

dark, Hunter couldn't read what was beneath it. He sounded pensive. And sullen. "I came to check on your well-being. But you were already asleep."

"My well-being," Hunter repeated. Was he feeling guilty for the stunt he pulled?

The narrow distance between them felt oddly dangerous. Hunter kept his eye off the line of light that traced Dax's bare shoulder and tricep. He leaned back, propping his torso up with locked arms behind him—mainly to put a little distance between them.

Dax's chin lowered to his chest and silence settled over them. He was loitering. Stalling. But Hunter had no idea why. He was naked and cornered with no idea where this was going, and it made him want to squirm.

"It has taken some wrangling," Dax said after a time, "but for the most part, the council has been pacified. With some promises made."

What did that mean?

"I would counsel you, however," Dax continued, "to remain low for a time. Try not to bring attention to yourself. Or give people a reason to be wary of you."

Was this supposed to make him feel relieved? Grateful? "Sure. I'll hide out here in the dark until things blow over."

Dax's head lifted. Hunter could feel his eyes drill into him. "Give people time."

Time? That was something he didn't have. Every day that ticked past here, he lost ten times more back home.

"The council can be vexing, I admit," Dax went on. "Simultaneously willful and indecisive." His voice in the dark hinted at something underneath that hard shell. Maybe it was the alcohol greasing his wheels, but Hunter glimpsed something unexpected. Something other than the hard-bitten solider. "But these are not lifelong radicals, hungry for unrest. They are merchants, artisans, a few nobles, all thrust into a conflict they did not foresee. They have lost much and stand to lose more. You can't blame them for being afraid."

A surprisingly generous defense of them. Hunter wouldn't have expected it from Dax. "I don't, I suppose. I am too."

Dax's head lifted a fraction. Hunter's admission was clearly unexpected. He nodded after a moment, as if accepting it as truth. "Is there anything you require?"

Hunter bit back all the obvious snarky retorts and tried to wrestle his tongue into a more civil tone. Dax was obviously trying. He could make an attempt too. "A drink. A strong one. I'd like a strong drink."

"You are entitled to one, I suppose."

"Have one handy?"

Dax stood and crossed the room, back to where he was sitting when Hunter first woke. He returned, and this time sat down next to Hunter on the same cot and handed over a large steel flask encased in leather.

Dax's new proximity made Hunter's heart lurch. He was keenly aware of how close his own naked thigh was from Dax's leg, and he itched to pull more blanket over his lap, but Dax was now sitting on the bulk of it. Only a small bit of the blanket covered his groin.

Was Dax so obtuse as to not realize how intimate this appeared?

Hunter kept his eyes forward as he pulled the cork stopper from the neck and tilted the opening to his mouth. The sharp liquid stung the back of his throat and ran a warm streak under his sternum. His throat constricted, and he fought the urge to cough. Dax had delivered—this was strong stuff.

"A few answers would be nice too," he said. "Since you're here."

"You are entitled to that too."

"Your boyfriend won't complain I know too much now, will he?" He winced inwardly after the remark slid from his mouth. He couldn't help but add a bit of snark, could he? Why was he always awkward and stupid in quiet moments like this? He was thankful Dax had come, but at the same time, he was uneasy. Anxious.

Dax had made the effort to come here—whatever his reason. Hunter could at least try to be cordial.

Thankfully, Dax ignored the comment. Instead, he leaned forward again, resting his elbows on his knees.

"All right," Hunter said. "My mom's broach. What's so important about it?"

Dax began with a long, full breath. "A public gift from King Ruzad to his bride Queen Jenora on their wedding day. The jewel in the amulet was enchanted to glow when she wears it upon her breast."

"Ah," Hunter said. It took him only a moment to deduce this plan. "Get her to put it on, expose her as an imposter."

Dax nodded. "Yes."

"I never saw my mother wear it," Hunter said. "Not once. She made sure I knew where it was, though. At all times. And always kept it locked away in that little box. I never understood why it was so damn important to her." An image of the broken box on his bedroom floor, with its red velvet lining exposed, flashed into his mind. He took another swig from the flask. "Where is it now?"

"Safe. Until we figure out our next move."

Hunter wasn't nearly ready to even accept his mother was from this world. Trying to imagine her as the queen was going to break his brain. "This plan seems rather absurd, if you ask me. How do you get her to put on something that she knows will expose her as a fraud?"

Hunter expected Dax to defend it, but he didn't respond. He continued to stare down at his hands. The cold silence said plenty—he thought the same thing.

"Can't imagine doing what you did. Blindly leaping into another world? If you had doubts about this plan, why'd you do it?" Hunter held out the flask to him, but Dax rejected it with an outward palm. This was not his first flask of the evening, Hunter surmised.

Dax sighed and kneaded the center of his palm with his

thumb. "There is growing dissonance between the members of the council. Spawned by fear. The palace has started using innocents to flush us out. Executing people they know are not involved. Loved ones targeted. No one can agree on how to combat this, so the coalition is spiraling off into factions. Quinnar is fighting to keep the resistance intact and focused. This mission was supposed to unite us again."

"And you volunteered for it?"

Dax nodded.

"You're insane," Hunter replied. "You know that?"

Dax made a low grunt in his back of his throat. "No one else had the necessary skills. And I work better alone."

The ever-faithful soldier, following orders. Doing what was expected of him for the cause.

Hunter took another swig from the flask, and as he wiped his mouth with the back of his hand, he studied Dax's face. The light from the corridor dusted the contours of Dax's profile. The sharp edge of his steely confidence seemed quietly blunted.

"How'd you even know where to look for it?"

"Sorcery," Dax replied as if it were obvious. "We managed to pluck a viable witchstone from a connected nobleman."

That again. Hunter held out his hand. "Hold on. What exactly is a witchstone?"

The corner of Dax's mouth lifted in what might have been a smile. "I forget how different your world is. A rare crystal. Fyrollite, but most call it witchstone. It has a particular quality. It can absorb an ambient power that leaks into our world from another."

"There's an opening between two universes?"

"It's a fissure of some kind, natural perhaps, but no one knows for certain."

Hunter couldn't help but wonder if such a connection existed between his own world and this one.

"Some believe," Dax continued, "that it was caused by a

portal stone, like the one I used. Only it never closed. The power seeps into our world slowly over time. Some are born sensitive to it. They can perceive it, manipulate it. However, in its ambient form, it is weak."

"Is it common? To be able to use this power?"

"Among our kind, no. Rather rare, in fact. Henerans appear to have a more innate aptitude for it and can harness it more readily, but even they are limited in their ability to utilize the ambient source. To truly tap its full potential, you need fyrollite."

"Witchstone," Hunter said. "What does it do?"

"Over centuries, the ambient power is absorbed by the stone, and it becomes concentrated in it. Enough for sorcerers do more with it. Much more."

"A magical battery," Hunter said, more to himself.

"We were lucky to get our hands on it," Dax said. "It's highly controlled. The mine's location in the Crags is a closely guarded secret."

"Of course it is," Hunter commented. Government 101. Anything that provides that much power is always strictly monitored and regulated. Everyone running around with magic stones would upset the balance of how things work.

But if he was going to find a way home, he needed to get his hands on a chunk of fyrollite.

"It took a bit of cajoling, but the council approved of Quinnar's plan to use the witchstone to locate the amulet."

"And you found it in my world," Hunter said.

"As well as who was in possession of it—"

"Me."

"The witchstone had enough power to create the two portal stones."

"One to get you there. One back." But not enough for a third. Quinnar made sure of that when he used it to find Dax.

"It was a huge gambit," Dax added. "A desperate move. And the cost was too high. It drained our coffers. Sorcerers do not work for free."

So, Hunter mused, he would need three things to get home. A chunk of fyrollite, access to that sorcerer, and the currency to pay him for it. No problem.

It felt like a brick had been dropped into his stomach.

He offered the flask to Dax once again. He hoped to keep him talking—as long as he was answering his questions Hunter was going to keep asking them. He expected Dax to reject it again, but this time, he took it and bent it to his lips.

"How did people figure out that the queen was an imposter?" he asked. The queen. Saying it out loud made his stomach sink. That woman had once been his mother. How would he ever get used to that?

"A cruelty that wasn't there before. She became vindictive. Ruthless. Arrests were made against anyone who slighted her in some way. At first it was quietly done, but such things are hard to keep concealed forever. Eventually, she didn't bother hiding it, and the executions became public. And more brutal. She made changes in laws without warning, ending centuries of custom. It all pointed to something."

It didn't surprise him people picked up on the change. His mother had a gentle way about her that seemed to affect everyone she came across. Including himself. He was a better person around her. When he saw the woman on the balcony, he recognized its absence even from that distance. "The king doesn't seem to notice."

"Enchanted as well, we presume. Perhaps into a dulled complacency."

Hunter took the flask back from Dax and took another hearty slug from it. They were getting to the bottom of it. His forehead felt heavier, and it was harder to focus his thinking. The booze was taking hold.

His thoughts drifted to memories of his mother, moments that stood out like roadside flares in his mind, and he tried to picture her as a queen. It all made sense in an unexpected way. She had a dignity and strength about her that was unmatched. But the melancholy in her, residing just beneath the surface of her skin—well, that made sense now too.

"You have no idea who this imposter is?" he asked.

"Specifically? No. Her identity is hidden through sorcery. But we have a clear idea who is behind it."

"Henerans." Hunter had no idea how he knew that. Of course they were behind this. "What are they trying to accomplish?"

"What they have always hoped to accomplish. Claim back the lands we took from them one hundred years ago. The Crags."

Ah. It was all piecing together. This was about power. The fyrollite mines and who controlled the witchstone.

"What they couldn't reclaim through war," Dax continued, "they now attempt through subterfuge and cunning."

"Seems to be working."

Dax didn't comment.

"Why didn't they just kill her?" Hunter asked.

"A simple enchantment could have located her here. Even dead. When suspicions arose, they didn't want her found. They hoped sending her beyond the veil of our world would conceal their ploy. They didn't anticipate us getting ahold of enough witchstone."

He tried to imagine what it would be like if something like this happened back home. Tried to imagine how much courage it would take to risk execution to fight back, to resist a tyrant. "So, how did you get involved?"

Dax thought a moment. "I was a scout, responsible for keeping an eye on movements. In a secret meeting, I was told that the throne no longer considered the Henerans a target of reconnaissance. That I was no longer to cross over into their territory. In the interest of improved relations, they said."

So, he was a spy. Just as the kug'ra and Henerans had accused him. It explained how they knew who he was. And how he knew his way through their territory so well.

Dax scratched at his beard. "The reason smelled false to me. I started asking questions. Too many, it turns out. I was branded a traitor. Luckily, I was alerted that my arrest was imminent, so I fled. And sought others in hiding like me."

Hunter was piecing it together. The weapons cache the kug'ra had in the camp. Dax telling Quinnar about the lack of guards at the border. The imposter queen was working from inside the palace to hide what they were up to.

Once again, the conversation stalled into a quiet intermission. Hunter fell into a booze-induced fog of convoluted thoughts. About his mother and her life here mainly. This was her world. Her *home*. And she was a fucking queen, ruling a kingdom alongside a man he knew nothing about until a day ago.

This was her world. The thought badgered his mind and refuse to relent. Her world, and by default, didn't that make it his too? Half of him came from here.

Dual citizenship, he thought dourly.

Had his father known? Maybe that was why he left, why he took off in the middle of the night without a single word of goodbye. Not that Hunter cared. The rat bastard never brought anything but shit-ton of misery and pain to him and his mother anyway.

He was pulled out of it when Dax's hand rested on his shoulder. The contact made Hunter's skin tingle with energy.

"I've kept you enough," Dax said. "I'll leave you to get some rest."

Hunter nodded, and Dax rose to his feet. He glided toward the doorway.

"One more question," Hunter said and stood too, holding the blanket in front of him. "Why did you do all this for me, Dax?"

Dax looked out into the corridor, and for a moment, Hunter wondered if he would leave without answering it. "You are the son of our queen. Although you are not of royal blood, in my view that affords you some consideration."

"And should Quinnar decide that I'm not worth the trouble?"

"Let's hope it doesn't come to that." Dax disappeared into the corridor and was gone. Hunter never heard a single footstep on the floorboards.

18

HUNTER NEVER thought a time would come when he would miss the stalwart blue-white glow of his alarm clock. When he opened his eyes, the tiny cave bedroom was unchanged. The hazy memory of troubling dreams told him he'd slept—but he had no idea if it was for an hour or ten. It could have been noon up above for all he knew.

Not that it mattered. His docket had plenty of vacancies. Only two things were on his must-do list. Use the bath and find boots.

Two chimes rang out from the corridor. It was still predawn. Which told him practically nothing. He let his eyes close again, and he lingered in the twilight between sleep and consciousness for a time until he heard a single chime announcing daybreak.

He wasn't sure why he'd waited. It was the arbitrary threshold, perhaps a way to force himself to maintain a conventional schedule down here. He had a new appreciation for those who spent time in a submarine. It was surprisingly easy to lose a connection to the outside world. He swung his bare feet onto the cold floor, arched his back, and stretched the stiff muscles of his shoulders and arms. The soreness felt good. Invigorating. A sign he'd accomplished something yesterday.

His conversation with Dax bounced about in his head like a bird trapped in a house. It felt more like a dream than something real, and the strange and inexplicable visit in the middle of the night spawned more questions than Dax had answered.

Specifically, why had he come? It wasn't a wellness check. Easy enough to peek in and see he was still alive. And any of the information he gave him could have waited until morning. So what was it really about?

He grabbed the tunic and pants from the foot of the bed and held them to his nose before he pulled them on. Finding somewhere to clean them would have to be added to his tight schedule.

He followed his nose back to the small mess hall, the pathway from his bedroom familiar enough now to find it without much thought. Another day or two and it'd become routine. The notion of that tugged down on his soul like an anchor. He didn't want to imagine a life down there. The idea of being stuck there for days was unnerving to even consider.

He could navigate around the basics now, take care of his immediate survival needs. But with Dax's appearances being erratic at best, he was going to have to be more self-reliant. Certainly no one else was eager to offer any help. It fell on him.

He scooped up another bowl of the thick gruel and took a quiet table well away from some others who were eating, a hardened and somewhat seedy group who looked like they'd just arrived from the wilderness. Hunter hadn't seen any of them before, which was evidently the norm down here. As Dax had implied, the hideout was a transient place. No one stayed down here for too long. Who would want to? But it was clear they knew who he was. Sidelong looks stabbed his way, and the talk among them quieted. One of them furtively, almost involuntarily, reached down to his boot and fingered the hilt of the dagger hidden there, tugging it upward a fraction to make sure it was readily accessible.

Carrying around a weapon of his own was starting to sound like a good idea. Not that he was proficient enough to defend himself yet. But it might act as a deterrent. It might also provoke some of these already jittery rebels into viewing him as a threat. He cringed inwardly, a part of him disgusted he would even consider it. He was a guy from Chicago. The idea of walking around with a sharp weapon at his hip seemed absurd.

Guttural talk ramped up among them slowly, though their voices remained low. They were uneasy about something. And angry. Hunter caught only fragments of it, and not enough to fully glean what had happened. They spoke of a raid. Someone dragged off during the night. And the deaths of comrades. Many, by the sound of it.

"They knew," one of them said, drumming fingers on the table. "They weren't just lucky this time, I tell ya. They knew." And Hunter could feel their attention again shift toward him.

Hunter's spine stiffened. His skin prickled in anticipation. He kept his eyes on the bowl on the table, but he was waiting for something to happen. Waiting for them to stand from the table. Their emotions were raw and itching for a direction. The slightest provocation would goad these men to violence. And Hunter was a convenient scapegoat.

Uri wandered in.

The shift in focus was immediate. For a moment Hunter was forgotten. They scrunched their noses as Uri made his way to the kettle. Uri kept his chin down and his shoulders hunched as if trying to will himself invisible. He chose a table nearer Hunter but sat on the bench with his back to him.

Hunter watched the rugged band in his peripheral vision, expecting one of them to now choose Uri as a target for their anger. It would only take one to start something. Only a trigger to set the violence into motion. But to his surprise, they let him be and left as a group shortly after.

Adrenaline still surging beneath his skin, Hunter took a few long breaths before he took his empty bowl and spoon to the wooden crate already heaped with dishes. More were stacked onto the floor around it.

He needed something to do, needed to focus this crazed energy somewhere, so he hoisted the crate with a grunt and carried it to the table where the same man from yesterday worked his way through a small mountain of potatoes.

He threw a hard glare at Hunter. "I'll get to it," he said with a scowl.

"Where do they get cleaned?" Hunter asked.

The man's brows drew together, and he leered at him like one might at a puzzle. "Leave it."

"I've got time and need something to do," Hunter told him. "Just point me in the direction."

The man eyed him with suspicion, as if trying to figure out Hunter's angle. He clearly doubted the offer was a genuine one. But he tilted his head toward a table across the room. Hunter nodded and carried the crate over, feeling the man's stare pressing into his back. A small cleaning station had been set up with an earthenware basin, a slop bucket, and a stiff brush. A barrel of clean water stood beside the table.

It took him perhaps an hour to scrub clean all the dishware, even the ones that had been placed on the floor. He stacked them neatly on a shelf. People came and went as he cleaned, but he paid no attention to them. It did his soul good to have a task that felt familiar and mundane. While everyone else left their dirty dishware on the tables or on the floor where the crate had been, Uri brought his empty bowl over to the table next to Hunter. He said nothing and quickly slunk away down a corridor. The cook came over once to inspect his work, and before he returned to his potatoes, told him where to dump the bucket and where to find the well to replace the water he used.

"Any idea where I can find a pair of boots?" he asked the cook once he was finished, wiping his pruned hands on his thighs.

The cook's eyes shifted briefly down at Hunter's bare feet. "Pernibran. She's the only cordwainer involved here."

"Pernibran," Hunter repeated. "Any idea where I'd find her?"

"Her shop, likely. Merchant District. Some masters and journeymen have set up workshops in the south caverns. Can't say if she's one of them."

Hunter pursed his lips. Well, her shop was out of the question. Finding which direction was south was another problem. The man seemed stiff and uneasy, as if nervous people would catch them talking, so he didn't press him. Instead, Hunter thanked him and left the kitchen. He'd figure it out on his own later.

HUNTER STARTED down tunnels with the intent of exploring more of the underground complex but found himself retracing his steps back to the practice field. An unplanned destination, but he decided to roll with what his subconscious was telling him. A workout had always been a part of his day and maybe, to stave off any impending madness, routine was what he needed.

He climbed out into the open air of the yard and immediately filled his lungs. An unblemished indigo sky reigned overhead, and a morning wind spawned little vortexes of sand that raced across the field. It was early still. Most of the yard was painted in shadow. Only the top half of the buildings on one side of the courtyard were lit with morning sun.

The yard was empty except for a crow perched on a post. Its black eyes followed Hunter as he moved into the yard, making annoyed little squawks. It was not thrilled with the interruption. It voiced one more complaint before it launched the air and came to rest on the railing of a balcony.

The sun hadn't broken over the top of the buildings yet,

so the sand was cool against the soles of his feet. Since no one was around, he pulled off his tunic and submerged it into the rain barrel and sloshed it about. The morning air was crisp against his skin. He massaged the tunic under the surface for a minute or so, then wrung it out fully and hung it on the post the crow had vacated.

He dug into the pine box for a practice sword, but beneath the cluster of wooden ones he used yesterday were ones of steel. Real swords. He slid one out and gripped it, swiping at the air in front of him. It was dented and tarnished, and the edges were dulled. Even the tip of it was rounded. But the weight distribution felt different than the wood swords. Substantial. Balanced. It felt the way he would expect a sword to feel.

Intrigued, he strolled out to the center and got to work.

He first ran through the drills Zinnuvial had taught yesterday, surprised at how much of it he remembered. He called off each guard position as he stepped into it. After a few minutes, his muscles warmed and loosened, the soreness from earlier melting away. Before long, as the sun line on the western wall almost reached the sand, his skin was covered in a film of sweat.

He took a break—ladled out a drink from the barrel and splashed chill water onto his torso and over his head. When he turned around to resume, swooping the wet strands of hair from his eyes, Zinnuvial stood by the horse corral, arms woven over her chest.

"In the future," she said, "please let someone know of your whereabouts. I wasted too much of my morning trying to locate you."

Hunter wondered how long she'd been there and if she'd been watching him practice. He marched back out to the center of the yard, feeling her scrutiny. "Perhaps next time let me know that we had an appointment." And precisely who would he have told anyway?

She studied him a moment longer before she strode to

the pine box, tossed back the lid, and pulled out a sword for herself. Hunter settled into the defense posture, shifting his weight to his right leg, as Zinnuvial glided out to meet him.

"A sword of steel today," she noted with a single brow raised.

"Figured I'd try it," he said. "See what it felt like."

"Ah. One lesson and you feel you have conquered the basics and are ready to advance."

"Not at all, Master Zinnuvial." She was goading him, looking for a reaction. But he'd learned his lesson from yesterday. Proving himself was only part of what he needed to do. He had to wait for the door to be opened, not kick his way through it.

She considered him with narrow eyes. Hunter could see her mind trying to work out if was mocking her.

He bowed his head. "I didn't know we would be sparring today."

She regarded him coolly. "Training takes place every day. That is how skills are mastered."

He would not argue with that. Even on days when there wasn't a scheduled practice, he was training at the gym or running skill and reflex drills alone on the pitch. Or both. "Should I exchange this for a wood one, then?"

Her lips pursed as she continued to watch him. "No. Experience with the genuine weight can be beneficial."

He shrugged. "I'm game if you are."

Her expression changed. Slightly. Her eyes seemed to alight with something that could have been amusement. She reached into the pouch at her waist and withdrew a pair of leather gloves. As she tugged them on, she swept her gaze down to his naked feet. "You are still without boots."

"I'm working on it."

She accepted his response with a nod and drew back into her offensive position.

And without preamble or small talk, she launched into the training. It advanced much as it had the day before, marching through the guard positions first, then switching to combat—where she came at him and forced him to defend against the assault. She was quicker to change out the guards, and the timing between her offensives was shortened, giving Hunter less time to recover. Often, she followed up with an immediate second offensive.

He reveled in it. Thrived on the flow and the physicality. He was invigorated and his mood lightened. The training required a cognitive focus that surprised him, not unlike what he had to maintain on the pitch when he was trying to follow the movement of the ball. He had to sustain a conscious awareness of how every part of his body was answering her attacks—feet, hips, shoulders, arms—all pivoting and twisting as her blade came at him in a blur. The heavier blade affected his timing at first, but he adjusted, and, in a way, felt he had more specific control of the sword's movement through the air and felt the contact with her blade more.

At the same time, he could feel his responses becoming programmed into his muscles. He started to act on instinct. Micro-movements she made tipped him off to what the next attack would be, and he found himself predicting the guard before she called it.

"You are quiet today," she said after at time. "No barrage of questions?" There was something slightly mocking about her tone.

He was reluctant to admit that her attacks were keeping his mind too busy. "No point if you won't answer them."

She responded with a simple lift of her chin. "More follow-through with your cuts. The objective is to not simply block my attack but to guide it aside." It was spoken directly, without emotion. But he glimpsed something, then, behind the stoic countenance. A shadow over her mood he hadn't noticed before. Something was eating at her. "Boar's tooth."

They ran through drills for perhaps another hour before Zinnuvial stepped back, lowering her blade, and called an end for the day.

"It is customary," she said, "to bow to your partner once the sparring has come to an end."

She demonstrated it—sword angled to the side and a bend at the waist. Hunter imitated it back to her, feeling clumsy. Her eyes revealed nothing as she turned and strolled back to the storage box to return the sword. Hunter followed.

"Something's happened today," he said. "Hasn't it."

She glanced over her shoulder at him with a raised eyebrow.

"I overhead some talk earlier," he said.

She seemed to weigh her response before turning to him. "It is none of your concern."

"Was Dax involved?" His heart lurched at the thought. It hadn't occurred to him to that Dax would still be out working for the resistance, on missions. Putting himself in danger. It explained his absence.

"You needn't worry yourself about Master Dax," she replied. Her tone had a mordant edge that surprised him. He'd seen Dax in action enough to know she was probably right about that.

Still, if anything did happen to him, Hunter was as good as dead.

"You would rather be out there, too, wouldn't you?" he said with a tilt of his head toward the large, barred door. "On missions. Fighting along with the others. Not spending your day here, babysitting me."

She was quiet a moment. "I do as I am instructed."

But that didn't stop her from resenting it. He was sure she felt her talents could be put to better use.

She tossed her blade into the box. "Since you evidently can find your own way, I will expect to find you here again tomorrow morning." She started toward the exit.

"I do have one question, actually," Hunter called out to her. "What's a skeg?"

She slowed and turned about. Lines above her brow line furrowed as her eyes narrowed at him. "A pejorative. It is the

Mazentian word for gray."

Referring to muted blue color of Uri's skin.

Zinnuvial swung open the door to the underground and disappeared, leaving it open behind her.

So, his instincts were right. Uri was both Mazentian and human, and yet, apparently, belonged to neither. Hunter couldn't help but wonder what circumstances would bring a boy like that here. And if he was treated this way all the time, why did he stick around? Hunter spotted him around every day. He was, it seemed, like himself, a permanent resident in this hole. As bad as it was down here for him, perhaps it was even worse topside in the city itself. At least here the boy had some allies. Dax, it seemed. Zinnuvial too. Maybe Quinnar.

Another trait that seemed to transcend universes. Pointless bigotry.

The afternoon sun pounded down over the courtyard, and the sand was getting hot on his bare feet. Today was hotter, and after Zinnuvial ran him hard through the paces, he would almost welcome the coolness below. Almost. Sweaty and stiff, he stumbled his way own back into the hole and steered himself toward the mess. His mind was running through the positions and their names when something broke the dense silence of the tunnel. It was the smallest of sounds—a stone crunching under the heel of a boot. Quick and sharp, but then nothing. Hunter wondered a moment if he'd imagined it. But no, it was too clear. Too distinct. Someone was behind him in the tunnel, shadowing his movements.

Against his better judgment, he turned on his heel and doubled back the way he had come, toward the sound he'd heard. Even barefooted, his footfalls crunched conspicuously. As Dax was quick to remind him, he had no skill to move with any stealth, so he didn't bother trying. Again, he wondered if he should have a weapon on him. He rounded a corner, close to where he'd heard the sound. No one was there.

Whoever had been shadowing him had scampered off.

People were keeping an eye on him. Distrust of outsiders

had trumped the orders to leave him alone.

When he was on the Dragons, the all-gay team, the squad was amateurish at best. The coach did what he could to get the players in line, but they were marginally trained and wildly undisciplined. Matches dissolved into chaos because the players didn't adhere to established gameplay tactics that the coach tried, in vain, to impart to everyone.

This resistance was no different. It wasn't some refined military establishment, and the people involved here weren't soldiers. They were rebels. Insurgents. Malcontents fighting for a cause in their free time—who wouldn't adhere to the chain of command if pushed and didn't have the discipline to blindly follow orders.

How much longer before someone made a move against him?

19

THE THIRD and fourth day had a weird Groundhog Day, déjà vu-esque quality that was getting under Hunter's skin, carving Hunter out from the inside.

The only discernable difference was on the morning of the fourth day, he woke up to find a pair of boots on the floor next to his cot.

He tugged them on and laced them up. They fit fairly well, if a bit odd in their shape, but in a world that hadn't figured out things like indoor plumbing or the assembly line, he couldn't rightly expect high-comfort footwear.

Four days.

And he was no closer to figuring out a way home. No closer to finding out what the resistance planned on doing with him. He was stuck in this shadowy limbo with no purpose and little hope. An urgency was starting to eat away at him, and he fought a rising tide of despair. How much time had passed back his own world already? Weeks? Months?

And no word from Dax. Nothing since his mysterious midnight visit two nights ago. He'd been involved in whatever crisis had taken place. Hunter was sure of it. Dax didn't strike him as the kind of guy to stay out of a fight. Hunter realized he was worried about him. Selfishly? Was it his own safety he was worried about? He couldn't tell. And that bothered him too—but he wasn't even sure why.

He'd noticed lately, in Dax's absence, his thoughts always seemed to drift back to him. His face would appear in his mind's eye, unbidden, or Hunter would catch himself daydreaming about the shape of his arms or the texture of his skin. It irritated him—and each time he would shove the images from his head. But they always crept back into his thoughts again when he wasn't expecting it.

He would have heard if something had happened to him, right?

He'd added peeling potatoes to his morning routine, tackling a bushel of them after the dishware was cleaned and put away. He needed more things to do. Training helped with his restlessness, but that covered only so many hours of the day. Too much of the day was spent without purpose or direction. And the mundane activity reminded him of home. If he closed his eyes and ignored the smell of old grease and woodsmoke, he could almost pretend he was standing in his own kitchen.

He cleaned up the workstation and headed to the practice field. His legs took him there as if on autopilot. Training with Zinnuvial was the only part of his day that occupied his mind enough that he didn't think about anything else.

Zinnuval waited for him as he climbed out of the hole, arms folded, looking impatient. Upon seeing him emerge, she took her place in the center of the practice field without saying a word while Hunter selected a sword from the box.

"You have boots," she commented dryly as she took her position.

"Found them in my room this morning," Hunter replied as he stepped opposite her and arranged his feet into the proper stance. It had become almost second nature to him now. "Do I have you to thank?"

She lowered her eyes at him, her expression annoyed. "I have more pressing concerns than seeing your feet properly attired. Those were compliments of Master Dax."

Dax? Hunter straightened his back and brought his feet together, taking him out of his stance. Certainly not what he expected. And for some reason, it irked him.

He hadn't seen Dax around for days. And in the middle of the night he snuck in and left the boots without waking him, without saying a word? Then, he scoffed and pushed back on the idea—why did it matter that Dax didn't wake him up to talk to him?

"Spared no expense either, it appears," Zinnuvial added. "Those are well made." She looped her finger in the air, a signal for them to begin. "Let's see if they impact your performance."

After an hour of drill work, they transitioned into combat work. Zinnuvial drove at him hard for a time, but then unexpectedly pulled back and stepped away from Hunter. She extended a bow to Hunter. An unplanned break in their training. Surprised, Hunter returned the bow and stepped back too. He watched her, brow knitted.

"You lack focus today," she announced. "Your mind is not in the fight."

Hunter used his forearm to wipe sweat from his brow. It was another hot day. He narrowed his eyes at her. "Excuse me? I thought I was keeping up just fine."

"Keeping up, as you say, is not taking control of the fight. I have provided several openings for you to make an offensive move, and they were ignored."

Hunter closed his eyes a moment to mine for patience. She'd moved the posts again without letting him know.

"All right. Now that I know they're coming, I will keep an eye open for them." He moved to show her he was ready to resume, but she made no change in her own stance.

"I doubt it will change the outcome," she said.

"So… that's it? We're done?" He fought to keep the

irritation from his voice.

"You have questions. Easy enough to see that they are the distraction. They are burning a hole through your tongue."

He didn't think that was at all the case. "I was heeding your advice and keeping my questions to a minimum."

"But they are affecting your performance. We will take a short respite," she announced with a sharp and definitive proclamation. She stepped away and tugged off one of her gloves. "We must clear the mind so you can regain your focus."

"Clear the mind," Hunter repeated warily.

"Yes. And to do so, we must address the distraction itself. I am willing to suffer your inquiries if it will bring you back to a state of concentration and the task at hand."

"Will you now?"

"But," she added as if it were a thought that had just occurred to her, "I think it only fair that you answer an inquiry of mine first."

Hunter felt the tug at the corner of his mouth but forced his lips to not break into the smile. This wasn't about his combat performance at all. This was about what was on her mind. He took in a breath. Something about the request made him uneasy. It had the feeling of a trap. "All right," he said. "Fire when ready."

Her mouth pressed into a line. "You are the witness Quinnar cited."

It wasn't a question, but she was still looking for confirmation. She hadn't been told anything, which surprised Hunter. He would have expected her to be more informed.

"I am."

"Then you are from the other world. The world where Master Dax went to retrieve the amulet."

"Yes."

"I suspected that. The garments you wore were unlike anything I'd seen. So, you knew her. Queen Jenora."

Hunter hesitated, unsure how much he should say. A part

of him felt he should consult with Dax first—there must be a reason she hadn't been told anything. But another part of him felt no obligation to lie for any of them. And he could use another ally here.

"She was my mother."

Her eyebrows arched and her eyes widened, the shock evident. "Then she broke her vow to her king."

Hunter hadn't considered that. His mother was already married before she met his father. "I suppose she felt she had no choice. She was alone and lost in a strange world with no hope of ever returning home. She did what she had to do to survive. Maybe felt she had to move on."

Zinnuvial's eyes lowered as she pondered that.

"Unfortunately," Hunter added, "she latched on to the wrong guy. My father wasn't a great guy. Not a great father and not a great husband. Bit of a bastard actually. He left us when I was around ten. After that, it was just the two of us."

She nodded, seemingly accepting that answer. Her hard countenance wavered, and Hunter caught a glimpse of something that struck him as vulnerability. Her lips thinned as she stepped closer, but her sword remained lowered. When she spoke, her voice was soft, nearly a whisper, like a child telling a secret. "What was she like?"

His throat tightened. It was not what he expected her to ask, and it caught him off guard. The question pierced him somewhere in the soul. He wasn't sure he wanted to remember her right now. Seeing her on the balcony was hard.

No, that wasn't her, he reminded himself. He had to stop thinking about that *thing* as her.

"You arguably knew her the most intimately," she continued. "Save the king."

"Why do you want to know?"

She considered that with a purse of her lips, her eyes lifted toward the sky. "Curiosity, I suppose. Learning that she is gone has affected me. More than I would care to admit. I only wish to know if my perception of her matches her true nature."

Hunter let the tip of the blade sink into the sand as he reluctantly cracked open the door in his mind that held back his memories of her. "She was an astounding woman, Zinnuvial. Strong. Resilient when she needed to be. But also uncannily gentle and caring. Elegant too. She never complained or had an unkind word to say about anyone. Even my father, who was a rare kind of asshole."

He took in slow breath. "But she suffered. Depression. It was always there, just under the surface. She did her best to hide it, always put on a brave face for me, but I could see it in her eyes. I thought it had to do with my father. I understand the real reason now."

"How did she die?"

"Cancer." He could tell from her expression the word confused her. "She had tumors."

"You were close."

"For a long time, it was only the two us. 'Two warriors against a strange world,' she would say." Those words now had a new sharp point that stung. "I took her death pretty hard. It wasn't fair."

"I am sorry," Zinnuvial said in a low voice.

Hunter shrugged dismissively. "Was she liked? You know, as queen?" He didn't know why he asked that. He already knew the answer. Everyone loved Jenny.

Zinnuvial looked at sand. "Beloved. It is what made this transformation in her so troubling and painful."

For a time, they didn't speak. Zinnuvial seemed to retreat into herself. Hunter began to wonder if they were indeed finished for the day.

"Appears it is your turn," she said. "What is it you wish to know?"

He wasn't sure he wanted to ask anything now. He was too busy trying to push the door shut again and lock away those memories of her once more. "Just tell me something about you."

Her eyes narrowed at him. It was not what she expected him to say. Hunter thought briefly she'd refuse to answer, but she took in a long slow breath before she spoke. "My father was an outlaw. A highwayman. Relieving travelers of their gold at the point of sword."

She said it with a cool, unvarnished candor. Her eyes held to him, studying his reaction.

"That surprises you," she added, a challenge lacing her tone.

It was meant to. This was some kind of test. "Yes," he admitted. "Only because people aren't typically so forthcoming about such things."

"He wasn't always one. He began as a carpenter's apprentice but was recruited for a time to fight in the war against the Henerans. Soon after he returned, his master accused him of stealing a pig. In truth, the man was drunk and left the gate open himself but refused to admit it. My father fled, knowing the punishment would be the loss of his hand. At the least. His years of service to the crown now meant nothing. From that time onward, all options for a lawful life were closed to him. So he forged a path of his own."

Hunter puffed out his cheeks and kicked at the sand. "Rough life. Especially while raising a daughter."

"Hard circumstances make for hard choices. Like your mother, he did what he needed to do for us to survive."

They had some common ground, it seemed. "He taught you to fight?"

"It was a difficult life. With many dangers. It was important to him that I was able to protect myself."

"So what happened to him?"

"He was captured and executed by the city guard."

"And you?" he asked.

"Captured as well. Spared. But forced to witness his execution."

Hunter's lungs constricted. He lowered his head and closed his eyes. "Shit."

"I escaped when a guard cornered me in my cell and expected me to either be weak or willing to accept his advances. I was neither."

Hunter was quiet as he let her story settle in. "Is that why you're here, a part of this resistance? Revenge?"

Zinnuvial shook her head. "I was witness to what happens to good people when faced with injustice. When forced down a path not of their making. My father was a good man once, but was broken and discarded, even by the same people he once fought alongside. Injustice is why I'm here. Under the tyranny of this imposter, there seems to be no end to those suffering from it. I wish to save any from the fate I witnessed."

"An honorable reason," he said.

She scoffed. "Honor. Integrity. Just words that men like to throw around. What matters is action. Not high-flown words."

A chuckle escaped Hunter's throat. "Well... call it whatever you want, then. It is a reason I can respect."

She waved him off, adjusted her grip on the hilt, and stepped forward again. "Enough of that. Your curiosities are placated, I trust? Your mind cleared of its distractions? Let us resume."

As if nothing had transpired, she stepped into her stance again and began anew. But the climate between them had changed in a quiet, almost imperceptible way. It might have been his imagination, but he didn't think so.

The door leading to the underground squeaked open, and Uri emerged into the afternoon sun. When Zinnuvial pulled back from her stance and looked his way, Uri nodded to her. Then he ducked back inside and pulled the door closed.

"Appears I am being summoned." She stepped out of combat range and bowed to Hunter, who responded in kind.

He wiped sweat from his brow, then extended his hand to her. "Here. I'll put them away."

Zinnuvial put the hilt of her weapon into his awaiting

hand, and the two walked off the field together.

"Will you be meeting up with Dax?" he asked.

"Possibly. He is with Master Quinnar today, I understand," she said.

Hunter nodded. So he was around, here in the hideout, not out on some mission. Knowing that prickled at him. "Any chance I could go talk to him? Could you take me to their quarters?"

"*Their* quarters?" she asked, her brow knitted.

"Yeah. Where they stay here in the hideout."

"Master Dax and Master Quinnar have separate quarters, Hunter."

That surprised him. "Oh. Sorry. I just assumed they shared a bunk."

She took a step closer. "And why would you assume that?"

"I don't know… because they're together."

Zinnuvial's dark gaze tightened. "What has Master Dax said to you?"

"Nothing. At least nothing specific. I made a comment or two. He didn't deny it."

Zinnuvial stared back at him.

"Did I miss something?" Hunter asked.

She closed the distance between them again and spoke low. "They are not 'together,' as you say."

Hunter blinked back at her, stunned. "I saw the way Quinnar greeted him. That didn't appear very platonic."

Zinnuvial seemed uneasy. "They were coupled for a time, yes. Master Dax ended their association."

Hunter was too surprised to respond. Dax had deliberately let Hunter believe he was still in a relationship with Quinnar. And the reason was rather obvious, he realized. Dax didn't want Hunter getting any ideas.

He hated to admit it, but it stung a bit.

"Why'd he break it off?"

"It is not my place to say…." Zinnuvial turned to leave.

"I'm just curious, Zinn. Trying to understand what makes the guy tick."

Zinnuvial took in a breath. "Master Dax is not one to share his thoughts, Hunter. If there is someone he talks to, it isn't me." She paused and considered a moment before resuming. "However, one can speculate, I suppose."

Hunter waited and didn't speak.

"Things ended between them soon after Dax heard news of his brother."

"His brother?"

Zinnuvial's lips pursed and she shifted on her feet. For some reason, she must have assumed Hunter knew more than he did. "When Master Dax learned he was to be arrested, he went into hiding. That is how he came to be a part of the resistance."

Joined the resistance? Hunter had a burning suspicion that he was a founding member.

"Unbeknownst to him," Zinnuvial continued, "the palace had his brother and his brother's wife imprisoned, and as I understand it, they were tortured to learn of Dax's whereabouts. Neither survived."

Hunter exhaled and stared at the ground, stunned. "Oh shit," he whispered.

"He had severed all contact with them with the hopes of keeping them safe. So, he did not learn of their deaths until much later."

While his brain wrestled with this new information, he was hardly aware that Zinnuvial had left the field.

20

IT EXPLAINED things, certainly.

Dax's brooding nature, for one. And self-induced isolation. Hunter couldn't begin to imagine the guilt and shame he carried. It also explained his hatred of the queen and his unyielding drive to bring an end to her.

His mind sprang back to the night Dax had shown up in his room unannounced. At the time, he still believed Dax was with Quinnar, so he didn't think much of it. He'd taken Dax at his word that he'd needed a quiet place to think, and Hunter assumed he only needed someone neutral to talk to. Yet looking back, the whole experience had a strange intimacy. Dax had revealed an almost tender side Hunter hadn't seen before. What were Dax's actual intentions that night?

There'd been an unexpected warming between them lately, a slow turn in the tide. Besides the embarrassing fact that he'd saved his life more times than Hunter wanted to admit, Dax had stuck up for him, kept him safe… even found a pair of boots for him. None of which he was required to do. Dax could be aggravating as all fuck, but in his own way, he'd accepted him into his very tight circle.

Did that mean something?

Hunter swatted aside the thought like a pesky gnat buzzing in his ear. He was being ridiculous. Dax broke it off with Quinnar over what happened. And now kept everyone at arm's length, and took on crazy dangerous missions solo. Clearly, he wasn't interested in pursuing the most basic relationships with anyone, let alone something romantic. And even if Dax was attracted in him—which was almost laughable to consider—what did it even matter? Hunter wasn't planning on sticking around in this insane world for one second longer than he had to. First chance he got, he was snagging it. He just had to stay focused and figure out a way to get his ass home.

All the same, Hunter couldn't shake the memory of Dax sitting next to him, their legs touching....

He grunted and shook his head. What the hell was he doing? Holy fuck, he was an idiot.

Once, soon after he'd been accepted onto the Lions, he allowed himself to develop a crush on a member of the team. Trevor Hopper, the flyhalf. Everyone on the team called him Bunny. Hunter had confused kindness and acceptance for affection, and convinced himself there was something going on between them. After working continuously for months to gain acceptance among them, he very nearly ruined everything—all because he was jonesing for a tight body and an adorable smile.

And here he was again, behaving like a horny teenager.

When would he ever learn?

His mood had soured, the benefits of the workout gone. He had to shake these ideas out of his head. He needed something to do.

Fuck, he missed fidgeting with a rugby ball. Missed the soft curve of the leather against his palm. It was the sort of thing that would bring him a sense of normalcy. He wouldn't even need to throw it around with someone, just hold it or spin it in the air. That would feel like home.

What would it take to have someone sew one up, he wondered. Someone who worked with leather could do it. The bootmaker—what was her name? Pern something.

He took to the passageways with a fresh purpose. He'd explore deeper into the tunnels, he thought, hoping to stumble upon the area where the workshops were located. There, he'd find someone who would make him the ball. That would take his mind off Dax and all the other bullshit that was happening around him.

He set off to explore. The notion of getting lost in this complex network whispered to him in the back of the head, but if he stayed within the corridors that were well traveled and framed in, he'd be fine. He ventured off in the direction he thought was south, but he discovered quickly that bearings in these tunnels were meaningless. Somehow he'd looped back around and stumbled on the common area he'd passed through when he'd first arrived several days ago.

The room was mostly quiet. A small group was seated around a round table. They leaned in on their elbows, faces close, and spoke in low conspiratorial voices. Someone else was passed out on the floor. No one seemed to notice him as he stepped in farther.

At the far end, Uri was seated on the floor, back to the wall. He had a pack between his knees and he rummaged through it, taking out belongings one by one and arranging them around him. Corrad was on the far wall across from him. He had a chair leaned back onto two legs, his butt on the edge of the seat and his boots on a barrel top. Hunter recognized the boots. Seeing them on the greasy thug, knowing his own feet touched the inside of them, made his toes itch all over again. Next to him was an equally brutish and ugly thug, elbows on his knees and a permanent scowl on his face. He flipped a coin off his thumb and caught it on his palm.

Slowly, some became aware of Hunter's presence and they turned their eyes on him. His skin tingled. There was a thick energy to the room—like he'd walked into the wrong locker room. He'd violated some sanctuary and was clearly unwelcome here. He forced a casual gait as he crossed the room and headed for a different corridor. But something made him slow.

Corrad and his goonish buddy were glaring down at Uri.

The two looked bored. Which Hunter knew made them dangerous. For men like these, there was a thin line between boredom and aggression. Corrad had a bowl of nuts in his lap. In an almost hypnotic routine, he cracked open the shell, plucked out the insides, and popped it into his mouth—all while staring down at Uri. As if he was angry at the floor, he'd chuck the shell down and reach for the next nut from the bowl. His friend repeatedly flipped the coin and snatched it from the air.

Hunter knew he should leave. He'd be a convenient trigger if he pulled their attention somehow. Corrad had been gunning for an altercation since they'd met. Instead, he drifted toward a heavy wooden bookshelf and slipped a leather-covered volume from the shelf. He leaned a shoulder against the wall, flipping through the yellowed pages, pretending to read, but watching from the corner of his eye.

The book was filled with a delicate but strange handwritten script, unreadable to Hunter. Spoken language was somehow the same here, but the written text was nothing like the alphabet he knew.

Uri made a sharp little cry. Hunter looked up to see him rubbing the side of his head. Uri glowered at the two men, his mouth in a tight line, before he returned his attention to the leather sack between his legs. Corrad and his friend snickered, exchanging glances.

"Why aren't you manning the door, skeg?" Corrad asked.

"My shift's over," Uri grumbled. He kept his chin low, staring down into the sack.

"Time off?" The man chucked another shelled nut at him. Uri ducked, and it ricocheted off the stone wall. "You got to earn your keep here, skeg. Who said you get time off?"

"Master Quinnar." His voice had dropped to barely a whisper.

Corrad made a face at the mention of Quinnar, and he exchanged a look with the brute next to him. It was clear they didn't care for him much. "Ask me, you should be chained to that door. Like a dog."

Uri hunched his shoulders, shrinking into himself. He started to gather up his belongings and dump them back into the sack. The situation was escalating, and he had the instinct to know it was time to bug out.

"Will never understand why that kug'ra fucker lets you stay here," Corrad said. "You'll never be one of us, skeg." The goon next to him rewarded Corrad with a grin of four yellow teeth.

Uri's cheeks darkened to a purple. He rose to his feet, clutching the pack to his chest.

Hunter snapped the book shut and set it horizontally on the shelf atop the others.

Another nut rifled through the air. Uri tried to lift the pack to deflect it, but he was a fraction of a second too slow. The nut struck the edge of his brow, missing his eye by an inch. Uri winced and shut his eyes, clearly in pain, but he didn't make a sound.

The goon chuckled and flipped the coin into the air again.

"If it were up to me," Corrad said, pulling his legs off the barrel and dropping his chair back onto all four legs, "you'd be on the street where you belong. Beggin' for scraps."

Uri stared back at him, his breathing coming in short bursts.

Corrad rose. "Nothing to say, skeg?"

Uri shook his head. He'd waited too long, and the window to escape had closed and nothing was going to derail Corrad from this path.

"I asked you a question," Corrad hissed as he reached

over and set the bowl of nuts on the barrel. His fingers were twitching. "Seems you need a lesson in how to respond to your betters."

It was at the cusp of getting ugly. Hunter had to act. He stepped closer into Corrad's line of sight.

"Betters? That's rich. Coming from you."

Corrad's eyes, dark with malice, shifted toward Hunter and narrowed. Hunter had interrupted his sport and he wasn't happy. The edge of Corrad's lip curled into a snarl. "You."

Hunter kept his gaze locked onto Corrad's. "Yup. Me."

Corrad lifted a thick finger and jabbed the air. "Stay out of our business, outsider. You don't belong here either."

Hunter put himself in between the two thugs and Uri.

Uri was instantly behind him, grabbing at his sleeve. "No, no, no. They were only playing." He tried to force a laugh.

Corrad stared at Hunter with narrow eyes, the corner of his mouth lifted in a satisfied smirk.

"Sit your fat ass back down," Hunter said. "And leave him alone."

Corrad chuckled down at his toady as if Hunter was a charming distraction. "You defending this skeg?" The goon took his cue and stood, taking his position at Corrad's shoulder. Both men were thick and formidable, massive arms flexing at their sides.

This would not end well for him. But he kept his eyes firmly locked onto them and didn't respond.

Uri was tugging on him harder. "It didn't hurt. Honest." Hunter could hear the panic in his voice. "It was all in fun."

Hunter knew what Uri was afraid of—that he'd be blamed for whatever happened and punished later. He looked over his shoulder at him and tried to give him a reassuring smile. "It'll be okay. Leave the room. Quickly."

Uri didn't respond right away. He stared back at Hunter with wide, terrified eyes.

"Go," Hunter said in a calm and quiet voice. Uri let go

of his sleeve and scurried away.

Hunter was aware the room had fallen into a prestorm hush. The group huddled around the table stood. Hunter understood what was happening. It was the catalyst they'd all wanted from the beginning. He was an outsider, untrusted, his presence here dubious. And their tribal thinking dictated that a threat against one was a threat to all. If this turned physical, it would quickly spiral into him against everyone else.

"He's done nothing to deserve this," Hunter said in a low and calm voice.

"His presence offends me."

"Get over it," Hunter replied.

Corrad took a step forward. "You tellin' me what to do, outsider?"

"Leave him alone, and we don't have a problem."

"Oh, you see, we already have a problem, outsider. You put your nose where it doesn't belong."

The second man started to make a move, but Corrad, the clear alpha of the two, held out his arm and put him to an immediate halt. His face fell, looking like a child's denied an opportunity to impress his father.

Corrad stomped closer like a bull squaring off against a threat. A move meant to intimidate, but Hunter held himself perfectly still. He wasn't going to let him see anything that might be interpreted as fear.

In the back of his mind, he knew what to expect. He'd been in brawls and could handle himself well enough. But this ogre had trained his whole life for combat. Plus, the man was likely armed with a sharp and pointy object that could do him real damage.

There was only one possible way this could end.

He came at Hunter with a sudden lurch and an angry shout. His fist circled around toward Hunter's head—all power and no grace.

Years of rugby had given Hunter quick reflexes. He twisted, putting himself out the path of the swing. Instinct told him another swing would follow immediately, and he readied himself. The other fist came up at him in a hard jab toward his abdomen. Hunter used his forearm to guide it to the side, then thrust his own fist straight out.

Pain exploded in his hand and shockwaves reverberated up his arms as his fist connected with the hard side of Corrad's head. It was a lucky hit, and Hunter knew it. Corrad expected an easy takedown and left himself open. It wouldn't happen again.

The punch hit hard bone and probably did more damage to Hunter's hand than to the skull. Corrad staggered a moment, looking a little rattled and surprised. The side of his head was red, but the impact hadn't broken the skin. He shook it off and turned his attention back toward Hunter.

His eyes flared with rage.

He reached down and extracted something from his belt. Dim lamplight glinted off the metal blade.

Four days of training with a longsword hadn't prepared him for a knife fight. Especially when Hunter was unarmed. He was going to be gutted like a trout. So he did the one thing he could do. He charged.

As Corrad lifted the weapon, Hunter kicked off and flung up his forearms. His only prayer was to knock the weapon out of Corrad's hand before he had a chance to use it. He barreled into Corrad, sending him backward into the tapestry-covered wall. It was solid stone behind it, and Corrad felt it. He grunted as his back slammed against it, air exploding from his lungs. He was stunned a moment. Hunter tried to grapple for the wrist that held the dagger, hoping to pin it to the wall, but Corrad evaded the grasp. Corrad, recovering quickly, shoved Hunter back and lunged, the dagger raised.

His rugby reflexes served him yet again. He knew how to move his big body quickly.

He rotated his trunk, throwing one shoulder back, and the blade just missed his collarbone. Corrad came at him again with a thrust straight for the gut. Hunter swept his forearm out and guided the arm to the side. Some of Zinnuvial's training had sunk in.

But Corrad was fast too. Hunter saw his left fist as a blur at the edge of his vision just before it clouted him in the temple. Lights flashed behind his eyes, and the room tilted. Hunter knew Corrad would take advantage of him being stunned. A blade strike was next. Desperate, he jabbed out with his elbow and struck something hard. Corrad's jaw.

A sharp groan burst from deep in his throat and he staggered backward.

With the room still spinning, Hunter bounded forward, shouldering him in the midsection, and he tackled him to the floor.

The two collapsed with a hard crash as a wood chair shattered beneath them. A shard jabbed into Hunter, and white pain exploded in his side. Corrad moaned and twisted with most of the destroyed chair under him. He flung his arm, attempting to stab Hunter's back, but his arm was partially pinned under Hunter. So he punched with his free hand, and the fist grazed the side of Hunter's head. More stars swam around his vision. He tried to push him off and roll away, but Corrad gripped him by the throat and shoved Hunter to the floor. Corrad was strong. And in his dazed state, Hunter was no match for him. Corrad sprang up and dropped a knee onto Hunter's sternum.

Hunter looked up, his vision a swirling confusion. Corrad glared down at him with wild rage in his eyes and a satisfied smirk on his lips. His rancid breath blasted hot into Hunter's face. With one hand still on Hunter's throat, Corrad lifted the dagger high, ready to plunge it into his chest.

Before he could thrust the weapon downward, another knife materialized at his throat. Dax's face came into view over the Corrad's shoulder.

"Drop it," Dax said.

Corrad hesitated.

"Drop it or I will slice your throat."

"You sidin' with him?" the man hissed through his teeth. Scowling, he pulled his neck back away from the sharp edge.

"Put it down."

Corrad complied by tossing the dagger across the room. It hit the wall and tolled like a broken bell. Dax relieved the pressure against his neck and pulled the blade away. He stood and allowed Corrad to do the same. Glowering down at Hunter, the ox rose to his feet.

"Take a walk," Dax told him. "Outside."

"Fuck off," the man said. "I belong here, not this—"

Dax stepped closer. "Walk." His voice was low and dangerous.

Hunter made a slow climb to his feet. Each heartbeat felt like a detonation, again and again, pounding with staggering and worrisome force. His entire side was in pain. He laid his palm against it, then looked at it. The palm was dry. No blood. The wood piece hadn't skewered him at least, but he'd have a magnificent bruise there tomorrow to show for this fight. Once again, he'd come within a hair's breadth of losing his life. It certainly settled the question of whether he should carry a weapon around. He was going to find one as soon as possible.

Was this the fourth time Dax had saved his life? Or the fifth? He was losing count. It was embarrassing.

Corrad spit onto the floor. "This isn't over." A dark stain splattered on the gray wood of the plank floor. One of Hunter's blows had done some actual damage.

Dax looked to be half his size. Yet something about his stance made him seem the bigger threat. "It is. I just ended it."

To Hunter's surprise, the man complied and stomped off. His henchman looked a bit confused as to what to do but ended up following in his wake.

So much for making more friends today.

Dax wouldn't look at Hunter. "Follow me."

HUNTER FOLLOWED Dax into an unoccupied storeroom.

Shelves with crates lined the walls, leaving enough space in the center for Hunter and Dax to stand and face each other. The room was dark, but enough light pushed in through the open doorway to illuminate Dax's face. His lips, pressed into a tight line, had disappeared. With hands on his hips, Dax looked at the ceiling. He still wouldn't look at Hunter.

He took several full breaths and spoke in a low growl. "What part of keep low was unclear?" He was furious and fighting to maintain control.

Hunter could sympathize. Adrenaline from the fight was still pumping through his system. His hands shook, and his heart pummeled against his rib cage. He didn't trust himself to not shout back at him, so he forced himself to stay quiet.

A hard, ugly silence filled the space between them.

"You have no idea the harm this will cause," Dax finally said.

"I don't care," Hunter answered.

Dax's eyes shot up to meet his for the first time. "Use your head. This threatens everything. Corrad has influence."

"He's an asshole."

"An asshole with a devoted following. He could undermine what we are trying to achieve."

"You seem forget I'm not part of any of this. Certainly, no one else has."

Dax glowered up at him. "I won't have it brought down. Not because of this. Not because of you. It's too important." He turned his back on Hunter and massaged the base of his neck. "Of all the people to provoke...."

"You think I planned this?"

"You'd be dead now had I not come in."

"A humiliating pattern, I admit," he replied, lifting his eyes to the ceiling. He wasn't sure what stung more, that Corrad had bested him or that Dax still saw him as weak. "Care to hear why it happened?"

"The damage is done," Dax grumbled. "Doesn't matter."

Hunter pulled in a long breath. This was the first he'd

seen Dax in three days. Hardly what he'd imagined their reunion would be like. But seeing Dax this angry with him struck him harder than he would have expected. "Listen to it anyway. They were harassing Uri, Dax. Tormenting him."

Dax stiffened. That seemed to get his attention. "You're mistaken. You don't understand our ways."

"I know abuse when I see it."

"It's taken time, but Uri has grown to be welcome here."

"Then what's a skeg, Dax?"

Dax's eyes jolted to meet Hunter's, a new surge of anger flaring his nostrils.

"Corrad," Hunter continued, "and everyone else in this hole, is savvy enough to not show their hand around you. But it's happening. The boy is being persecuted. Daily."

"Uri would have said something—"

"Not if he's afraid."

Dax fell silent. He knew that was true.

Hunter stepped closer. "All I did was stand between them to put an end to it. Corrad's been gunning for a confrontation since I arrived, and like an idiot, I played right into it."

"Corrad goaded you into this fight?"

"Not precisely. But I was a convenient excuse to start one."

"And you've witnessed this harassment?"

"Enough to know it's not isolated."

Some of the anger seemed to drain from Dax, or at least its focus shifted away from Hunter. "I'll address it. And do what I can to mend this disaster before it reaches Quinnar's ears. For now, follow me to the council room. You've been summoned."

"Summoned?"

Dax marched out of the storeroom. "Quinnar wants to speak with you."

21

THE LOW talk among the council members tapered quickly to silence as Hunter stepped into the packed conference room. All eyes lifted his way. Expressions pressing on him were a mixed bag ranging from the slightly hostile or annoyed to some undefined concern. None acted surprised to see him as he broke the threshold.

Zinnuvial was in the room as well. Her back was to the wall, her arms crossed. She lifted her chin at Hunter when he glanced her way, but she said nothing.

Quinnar sat at the head of the table, tenting his fingers in front of his lips.

"What kept you?" he asked, his tone somber.

Dax stepped in closer to the table. "A complication. To be addressed later."

Quinnar's eyebrow lifted a fraction, and his eyes shifted briefly to Hunter, but he didn't comment. News of his scuffle with Corrad hadn't reached him yet.

He passed his eyes over their faces. Each occupied the same space around the long central table as before, give or take one or two exceptions. No one spoke. All seemed to hold their breath and wait for Quinnar to lead into whatever this was about. Tension choked the room. They were uncomfortable. Or anxious. Or both.

This couldn't be good, Hunter thought. It felt like he was standing in front of a jury box, awaiting sentencing.

Quinnar's eyebrows knitted closer together, and he looked for a moment like he might respond with more force, but he seemed to rein himself in and the expression softened. He gave a curt nod instead.

"Can we proceed now?" said the balding man with a huff of impatience. Ronlin. "It has been too long already, and my absence will be noted."

"Go," said the older woman with the gray braid with a threat of impatience. She'd switched out her colored ribbons from green to powder blue. "If you must. Everyone here knows where you stand anyway."

"You are not the only one who has taken risks to be here, Ronlin." The speaker was a middle-aged man with smooth caramel skin and dark eyes. The band collar of his brocaded coat was buttoned up to the throat. He had a regal air that made him seem wildly out of place in this gloomy hole.

Ronlin scowled but didn't move.

"Take a seat, Hunter." Quinnar's voice always had the conceit of expected compliance. He gestured to an empty seat to his right and smiled. Hunter knew it was supposed to be warm and welcoming but it came off as awkward in the cold tenor of the room. Quinnar's clearly intentional use of his name grated him. They were friends now?

"I'm fine standing," Hunter replied. This whole business was making his skin prickle. He felt like there was a guillotine dangling over him.

He noticed some eyes glancing expectantly in the direction of the far corner to Quinnar's left. The light from the irregularly placed candles didn't reach that corner of the room, cloaking a man Hunter hadn't seen before in shadow. He was seated on a stool with his back to the wall, arms folded over his chest. He was dressed in the same red and black uniform

186

the guards at the city gate wore, but the front was unclasped and loose, exposing a white tunic beneath it.

Somehow, his presence explained the grim tone in the room.

"Hunter," Quinnar began. He lowered his hands to the tabletop and leaned in. "The council has concluded that we could use your aid."

Hunter shook his head not sure he'd heard him right. "My aid?" His face flushed with sudden heat. Something about the casual, almost friendly use of his name made Hunter's blood pressure rise. "You were pretty damn clear that you didn't even want me here. And now you want me to help you out?"

"Circumstances have changed."

"My lucky day."

"We understand your hesitancy—" Ronlin began.

Hunter spun on him. "Do you now?" He was angry, and he had no interest in hiding it. He'd almost had his throat slit twenty minutes earlier, and now they were going to sit here and pretend to play nice with him?

Ronlin shrunk down in his chair. Eyes wide, he looked about to squeak out an indignant complaint, but Quinnar's glare silenced him.

"We would not ask this if need were not so great," Quinnar said. "We recognize that it's perhaps not fair to ask this of you—"

"You're right. It's not."

Quinnar took a deep breath. "But we are prepared to offer something in exchange."

"Is that so?" His throat constricted. It couldn't be this easy. "Well, you know what I want, Quinnar."

Quinnar pressed his lips together and tilted his head. "Unfortunately, that is not something we can promise at this time. Once this business is over, perhaps…."

"So your opening offer is a maybe later, something… maybe," Hunter replied.

Everyone around the table looked at their hands or at the wall—anywhere but at him. Quinnar was the only one who held his eye firmly on Hunter. "If that isn't suitable, make a request of us."

Hunter folded his arms, shook his head, and chuckled low in his throat.

"Is something funny?" Quinnar asked.

"Yes. I find all of this rather laughable."

Ronlin leaned back in his chair. "I said this would be a waste of time."

"Patience," Quinnar said to him, irritation rising in his voice.

"You haven't even told me what you want from me," Hunter said. "I'm not agreeing to anything—"

"A place to live," Dax broke in. "Above ground."

The room was jolted into silence.

Dax swept his eyes around the table. "That would be a place to start, I think. Something he would desire, something we can provide."

Quinnar's mouth pursed, his gaze hard on Dax. "It was your idea to keep him here, Dax."

"But he cannot be expected to live here indefinitely," Dax replied. "He needs something permanent." It wasn't about that, Hunter knew. Dax had come to realize it was no longer safe for him here. Despite Quinnar's decree of not being harmed, one of Corrad's sycophants would gladly take the first opportunity to finish the job. Dax was working to get a deal in place for him now, before the news about his skirmish with Corrad broke.

The darker-skinned aristocrat frowned and shook his head. "For how long? Our resources are rather thin, Master Dax."

Dax lifted his brow. "Do you require his cooperation or not?"

The council members exchanged nervous glances.

"Knowing you, Master Dax," the gray-haired woman

said with a silky lilt to her tone, "you have already figured out where."

Dax's expression remained unchanged. "We have safe houses, yes?"

Each head turned to Quinnar, who seemed to consider the question by leaning back against the chair and drumming fingers on the table. "None available. They are all in use currently."

"I'm certain you can make some changes," Dax pressed. "Seems a reasonable solution."

"How can we even consider letting him roam freely in the city?" Ronlin said, shaking his head. "If he is captured, or the safe house discovered… and ends up in the hands of the palace, he could expose us all."

A wave of nervous grumbling circled the table.

"We already agreed to trust him with this mission." The speaker was a thin-faced woman with her head mostly concealed in a brown linen wrap. Wisps of ruddy hair escaped the edges of it to frame her delicate features. "We will need to concede something."

No one had a response.

"Fine," Quinnar said. "I will make arrangements to have one of the safe houses made available to him."

"And in the interim?" Dax pressed. "Quarters that are not public?"

Quinnar narrowed his eyes at Dax. Hunter could tell he sensed something was amiss. "Offer him your own chambers if you like."

Dax made a single curt nod. "Very well. Until arrangements are made, I relinquish my private quarters to him."

Quinnar continued to drum his fingers on the table while he considered Dax with a furrowed brow. His eyes shifted to Hunter. "Are these terms agreeable to you?"

Hunter swept his gaze over the faces in the room. "Depends on what you want from me."

Quinnar and the man in the guard's uniform exchanged a look, then Quinnar straightened in his chair. "One of the benefactors of our cause has been identified. Her name is Yvenne. She's a textile merchant, supplying the cloth used for the city and palace uniforms. She isn't directly involved in operations here, but she has been a powerful ally, backing us financially and providing us with valuable information from inside the palace. She's been an effective runner of supplies for us too. Steffor, here"—Quinnar indicated the guardsman with a tilt of his head—"tells us her association with us has been uncovered. She needs to be warned."

"So send someone to warn her," Hunter replied.

Out of the corner of his eye, he caught movement by the door. He glanced over to spot Uri slinking in. His head was low, his body tense and pulled into itself. From his body language, Hunter worried something else had happened after the scuffle in the common area. Uri threaded his way through the room, handed a roll of parchment to Quinnar, and worked his way back to the door. He didn't look anywhere other than at his feet.

"It's not that simple," Steffor said. "They were sloppy with this information. Too sloppy to be believable. They wanted the information leaked."

He was young, likely no older than twenty. His beard wasn't even filled in all the way along his jawline. He had a cocky edge to him—the brand of arrogance youth can transmit so effortlessly.

"So it's a trap," Hunter said.

"I came to assure no one falls for it," Steffor said.

"At great personal risk," Quinnar added.

"The risk of a message getting intercepted was greater still," Steffor said. "I chose to ensure the intelligence reached you." He rose to his feet. "But the hour does grow late. I should return."

"Of course," said Quinnar.

Steffor bowed to the council. "I take my leave." He

followed around the wall and exchanged a look with Zinnuvial before he slipped out of the room.

Quinnar turned his attention back to Hunter. "Yvenne has been loyal to us and deserves our aid. I will not abandon her. That is why you've been asked here."

Hunter could see how this was weighing on him, could hear the heft of it in Quinnar's voice. He understood where this was going. "You want me to deliver the message to her."

Quinnar nodded. "The palace has spies throughout the city. Somehow, they have learned the identity of many who fight for our cause. How many, we cannot be certain. But some have already been killed. Others imprisoned. We have no idea who is known to them. So anyone we send could potentially be recognized and seized. However... we can say with certainty, they have no idea who you are."

"So I just walk in, deliver the message, and leave? What good will that do? You know she's being watched. If she tries to leave the city, they'll assume you got to her and nab her then."

"Which is why we need to get her out ourselves. Get her back here. Then we can smuggle her out safely."

"And how am I to do that?"

"We will dress you as the man supplying her dyes. You resemble him. He's a bit smaller than you, though I doubt anyone will take notice. Zinnuvial will be hiding inside a cart you will bring with you to Yvenne's shop. Pull the cart inside the shop, Zinnuvial trades places with Yvenne, and you bring Yvenne back here, hidden in the cart."

Hunter glanced over at Zinnuvial. "Seems pretty dangerous for you. You agreed to this?"

"I did," Zinnuvial said, her face unreadable.

He turned to Dax. "And what do you think of this plan?"

Dax's lower lip tightened. "Too risky," he replied in a deep whisper. "This is a task better suited for me than you. But I was not considered."

Because the palace certainly knew him. He worked

there.

Hunter turned back to the table at large. A heavy silence consumed the room. The only sound was the creaking of a chair as Ronlin leaned in.

"When do you want this done?" Hunter asked.

"Immediately," Quinnar replied. "There is no time to waste. The longer we wait, the more risk to Yvenne."

Hunter tugged on his ear as he thought about it. "Okay. I'll do it."

From the corner of his eye, he saw Dax's expression harden. Hunter couldn't tell if he was angry or troubled. Maybe both.

Quinnar blinked back at him, clearly a little bewildered. He'd expected more of a fight.

Hunter understood the reaction. He was just as surprised himself he agreed to this. "I do have one more condition, though," he added.

Quinnar stiffened. "I'm listening."

"This is no place for a kid like Uri. He leaves this hole and lives with me."

QUINNAR ORDERED preparations to be made, then adjourned the meeting. Hunter drifted back toward the wall as everyone shuffled out into the corridor, quietly mumbling to themselves. A few glanced Hunter's way as they passed, but none said anything to him. Apparently, a word of thanks for what he was about to do was too much to ask. He wasn't doing it for any of them, anyway.

As the room emptied, Hunter spotted Uri lingering outside in the corridor, likely waiting for a response from the message he'd delivered to Quinnar. Hunter moved out into the corridor to intercept him.

Uri flinched as he spotted Hunter approaching. His face contorted into a hard grimace and he pushed his back against the wall.

"Are you okay?" Hunter said.

Uri glared up at him, his gaunt frame stiff and unyielding.

"They haven't bothered you again, have they?"

"You shouldn't have interfered."

"Uri, the way they treat you—"

"It doesn't matter."

"It does—"

"I'm not leaving. This is my home."

Hunter took a step closer, but Uri slid down the wall away from him. "Uri, I don't think it's safe for you here."

"Leave me be," Uri replied, and he marched off down the corridor.

"Uri," Hunter called after, and moved to follow him, but Dax placed a hand on his forearm. Hunter hadn't even been aware that he was still beside him. The touch was unexpectedly gentle and warm.

"Leave him for now, Hunter," Dax said. "I will speak with him later."

Hunter sighed. That hadn't gone as he'd expected. Maybe it wasn't his place to try to rescue him. Maybe he should just stay out of it.

"I'm real good at making friends, aren't I?" Hunter said.

Dax lifted the corner of his mouth in a sad facsimile of a smile and turned to leave.

"Wait," Hunter said. His conversation with Zinnuvial had stirred up memories that he'd wanted buried and forgotten, but now that she'd pried them loose again, they'd lodged themselves in the back of his brain like a corn kernel in his teeth. "Tell me something. You told me you spent time in the palace. Did you know my mother? Before she was sent to my world."

Dax's eyes crinkled at the corner as he looked at Hunter. It was not a question he expected. "I'd had audiences with her, yes."

"What was she like? Not as queen. Just as a person."

Dax's lips pursed as he considered the question. "Kindhearted. Compassionate. Courteous and respectful to any and all that spoke to her, regardless of station. I was always made to feel welcome in her presence."

None of that surprised Hunter. "Was she happy?"

Dax scratched at his jawline. "Hard to say. My only meetings with her were about official matters, and she tended wield a statelier countenance when speaking publicly. But even so, she had an easy smile that filled the room and put all at ease. So, I would say yes. She was happy."

Hunter's throat constricted. He raked his hair back from his eyes and stared at the floor. When he spoke, the words were a husky whisper. "My whole life I never knew her to be happy. Truly happy. I hate that they took that from her, you know?"

Dax studied him a moment before replying. "I am struck at times by how your mannerisms are uncannily similar to hers. You gesture with your hands as she did, and the cadence of your voice is the same. But I see her in you in other ways as well. Queen Jenora had a unique power about her. She could command a room with a look, but there was never a question that she cared deeply for those around her. And she had a particular regard for the downtrodden or dispossessed. Appears you take after her in that respect as well."

Dax's words carried an uncharacteristic tenderness that caught Hunter off guard, and for a moment, all Hunter could do was stare back at him, his mouth slightly open. And before he could conjure up a response, Dax put a hand to his shoulder and Hunter's muscles vibrated beneath the touch. "Come. There is much to prepare," he said, and left him standing in the middle of the corridor alone.

22

DAX LEANED against the fractured plaster of the wall at the opening of the alley, arms folded, glaring out at the street, keeping watch. He looked like a sullen teen who had separated himself from the group.

Hunter ignored him. After they left the hideout and made their way to the meeting point, the brief and inexplicable warmth of earlier had steadily cooled back to the familiar icy indifference—to the point that Hunter wondered if he'd imagined the whole exchange in the corridor. Since they'd arrived in the alley, Dax hadn't said two words to him. The reason for the shift in mood was obvious. Dax already made it clear he was sore about being left out of the mission, and now that Hunter was minutes away from leaving, he was going to be surly about it. Also, he likely believed Hunter would ultimately fuck it up and get everyone killed. But Hunter didn't care what Dax thought. He wanted out of the hideout for good and wanted Uri out too. He'd get it done, one way or another.

He positioned himself between the two shafts that extended out from the front of the cart, assuming his role as the beast of burden. The cart was somewhat bigger than a rickshaw, with a longer, flat bed and comically sized wheels. He secured his hands around the leather grips and as Zinnuvial climbed up onto the back, the shafts pressed against his palms. She ducked inside a large crate turned on its side and pulled a tarp over the top, concealing herself.

Two others unfamiliar to Hunter loaded the back of the cart with an unruly pile of sacks and jugs, creating the illusion of a full load of supplies.

He drew in a long breath, which smelled of piss and decay. Like all shadowy back alleys, it was clearly used by a multitude of drunks as a convenient, out-of-the-way place to relieve themselves as they stumbled home. Still better than the dank of the caves, he thought. It felt like he was on furlough from a prison term. Despite the potential danger, he was unexpectedly eager to delve back into civilization. A twisted medieval version of it, but civilization nonetheless.

Dax left his post at the alley's entrance to stand next to Hunter. "Stay to the route I showed you."

"Of course," Hunter replied.

"These streets are confusing to those unfamiliar—"

"So you've reminded me. Multiple times."

"Your name is Maxence."

Hunter gave him a long side-eye. "You know, it's entirely possible I'm not the fuckup that you think I am."

"However unlikely," Dax replied dryly. The comment didn't have the normal bite it usually had. If Hunter didn't know better, he'd think Dax was concerned about him. "Speak little. Your strange tongue will give you away."

Hunter closed his eyes and fought against the retort bubbling up to his tongue. "Are you ready, Zinn?" he said over his shoulder. He was answered with a double knock from within the crate.

"A sword's in the cart. Last resort only. If anything appears wrong—" Dax added.

"Abort and return immediately." Hunter was fairly

196

certain that Dax had inserted that final bit of instructions himself. He doubted Quinnar would be keen that Dax was encouraging him to bail on the mission.

"Bring Yvenne back here. I'll be waiting."

Hunter adjusted his grip again on the shafts. Dax hated he wasn't part of this. He wanted to be the one going in to bring her back. But Hunter knew him well enough already to know this wasn't his type of mission. Dax worked alone.

And he likely wasn't strong enough to pull the cart.

Dax grabbed Hunter's forearm and looked at him directly. His jaw was tight, his lips pressed into a thin pale line, but Hunter caught a glimpse of something behind his eyes. When he spoke, he had a different edge to his voice. A note of unease. "No unnecessary risks."

"Careful, Dax. You almost sound like you care."

Dax's expression hardened and he pulled his hand away. "I care about the mission."

"Get me started," Hunter said over his shoulder. The two behind the cart pushed to get it rolling. The wheels rolled with a squeak and a groan as they crunched over the cobblestones. Hunter leaned in and hauled the cart down the length of the alley.

The first leg of the journey followed the narrow gully made of buildings covered in pale yellow plaster. The street had a slight incline that Hunter could feel in his calves as he tugged the cart along. Cobblestones were missing everywhere, and the wheels dropped in the holes, forcing the cart to lurch and threatening to bring it to a halt. Hunter grunted and put his back into it to keep the cart moving—and imagined how sore his legs were going to be later. He'd suggest this to Coach Titan as part of his training regimen. If he ever made it back, he thought ruefully.

On his own, exposed in the open city and surrounded by people, Hunter had to admit it felt more strange and unnerving than he had anticipated. Curious eyes surveyed him as he lumbered past. He felt conspicuous, an obvious fake that stood out like a bad toupee. And every shadowy corner or alleyway seemed to mask a hidden, unknown danger. He wondered if he'd been too quick to agree to this. Maybe Dax had been right.

More unease needled him as his mind chewed over a new thought: Quinnar had an ulterior reason in selecting him. If the mission worked out like it was supposed to, great. But if it didn't, Hunter was expendable. If something happened to him, it would put a neat end to one of Quinnar's many headaches.

The narrow street entered a plaza, which was a frenzied knot of congestion. Everyone acted as if they had somewhere to be immediately, and people swarmed about without any discernable traffic flow. Hunter guided the cart across the confusion toward the landmark he was instructed to find—a statue of a woman with a golden orb resting in her palm and lifted toward the sun. Then, down a wider street toward the next landmark. Then a right turn toward the next.

The street leveled off, making progress easier on his legs and back. He rounded the corner and was thrust into the perimeter of a broad market square. Brightly colored tents piled around a towering red marble obelisk at the center. Merchandise spilled out from under each canopy—bolts of fabric, earthenware jugs, stacks of cast-iron pots—and midday shoppers strolled about like wayward sheep, scrutinizing the wares on display. A long bank of food stalls had taken position along one side of the square and a separate but more fervent crowd pressed in hard, demanding their lunch. The breeze shifted, and the smoke from their fires wafted in Hunter's direction, carrying the smell of cooked meats and unfamiliar spices.

The city was alien and strange in so many ways. But at the same time, it had a deeply rooted familiarity that resonated in him. It had the same pulse every city seems to have. The same energy.

He pushed into the teeming square and the thick ambling crowd swarmed around him and the cart like flood waters and forced him to slow. People pushed against the cart as they flowed around him, rocking it. His unease spiked. Sweat cascaded down the center of his back. The crowd was too tight around him and felt turbulent and erratic. He picked up the pace, heedless of those in front of him. People shouted and cursed at him as they leapt aside.

From the corner of his eye, Hunter caught sight of a statue—a woman, standing on a massive black marble plinth. She was wrapped in flowing robes and gripped a sword in her right hand as if she was on a battlefield. Her chin jutted outward toward the sky in a haughty and contemptuous expression of power. Hunter involuntarily slowed.

The statue was splashed with bright red paint, and part of the side of the face had been cracked and broken off, but the resemblance was undeniable.

His mother.

His cheeks flushed with sudden rage. This was how she was viewed now. Detested and feared. She would forever be remembered as a villain. A monster. The unfairness of it, after how she was made to suffer, made his insides burn like a kiln.

People around him were shouting for him to move. Two guards threading through the crowd craned their necks to see what was causing the commotion. Heart thumping, Hunter ducked his chin to his breastbone and lurched into motion again. The cart creaked and rocked behind him.

Yvenne's shop was at the far end of this chaos somewhere.

After he rounded the perimeter of tents, he fought the urge to look back over his shoulder to see if the guardsmen trailed him. But a bored patrol, maintaining a visual presence at a public event, was less a concern, he told himself. Agents of the palace, on the lookout for resistance members they recognized, were the real danger. And they wouldn't be cloaked in black and lurking in shadows. Any one of these shoppers could be on the lookout for him. Every turn of a head in his direction made his chest constrict.

He caught his first clear view of the far side. The workshop was hard to miss. It was one of the largest on that side of the square, and vibrant lengths of silk hung from posts outside the building, flailing in the air with theatrical, almost comical, flourish. He half expected a drag queen to march out of the open barn-style door and start a fierce routine on the plaza.

He dragged in a full breath to shore up his nerves, the air tight in his lungs. He straightened his back and angled toward the shop. No one paid him any attention as he hauled the cart through the open doorway. With any luck he'd be in and out in under twenty minutes.

He lowered the front of the cart and let go of the shafts.

The sprawling workshop wasn't as dark as he expected. Light streamed in from four skylights in the high ceiling. The warm sunlight illuminated a host of earthenware vats, each large enough to bathe in, all neatly arranged in a grid. The back wall was a row of heavy shelving that looked more like scaffolding, laden with stacked rolls of fabrics. As warm air rushed past him to escape out the door, it carried with it an odd fusion of odors. Somewhat floral. Somewhat acerbic. Somewhat chemical and identifiable.

"Hello?"

He circled around to the back of the cart and rolled the barn door closed, shutting out the din of the market. The room was thrust into a pregnant silence. No one was around, no one tending to the vats. What should have been an industrious workshop was abandoned and still.

Movement caught his eye. He looked up, past the cart and across the front line of the vats. A woman emerged from somewhere, shuffling along slowly as if sore from a marathon. She fit the description Dax had given him—thin, angular frame, dark-skinned like Zinnuvial. Her hair was longer than Zinnuvial's, and streaked with gray. They didn't look that much alike, but Hunter hoped it was enough to fool anyone long enough to get Yvenne away. She wore a nondescript linen dress with a tan leather apron over the front.

Hunter dropped the sacks onto the ground. "Yvenne?"

The woman stopped at the front line of vats and came no closer.

Hunter circled back around to the front of the cart. "Are you Yvenne?" he asked again.

"Bring the supplies to the back," she said in voice that was too loud for the distance between them.

Hunter stepped closer, and Yvenne stiffened. Something was wrong. Her eyes were wide; her chest rose and fell in quick succession. She was afraid.

Her mouth formed silent words. *Go now.*

A trap. They knew they were coming extract her. They knew when and they knew how.

Behind him, he heard the tarp over the crate get thrown back and the cart creak as it shifted. Zinnuvial was leaping out of the back. She'd picked up on it too.

Hunter lunged forward and grabbed Yvenne by the wrist.

"No, no," she yelped as Hunter flung her behind him.

More movement—dark hooded shapes rose from behind vats throughout the workshop, and more still appeared on the shelves in the back. The figures on the shelves army-crawled forward to the edge of the high stack, and Hunter caught the front curves of crossbows aiming down at him.

The twang of a bowstring came from his left. The arrow shot across the workshop and with astonishing precision, impaled one of the dark figures on the shelf. The figure spasmed and went limp. The weapon tumbled to the floor. The reaction from the others was immediate—they all shifted to get better cover.

Zinnuvial dropped again behind the cart, notching another arrow. She'd bought them a few seconds.

Still gripping Yvenne's wrist, Hunter flung his arm over the side of the cart and fumbled around until his fingers touched the hilt of the sword. Right where Dax told him it would be. He slid it out and dragged Yvenne behind the cart with him.

"Stay low," he told her. The downward angle of the bed should give them enough cover from the crossbows. At least until the other attackers came around and flanked them.

"I'm sorry," she said as they ducked under. She was borderline calm—more angry than afraid. "There was no way to warn you."

He considered pulling the door open again and dodging out with Yvenne in tow, but he knew it was pointless. The palace agents would already be moving in to block any escape. Hunter sprang up and threw a large iron latch that locked the door in place. It trapped them inside, but it would slow down others from storming into the warehouse.

A crossbow bolt slammed into the door with a sharp thud a foot to his left as he dipped back behind the cart. "We'll get you out." It was an empty platitude. He had no idea if there was any way out of this. "Is there another exit?"

"In the back."

It would be watched too. Or blocked.

Another bolt ricocheted off the wooden spoke of the wheel. A splinter of wood slammed into his cheek.

Zinnuvial popped up and fired off another arrow. A moment later—a brief but satisfying cry.

"How many more archers?" he asked her.

"Now three," Zinnuvial replied.

"And on the ground?"

"At least four."

At least. That didn't bode well.

His body and mind fell into a state of focused calm. Like they always did when the whistle blew at the start of a match. But this was no game. There was a solid chance he was going to end up captured or dead. The latter, most likely. But his brain was conditioned for conflict. It just hadn't figured out yet the stakes were higher. Much higher.

"Keep them busy for me." He couldn't believe what he was about to do. But acting without thinking was his specialty.

He hadn't had enough training at this—he knew that—yet all his instincts told him to throw himself into the action. It was what he did.

Only this time he wasn't chasing a swollen oblong ball.

Zinnuvial grabbed his arm as he started to move. "Do not stay your hand. Do what must be done."

Hunter swallowed. She meant he would have to kill.

She sprang up to fire off two arrows in quick succession, and he dashed left along the wall, sword raised.

The first attacker rounded a vat and lunged for him. He was clad in the same thick black leather Hunter had seen before. The Black Brotherhood. Queen Jenora's personal elite force. And Hunter faced him without any sort of armor protection. He might as well have been naked.

The attacker came at him, sword high in an angle swipe. The blade was smaller than he used when he fought against Zinnuvial. A short sword. It cut the air faster. Responded quicker. Panic flooded his head like a gas leak. He had no idea how to defend against it.

But his body reacted as if it had been hacked.

His feet snapped into position. The blade seemed to pull his arms as it twisted up to meet the attack. Metal clashed and sang as the edges slid against each other, and the short sword was guided to the side. The attacker responded with a quick step inward and came at him again. Hunter pivoted back a step and met that one too.

The attacker was fast—but not as fast as Zinnuvial.

He'd thank her for that later.

A third attack drove him back farther. He was losing ground, and he'd run into a wall soon. Then what? He knew he couldn't spend the entire afternoon deflecting attacks. From the corner of his eye, he could see more of the attackers moving in.

Zinnuvial had chastised him for not striking when there was an opening. He caught himself doing it now. He was keeping him at bay without taking the offensive when he had the chance. This wasn't practice. The man would not stop until one of them was dead.

The attacker saw it coming and warped his trunk to avoid it—but not quite fast enough. Hunter's sword ran across his flank. A lucky strike enabled by the man's overconfidence. He hadn't expected Hunter to be a challenge. Hunter felt the push against his hand—felt the cut—and he recoiled from the sensation. Involuntarily, he relaxed the pressure, and the blade sliced open the leather only. Not the skin.

Fear had held him back. Fear of killing. He had to get out of his head and stop pulling punches.

His opponent stiffened a moment, expecting pain. He should be dead, and he knew it. A grin split his face.

Something whizzed past Hunter's head and thumped into the wall behind him. Another crossbow bolt. And the others were closing in.

No time left.

An earthenware jug tumbled through the air and shattered next to the man. Yvenne had heaved it from behind the cart. The man jolted, his grin evaporating. Hunter took advantage of the moment and lunged, closing the distance between them. The attacker brought up his sword in defense, but Hunter snatched the wrist of his sword arm, freezing it in place. Gripping the sword with only his right, he thrust it forward. This time, he grit his teeth and didn't hold back.

He closed his eyes and winced as the tip impaled his midsection. He felt resistance for a moment, like when sinking a knife through the hard rind of a melon, then nothing. The sword sank deeper. The man's sword arm spasmed in Hunter's grip, and his other clasped the sleeve of Hunter's tunic. Then he went limp and fell to the floor.

Hunter pulled out the blade and turned from the body, averting his eyes. Bile burned the back of his throat, and he fought to keep his stomach from emptying. He'd killed a man—didn't matter that it was in self-defense. This would forever change him.

Well… if he survived this. At the moment it didn't seem likely. Two more were rounding the closest vat. He caught dark glimpses of others circling around to come at them from another direction. And there was at least one crossbow sniper still on the stacks.

As the two sprang for him, an arrow struck the curved side of a vat, splintering it apart, and pieces of it ricocheted off. The man closest to it cried out and ducked, an arrow fragment narrowly missed his head. Zinnuvial was still providing Hunter some cover.

Hunter launched at the other one.

He stepped in hot, first making a low cut to the left. The man met it easily and pivoted sideways and tried to force the blade up to expose Hunter's torso. A move he was ready for. Zinnuvial had run him through that drill a thousand times. He shifted and stepped in again, spun his sword around in a downward cut aimed at his neck before the attacker could take advantage of the opening. But the sword cut only air as the opponent pivoted beyond Hunter's strike zone.

More shouts. Barking commands from somewhere deeper in the shop. Were more entering from the back?

Zinnuvial fired off more arrows in quick succession, forcing the farther attackers into cover behind vats. But it provided an opening for the second attacker to close the distance on Hunter. From the corner of his eye, he saw the flash of the sword.

He lunged back. The blade missed him by inches.

As he recovered and sprang back into his stance, ready to face the newer opponent as well, an arrow whistled through the air to his right. Hunter heard a soft gasp, almost a sigh, and turned to see the shaft protruding from the man's throat. As his eyes rolled back and red bubbles gurgled out from the wound, his legs gave out and he sank to the floor.

A splintering crash came from above. Shards of glass showered down as the skylight blew apart. A large stone careened down in the center of it all. Rectangular, like a cinder block. As the glass splattered on the stone floor, the brick struck a vat. With a crack that sounded like a gunshot, the vat broke apart and viscous orange liquid exploded out the side.

Hunter's opponent leapt backward, startled. That wasn't part of their plan.

A second object plummeted from the hole in the ceiling.

It soared down like a meteor—a streaking ball of fire. It hit the wet ground where the vat had come apart. Yellow flames rolled out from the impact. Then, a moment later, the wet floor erupted in dancing blue fire. A wave of intense heat pressed against Hunter's face.

Cries rang out, and black-garbed soldiers scattered in all directions.

Whatever chemicals were used in those dyes, it was flammable. And there were more than a dozen filled vats. The building was doomed.

Hunter took advantage of the sudden distraction and thrust the blade. The man's attention snapped back to Hunter, and he stepped back and turned to avoid the point. But he wasn't quite fast enough. The edge caught him under the unprotected sword arm. Blood jetted from a wide gash, and the man screamed. The sword tumbled from his grip. He recoiled from Hunter, grasping the wound with his free hand, blood oozing out from between his fingers.

Hunter hadn't killed him, but he was out of the fight.

More heavy bricks hailed down from the hole in the ceiling. Some thumped harmlessly on the floor but one smashed into another vat, shattering it apart. Purple-black liquid gushed out, and as soon as it reached the line of blue fire, it, too, erupted into flames. Sacks underneath the lowest shelf caught fire, and flames lapped up to reach the rolls of fabric on the shelves.

Zinnuvial, bow gripped tight in her right hand, appeared at his side. Yvenne was pressed in close behind her.

Through the haze of gray smoke that rose up to escape through the shattered skylight, Hunter caught a glimpse of figures on the roof. Three, by the looks of it. One sidled right up to the edge of the jagged opening, crossbow in hand. He fired several bolts down at the men scattering about and looking for cover, then repositioned himself out of sight. Hunter almost laughed. He recognized the silhouette.

Dax. Saving his ass again.

"That's our way out," Zinnuvial said, pointing up to the shattered skylight with her bow. The edge of it was directly above the top of the stacks. Which were now on fire.

"We better be quick about it," he said. It wouldn't take long for all that fabric to catch fire. The building would be a full conflagration in minutes.

He circled the workshop, hunched low and hugging the wall. The other two were close to his heels. More smoke billowed into the workshop than could escape through the skylights. It swirled over their heads, a disorienting and toxic cloud that pressed down on them. It provided cover, but Hunter's eyes stung, and each inhale burned down into his lungs.

Crossbow bolts flashed over their heads like mad starlings, impaling the wall behind him with sharp thuds. The archer on the high shelf was shooting blindly through the haze. Others across the workshop were shouting orders.

Another attacker sprang from the haze. Zinnuvial loosed an arrow and the shaft skewered his shoulder. The force of the impact threw him back with a splatter of blood. As Zinnuvial stepped over the body, she ripped the arrow free from the wound and renotched it.

Red and orange heaved to life on the first shelf. The fabric had caught fire, and the flames ate it greedily. It spread outward and climbed higher.

A river of blue flames ran between them and the shelves.

"Jump it," Zinnuvial barked from behind.

Hunter didn't hesitate. He took a short running start and heaved his bulk over the narrowest vein. Intense heat seared his exposed skin as he sailed over it. He landed hard on the far side, and as he staggered to keep his balance, an attacker leapt for him, sword high.

He ducked and threw up his sword in a desperate parry. Steel clashed and sparked as the new attacker's blade ran the length of his to catch against the guard. The shockwave ran through Hunter's forearm, and the force twisted his wrist and threatened to dislodge his own grip on the hilt.

He punched outward with his elbow, putting the full strength of his arm behind it. The blow clipped the man's chin, and his head jolted back. The attacker stumbled sideways.

An arrow shaft sank deep into the man's collarbone. He spun about from the impact and collapsed.

A moment later, Zinnuvial jumped the river of blue fire and appeared at his side. Yvenne hoisted her shift above her knees and leapt over the flames as well. The hem of the fabric caught as she landed, but Zinnuvial was quick to pluck the flames from her before they spread.

In the corner of the workshop, the shelves were now a tower of swirling flames. Eating away at the rolls of fabric, they quickly lapped up toward the ceiling. The crossbowman positioned near the top, clearly growing nervous, climbed to his feet and scurried to the far end, ready to climb down. But that option seemed fruitless now. A shocking mix of blue and orange flames had consumed most of the ground beneath him.

Hunter leapt and grabbed the lip of the first shelf. He hoisted himself up, dropped to his belly, and offered his hand down to Zinnuvial and Yvenne. Heat pressed on his side like an open blast furnace. The flames drew closer with every second.

"Keep going," he shouted over the roar of the flames as soon as Zinnuvial and Yvenne were hauled up. Smoke filled his throat like a hot rag, choking him. His eyes burned. He wove his fingers together in front of him. Zinnuvial stepped in the center, and Hunter hoisted her up to the next level. Yvenne followed, with Zinnuvial helping her.

Movement caught his eye. Across the sea of flames, a

darkly clad figure emerged from a separate room off to the side. His pale skin reflected the firelight like porcelain, and the black hair caught the swirling eddies caused by the fire and flew outward like bat wings. Charcoal blue ram horns twisted out of his temples.

The Heneran strolled out into the workshop, heedless of the inferno around him, looking like a demon of hell. Flames rolled away from his feet as if terrified of him, and as he crossed the floor, he glared up at the three of them, his eyes piercing into Hunter's soul like an arrow. Despite the heat pressing in around him, it sent a cold wave racing down his back.

He wondered, for no more than an instant, if this was a projection like before. But no—his form was solid, and he commanded the flames around him as if they were his children fawning for his attention.

The Heneran lifted his arms out to his sides. The crystal at his breast surged with light. Blue flames rose from the floor to meet his palms, then spun themselves into churning orbs. He extended his hands out toward the shelves, and the orbs shot through the air.

Hunter flung himself up. One hand grasped the edge of the shelf above him as the two balls of fire pounded into the shelf under his feet. Flames exploded underneath him, searing heat surrounding him. If not for the heavy boots he wore, his feet would have been charred. The shelf beneath him disintegrated, and rolls of burning fabric cascaded to the floor.

Zinnuvial lifted Yvenne up to the final shelf while Hunter pulled himself up. He scrambled to his feet, ready to jump again. The blast had weakened the shelving—Hunter could feel the entire structure shift under him. It was losing its integrity and would soon all crash down. He stole a glimpse of the Heneran. More flames were rising up into his hands.

Above him, a hand was reaching down from the broken skylight to pull Yvenne to safety. She at least would make it out of this alive.

Zinnuvial notched her last arrow and let it fly. Hunter froze a moment to watch it soar across the workshop. It impaled the shoulder of the Heneran, throwing him back. The blue orbs lost their structure.

She had bought them a little more time, but already the Heneran was attempting to recover, and the shelving groaned and started to list.

Hunter again hoisted Zinnuvial up. She threw down her bow and leapt for the skylight. Hands seized her and hauled her onto the roof.

He scrambled up, feeling like he was on a capsizing ship. Everything was twisting under him, wood groaning. He jumped—but the shelf gave way. He couldn't push off hard enough. He flailed his arm upward in a desperate attempt to grab anything. Four fingers caught the lip of the skylight, but a shard of glass embedded in the edge stabbed into his palm. He cried out. Pain exploded throughout his hand, and as he dangled over the inferno, the shelving collapsed into a burning heap. Smoke swirled thick and gray around him, forcing his eyes closed, and he couldn't pull any air into his lungs. Another blast hit near the skylight. The Heneran was back to throwing fireballs at him.

"Give me your other hand, idiot!" Dax shouted down at him.

Hunter knew that Dax would never have the strength to pull him up. Hunter was more likely to pull Dax down and they'd both plummet to their deaths. But he flung an arm up blindly anyway and felt a hand snatch his wrist. Then more hands were grasping any part of him they could reach, and his body was hauled upward. Slowly. Once his waist was at the edge, he threw his leg up and rolled onto the roof.

He lay on his side, coughing smoke from his lungs. He felt dizzy and nauseous and wanted to do nothing but remain curled up in a ball. But Dax was already pulling on him.

"We have to move," Dax said. "Now."

He forced himself to his feet again, choking down vomit

that lifted into his throat. And they all started to jog across the rooftop.

23

"HOLD STILL," Dax grumbled.

Hunter drew in a breath and tried to keep his arm steady while Dax prodded away at the gash in his hand with the tip of a knife. "You almost done in there?"

The two of them occupied a small store room. Hunter straddled a barrel, facing Dax, who sat on a low stool. Hunter's arm lay across a wooden crate positioned between them, with a lantern burning next to his hand.

"There's one more shard," Dax replied as he tightened his grip on Hunter's wrist. He leaned in, squinting at the angry red line across the center of his palm. "And every time you talk you move your hand. So, stop talking. If you don't want the wound to fester, remain still so I can remove it."

An infection was the last thing Hunter needed. Safe to assume antibiotics weren't a thing here. He grunted, but then held the air in his lungs to keep his arm from moving. But with each heartbeat, he could feel his arm twitch. With Dax poking around inside his hand, it felt worse than when he got the wound in the first place. He squeezed his eyes closed, clenched the fist of his other hand, and tried to ignore the sharp bite of the knife point.

"I warned you not to take this mission," Dax said.

"You did no such thing," Hunter replied.

"I told you it was too risky. That should have been enough."

"You're the one that offered up the suggestion of me staying at one of the safe houses. You expected me to turn down that sweet deal?"

"I could already tell you were going to agree to the mission," Dax replied with a huff. "So, I wanted to get you something out of it that would benefit both of us."

Meaning Hunter would be out of his hair and no longer his problem.

Dax set the knife aside and reached into the gash with his thumb and forefinger and pinched. He slipped out a thin blood-covered shard. "There." He wiped blood from his hands on a rag, grabbed the bottle of spirits from the floor and doused the wound in the amber liquid.

Hunter hissed through his teeth as his hand erupted in stinging pain.

They were silent for a time as Dax gathered up the strips of khaki-colored linen. He none too gently repositioned Hunter's hand in the center of the crate, shook loose the first strip, and began wrapping it around the hand. A spot of red immediately appeared on the linen over the wound.

"You should have turned around at the first sign of the trap."

"And left Yvenne in the hands of that Heneran?"

Dax tucked the end of the linen bandage under itself, and his finger poked at the wound. Hunter clenched his teeth. "You'd be dead if I hadn't followed you to the warehouse. Yvenne and Zinnuvial too."

"You think I like playing the role of damsel in distress all the time? I went into this knowing there'd be risks, Dax."

"You did not understand what the risks were." Dax started wrapping another bandage around his hand, but his bedside manner was getting rougher. Hunter breathed through his teeth while Dax squeezed his hand tighter and looped the straps around his palm like he was winding a crank.

"It was my choice to take them. You're not the only one here taking risks."

"But when you take risks, it means I have to rescue you. Which, as it turns out, is taking far too much of my time. You aren't prepared for the dangers of this sort of thing."

That stung more than the gash in his hand. "I actually think I held my own pretty well."

Dax scoffed. "You were lucky."

Hunter tugged his hand away from Dax's grip. "This isn't about me at all, is it? This is about your brother. You're the only one allowed to assume any risk around here because you don't need another death on your conscience. Is that it?"

Dax froze a moment, and the temperature in the room seemed to drop ten degrees. Rage flashed in Dax's eyes as he turned his head. "We need to report to Quinnar."

He stood from the stool and left the store room.

QUINNAR STEEPLED his forefingers against his lips in thought. "Do not misunderstand me, Hunter. I am grateful for your contribution, of course," he said to Hunter, breaking his long silence.

His contribution? Quinnar made it sound as if he'd spent the afternoon volunteering at a youth shelter or cleaning out an abandoned lot. Just as Dax liked to remind him, there were at least a dozen ways he could have died back there.

"But," Quinnar continued, "with respect, there is much you do not know. I am disinclined to fall to that conclusion so quickly."

"He is not wrong," Dax replied. "They were ready for us. They knew the plan."

Hunter wondered how hard it was for Dax to admit that.

Quinnar stared back at Dax a moment, lines appearing at

the corners of his eyes. "Or, more likely, they outmaneuvered us. They leaked the information to us and predicted how we would respond. We played into their scheme exactly how they wanted us to."

Dax's face remained hard and Hunter could feel anger radiating off him. He had refused to discuss the outcome of the mission openly with the council, so the four of them were crammed into Quinnar's private office. The reason now was clear—Dax suspected someone in the council could have tipped the palace off. Watching Dax's eyes on Quinnar, Hunter couldn't help but wonder, too, if Dax suspected Quinnar himself.

Gingerly, Hunter prodded his thumb over the bandage wrapped around his palm, exploring the boundaries of the pain. His hand was throbbing from deep within—a pain different than the typical bruising and muscle soreness he was accustomed to. "And if you're wrong?"

A flash of annoyance burned in Quinnar's eyes. "Your hunch is not enough to sow seeds of doubt among us."

"My hunch?" Hunter asked, stepping closer to the table. He was trying hard not to care about any of this. None of it should matter to him. He'd done what they'd asked, and now it was time for him to get on with the task of finding a way home.

"The only ones that knew of the mission were those in the council room. They all have earned my trust."

"It does us no harm to take further precautions," Dax interjected.

"Don't presume I am being naïve," Quinnar replied directly to Dax. "We have all heard the rumors of a spy among us. And despite what people think, I take the rumors seriously. But there is already too much discord. Factions splintering our resolve. I will not have the council now turn on itself. I need evidence. Better yet, a name."

A grim silence followed. There was no solid evidence, and Quinnar knew it. Even Yvenne couldn't provide anything substantive to prove one way or the other that the Heneran knew the specifics of the plan. Hunter knew that Quinnar would not act.

It didn't matter anyway, he reminded himself. This wasn't his fight, and he'd be smart to remember that. He'd held up his end of the bargain, and as long as Quinnar did the same, he could now at least put some of this insanity behind him. He'd be a surface dweller again, topside.

"What will you tell the council?" Dax asked.

"That there were complications—"

"Nothing like understating the obvious," Hunter grumbled.

Quinnar's eyes shifted to Hunter before returning to Dax. "But the mission was ultimately a success."

"They will come to the same conclusion we have," Dax said.

"Leave them to me." Quinnar leaned against the back of his chair and pinched his chin with his forefinger and thumb. "The bigger concern is the Heneran. You're certain it was there in the flesh? Not a projection?"

"Positive," Hunter replied. "It shot balls of fire at me."

"And there was only one of them?"

"One was enough," Hunter said. "It had one of those glowing stones around its neck. A big one." He gestured the size of an apple with curled fingers over his chest. "If there'd been more, I'd have been toast. Burnt toast."

"If there was one...," Zinnuvial said dourly and left the rest of her thought unfinished.

Quinnar nodded with pursed lips. "Then there are likely more. Any kug'ra?"

"None that I saw," Hunter said.

Zinnuvial folded her arms. "They would be much harder to smuggle in."

"How did that Heneran even get into the city?" Hunter asked. It wouldn't be easy to simply hide those twisting horns under a hood. "The gates were heavily guarded when we got

216

here, and every cart was searched. Would guards knowingly let any in?"

Quinnar shook his head. "Illusion, most likely."

"Is it that easy?" Hunter asked.

"Not hardly. Few sorcerers know the spell, and even fewer have the competency for it. It is a costly spell, demanding much power to maintain, but that doesn't seem to be a problem for the Henerans since they obviously have ample witchstone at their disposal. But it's a lengthy ritual to conduct and requires specific components."

"Components?"

"Supplies needed to make the spell work. Not least of them, I understand, is flesh from the one they wish to impersonate."

Hunter's heart skipped. The missing part of his mother's hand. Before they'd sent her to his world, they had cut it off to use for their illusion.

Dax made a low noise in his throat. His expression had darkened. His brow pulled in tight over the bridge of his nose, and his mouth twisted to the side. "They grow bolder. Explains the weak defense we noted at the border. She is providing them covert access into our lands to establish a position. And now they have occupied the city. No telling how many Henerans are already here."

"We are running out of time," Zinnuvial whispered.

"Why? What does that mean?" Hunter asked.

"Their plan is nearer to fruition."

"And that plan is?"

Quinnar drummed his fingers on the desk. After everything Hunter had gone through, was he still debating whether to share what they knew? "Seize control the kingdom, of course. And return the Crags to Heneran control."

"They want the witchstones mines," Hunter said.

"Yes... but it is not as simple as that," Zinnuvial replied. "The Henerans claim the Crags are their ancestral home. And the home of their gods."

Hunter took a step back. "Hold on. The land you took from them is their *holy land*?"

Quinnar shook his head. "The Crags were taken during the Ghu'doric Wars more than a century ago—"

"Doesn't matter. They still view it as theirs. That is the sort of thing that lives a long time in the memory of a people."

"The lands were won fairly—" Quinnar continued, leaning in on his elbows.

Fairly? Hunter doubted that. "So, they're supposed to just walk away and forget their homeland is occupied by their sworn enemy? This whole thing isn't about them gaining power, is it? It's about you keeping it."

"I don't expect you to understand. This isn't your world—"

"That's bullshit and you know it." Most of the wars that ever occurred in his own world had their roots in religion. "Certainly explains why they're fighting so hard to get it back." And why they hated the humans so damn much.

"Do not sympathize too deeply with them, Hunter," Zinnuvial said. "Their beliefs also allow for the enslavement of the kug'ra. A right bestowed upon them by their gods."

That did give him pause.

"Regardless of their motives," Dax added, "if the Henerans are successful, it could trigger a new war between us. Thousands could die. Thousands more driven from their homes to become refugees."

"Or enslaved," Zinnuvial said. "As the kug'ra are. Punishment for us defiling their lands."

Quinnar leaned back in his chair again, drummed his fingers on the arm of it. "The presence of the Heneran in the city cannot be ignored. It forces our hand. And I've recently received word from inside the palace. The imposter queen has spoken to her court about her attempts to bear the king's child. That may have been their plan all along. Create an heir."

Zinnuvial and Dax exchanged looks. "Which would legitimize their ownership of the land," Dax said, nodding.

Hunter looked into Dax's eyes and saw cold concern there.

"Is that even possible?" Hunter asked. He had no idea how different they were from humans.

"A human-Heneran crossbreed? I know of no such occurrence," Zinnuvial replied, weaving her arms over her breast.

"Yet it is possible with the Mazenti," Quinnar said. "Are we willing to gamble that it will not work?"

"Well, if it is possible, and a kid is born, those horns would be a dead giveaway," Hunter said.

Dax shook his head. "They would extend the illusion to include the child as well. Otherwise the child would not survive the hour."

Quinnar said, shaking his head, "My thoughts exactly. Which means we need to consider taking bolder action. We should act on the imposter sooner than we planned."

Dax lifted his brow in a high arch. "We are not nearly in place to expose her."

"I'm not speaking of exposing her."

Silence fell among them. "What then?" Zinnuvial asked in a very quiet voice. She already knew the answer.

"Something we should have done at the beginning. Before it got this far."

"Are you seriously suggesting—" Hunter cut himself short. He heard a noise behind him, out in the corridor. He turned around to find Uri standing there by the open doorway, bearing a tray.

"My apologies," Uri said with a bow. "I was sent with Master Quinnar's evening meal." In the center of the tray was a plate of steaming meat and potatoes and a heavy wooden mug. Quinnar waved him in. As he circled around, Hunter tried to catch his eye, but the boy avoided Hunter's gaze. As soon as the tray was set on the edge of the table, he quickly dashed from the room and disappeared into the corridor.

"You cannot be saying what I think you're saying," Hunter continued quietly once Uri was gone.

"I know it sounds distasteful—"

"No, it sounds barbaric, actually."

"We need to consider it. If we are to survive."

"Assassination is not the answer," he said with a shake of his head.

Quinnar frowned and took the mug of ale from the tray and set it front of him. "It may have to be."

Quinnar must be feeling desperate, feeling his influence within his resistance slip from him, to even suggest this. And the subtext here was clear, especially with the way Quinnar's eyes lingered in Dax's direction. Hunter knew exactly who Quinnar had in mind for the job. "Even if you're successful, it will not turn out the way you think. It never does."

Quinnar took a drink from his mug but stayed silent.

Zinnuvial and Dax were quiet as well, their expressions hard and unreadable. Did they agree with this?

"Bring this up to your council," Hunter pressed. "See what they think."

"Were you not just advocating for more secrecy? That the council could not be trusted?"

"It's a terrible idea. Others will agree."

Quinnar's expression darkened, his eyes lowering to the table in front of him. He looked as if he was struggling with some internal fight, trying to not say what was on his mind. Eventually, he sighed and said, "You did far more today than we asked of you. For that, we are grateful. But this is now a matter for the resistance."

"So, butt out," Hunter said.

"Yes."

"Speaking of the arrangement," Dax put in, his words wedging the taut air between Hunter and Quinnar. A deliberate subject change. The way Dax and Quinnar met eyes, it was clear they were shelving this conversation for later.

Quinnar nodded. "A small tenement has been procured. As promised. He will be delivered there in the morning." He gave a Hunter a cool look. "Until then, avoid any more contact with others. We don't need another altercation."

The frosty note in his voice told Hunter he was sore about his clash with Corrad, which had never been directly addressed between them. Despite what he'd been through today, clearly all was not forgiven.

Dax seemed to accept this with a curt dip of his chin, and his head turned slightly toward Hunter. "He will occupy my quarters."

Quinnar lifted his eyes to the ceiling. "With the door locked, I'd advise."

Hunter scowled. The appreciation for what he did today didn't extend very far into the organization, apparently. "What of Uri?"

"He's expressed no interest. This is his home, Hunter."

Hunter refused to believe that and wondered if Quinnar had even approached him with it. The boy needed to be out of here, in a place where he could be treated like a human being. He'd likely been mistreated so long, this had become normal and expected.

But he didn't push it. He'd find Uri later and speak to him privately, convince him it was better if he stayed with him. Uri didn't have to leave the resistance—but he didn't have to spend all his days in a dark hole underground getting kicked around like a rodent.

Dax nodded to Zinnuvial as he turned to leave.

Hunter followed. "You don't need to give up your room. I'll be fine where I was."

Dax's head tilted a bit in front of him, but he didn't look back at him. "It is one night."

DAX LED him to the door of his personal room, which was tucked in an out-of-the-way corridor, alone and inconspicuous. He presented an iron skeleton key and dropped it into Hunter's palm.

"You were not shown due gratitude," Dax said from

deep in his throat. He looked pensive. Dour. "For what you did today. Not from Quinnar. Nor from me."

"I didn't do it for that," Hunter answered.

"Nonetheless." Dax looked down at his boots, quiet for a time. "You fought well today."

Hunter shrugged. "Finally got that stance figured out."

Dax's eyes swung to meet Hunter's, and even in the dim corridor, Hunter caught a glimpse of mirth behind them. "Your courage has not gone unnoticed. By many."

Evidently not enough, though. Otherwise he wouldn't need to sleep in a locked room.

Dax appeared as if he had more to say as his attention turned to the long corridor, and he stared off at nothing in particular. Hunter could almost hear his mind whirling. The silence between them grew prickly, and for a moment, Hunter thought he would speak what was on his mind. But instead, Dax straightened his spine and tugged on the bottom of his jerkin. "Rest well."

He marched away then, leaving Hunter curling his fingers around the key and wondering what he'd wanted to say. No one needed to tell Hunter, though, where Dax was going. He was heading back to talk to Quinnar.

Frowning to himself, he turned the key in the lock and let himself into the room. Some light from the corridor pushed past him into the vacant room. A bed, a nightstand, a table, a wardrobe. Neat and orderly, which didn't surprise him. He stood at the threshold, reluctant to let himself step into the room.

It smelled of Dax. The ghost of him had absorbed into the walls and the simple furnishings somehow. And it amplified his absence. Hunter couldn't help but drum up imaginings of Dax during his private moments in here, and it made Hunter feel like an intruder. A voyeur.

He would sleep here… later. He wasn't about sit in here all evening with nothing to do but mull over what had happened at the warehouse and wallow in Dax's absence. That felt a little pathetic.

He pulled the door shut again and locked it back up, then worked his way through the network of corridors, led by some inner compulsion. He let his feet steer him, and he knew where they were headed—back to the training yard. The fight in the warehouse now felt like a cold iron lump weighing down his soul. He felt restless, agitated, and needed to give his muscles something to do.

In the fading light of the courtyard, he peeled off all his clothes and left them in a pile. They were stained with blood and smelled of smoke—and he couldn't stand to wear them any longer. He grabbed a practice sword, and naked, he ran through all the drills Zinnuvial had taught him, one after another. Then ran through them again, until it was too dark to see. He gave himself over to the workout, despite the protest of his muscles and the stinging of the puncture wound in his hand. He worked until his skin was covered in a sheen of sweat. For a time, with his muscles aching, his heart rate elevated, his mind almost forgot what it was like to dangle from the ceiling, seconds from dropping to his death. Or the heat of the fireballs as they exploded around him, threatening to burn him alive. Or the grim sensation, felt in his hands, of a sword pushing through soft flesh.

At the point of collapse, he returned the sword to the box. The cool night air nipped at his damp skin, and the center of his hand now throbbed, but he didn't care. It was pain he'd rather feel than the one his heart held at bay. He used the water from a barrel and a thick horsehair brush he found to scrub the soot and sweat from his skin and hair. He scrubbed until his skin burned. But even then, it didn't feel like enough. The taint of death still clung to him.

He dunked the clothes into the water as well, wrung them out, and hung them over a railing. As they dried, he lay out naked over the pine box and watched the moon drift upward into the sky.

Tomorrow, he thought. Tomorrow he would be away

from here. Which meant he had to figure out a way to put all this behind him. Somehow. He had to. It was time focus all his energies on finding a way home. On finding a way of leaving this godforsaken hell.

24

HIS CLOTHES were still damp when he eventually decided to head in. He couldn't shake the feeling that they were still soiled with the events of earlier, and he was loath to put them on again. It didn't matter to him if anyone saw him naked and roaming the corridors. He hoped to never see any of these people again anyway. But Quinnar's request to not draw unnecessary attention to himself loitered in the back of his head. Despite his opinion of Quinnar, the advice was sound. So he settled for only wearing the pants, which were cold and clammy against his skin as he slipped them on. Boots and tunic held against his side, he wandered the vacant corridors barefoot.

In the morning, Hunter would be quietly stowed away in an apartment somewhere in this city, out of sight and likely forgotten. Safer probably, but minor details like how he was to buy food and necessary supplies hadn't been told to him yet. He was going to have to learn how to survive on his own in this city. Which would take time—time needed to begin his search for a way home.

A daunting prospect—and after today, it fell entirely on

him. No one in the resistance was going to help him, that was certain. He sighed. Home felt so far from him. It seemed beyond his reach. But he didn't want to think about that right now. He was morose enough.

He rounded the final corner leading to Dax's room and stopped. A thin streak of light cut across the floor. The door was ajar.

His heart lurched. He was certain that he'd locked it. He crept closer and stood outside, holding his breath and listening. He didn't hear anything. Had one of Corrad's thugs snuck in looking to finish him off, discovered he wasn't there, and bolted?

With one hand, he swept the door open farther.

Warm light spilled out to greet him. A lit lantern was on the table. Dax sat on the edge of the bed.

For a moment, his breath caught in his throat, surprise segueing into an unexpected buoyancy. As much as he didn't want to, he was glad to see him here.

"Forget you loaned out the room for the night?" he asked, trying to sound indifferent. A part of him wondered how he'd gotten in, but it didn't matter.

Dax's eyes made a quick tour of Hunter as he stood in the doorway, from his bare feet on up, but he made no question of why Hunter was wandering the corridors half-naked. He kicked at a sack on the floor near his feet.

"Your belongs. From the other chamber."

Hunter stepped into the room, dropped the boots, and tossed the damp tunic over the back of a chair. Of course, Dax could have simply dropped the sack on the bed and left, or had it delivered in the morning. But he chose to bring it himself, and then wait for him. Dax's expression, as always, was unreadable, giving Hunter no indication as to why he was really here. "Thanks," he replied, not knowing what else to say.

Dax lifted a dark glass bottle from the floor by his feet. "Brought this as well." Gripping the bottle by the long neck,

226

he rose to his feet. "The same batch as the other night. You seemed to enjoy it."

As Hunter took the bottle, their hands brushed—and contact with Dax's skin sent a jolt through his body. He struggled to pull a breath into his constricted lungs and tightened his fist on the bottle's neck to stop his hand from shaking. His insides quivered.

What the hell was wrong with him?

"Thought you could use it," Dax said. "After today. Numb the pain."

He had cleaned up as well, and Hunter caught the warm scent of something like sandalwood coming off his skin.

From the weight of the bottle, Hunter could tell half the contents were gone. Dax had been waiting here a little while, it seemed. Hunter pulled out the cork stopper and inhaled the contents, mostly to get Dax's virile scent out of his head. The sharp aroma lit up his sinuses. He tipped the bottle to his lips and opened his throat. The spirit rushed in, burning momentarily, and Hunter swallowed. He closed his eyes as heat trailed the length of his sternum to settle in his stomach.

When he opened his eyes, Dax was seated on the bed again. His attention was on the wall, unfocused, his mind elsewhere. Something was different about him tonight. Hunter couldn't pin down the source. It wasn't anger. It was something darker.

Hunter extended his hand with the bottle. It took a moment for Dax to notice before he took it back.

"I can change your bandages for you, if you like," Dax said.

Hunter turned his hand around. The blood had soaked through all the layers now, and it stung when he bent his fingers. He didn't feel like messing with it tonight. "I'm good."

Dax took a long draft, wiping the corner of his mouth with the back of his hand, then propped his elbows on his knees with his eyes on the floor between his feet.

Hunter sat on the chair with the back of it against his chest, facing him.

What was Dax doing here?

Tomorrow, Hunter would be gone from this place forever, and out of Dax's hair for good. Dax could happily return to his mission without having to worry about Hunter ever again. Hunter would have thought he'd be thrilled. So why was he lingering about?

Hunter hated to admit it, but he was glad he was here. The notion of never seeing Dax after tonight filled him with a sudden and unexpected pang, and he caught himself not wanting Dax to go anywhere. A part of him knew he should ask him to leave—tell him he was tired and he wanted to go to bed, but he couldn't bring himself to do it. But also, having him here ached. It felt like someone was poking at a wound.

This was not like him. He didn't pine after guys, didn't get swept up like this. But he caught himself grasping at this moment, relishing this chance to be alone with him, knowing full well Dax didn't feel the same.

Why else would he have let Hunter go on believing he was still with Quinnar? He didn't want to give Hunter any ideas.

Hunter took the bottle again and let the fiery liquid lave over his tongue. If only he could have remained blissfully ignorant of what it meant to fall for someone. It was terrible, and he never wanted to experience it again.

Dax reached for the sack on the floor between them. The sack containing his own clothes. Dax set it into his lap, dug inside, and pulled out Hunter's jeans.

Seeing them felt like a sharp stab to his heart. Something so ubiquitous back in his world, but here so harshly incongruent. A bitter reminder of how far away he truly was from his home.

"I was going to let you find this on your own," Dax said.

Hunter watched as he slipped his hand into the front pocket. Something about his hand probing inside his jeans made his heart race.

"But," Dax continued, "now that I think on it, I've no idea how long it would be before you wear these garments again." He extracted something from the pocket, stood, and presented his open palm to him.

His mother's amulet.

Hunter could only stare at it.

"Take it," Dax said.

Hunter couldn't move. He'd been chasing after it since he arrived here, but now that it was right in front of him, he was strangely reluctant to take it. "Why now, Dax?"

"The plan was never going to work. Might as well return it to its true owner."

Did Quinnar know Dax was doing this? Hand quivering, Hunter lifted the amulet from Dax's hand. His fingertips brushed Dax's palm. The touch sent another jolt through him.

He curled his fingers around it. It felt weird to hold it again. Almost sad. An exclamation point that everything the two of them had gone through together was for nothing.

"I take it that this means you're going through with Quinnar's plan."

Dax frowned. His *this doesn't concern you* face. "No decisions have been made."

"If it comes up again, you could say no. That's an option. You know that, right?"

Dax didn't reply. He instead took the bottle again and lifted it to his lips. He held there. A heavy shot that would have left Hunter sputtering and choking. Dax eventually let the bottle lower with a gasp as if emerging from underwater, then set it down on the end table with a decisive thump.

In a flash of movement, Dax closed the distance between them. Before Hunter could process what was happening, Dax slid a hand behind Hunter's neck. And then his lips were pressed to his mouth.

Hunter's heart sprang into his throat. He flinched and gasped a startled breath, tasting Dax's scent. His brain rolled over in his skull. He had no idea why this was happening and struggled to accept that it was. But his body was way ahead of his brain and responded on impulse. Hot euphoria pulsed through him in a scorching wave. Dax's lips were warm and soft, but his beard sweetly scoured the sensitive edges of Hunter's mouth.

But something about it felt wrong.

It felt desperate. Frantic.

Hunter put his hands on Dax's shoulder and pulled away from him. The sensation of the kiss was still hot on his lips.

"Dax...."

"Don't," Dax replied in a low voice that was almost a growl. "Don't say anything."

There were a thousand things he wanted to say. A thousand more he knew he should say. The liquor had kicked in, and his head was swimming. He couldn't get his brain to form any words.

Dax's mouth was against his again, the force against his lips almost angry.

This time, Hunter didn't have the strength to resist. He closed his eyes as he gave in to it, and his lips parted.

Dax pushed in harder with a surge of raw hunger. His hands slipped around Hunter's torso, sliding across the skin and setting the muscles of Hunter's back alight with fire. The sensation flooded his brain; his head swooned. Dax pulled him in tighter, and his tongue thrust into Hunter's mouth, plunging deep, and Hunter sucked on the thick muscle to pull it farther into his throat.

Dax groaned. The vibrations reverberated through Hunter's chest.

He coiled a thick arm around Dax and squeezed him tight against him. The muscles of Dax's back constricted against his touch. Hunter was lost in the taste of Dax's tongue and the feel of his body against his own. Nothing existed beyond the two of them.

Dax broke off contact long enough to strip the tunic off

over his head and toss it to the floor. Then he plunged back in. Hunter's skin drank in the feeling of Dax's chest pressed against him, and a wild surge rushed to his groin.

Hunter slid his lips to Dax's neck under the ear and a groan escaped his throat as salt and sweat delighted his tongue. Dax's head fell back. The heady aroma of Dax's skin flooded Hunter's nostrils and sent dizzying explosions to his head. He cupped Dax's pec and thumbed his hardened nipple while he glided his other hand down his lower back to dig under the waistline of his pants. Dax palmed the curve of his ass, then a hot finger coaxed its way into the deep cleavage between his cheeks.

Hunter's head whirled. He was fully erect now and pointing straight up, wedged between both their bellies. Dax playfully gyrated his hips against it and lifted a knee between his thighs. The head of his cock tingled and pulsated. Hunter's entire body shuddered, and his knees almost gave out.

His mind screamed at him to stop, but it felt distant and weak, as if his desire had it chained up in a dark basement somewhere. His body was in control now, and he was powerless against it. He knew he was going to regret it, knew that afterward his heart would punish him.

This would only make leaving tomorrow more painful.

He secured his arms around Dax's frame and lifted him off the ground with little effort. Dax curled a leg around the back of his thigh. Gently, Hunter carried him to the bed and lowered him down to the mattress. While Dax unpeeled himself from Hunter's body, Hunter hovered over him, drinking in the sight with a lump in his throat.

A thin smile broke Dax's face, but it was cool and hungry.

Dax's arms stretched over his head, relaxed and waiting. The glorious curves of his torso and biceps made Hunter almost delirious with yearning. Hunter savored the vision a moment before he traced one hand down the length of Dax's flank, from his armpit to his hip, muscles and ribs pressing against his palm, skin like silk. His cock throbbed painfully in his pants, begging to be released.

He took Dax's hard nipple into his mouth, flicked it playfully with his tongue before he bit down on it. Dax groaned again and arched his torso. Hunter slipped a hand under him, pressed the small of his back as he explored the hard, spasming muscles of Dax's abdomen with his lips and tongue. The skin was spiced with sweat, and the scent made the room spin as if he was intoxicated.

He drifted his hand across Dax's groin and felt the swollen cock beneath the fabric lift to meet his touch. He explored the shape with his fingers, his thumb gently brushing the round head. Dax pulled in a sudden breath.

"Get these fucking clothes off me," Dax breathed.

Hunter grabbed a leg and braced a booted foot against his bare chest. With deliberate slowness, he undid the laces. Then he pulled off the boot and tossed it unceremoniously to the floor. He explored the toes and the arch of Dax's foot with his tongue, pulling the big toe into his mouth to suck on it as he breathed in the delicious heady scent. Once both boots were on the floor, Hunter loosened the laces crisscrossing Dax's bulging crotch, and when Dax lifted his hips, Hunter used two hands to rip the trousers away.

The unprecedented beauty of Dax's nude form made Hunter forget everything. His form was something divine. A godlike beauty. Proportioned with such transcendent perfection it almost hurt to look at it. His skin caught the lamplight like burnished copper, and the assortment of scars only accentuated its succulence. Dax's cock was no exception—a sublime testament of his potency. Thick and exquisitely formed, it rested against his belly, inviting Hunter in.

Dax slid his foot up the mattress, raising his knee. "What are you waiting for, dolt?"

Hunter allowed his own trousers to drop to the floor.

As if wielding the most precious of relics, he cradled

Dax's sac in his hands, let his fingers massage the slightly tightened skin. Hunter brought his fingers to the base of the shaft, which throbbed in anticipation of what was to come. He curled his fingers around it—felt his heart race with the thrill of it in his palm. Dax exhaled and pushed up his chin.

Hunter let his eyes take in Dax's perfect yet squirming form while his hand slowly slid up the length of his cock. He wanted to devour every inch of his body—but he forced himself to keep it slow. When Hunter's hand drew close to the head, Dax's shoulders shuddered and he let out a soft moan. A gush of clear fluid oozed from the slit and beaded on the side.

Still gripping the hard shaft, Hunter slid Dax's leg up and ran his tongue in the crevice between his inner thigh and sac. More fluid seeped down the side of his cock and drizzled over Hunter's finger. Hunter ran his tongue over the finger and up the side, lapping up the clear juice like melting ice cream running down a cone. Sweet exploded on his tongue.

Then he took his shaft into his mouth.

Inhaling through his nose, he tightened his eyes and allowed all of Dax to enter his throat until Hunter felt his lips reach the bottom and the pubic hair tickle under his nose. Dax cried out, and his entire body spasmed as if shocked. Hunter's mouth was filled to capacity, his jaw stretched to its limit. Dax throbbed against the sides of his throat. Hunter tightened his lips around the shaft, pulled back and slid off of it—then sank down onto it again.

Dax began to squirm his hips about and groan louder. Fingers twisted in Hunter's hair, and he was tugged downward again and held there. The gyrating of his hips increased, and his back arched. With Dax's sac still in his hand, Hunter used his forefinger to explore upward, trace Dax's opening and massage the skin around it.

"Stop," Dax said suddenly, and tried to push Hunter off his cock. Hunter smiled inwardly, feeling the tightening of his ball sac in his hand. "*Stop*," Dax cried out again.

Hunter complied, pulling off his cock with a pop of his

lips. He grinned up at Dax.

"Not yet," Dax told him. He dropped his head back, panting. "Not yet. My bag. On the floor. Grab it."

Hunter reached down and snagged it. He loosened the drawstring and reached inside. A quick search revealed a small earthenware jar with a cork stopper on top. Inside was a white creamy paste. Hunter dragged his forefinger across the top, leaving a trench, and rubbed the material between his fingers. The paste was slick.

He gave Dax a sideward glance. "You planned this all along."

Dax said nothing.

Again his mind sent off a warning klaxon. But there was no chance of stopping this train now.

Hunter took in slow breath as he slid his hand back under Dax, who bent his knee to allow Hunter's slickened forefinger freer access to explore.

Hunter sat back on his heels and generously applied the white cream over the full length of his cock. It was warm against his skin and as he cupped his hand over the head, his entire body shuddered.

Dax lifted his hip and pulled a knee back to his chest. Hunter scooped more white cream onto his fingers and gently worked the lubricant into the welcoming hole, first massaging his thumb around the perimeter, then probing inward with his forefinger. Dax's chin jolted upward and his chest heaved as the finger glided in its full length. Hunter twisted his wrist back and forth, then coaxed his middle finger inside as well. Dax put his heel to Hunter's collarbone, and a low moan escaped his throat.

Hunter took his time, working his fingers in and out, turning his hand about until he could feel the muscles around his two fingers begin to relax. Dax's breathing quickened. He lifted his hips and pushed himself onto Hunter's fingers with intensifying desire. With one hand, he grabbed Hunter's forearm to encourage him to thrust harder while the other tugged on himself.

"Let me," Hunter whispered, and gently replaced Dax's hand with his own, curling his fingers around Dax's thick cock. He gave it a squeeze and slid his grip up and down the shaft. It pulsated against his palm. Dax spasmed against the mattress, helpless. His head thrashed side to side.

Dax was ready.

Hunter pulled out his fingers and shifted himself closer. Still stroking Dax, he gripped the base of his own cock and guided it toward Dax's opening. He didn't think he'd ever been so hard—surges of both pleasure and swollen pain ran through him as he maneuvered the head into position.

Slow and gentle, he thrust his hips. The head of his cock broke the threshold. Dax took a sudden intake of breath and arched his back. He cried out. Hunter was ready to pull out again, but Dax lifted his hips farther, inviting him in deeper.

Dax's tight muscles squeezed around Hunter and sent tingling waves of euphoria through his body. The muscles of his ass and thighs contracted involuntarily. His chin lifted as his lungs pulled in sputtering breaths. He wanted nothing more than to push, but he forced control and only eased in a bit farther. He watched as more of him disappeared inside. Dax cried out again as his fingers tangled within the sheets.

Hunter forced himself to work slow. He pulled out a little, then drove in even more. Then again. And again. Dax showed no signs of resisting, no sign that Hunter's girth was too much. So, Hunter gave in to his own desire and thrust his hips until all of him was inside Dax.

Still massaging Dax's cock, he fell into a rolling rhythm. His thighs slapped against skin, and Dax roiled and twisted beneath him. Ankles moved to his shoulders as Hunter leaned in. Dax lifted his shoulders to bring his mouth against his. Hunter grunted into Dax's awaiting mouth, and Dax's hot breath blasted into his. Hunter's tender lips burned with the rasp of Dax's beard.

Every one of Hunter's senses was on overload. The

musky smell of Dax made his head swim. The salty taste of his sweat was like wine on his tongue. The electric contact of their skin made every muscle convulse. The look in Dax's eyes as he stared up at him, it was more than his brain could handle, and he was aware of nothing other than the joining between them.

He was lost in the rhythm. Lost in the desire. His hips rolled against Dax in steady but powerful thrusts. Energy was building in him. Escalating ecstasy coursed through his groin and he felt his sac tighten in anticipation. The sensation rose with sudden intensity, and tremors rocked through him. He was tormented by the promise of what was to come. His face flushed with fever, and sweat cascaded from his brow.

Dax's ankles tightened on the side of his neck; his hands clung desperately to Hunter's back, pulling him closer. He bit down on Hunter's lip. He felt it too.

Release came for both of them at the same time. As Hunter's cock erupted inside Dax, sending exquisite convulsions through him, Hunter felt sudden pulsating warmth coat the hand around Dax. Their cocks surged in unison. Wave after wave of quaking pleasure. Hunter surrendered to the power of it. It was like nothing he'd experienced before. Each pulsation made every muscle seize in an almost violent onslaught on his body. Dax thrashed under him.

When it was over, Hunter was light-headed and drained. He removed himself from Dax, whose legs dropped to the mattress like a ragdoll's. Hunter lowered onto his side next to Dax, his hand drifting from Dax's still hard cock to cup the tight scrotum. Hunter's chest was varnished in Dax's seed. He used two fingers to scrape up some of the creamy fluid from his skin and slid the fingers into his mouth. He closed his eyes to savor the sweet taste of Dax's ejaculate on his tongue.

Dax was already asleep. The sound of his gentle snores made Hunter's heart ache for a reason he couldn't explain. A part of him still couldn't believe any of this had happened.

His breathing and heart rate were returning to normal

now, and his cock had started to reduce. He thought about wiping up before he drifted off too, but he didn't want to peel himself from Dax, and besides, he liked the idea of Dax's sweat and cum coating his skin. He enveloped Dax in one of his thick arms and snuggled in close. The heady smell of sex filled him with each breath. Spent, he too was asleep in moments.

When he woke up later, Dax was gone.

25

HUNTER SAT on the edge of the bed and rubbed the corner of his eye with the heel of his hand.

Of course he was gone.

Dax had gotten what he'd wanted from him and moved on. Hunter had allowed himself to believe that perhaps it had meant there was more between them. But he knew all along exactly what it was—a hookup. Netflix and chill. Hunter chose to ignore the warning signs.

And he was right about one thing. His heart was going to punish him for a long time.

With a certainty he couldn't explain, he knew that Dax had lied to him. He'd already agreed to take up the mission. Because that's what he did. He followed orders. And this time, Dax didn't think he'd be coming back.

Hunter was Dax's steak dinner before he walked the long mile to his execution.

His sleep-clogged brain, still fuzzy from the strong liquor, was slow to realize that something other than Dax's absence had woken him up.

Noises. Shouting.

Something was happening.

He sprang up. Crusty remnants from earlier pinched and tugged the skin of his abdomen as he moved. A bittersweet reminder of what he'd experienced only hours before. He pulled on his tunic and pants. The memory of Dax's warm body against him lingered on his skin, but he shoved the sensation aside.

He'd be angry about it later.

He dashed out into the corridor, barefoot, still tying the drawstring at his waist. The shouts were growing louder. And closer. He headed toward them, rushing back toward the areas of the hideout he knew. The kitchens. The common area. As he drew closer to the sound, he heard the clash of steel.

He rounded a corner and skidded to a halt. A figure stomped toward him. Dressed in a familiar uniform. A *guard's* uniform.

His brain fought to make sense of it. What was a city guardsman doing here? The man had his sword drawn, and Hunter's blood went cold. The hideout was under attack.

The guard charged him, sword arm back, preparing a thrust. There was not enough room to swing the sword in the narrow corridor. Muscle memory seized control of Hunter's body. He twisted, throwing his back against the wall. The sword's point caught the front of Hunter's tunic and ripped through it but made no contact with Hunter's skin. He snatched the guardsman's wrist and slammed his gauntleted hand against the opposite wall, pinning it. The guardsman squawked in surprise and tried to pull free, but he was no match for Hunter's strength. Hunter kneed him in the groin. The attacker lost all the air in his lungs in a sudden whoosh and doubled over. Hunter grabbed him by the neck and bashed his head against the wall. Protected by a helm, the head took three impacts before the guardsman fell limp and slumped to the floor.

Hunter snatched the sword from the man's loose hand.

Where to go now was the question. By the sounds around

him, the hideout was overrun. He'd been right—the resistance had been betrayed by a mole. Cold consolation considering he'd likely be killed along with the rest of them. Finding the nearest way out was the smart thing to do. But where? The main entrance was being watched, surely. The only other way to the surface that he knew of was the enclosed training yard.

But people were dying down here. Maybe in their beds. Could he just leave?

Sword in hand, he took off in the direction of the noise.

He pounded on each door he passed, calling out "attack, attack" and waiting only long enough to hear if anyone responded. Some doors flew opened, and a few resistance members stumbled out into the corridor half-dressed and bleary eyed.

"Get out, get out," he shouted at them.

Another city guardsman barreled around a corner. Hunter sprang and tackled him to the floor before the man could lift his weapon. He wedged his knee to the man's chest, pressing his full weight on him, then punched his temple until the man was out cold.

A small group of resistance fighters, swords in hand, rounded the corner. The mess hall cook led the charge. They skidded to halt as Hunter rose to his feet.

"You!" one of them cried, pointing. "You're behind this."

He lunged for Hunter, but the cook shoved him back into the wall.

"Dolt!" the cook shouted at him. "That's a city guard he just took down."

The others froze, eyes lowering to take in the body on the floor.

"Corrad said—"

"You going to believe what that hood tells you or your own eyes?" The cook didn't wait for a response, but stepped closer to Hunter, lowering the blade. "Where are they?"

"Not sure. But the hideout's overrun. You need to get

out."

Someone cried out from somewhere, their anguish reverberating against the wall, and the sound cut off abruptly. Hunter's stomach wanted to empty. The faces of the men hardened into anger and bloodlust as they adjusted their grips on their weapons. They were going to run into the fray, ready to defend the hideout.

Hunter grabbed the cook by the bicep as he tried to push past him. "It's too late," he growled at him. "Warn as many as you can. Fight another day."

After several sharp breaths, the cook nodded, and the group dashed off down the other corridor.

Hunter knew he should heed his own advice and head toward the exit. But someone needed to fend off the attackers to gain time for others to escape. Someone had to draw their attention. Might as well be him. Get to the action. Hold the line. Protect the others. Wasn't that his role in life?

He sprinted down other passages toward the cries. More bodies. Brutally slain. Hunter tried to divert his eyes from the carnage, but his bare feet slipped on blood pooled on the stone.

A man dragged himself across the floor toward Hunter, a long streak of red behind him. Hunter darted to him, but the man collapsed facedown at his feet and went limp. Hunter gently turned him over, but the man's eyes stared up at nothing. He was dead.

Rage flashed through him and made his vision blacken. This killing was pointless. The victims didn't even have weapons to defend themselves.

Hunter pounded on any door that was closed, but the deeper he went into the tunnels, the more doors were left open. In some of the rooms he saw motionless bodies. Others were empty. The attackers had already swept through these passages, and Hunter was coming up behind them. He could hear the shouts and cries of agony coming from up ahead.

Maybe he could take them by surprise—put an end to their massacre.

Then Hunter heard another sound. Closer. Quieter. Sobbing.

A door near him was ajar. The sound came from there. Hunter pushed the door open, allowing the soft yellow light from the sconces in the corridor to reach inside. A figure was hidden in the back, huddled in a ball.

Uri.

His face was in his knees and his shoulders quaked as he tried to muffle his cries. Hunter reached into the room, grabbed him under the arm, and hauled him to his feet. Uri called out and thrashed out in sudden terror.

"It's me," Hunter told him as he dragged him behind him. "I'm getting you out of here."

"No, no, no," Uri barked between sobs, and tried to squirm himself free. "Leave me alone."

Hunter ignored him.

Another figure whipped around the corner. Hunter nearly let go of Uri, ready to fight. He stopped short. Zinnuvial.

"Hunter," she said. She looked him over, and then Uri. "You are unharmed?"

Hunter nodded. "I was about to head to the training yard."

"Blocked," Zinnuvial said. "It is how they got in."

Someone had to have removed the bar from the gate. It was an inside job. Hunter wondered how many others had thought to exit that way and run right into an awaiting force.

"Follow me," she ordered, and took off at a jog. Hunter followed without question, Uri's wrist still in his grip.

A shout came from behind. "Halt!"

A guardsman. With a crossbow. Hunter tackled Uri to the floor, landing on top of him. Hunter heard the bolt whiz overhead and chink against the wall. Chips of stone fell on top of him.

He jumped up and sprinted for the attacker. Before he could load another bolt, he ripped the crossbow from his grip and tossed it behind him; then he punched the man hard enough to throw him clear off his feet. The guardsman hit the ground and didn't move.

Hunter grabbed Uri's wrist again as the boy tried to regain his feet. He took off again, steps behind Zinnuvial.

They rushed through the corridors and ducked into another room. A storage closet, filled nearly to capacity with stacked crates. The three of them crammed inside made for a tight squeeze.

"Zinn, hiding is pointless," Hunter said. "We need to get out of here." He had been willing to stay and fight the attackers until more got out—until he found Uri. Now, getting him to safety was his sole priority.

Zinnuvial lifted a crate from one corner of the closet and handed it over to Hunter. "Stack that over there."

What was the point of this? But Hunter obeyed, setting the crate on the other. "How'd they find the hideout?"

"No one knows." She climbed up on the crate and reached up toward the ceiling. Her fingers fumbled around in the dark. "Doesn't matter anymore. It's done."

"So, what now?"

She punched up at the ceiling with the heel of her hand. Hunter heard a wooden thump and a squeak of a hinge. Pale light spilled down into the small room from a line that appeared in the ceiling. "We go to one of the safe houses."

She shoved the trap door open, then hoisted herself up through it. A moment later, her face appeared, and she reached down.

"Come on," Hunter told Uri. "You're next."

Uri hesitated, looking anxious. He looked like he might bolt out the door instead. With a whimper and a sound somewhere between a sob and hiccup, he climbed up onto the crate. Hunter gently lifted him by the waist as Zinnuvial grabbed his forearm and heaved him upward.

Hunter followed. He pulled himself up and rolled onto a wood-planked floor. Zinnuvial slammed the trap door closed again. The room was lined with shelving loaded with wooden crates and sacks. They were in the backroom of a shop.

"How many of these little secret exits are there?"

"Hopefully enough," she said. "We aren't safe yet, Hunter. Guards are going to be searching for those that reach the streets."

A flight of stairs brought them to street level, into a shop of some kind, dark and closed up tight for the night. Faint bluish light filtered through the thick warped glass of the paned window. They were still an hour before dawn.

Hunter drifted to the window to scope out the street. It seemed empty, so he moved for the door.

"Don't be daft, Hunter," Zinnuvial growled. She was climbing up the thick wooden shelves like a ladder. "We can't stroll out the front."

Once again, she punched up upward at the ceiling and a section popped out. Zinnuvial climbed up into the rafters. Hunter prompted Uri to follow her, then trailed behind. A quick hunched scurry through the attic and through one more hatch overhead, and the three of them were on the roof of the building.

In the predawn light, Zinnuvial led them at a crouch from rooftop to rooftop. Some flat, some with dizzyingly steep angles. Gusts of morning wind threatened to dislodge Hunter and send him sliding down to plummet to the street. Cresting the peak of a high roof, Hunter risked a look down. Night and shadow still governed the bottom of the human-made caverns between buildings, but Hunter could see figures drifting through the streets with purpose. Too many for this time in the morning. Zinnuvial was right. City guards were hounding down the fleeing rats that escaped to the surface.

A whistle blew, and the dark shapes sprinted off. They'd spotted someone.

The pounding of his heart reached his ears. If not for Zinnuvial, that might have been him.

On the way down the other side, Uri slipped on the dew-covered cedar shingles. He gasped with sudden fear, his eyes wide as his body started to slide. He kicked his feet to stop the descent, but they couldn't find purchase. Hunter snatched his flailing wrist with one hand and gripped a cast-iron pipe protruding from the roof. Uri jolted to a stop.

But with the sudden lunge for Uri, he was forced let go of the sword. It slid over the slick shingles with a metallic hiss, down the length of the roof. Hunter locked air into his lungs as he watched it skate toward the edge. If it fell to the street, it'd alert all the guards below to their presence.

The sword caught on something and spun, slowing it down. It reached a raised lip at the base of the roof, and the blade protruded out over the open air. But the hilt remained on the shingles. It dangled precariously, teetering. The slightest wind might upset the balance and send it tumbling downward to the street. But for now, it remained.

Uri reached up and clung to Hunter's arm, panting. He buried his face in Hunter's sleeve, and Hunter could hear the boy's quiet sobs.

"Be careful," Zinnuvial snapped back at them in a whisper.

Hunter allowed himself to exhale. "It's okay," Hunter whispered to Uri. "I won't let anything happen to you. Stay close to me."

Uri, eyes still buried in his sleeve, nodded.

The sky was turning a brighter blue, and the morning light reached down to the cobbles. They scurried over a few more rooftops before Zinnuvial dropped down to a balcony and crawled through a window.

Hunter lowered Uri down first, then followed. He reached his foot through the window and ducked his head under the frame. He felt the presence of others in the room already as he came in. Several others. He lifted his head.

"Fuck."

The first two faces he saw as he straightened his back were Quinnar and Corrad.

26

ON INSTINCT, Hunter's hand dropped to where a sword would have been—only to remember that it was lost on the roof. Inwardly, it amazed him how quickly that response had been now programmed into his brain, how quickly he relied on having a deadly weapon with him. An unsettling reality of this world he was in, and how even in the short time he was here, he was already changing to fit into it.

Corrad, unsheathing his sword, took a heavy stomp closer.

Uri shrunk back along the wall to squeeze himself into the corner. Zinnuvial moved to put herself in front of Hunter, her hand at her waist, circling a hilt.

Hunter gripped Zinnuvial's forearm at the same time to stop her unsheathing the weapon. Enough bloodshed had already happened—he wasn't going to be the cause of more of it. At the same time, Quinnar thrust a palm to Corrad's chest.

"Enough," Quinnar growled through his teeth, giving Corrad a hard glare. "I told you the matter's done." His tone had more force and authority than Hunter would have thought possible from him.

To Hunter's surprise, Corrad stood against Quinnar's hand but did not push past it. His eyes narrowed at Hunter, his wide jaw clenched tight. "Not to me. He's likely the one who betrayed us."

"Witless ox," Quinnar replied. "He's proven himself more trustworthy than you. And with twice the sense."

"Agreed," Zinnuvial said flatly.

The sudden and unexpected votes of confidence from both Quinnar and Zinnuvial stunned Hunter a moment. He wasn't sure which surprised him more.

Corrad's cheeks turned crimson in anger, and his nose flared outward. He looked dangerously close to ignoring Quinnar's hand and lunging for Hunter. But with Zinnuvial and Quinnar between him and Hunter, he had to know it would only end in more humiliation for him. Instead, he spit on the floor.

"For fuck's sake," Hunter said, lifting his eyes. "Give it up." He knew he was poking the bear, prodding Corrad into a rematch. He didn't care.

Quinnar's hard gaze refused to veer from Corrad's, as if it was his eyes that somehow held him back. "Leave," Quinnar told him. The single word was dropped like a sledgehammer striking stone with a firmness and certainty that it would be obeyed.

Corrad's eyes widened as he turned to Quinnar, and his expression turned to rage. His fists opened and closed. For a moment, Hunter wondered if Corrad would dare attack Quinnar. But to his amazement, Corrad took a step backward, then stomped away. He shouldered his way through a door and was gone. This wasn't over. The brute would try to get his revenge at some point.

Hunter puffed out his cheeks. "That dude is unstable and dangerous."

Quinnar, too, seemed to relax once Corrad was gone. "You are not wrong. Made more dangerous by the fact that his power here has diminished." In the midst of the confrontation,

Hunter hadn't noticed the gash just over his ear at the hairline only beginning to harden over. A swath of crusty brown-red covered his temple and clung in the recesses of his ear. He'd seen some action too. "His support was already declining, but it appears many of his toadies either died or fled during the attack. Seems they were involved here more to stir up trouble than stand for something."

His voice remained low and severe, bitterness and anger lacing every word.

The room was a small single-room apartment, with a bed against one wall and a round table in a corner. The table and the floor around it were buried beneath books and rolls of parchment documents, hastily deposited. Rescued from the hideout, no doubt. Incriminating details that should they fall into the hands of the palace could put even more people in danger. The cupboard was stocked with various bags, jugs, and crates. More were stacked in the corner. Provisions for long-term hole up.

"How many made it out?" Zinnuvial asked.

"Yet unclear," Quinnar said. Now that Corrad was gone, his air of dominion seemed to languish. The Quinnar of before, who flaunted his superiority like a parade float, was gone. Now Hunter faced a man crushed beneath the heft of fatigue, grief, and failure. "We are still trying to ascertain the damage. Scouts have only started to report in." He leaned his backside on the edge of the table and entwined his arms. "I am sorry, Hunter, this means I will not be able to honor our agreement quite yet."

Hunter's insides twisted. He'd already figured that to be the case, but hearing Quinnar say it stabbed at his hopes. Another delay before he could begin his search for a way home. How many more days before he could put this resistance fight behind him once and for all?

He sighed inwardly, feeling like a self-absorbed ass. People died tonight, he reminded himself.

"What of Dax?" he asked. He was afraid to hear the

answer.

Silence.

Quinnar lifted his eyes Hunter's way, as if to read how much Hunter might now know or had guessed. "No word. He left before the attack began."

Hunter rubbed the corner of his eye where a pain flared behind it. "Because you sent him into there on this stupid and reckless mission of yours."

Quinnar looked off at the wall in front of him. "He volunteered. He came to me last night and said he was going."

"Of course he did." Hunter wanted to hate Quinnar but was surprised he couldn't. Not now. Not after what happened. His simmering anger was aimed more at Dax. The fucker could have declined the mission. But his maddening sense of duty governed every decision he made. Underneath Hunter's fury, a sickening pool of worry ate at his insides. "If he fails, he's dead. And if he succeeds, your problems have only just begun."

Quinnar let his chin drop. "I'm quite certain our problems cannot become worse."

"I wouldn't count on that."

Quinnar tried to smile, but the attempt was largely a sad failure. "Rest," he said. "We control all of the tenements on this floor. But I would ask that you remain here for now."

"Anything I can do to help? Since I'm here."

"A generous offer. Considering. But… best, I think, if you remain here and out of sight for the time being."

Hunter nodded. Quinnar moved toward the door, and Hunter and Zinnuvial exchanged a glance.

"I will keep you apprised," she said over her shoulder.

"Thanks," Hunter replied. It was all he could ask for at the moment.

She followed Quinnar out of the room, leaving Hunter with the quiet sobs of Uri in the corner.

Hunter frowned. He could understand Uri being upset by the attack—the loss of life, loss of his home, the fear for his own life as they fled—but Hunter suspected there was more to it. Uri's reaction seemed triggered by more than just fear and grief. The members of the resistance were at best tolerant or dismissive of him. Others were outright hostile. His reaction didn't seem to fit.

He crossed the room, sat on the floor next to him, and leaned against the wall.

"Uri, what's going on?" he asked.

Uri's eyes remained downcast. He tried to rein in the sobs, and hiccupped instead. He wiped his cheeks and under his nose with his sleeves. "Didn't think they'd—" He cut himself off, a lump forming in his throat as if he'd swallowed his tongue. His shoulders constricted, and he turned his face away.

Sudden dread burned a hole through Hunter's gut. "Didn't think they'd what?"

Uri didn't reply.

Hunter took in a long breath to calm himself, but he felt the tide of panic and horror pressing in under his skin. "Who are you talking about, Uri?"

Still, Uri remained silent. His breathing was hard, like a trapped animal.

"Holy shit, Uri," Hunter breathed. "What have you done?"

A sharp defensiveness leapt into Uri's voice. "I don't know what you mean."

"Do you hate them so much that you would do this?"

He looked up, a flash of fire in his red and puffy eyes. "I don't hate them! They are my friends."

"Some are. Some were cruel to you." Hunter bent and turned his head to look directly into Uri's eyes. "You were the one who gave up the location of the hideout."

Uri turned his eyes away with a sudden intake of breath but didn't say anything.

"I suppose," Hunter continued, "you were the one who tipped off the Black Brotherhood, too, when I was sent to warn

Yvenne." A knot of anger flared in his stomach—that betrayal had almost gotten him killed as well—but he forced the anger to remain out of his voice, forced a level of calm he did not feel. "I remember how you came into the room during the meeting just long enough to hear the plan."

Uri's face hardened. He huffed and stared down at his boots.

"No point in denying any of it now," Hunter said. It made sense now why Uri resisted Hunter's plan to get him out of the hideout. He was the mole, and if he left, he couldn't fulfill the mission.

Why now, though, he wondered. Why did the raid on the hideout happen now? What was the trigger? He considered that maybe Uri was nervous, that he was close to being found out. But that wouldn't have mattered to the palace. They wouldn't spring the ambush on Uri's outlook. Then Hunter remembered that Quinnar had sent word to have many of the resistance's supporters retreat back to the hideout. It explained why so many were in the tunnels tonight. Members from all over the city had fled into the hideout to avoid getting picked up by the city guard. Had that been the plan all along? Trick the resistance into calling back their members, then strike?

"Tell Quinnar whatever you want," Uri grumbled. "It doesn't matter."

Not exactly an admission, per se, but it was enough to convince Hunter he was right. "I think it does matter. I've no intention saying of anything to Quinnar. Not yet. Because I suspect you had a good reason to do what you did."

"You should have left me in there."

"So you could die with the others? No. That's not the way this ends. Talk to me. Or I will get Quinnar and you can tell him."

A thick silence settled between them while Uri stared at the floor between his boots.

"I didn't want to," Uri said eventually in a very small voice.

"I believe you," Hunter replied. "What did they have over you?"

"Over me?" Uri asked, confused.

"How did they force you to do this?"

Uri looked tentative, afraid to speak. "You'll not tell Quinnar?"

Hunter bit the inside of his cheek in thought. "Not if I can avoid it."

Uri took in a prolonged breath and let it out slowly—a stalling tactic. He was clearly still reluctant to own up to it. "My mother."

Hunter stayed quiet and let him talk. After holding this secret in, he knew that once Uri's words started to flow, it would be hard to stop them.

"I started running errands for the resistance about a year ago. Didn't know what I was running, but they gave me a coin each time. Over time, I learned more. Did more. Ma found out what I was doing. She was really mad about that—mostly because she feared it would get us kicked out of the city. We struggled enough as it is. Scared, she asked someone we knew what we should do."

"And they turned you in."

Uri nodded. "Came home and she wasn't there. But two city guards and a man in black leather armor were at our table eating our food. The man in black said they had her in the palace dungeon. Said if I didn't do what they told me to do, they would execute her. Put the head on a spike where I'd see it. But if I helped them, they said they would let her go. I don't think they ever intended to do that. But I hoped they would."

"Bad men are like that."

Uri made another slow affirming nod.

"They told me how to infiltrate the resistance. Build their trust. It worked. But when I began to know some of them better, like Dax, men who were kind to me despite my skin, I started to hope that the resistance would win and stop the men who had my mother. It felt good to be a part of what they were doing. I pretended that the time I was to betray them would never come."

A fresh batch of tears pooled at the corners of his eyes.

"This isn't your fault, Uri." He tried to force confidence into the words, but his voice was weaker than he intended. Images of bodies on the ground, the blood that was everywhere—all of it shouldered its way into his mind.

"It is," Uri replied. "I know what I've done. And when they find out, they will kill me."

"They won't find out," Hunter said. "Not from me."

Uri made a face that said he didn't believe him.

"You have my word," Hunter added. The boy had been played. Used. And left to face the consequences of what he'd done. But it wasn't his fault. Hunter forced himself to repeat his own words in his head, forced himself to at least pretend he believed them. Regardless of the carnage his actions had caused, it wasn't his fault.

"I betrayed everyone," Uri continued. His voice took on a strange and cold quality that made Hunter uneasy. Uri's affect became detached, and it made the hair on Hunter's arms lift. "Even those that treated me kindly. And for what? They probably killed my mother weeks ago. I don't know, maybe I'll just tell Quinnar myself."

Hunter grabbed his arm. "Listen to me. They gave you no choice but to do what they said."

Uri didn't respond. Instead he stared at the ground between his bent knees.

But something that Uri said made Hunter's inside congeal into cement. Even those that treated him kindly.

He rose to his feet and crossed the room, fingers raking through his hair.

"Dax," he said. He kept his back to Uri, unable to bring himself to look at him. "You told them of the plan to send Dax into the palace."

A long, thick silence followed that felt like waiting for an executioner's ax. "I had to."

Did he? Hunter screamed into his head. Did he have to tell them about Dax? He fought the urge to spin about and drag Uri from the floor and shake him. The acidic truth ate at his gut. They knew about Dax. They knew he was going to enter the palace and try to assassinate the imposter. Uri might as well have slit Dax's throat himself.

His feet stammered. His insides retreated until nothing remained but a cold void. He wanted to launch out of the room and call for Quinnar. He had to be told. Maybe something could be done to get a warning to Dax. Find a way to abort the mission. Get him the fuck out of there. Something!

But if Hunter told Quinnar what he knew, he'd also have to tell him where he got the information. Exposing Uri.

He'd made a promise. And if he broke it, Hunter knew what would happen to Uri.

Dax was smart, he told himself. Skilled in ways that Hunter would never be able to understand. There was a solid chance he could slip through their net and escape unharmed. There was a chance. But all Hunter could do now was wait. And hope.

But hope was in thin supply.

27

MOUSE WAS beginning to wonder if Jardem would show after all.

Seated in a high-back chair he'd positioned on the dais, he felt rather like a sad king holding court in an empty chamber. Bored, he stabbed at the arm of the chair with his dagger.

Dusk had come and gone. The gaping hole in the old temple's roof had gone from azure to red-orange to indigo…to finally black. And Jardem still hadn't shown himself.

Perhaps the message had never reached him. He was beginning to feel a little foolish for the elaborate setup he'd created.

He'd arranged lanterns throughout the ruins in a dramatic display of lighting. They cast warm light around the ancient temple and created histrionic shadows among the broken stone and wood cluttering the temple's center, material that had come from the collapsed roof. A few statues that once stood in alcoves along the walls had been pulled down, and their broken pieces added to the rubble.

He'd chosen the location carefully—an abandoned

temple in the Hollows. The deity it once honored was lost to time. It was neutral territory, and Mouse felt he had an advantage here. He doubted Jardem spent much time here in the Hollows. The temple had the added advantage of having only one entrance at the opposite side of the dais. There was no way anyone could enter without him knowing it.

If Jardem ever arrived.

Mouse had given him instructions to come alone. Jardem would know he wasn't in physical danger from Mouse. If something happened to him, the information about Mouse's real name and where his father was located would be released automatically. But still, it was likely a fantasy to think he would abide by that. Jardem did what he wanted. But if he did bring others, Mouse would know.

A new light appeared in the corridor beyond, and the crunch of boots on stones and grit signaled someone's approach. The light pushed its way into the opening first, followed by a figure.

Then a second.

Mouse growled inwardly. "I asked you to come alone."

Jardem stepped further into the long chamber. Holding the lantern aloft, he stepped over sections of the collapsed roof, scowling. He was dressed in an auburn doublet. A fine one, by the look of it. As if he had stopped by on his way to some well-heeled event.

Ludvic was close behind him.

"As if I would ever take direction from you," Jardem replied.

"We have important matters to discuss, Jardem. Matters that you may not want others to hear."

"So you said in that missive," Jardem said, sounding bored. "Your boldness is staggering, Mouse. Even for you, this is beyond anything I would have expected." He stopped in the middle of the chamber, apparently not wanting to step over a larger portion of the roof that was blocking his direct path. "I nearly didn't come. Felt the wiser choice would be to leave you here to reconsider whatever foolishness you dreamt up. But…." He shrugged, hands out. "Curiosity got the better of me. A weakness of mine. I like to know all the answers. And I very much wanted to know what would possess you to make such a dangerous ploy as this." He dusted off the front of his doublet as if the room was collecting on him. "Now, let's get this over with. I have important clients to entertain this evening."

Mouse glanced at Ludvic, who glared back at him.

He leaned forward in his chair, elbows on knees. "I would like to propose a deal, Jardem. A deal that will secure my liberation from the Night Fingers. Forever."

Jardem threw his head back and laughed. "Oh, isn't this rich!" Grinning, he glanced back at Ludvic. "Hear that? He has a *proposal*. Glad I came after all. This is bound to be entertaining." His eyes narrowed back at Mouse, one side of his mouth lifted in a sneer. "Dear Mouse, you belong to me forever. Nothing short of your death—or your father's death, I suppose—will put an end to that arrangement."

"We shall see," Mouse replied. "This conversation will go one of two ways. To your benefit…or your ruin."

Jardem chuckled. "You intend to kill me?" He looked at Ludvic again, who shrugged back at him. "You know what that would mean, yes?"

"I have not forgotten. And killing you, as pleasing as that would be, is not my intention here. Is that why you brought Ludvic? You feared that I would strike you down?"

Jardem stared back at Mouse. "There is nothing I fear less than you, little Mouse."

Mouse allowed a smile to break his lips but said nothing.

Jardem threw up his hands. "By the gods, get to it, man. I haven't all night, you know. Speak your proposal so I can reject it and get back to the day-to-day pleasure of controlling your every move."

Mouse sat back and leaned against one arm of the chair. "It may behoove you to take this parley with more gravity. Do you think I called you here on a whim?"

"No, Mouse. I do not." A darkness took Jardem's eyes. "But I also know you are arrogant and reckless, and that will always be won out by cleverness and meticulousness."

Mouse chuckled. *He* was the arrogant one?

Mouse reached to his side and picked up the rock that was on the seat next to him. It was wrapped in parchment and tied with twine. He tossed it straight up into the air a couple of times before he lobbed it across the room. It landed two strides in front of the two of them.

Jardem frowned at it, then gestured with his head to Ludvic to retrieve it.

Ludvic stepped closer and fished it out of the debris. He pulled out a dagger, cut the twine, and unwrapped the parchment from around the rock. Dropping the rock, he opened it to its full size.

"What am I looking at?" Ludvic asked, his brow askew.

Jardem snatched it from him and scanned it himself. There was too much distance between them and not enough light to tell for certain, but it looked as if the color had drained from his face.

"Ludvic, leave us," Jardem spat.

Ludvic glanced up at Mouse, a curious expression on his face. "I think you were right, Quickblade. It may be best if I stay."

Jardem's face turned crimson, but he didn't respond.

"You have already surmised, Jardem," Mouse said, "that this is an invoice from your secret workshop."

Eyes filled with fire shot up from the parchment. "*You*!"

"Yes, I discovered your secret project, Jardem. And put an end to it."

Ludvic's attention shifted from Mouse to Jardem. "What secret project?" His voice was thick with fresh suspicion.

Jardem rounded on him. "*Quiet*!"

"I will tell you, Ludvic, since Jardem was insistent you come. I tried to protect him, but you know how he is. He

258

doesn't take direction from me." Mouse waited for those words to land. He fought the urge to grin like a drunkard and kept his face neutral. Jardem looked like his head might explode. "Our guild master had a side business of creating barbarian forgeries to sell to rich merchants and nobles craving pieces stolen from the wastelands. He was using guild money to fund the operation but keeping profits for himself."

Ludvic's expression turned cold.

Jardem's hands were shaking. "Idiot. You know how foolish this is? You sealed your fate, as well as your father's."

"Ludvic," Mouse continued. "I don't need to tell you that such an operation is a direct violation of the rules of the guild, established centuries ago."

"No, you do not," Ludvic growled.

"You have any idea how much coin you wasted?" Jardem hissed through clenched teeth. "Good coin that could be spent on guild improvements. That operation benefited everyone in the Night Fingers." It was a lie, of course. Mouse had enough documentation to prove that. "You will pay for this. I promise you. Come, we're leaving."

Mouse stood from the chair. "Leave, and all the documents I stole from the workshop will be handed over and made public. Not only to the guild, but to the city magistrate."

Jardem froze. "You think blackmail is going to free you? If the guild is taken from me, you will suffer along with me. I will see to it."

Mouse knew this wasn't enough to persuade Jardem to turn him loose. His pride was too great for that. He needed both the leverage and a reward so he could salvage this as a win for himself.

Jardem turned to leave again.

"Which is why I have another solution," Mouse called to him. "One that you would be keen to hear."

Jardem kept his back to him. "You best not be wasting my time."

"I know you want the writ of nobility for yourself,"

Mouse said.

Jardem turned about slowly. "And why would you think that?"

"Tenric, kept in a cage in the cellar underneath the guild. You were attempting to locate the lost king's seal."

"So that was you as well," Jardem growled.

Mouse smiled down at him. "Guilty. Easy enough to steal him right from under your nose."

"No point. Despite what I'd been told, the fool didn't know anything about the location of the seal."

"That is where you are wrong. A rarity, I grant you."

Jardem's gaze narrowed.

"I know where to find the seal," Mouse said. "The writ and seal can be reunited."

Jardem reached into his doublet and pulled out a folded document. Mouse caught a glimpse of the red wax seal. "I keep it with me now," he said softly. "After the raid on the workshop, I did not trust it out of my sight."

"Allow me to leave the guild," Mouse said, "and I will tell you the location of the seal and return all the incriminating documents I took from the workshop. I think that is a fair trade, Jardem. You become a noble, and no one learns of the business at your workshop."

"A tempting offer," Jardem said. "But the powerful client who hired me may take issue with the betrayal. I'd be dead in days." His eyes narrowed at Mouse. "And that would be very bad for you."

"Let's not pretend further, Jardem. We both know the client is dead."

Jardem chuckled. "Dead? Don't be ridiculous."

"Don't play the innocent fool, Jardem. I know you had him murdered."

Jardem regarded him a moment, blinking as if trying to solve a puzzle. Then he spun about, throwing up his hands. "Idiot. So that's what your message meant." He turned back around again to face Mouse, eyes alight with contempt. "I sent you off to discover what happened to him. Why would I do that if I was the one who killed him?"

"To cover your trail! Make it look like you had nothing to do with it."

"By sending *you*?" Jardem exclaimed, then his head fell back as he laughed. "What an imbecile! Gods, I forget how witless and naïve you can be, even now. Mouse, you'd be the last person I'd send if I needed some truth concealed."

Mouse's head whirled. Was that a compliment?

"You believe me to be that reckless?" Jardem continued with a shake of his head. "Thought I'd kill a member of the Shadow Elite?"

"To gain the writ for yourself."

"Me, a noble. Can you imagine?" Jardem threw a grin at Ludvic. "Lord Quickblade." He laughed and turned his gaze back to Mouse. "Alas, the notion never occurred to me, I promise you. I didn't have Darko Paine murdered, Mouse. However…now that he *is* no longer around to collect the prize…" His eyes shifted to take in the writ in his hand.

"I don't need a confession," Mouse said smartly, losing patience. "Doesn't matter. I only need you to agree to the deal. Though I would cheerfully kill you for what you did to Zel."

Jardem looked to retort, but he froze, whatever words he intended to say lodged in his throat. His voice dropped to nearly a whisper. "Zel?"

Anger flared and Mouse had no control of it. "Don't, Jardem!" he shouted. "Don't insult me. I discovered your handiwork myself." Remembering the scene brought new, hot tears to his eyes.

Jardem made a clumsy step backward. "What are you saying?" When Mouse didn't reply, his eyes widened with sudden rage. "*Tell me!*"

"You act innocent, even now?"

"No," Jardem choked. "That's not possible. I thought…She said she was looking into a matter and would not be…" He trailed off.

"She must have learned what you did with Paine. Maybe she confronted you, so you killed her."

Something in Jardem's eyes spoke of true horror. His face blanched of all color. "I would never…" He swayed and looked as if he might collapse at the news.

The truth of it was etched into Jardem's eyes, and it struck Mouse with a flash of lightning clarity. What had Zel said to him? *He knows precisely what he has with me.*

Jardem loved her.

Mouse could only stare in disbelief. Was he telling the truth? Did he not kill Pain? Or Zel? Then who?

Jardem took a step forward—then suddenly gasped, eyes wide. He arched his back, and his arms flew into the air. He spasmed again just before the blade pushed through the front of the doublet in a geyser of crimson. Ludvic gripped him by the shoulder as he shoved the blade in further. He yanked the sword free again as Jardem collapsed.

"*No!*" screamed Mouse as Jardem hit the floor. He rushed to the edge of the platform. "No, no, no."

Jardem landed in a heap on the floor. He panted, eyes wide as his life spilled from him, then he was still.

It was over. Once Jardem's death was learned of, the information about Mouse and the location of his father would be handed over to the magistrate. THE HOURS that followed in silence were agony. The two of them didn't speak again. Hunter couldn't bring himself to give the boy any more comfort even though he knew he should, and Uri clearly needed it. Hunter was too heartsick, too angry, and too worried for Dax to muster up the strength and put it all aside. Uri eventually curled up on the bed and fell asleep while Hunter sat on the floor and stared at the walls.

He must have fallen asleep himself for a time, because his eyes sprung open when he heard the latch on the door.

Quinnar, Zinnuvial, and Corrad moved into the room as

Hunter crawled to his feet. The three of them looked haggard, exhausted. Even Corrad, for all his conceit and bullishness, seemed defeated. He leaned against the doorjamb, blocking most of the light from the hall outside, looking sulky and hostile. Quinnar stepped into the center of the room, thumbs tucked into the front of his belt. He didn't waste any time on pretense, and Hunter could see on his face the news was not good. He had the look of a man who'd lost everything.

"We've received word from our sources inside. Dax has been captured. They knew he was coming."

The room seemed to shrink as a raw stillness filled the space between them like a toxic cloud. He forced himself not to look in the direction of the bed, at Uri. He wasn't sure if he was relieved or not that Uri was asleep and hadn't heard the news.

"I knew you'd want to know," Quinnar added as he turned to leave. Corrad and Zinnuvial moved to follow him.

"But he's alive," Hunter prodded.

Quinnar nodded, hand on the latch. "For now. His public execution is being arranged. For as early as tomorrow."

"The imposter made an unscheduled appearance on the balcony," Zinnuvial said. "Likely to send a message to us that the mission had failed and that she was still alive."

"What are you going to do?"

"My hands are tied, Hunter. There isn't anything we can do," Quinnar said.

No. That wasn't acceptable. "Someone has to go in there and rescue him."

"That is not possible."

"You're just going to sit with your thumb up your ass while he's executed?"

Anger flashed behind Quinnar's eyes as he took a hard step closer to Hunter. "I will not risk more people. Not even for him. Our losses this day have been too great already." His lower lip trembled as he spoke. This decision to leave Dax to his fate was shredding away at his insides.

Hunter understood. But he wasn't about to accept it. He closed his eyes and pulled in a breath. "Then I'll do it."

The words spilled out of his mouth before he was consciously aware of it. His heart rate quickened. He knew he was being impulsive and stupid. But why wouldn't he volunteer? How many times had Dax saved his life? Hunter owed him at least that.

But from a dark corner of his mind, Hunter knew he wasn't being fully honest with himself. That wasn't the real reason. He needed an answer. He needed to look Dax in the eye and ask why he came to him last night.

From the doorway, Corrad made a low grunt of a laugh.

"You?" Quinnar replied with genuine surprise.

He rested his thumb and forefinger on his hipbones and stared at the floorboards a moment. What the fuck was he doing? "Tell me how to get in there. And I'll do whatever it takes."

Zinnuvial shook her head. "You'll be captured or dead before you step one foot into the castle yard."

Corrad shrugged. "Let the dolt try. All the better, I say. He gets himself killed, problem solved."

Quinnar threw him a stern glare to silence him. "Zinnuvial is right. You wouldn't make it past the outer walls. Every inch of the perimeter will be watched. Dax was skilled at such matters, and we can see what happened to him."

Only because someone was tipped off, Hunter thought. "How did Dax get in?"

"Scaled the south wall," Zinnuvial said.

Hunter couldn't hide his surprise. "He climbed it?"

Zinnuvial nodded.

They were right about that, at least. He'd never be able to do that. Not without a grappling hook and rope anyway— and that would be rather conspicuous. "Well, no place is impenetrable. There has to be another way in."

The three of them seemed to stiffen, and Hunter felt some cryptic communication pass between them. Corrad raised his eyebrows at Zinnuvial. "Tell him," he prodded with a sinister grin.

Quinnar looked annoyed. "We've been over this. A thousand times."

Hunter felt the spark of hope renew in his gut. "I'm right, aren't I. You know of a way in."

Zinnuvial sighed, clearly reluctant. "There may be. It has not been tried."

"I'm listening," Hunter replied.

Quinnar shook his head. "This will only serve to get you killed."

"I'll decide for myself, thank you," Hunter said. "Tell me."

Zinnuvial put her hands on her hips and looked at the floor. "Water from the river is diverted through a conduit underneath the castle. It's their source for clean water and for removing waste. Some have speculated a person could swim through it to get inside."

"The conduit entrance is far west at the outskirts of city," Quinnar added. "It's there to prevent soiled water from the city contaminating their supply. We've calculated the distance, Hunter. It's too far for one person to traverse underwater."

"No other access points along the way?"

"None that we've found," Quinnar replied.

"If there are any, they are a safely guarded secret," Zinnuvial added. "The designers must have anticipated the potential threat."

Corrad leaned in with a grin. "And there is no guarantee there aren't any metal grates blocking access along the way or if the conduit is even wide enough throughout. It might narrow or break up into smaller pipes. No one knows."

Hunter wasn't small, certainly. But with all the cooking, cleaning, and bathing happening within the walls, the water needs of the castle would be extensive. It stood to reason that the conduit in would be big enough to sustain those needs.

"Even if the trajectory was clear and unobstructed, you'd

never be able to hold your breath long enough," Quinnar said.

Hunter paced the small room, a hard stone sitting low in his stomach. The very notion of this was terrifying. It roused his greatest fear—getting trapped in some dark and tiny space. Happening underwater was an additional bonus horror. This would send him into a panic attack for sure. But he wasn't about to let Dax go to the gallows without attempting to spring him first, and this sounded like the only way to get in undetected. Dax had saved his skin how many times now? It was high time he returned the favor.

The others were right, though. Thinking he could hold his breath that long was foolhardy and suicidal. He had a decent lung capacity, but certainly not anything Olympian. And he wasn't exactly the epitome of grace in the water. But there had to be a way to make it through that distance.

Something caught his eye on the shelf loaded with supplies. Sitting atop a crate was an empty leather wineskin. Hunter picked it up, pulled off the stopper, and blew into it. The bladder swelled up and Hunter quickly pushed in the cork stopper to keep it inflated.

Watertight also meant airtight.

"How many of these can you get me?" he asked. "Large ones."

The three stared back at him.

"How many?" he asked again. "I have an idea."

28

"THIS IS madness," Zinnuvial told him. "You realize this."

Hunter ignored her. "You sure it's down there?"

He stood on the edge of the wall and peered down into the river. Nothing remarkable or distinctive about the place, nothing to mark it as the castle's water intake. The wall simply made a sharp right angle, jutting out into the river, then it turned again to continue as before. He expected to see some sign on the surface—a disturbance in the flow of the river. He saw nothing but the churning reflection of the moonlight brushing the surface of the dark water.

His heart pounded with wild frenzy. Panic threatened to overtake him and shake him apart. He tried to force his breathing into a slower, steady cadence, and he tucked his thumbs into his belt to hide the quaking of his hands.

"Having second thoughts?" Corrad said.

Quinnar had ordered Corrad along to help, but Hunter was convinced he only came willingly to see if he backed out. Or if not back out, watch him dive on down to his death. Uri stood behind Zinnuvial, looking distressed. He, too, had refused to stay behind.

They all agreed to wait until the cover of night before they slipped unnoticed from the small safe house out into the street. Hunter had tried to get some sleep, but to no avail. He was too wired—like the night before a big match. He could only stare up at the ceiling. As they skulked through the dark and vacant streets, not a word was spoken between them. Zinnuvial led the way, taking them on a less direct route, concerned the city guard could still be lurking about.

A lingering smell of wood smoke and fish were in the air.

"It is down there," Zinnuvial said.

Standing there, looking down at the water, Hunter was beginning to agree with the others. The idea was preposterous. But with Corrad staring at him, waiting for him to cave, he swept the doubt aside and tightened his resolve.

"And the grate that covers it?"

"We removed the lock that was on it. Back when we were exploring the idea," Zinnuvial said. She dropped the loose-knit sack she carried on the ground. The bag of wineskins. "I doubt anyone noticed."

He wondered about the grate hinges, whether they had rusted shut. He wondered if he was hopeful they had. It would give him a reason to abandon this.

"I stand by my assertion that this is unwise, Hunter," she added.

Corrad chuckled. "Leave him to it."

Hunter responded by pulling the tunic off over his head. The cool morning air bit at his exposed skin. Zinnuvial and Corrad's eyes focused on his mother's amulet that hung around his neck to rest on his breastbone. Both lifted their brows in surprise.

"Is it wise to bring that?" Zinnuvial asked.

Hunter subconsciously pinched it between his fingers. He'd gone through hell to retrieve it. It wasn't going anywhere. "It stays with me."

Zinnuvial accepted that with a nod and dumped the

contents of the sack onto the ground. Empty wineskins and a coil of rope. "I gathered the largest skins I could find. Twelve of them. Once inflated, it'll be too difficult to pull them all down at once, so you'll have to do it one at a time. Dive down, tie it on the inside of the grate." She removed a dagger from a small hilt on her thigh and tossed it on the ground next to the sack. "Once they are all in, cut the lines and go."

Sounded simple enough. He pulled off his boots.

Zinnuvial pulled something out of a pouch on her belt. It was crystal of some kind, attached to a leather thong.

Corrad's eyes widened. "Quinnar know you took that?"

Zinnuvial ignored him. "This is a moonstone. It glows with a faint light. It isn't much, but it is something."

Hunter nodded and took the stone. It felt faintly warm in his palm. He took the two ends of the leather strap, reached behind his neck, and knotted the ends together. The stone rested next to his mother's amulet on his breastbone. He wondered if they could see the two pendants bounce with the mad beating of his heart.

"Better get started," he said.

One by one, the skins were inflated into sad, misshapen balloons, and the corks quickly thrust into the openings. "Tie the length of rope around your middle," Zinnuvial said as she secured a length of twine to each skin. "The current will be very strong at the opening. We will have to pull you up each time." She checked them one by one for leaks by squeezing them.

Which meant he was dependent on Corrad to help Zinnuvial. Her strength was impressive, but she wouldn't be strong enough to haul up his bulk on her own.

"You're going to have to be extremely careful, Hunter. If the current pulls you into the conduit before you're ready, you'll drown."

Hunter stripped off his trousers, leaving him naked and shivering. Every inch of skin on his body trembled. It was chilly—but not that chilly. His nerves were getting to him. He was starting to unravel. While Zinnuvial knotted the thick rope around a metal docking ring bolted to the rock wall, he slipped the other end around his waist and secured it as tight as he could with a knot.

He then lowered to the edge of the wall with his feet dangling and looked down into the water. A leaf spiraled below him for a moment before it was pulled under the surface. Like it was going down a drain. Yes, the conduit was down there.

He circled the twine from the first inflated skin around his fist, took a few long breaths to prepare, and pushed off.

The shock as the cold water squeezed around his torso and shoulders made his lungs hitch. His head dropped below the surface, and he was consumed in eerie green darkness. Already he could feel the staggering forces at work. The river's current tugged on his upper body, wanting to carry him off downstream while his legs were being dragged downward by a disconcerting and powerful undertow. He fought his way back up to the surface, heaving his arms behind him to fight being dragged down. But as his head broke the surface, the cold wouldn't allow him to pull fresh air into his lungs for a second, and it took a moment before he managed to pull in quick choppy gasps.

The inflated skin was bobbing on the surface and pulled the full length of its tether as it tried to drift farther out into the river. He lured it back to him and tucked it under his arm.

Three faces leaned over the edge and peered down at him. Zinnuvial cupped a hand against the side of her mouth. "Tug on the rope when you are ready to resurface."

He gave them a thumbs-up—absently wondering if that symbol meant anything here.

Then he filled his lungs to their capacity and plunged down.

The resistance of the single puffed-up skin against him was astonishing. It tugged, it shifted, it lurched—it did anything it could escape Hunter's hold on it and return to the surface. He pressed it up against his side like a rugby ball, careful not to squeeze it too tight and pop out the cork.

Downward he sank, letting the undertow do some of the work while he used his free arm to steer him. The water surrounding him was a thick green soup. A soft luminance emanated from the moonstone, providing just enough light to spot a gray circle below him. The entrance to the conduit.

The water towed him right to it.

He picked up speed at an alarming rate and slammed against the grate of the circular intake. It was wider than he expected—six, maybe eight, feet in diameter. It was hard to gauge in the murky water. The entire front was covered with a lattice of iron bands, covered in a wiggling green carpet of algae and milfoil.

The force of the impact caught him off guard, and he nearly lost the air in his lungs. The water pushed around him and pinned him to the fuzzy metal bands. He felt like he was at the bottom of a collapsed scrum, the entire squad on top of him.

Fuck, this is was such a horrible idea.

The space between the iron bands was large enough to squeeze the inflated skin through if he was careful. The last thing he wanted to do was puncture the skin with an unseen sharp metal edge. He first tied the end of the twine to a horizontal band. As he tried to negotiate the skin through, he lost his grip on it, and it launched upward as if shot from a cannon. He hauled it back down and tried again.

His lungs were beginning to burn. This was taking too long.

Inch by inch, he worked the skin through the hole. Once inside and free, it was at the whim of two different forces—buoyancy and the force of water entering the conduit. It darted up and deeper inside like a startled fish, and the twine was instantly pulled taut—but it held.

His lungs were desperate for air now. He had to get to the surface.

He tugged on the rope, worried that Corrad had already abandoned him up there, leaving Zinnuvial to the job on her own. If he had to swim back up to the surface using his own power, he would never make it. Terrifying seconds ticked by before the slack in the rope disappeared and his body was dragged away from the grate.

He broke the surface and delicious air blasted into his lungs. He tilted his head back and took a few moments to allow his breathing to steady.

"Well?" Zinnuvial said.

"First one is secured," he replied between pants.

"Only eleven more to go," she said dryly, and she tossed the next inflated skin down to him.

Again and again he descended into the dark depths of the river to tie the brown balloons to the grate. His fourth time down, one slipped from his grip and he lost his hold on the twine. Before he could react, the skin burst up toward the surface and was immediately taken down stream by the current. There was no recovering it.

He would have to make do with eleven.

The promise of dawn illumed the horizon with a streak of red when he at last climbed back onto the land again, shivering from the cold air.

"That's the last of them," Hunter announced when he rejoined them. "All secured and ready to go." His muscles were already burning from his fight with the current. He wouldn't have much strength if he ran into trouble down there.

"That was the easy part," Zinnuvial replied dryly. "When you swim down this time, take off the rope and tie it to the grate. We will pull it open."

Hunter nodded that he understood.

She handed him a short dagger and a leather strap. "Tie this to your leg."

He complied while she continued to bullet point off the instructions to him. His head was in a fog. He was having a difficult time concentrating on the words she said. All he could think about was what awaited him inside that dark tunnel and if it was going to end up being his grave.

What the fuck was he doing? This was insane.

Corrad shook his head. "The only good that is going to come of this is that your dead body is going to poison their water supply."

Hunter held his gaze. "I'm going to try to rescue a man who sacrificed everything for your resistance. What are you doing?"

Zinnuvial put a hand on his arm. "This is a brave thing you do."

"It's idiotic," muttered Corrad.

She threw Corrad a cold look. To Hunter's surprise, Corrad's mouth snapped shut as his eyes rolled up. "If you manage to do this," she said, "and get in unnoticed, no one will suspect you because they will believe the palace is impenetrable. Do not bring attention to yourself if you can."

"Sure," he said. "Where will I find him?"

"In the bowels of the castle is our best guess. The dungeons are said to be extensive and well guarded. It will not be easy to locate him. We'll take a position near the northern wall. There's a heavily armored door there that is seldom used. It'll be off a small yard by the stables. The wall around there will be well guarded, but if you can unlatch that door, perhaps we can get in and provide you aid."

Hunter glanced over at Uri. His eyes were downcast, and he wouldn't look him.

"I'll do what I can," he said. "Wish me luck."

He climbed over the edge one last time and dropped into the water.

29

WITH DAWN'S red glow filtering through the surface of the river, he descended once again into the green murk. The inflated bladders were in place. All that remained was to give himself over to the mercy of the water. And pray.

One last time, the river shoved him against the fuzzy covered lattice, the wide maw of the conduit drawing him in with staggering force. His heart thumped in his ears, but he pushed his fear aside and focused on the task of removing the rope from his middle. He fumbled with the knot, but it was too tight and too wet, and it wouldn't loosen. He didn't have the time to waste. Already his lungs were feeling the strain. With no other option, he instead worked the loop little by little down over his hips and buttocks and slipped it off his feet. He tied the end to the grate as best he could—then tugged on the rope.

Immediately the rope went taut, and the grate was pulled away from the opening. Gripping the slimy metal with two white-knuckled hands, he inched his way to the edge of the grate. He looped an arm through the hole at the end, circled his body around the edge, and put himself on the inside of it.

The force of the water tried to peel him off the grate. But

with the full strength of his arms, he held firm. If he lost his grip without the skins, he was dead for sure. The metal edge beneath the green covering bit into the bend of his elbow.

Now the hard part.

With his one free hand, he turned his wrist around the eleven strands of twine that held the bloated waterskins in place. The balloons bounced and jockeyed about like nervous horses ready to start a race. Hunter wrapped two complete rotations around his wrist; then he tightened the eleven strands inside his fist.

Then he let go of the grate.

His body was thrown out horizontal. The rough jolt cut the twine into his wrist, pinching off the circulation in his hand, as the water pushed his legs straight out into the conduit. But the cluster of twine held to where it was tied. He slipped the knife from his thigh, and one by one, sliced through the strands holding it to the grate.

As soon as the last was severed, he shot through the conduit like a bullet through the barrel of a gun. With a heart-stopping lurch, he was instantly in motion, his body spinning and tumbling out of control. Blackness swallowed him. The moonstone around his neck pushed back at it weakly. His stomach leapt into his throat, and he felt the terrifying speed even though he saw nothing around him except the faint blurred impression of the conduit's sides. His shoulder grazed the side. Stinging pain shot through his arm as if he were stung by a thousand bees.

He managed—somehow—to get control of his body again, force his body into a straight line. He oriented his feet out, locking his knees, as if going down a water slide. If there was anything blocking the way ahead, he wouldn't see it coming—and going headfirst was a death sentence. He'd knock himself out.

It seemed like an eternity already, but only seconds had passed since he cut himself free. His lungs burned and begged for release. *Longer*, he thought. A little longer. He had make his air supply last. The leather balloons bounced and jostled above him, trying to reach the top of the conduit.

When his lungs could bear it no more, he pulled one of the balloons in closer. Timing it carefully, he emptied his lungs, pulled out the cork, and shoved the end into his mouth. Even so, a bubble of precious air escaped into the water before he circled his lips around the opening. The air, tasting a little stale and mildly of leather, rushed into his lungs. The skin flattened—his lungs took all of it. He felt he could take more, even. The contents didn't add up to a full breath. He closed off his mouth, trapping the new air in, and cut the skin loose.

Ten remained.

The light from the moonstone seemed brighter now. But he knew that was only his eyes adjusting to the darkness. It cast a ghostly glow around him and reached out farther. Even so, there was little to see. The conduit walls sped past him in a blur.

The direction changed. He shifted suddenly right. His insides seemed to shift too, but at a delay. His body glided dangerously close to the wall. A sharper turn and he'd collide with it. Then he lunged left again. He was at the will of the water.

Too soon his lungs were begging for more air. He tried to wait, but the burning agony in his chest forced him to pull in another skin. He exhaled and drew in the fresh air like it was sweet wine. The relief was immediate, but not compete. He wanted more. He was tempted to use another, but he resisted. He had no idea how much farther he had to go.

Something whizzed by overhead. An opening? That meant there *were* more ways into the water supply. If there was one… there were likely more. If he could see one coming, he might be able stop himself, maybe haul himself up, take a breather, refill the skins….

But who was he kidding? He could barely see anything beyond the reach of his arm. He'd never see the opening in time. And there was no way he could fight the force of the water.

The conduit altered again. It threw him sharply left this time and he swerved toward the conduit wall. Two of the skins happened to land between him and the wall. They cushioned the impact, saving him from potential injury against the rough stone. With the speed he was going, he could have lost all the skin on his arm or shoulder. But something snagged. With a muffled pop, the skins ruptured. Air escaped into the water as one giant bubble and sprang to the top of the conduit, lost.

He was down to eight.

And then seven. Each time he pulled the air from skin, it seemed less and less sufficient now. His lungs wanted more. But he had to wait. He had no idea how much farther he had to go.

Another opening whizzed by overhead. Fuck. If there was only some way he could catch the lip of it as he passed it… but the notion was ridiculous.

He happened to look in the direction he was traveling, toward his feet. Something was visible up ahead. Approaching quickly.

Fuck.

His feet struck an iron grate seconds after his mind registered it was there. The force of the impact made his entire body jolt. A shock wave reverberated through his ankles and legs, pain exploding as if he'd jumped from the top of a building. He was lucky he hadn't shattered a bone. His jaw clenched to prevent the air from escaping his lungs. A fraction of a second later, his entire body was pressed up against the metal.

Another grate. The way was blocked. He was trapped.

Panic threatened to seize hold of him, but he choked it down. *Stay calm*, he told himself. *You're not going to die. You're not going to die.*

But a voice inside him was more realistic. If he didn't find a solution, he would die.

The entire grate was covered in slimy debris. His hands

fumbled around the circumference of the barrier, searching. His heart thundered in his ears and his lungs were already clamoring for more air. His fingers dragged over something different—roundish, cylindrical. A hinge.

That meant it was designed to open.

He made a frantic search on the opposite side. There had to be a release of some kind. His shaky hands touched and grasped at everything while the water pressed in around him to escape through the holes in the grate.

He found a metal peg wedged down through a hole.

He gripped it as tight as he could and tugged upward. It didn't give at all. He tried to wiggle it.

Nothing.

He couldn't wait any more. He needed air. He dragged in another skin and drained it of its contents. He had only six left now.

If he'd had his boots on, he could kick the damn thing, but his bare feet wouldn't likely do much to loosen it. And the force of the water wouldn't allow him the movement needed. He tried rattling the grate, hoping to initiate some movement, but it remained firm. He used the handle of the knife and tried to pound it up from the bottom. Still, the peg didn't budge.

Frustration and panic overwhelmed him. He pounded on the flat metal of the lattice with the heel of his hand.

Something snapped.

One of the strips of metal broke free. The old metal, after years, perhaps centuries, of being submerged down here, had weakened. Hunter pounded on it more.

Another section snapped loose.

He gripped the slime-covered slat and started rocking it back and forth. At first nothing—but then he felt the metal of the lattice start to give.

Another broke free. Then another.

Using all the strength he had left, he shoved on it. Again and then again. The grate bent back. A little at first, but then more. And then a little more. The opening was getting larger.

He just had to push it back enough for him to slip through.

His lungs forced him to stop and take in another skin full of air. He now only had five left.

He resumed his desperate effort to bend the broken section back. The metal was stubborn. It moved—but in tiny incremental amounts. And his strength was flagging.

He used another skin. Four left.

The gap he made was still narrow, but he judged it large enough for him to pass through. Desperation forced him to give it a try. Fighting the current, he turned his body sideways and slid his head through first. The slats of metal squeezed against his thick torso. He shifted, inch by inch. It grew tighter around him.

He was going to wedge himself in and be killed for sure.

His stomach was in his throat. Jagged edges of metal cut into his skin as he cajoled his thick form farther through the opening. If he survived this, his skin would be a road map of scrapes and gashes.

And then he was through it. He felt a momentary hitch— two of the skins caught the sharp edges of the broken slats and ripped open. More of his air bubbled out and was gone.

Two left.

He had no choice but to use another of the skins. The exertion of getting through the grate had made his vision blacken around the edges. He was near the point of passing out. He grappled for the skin, emptied his lungs and gulped down the air from the bag.

And then there was only one.

The relief the air provided had shrunk to nearly nothing. Immediately after taking the air, his lungs were already wanting more. But he waited, holding out as long as he could.

Free of the grate, he picked up speed again quickly. It felt even faster this time, as if he was moving downhill. Maybe he was. He had no way of referencing that.

Then, suddenly, the walls of the conduit were gone. His

body tumbled, and he plummeted in free fall. Sound crashed into his ears. The sound of a waterfall. He was no longer submerged. He was out of the water. His mouth opened and air that tasted like a cave rushed into his lungs. He didn't care—the sensation of full lungs was euphoric.

This lasted for a second—then he was underwater again. Plunging. The sound of the cascading water cut off to become a muffled roar.

The hard force of the water was now gone. Except beneath him. He could feel the water trying to tug him down into dark depths. He clawed at the water to pull himself up, praying there was a surface.

He broke from the water. He tilted his head back, and while kicking and swooping his exhausted arms through the water to keep himself afloat, he took long satiating breaths until his heart rate recovered.

He'd done it. He made it through and was now inside the castle.

Naked. And with no idea where he was supposed to go to find Dax.

But he was inside. And still alive. It was a start.

30

HUNTER LIFTED the moonstone from the water and held it aloft as high as the leather thong would allow. The soft light danced off the ripples of the water's surface and reached out to gently touch the cavern-like walls that curved up to form a rough dome. No brickwork. The cavern was cut from solid rock beneath the castle.

Water cascaded from the clay cylinder that protruded from high up the sandstone wall. The same cylinder he'd tumbled out from moments before. It struck the pool in a continuous deafening thunder that resounded off the walls.

He drifted away from the waterfall and deeper into the cavern, taken by a current. The walls tapered, and as he was funneled into a passage, he picked up speed. The roar of the falling water dulled to a deep hum as he drifted farther and farther in. Up ahead, he saw the passage split into two separate channels. The moonstone's light reached in the dark recesses ahead to reveal the hint of red brickwork lining their arched ceiling.

He was under the castle now and entering the network of passages designed to distribute the water. Water used for cooking, cleaning, drinking—which meant there had to be multiple places for people to access it. He hoped at least one was large enough for him to crawl through. Otherwise he'd end up flowing into where waste was dumped into the water. As disgusting as that would be, it wasn't the real danger. Eventually, he'd start to flow back out toward the river. If that meant another conduit, with no more wineskins left, he was dead.

He paddled toward the left opening.

The ceiling quickly lowered almost to the surface of the water. He had just enough space to allow his head to remain above it. The air was thick and stale and tasted like stone. The soft strokes of his arms through the water echoed around him.

The passage split again. He steered himself left again, only because the passage seemed wider. He'd had enough tight spaces for one day.

Up ahead, a section of the ceiling was no longer red brick—but black. The light of the moonstone touched on nothing but curved edge. A hole. He waited until he drifted under it, then quickly grabbed the edge to bring himself to a halt. The water tugged on him, coercing him to keep moving, but he held firm and peered up the round opening, the moonstone elevated in his palm. The light dusted the sides of the tight shaft that shot straight up but didn't reach the top. The walls were smooth—nothing for his fingers to grip on to. And it was too narrow for him. He'd never be able squeeze his thick trunk through it.

He let go and kept drifting.

He passed under two more openings, both no different than the first. Too small for him. The walls too smooth. Fresh apprehension blossomed in his gut. If all these water access points were the same, he was in real trouble.

The sound of a thump and a splash resonated off the stone. He could feel the force of it in the water as it passed him in a wave. His heart made a hollow dip. Something was in the water with him. Something living down here in the depths of the caverns. He hadn't considered that. Of course creatures would exist down here in this sprawling network of passages. Fish, certainly. Rats. Snakes. And probably other ungodly things he couldn't imagine. He could almost sense something moving in the dark water around him.

He forced his breathing under control again. *Get a grip*, he told himself. The sound wasn't something in the water, but an impact on the surface. It came from another nearby tributary, a passage that was even smaller than the one he was in. He shoved back his fear and diverted his course toward the sound.

The ceiling was even lower; he had to lift his chin up to keep his mouth above the surface and prevent his head from scraping the top. The channel curved, and he saw a light dancing on the ripples of the water ahead. Small waves rolled past him and splashed into his mouth. Something lifted out of the water.

A bucket with a rope tied to the handle. It wobbled a moment as it cleared the surface, water sloshing from its sides; then it disappeared through the opening in the ceiling.

The current was weaker here, and the passage was narrow enough for Hunter to brace his legs and arms against the walls to stop his forward movement. He brought himself to a halt just before the shaft and peered up. Warm light spilled down from a hole, illuminating the walls and the water, as the bucket was hauled up. The light seemed intense compared to the moonstone, and it stung his eyes as he gazed up at it, but it was likely only torchlight. He caught a glimpse of a silhouette and heard a grunt as the bucket was heaved out of the hole. Female, by the sound of it. Hunter then heard the creak of hinges, and a wooden lid slammed down, plunging the shaft in darkness once again.

Twenty, maybe twenty-five feet up, Hunter estimated. And this shaft was wider than the others he'd found. Wide enough for him to fit through. But in the brief illumination, he hadn't seen any rungs or handholds up the sides.

He reached up into the shaft and ran his palm around the wall, searching for a handhold. At the extent of his reach, his fingers passed over a protrusion, a single brick that extended out far enough for him to lock his fingers over the top of it.

Kicking his feet for added force, he pulled himself up out of the water with his one hand while his other slapped around the opposite side of the wall for something else to grasp. Finding nothing, gravity tugged him back down and his hand slipped off, and he collapsed back into the water.

He tried again. And again.

On the fourth attempt, his hand found purchase on another protruding brick, and he dangled there, half out of the water. He heaved, using the full extent of his upper body strength, and wedged himself into the shaft, pressing his back against the wall and lodging his feet opposite him. Water cascaded off his skin. The roughly cut bricks stabbed into his back, but he ignored the pain. He was out of the water.

Inches at a time, he trudged up the hollow shaft, feeling like the Grinch shimmying up a chimney in Whoville. He kept his eyes upward. At any moment the trap door might open again and a bucket get launched down onto his head. He strained his ears for any sound that would announce someone returning, but all he heard was the chiming drip of water as it fell from his skin to the surface below.

His legs cramped, and his back muscles were threatening to spasm. And he was afraid to see what the skin of his back even looked like now. Each time he shifted upward, it felt as if more skin was stripped away.

Closer to the top, he heard voices. Muffled and distant. But still not close enough to hear distinct words. He froze in place for a time, listening. Two women, by the tone, engaged in casual conversation. He had no idea how far they were from the opening at the top. He shuffled a bit higher. A whiff of something acerbic drifted down into the shaft. Urine.

His whole body stiffened. The last thing he needed was for this to be a latrine. He looked up, wondering if the next time the hatch opened it would be covered with two asscheeks, and he winced at the thought.

He hesitated a bit longer. But his back muscles started to seize up. He wouldn't be able to hold this position much longer, and the last thing he needed was to slip and plummet back down. He had no choice but to keep moving.

He shuffled the remaining few feet up and waited again. The voices faded as the speakers moved farther from the opening. With an awkward shove, he forced the hatch lid up.

Tentatively, he craned his head up through the hole. The smell of ammonia burned in his sinuses as he scanned the cluttered little chamber. It was cloaked in heavy shadow, but a light from the next room pushed through a cracked doorway. Voices were still audible beyond the door but fading.

Safe. For the moment.

He hoisted himself through the hole, and as soon as he was out, he lowered the wooden lid with a decisive thud, and he dropped his bare ass on top of it, panting. The worst of it was over, he told himself. The nightmare inside the conduit was behind him. He was out of the water and inside the castle. Hands on his knees, chin low, he took a few moments to savor that.

Now… to find Dax.

He peered through the gap in the door and, seeing no movement, gently pulled the door open a bit farther. Hinges squeaked, and his heart quickened, but no other sounds followed. The room beyond was quiet, the women apparently gone. Still reluctant to risk more noise, he slipped sideways through the door's slim opening.

Warmth greeted him, a welcome change from the chill of the water, but the air was swampy and dense. The chamber was large, but the array of a dozen or so stout pillars filling it made it hard to gauge its full size. Hooded lanterns that hung from chains cast a strange patchwork of shadow and light on the stone floor.

Crouched, he tiptoed on the balls of his feet along the

wall. One side of the room was lined with four colossal hearths, and inside, massive iron pots hung over shimmering coals. Tendrils of diaphanous steam rose from them like escaping spirits. Woven baskets overflowing with clothes were strewn about nearby like fluffy boulders after an avalanche. Earthenware vats, large enough for him to crawl into, were huddled around the pillars. Wondering if one was a place he could hide inside, Hunter shuffled over and leaned over the edge. Ammonia burned the inside of his nostrils. It was the source of the urine smell. White linens were soaking in it.

He wrinkled his nose. The thought of sleeping on sheets cleaned with urine made his stomach twist.

Of all the places he could have emerged inside the castle, this seemed the most fortuitous. The room, at least for the moment, appeared empty. The women must have gone off to gather more baskets of dirty laundry. No telling how much time he had before they returned. He had to move fast.

He scurried over to one of the baskets and made a quick rummage through the clothes. One after another, he held tunics up to his chest to gauge their size until he found one that seemed large enough—light brown, with conspicuous wine stains dribbling down the front. It smelled a bit ripe, but he tried not to think about it and pulled it over his head.

Other baskets carried women's garments mostly, simple ones that likely belonged to servants of the keep. He ventured deeper into the room, looping around pillars in search of baskets that held any men's clothing.

Voices reached his ears. The women were returning.

He all but sprinted toward an unexplored cache of baskets piled near the wall. Frantic, he tossed each rejected garment onto the floor as he dug deeper. More servants' wear. He unearthed a hooded cloak that was only long enough to just cover the shoulder, some sleeves with satiny ties at the arms but no vest to go with them, and a padded shirt—something Hunter guessed would be worn under armor.

The voices grew louder.

He dumped the contents of the next basket onto the floor. Rummaging through the pile, he unearthed a pair of brown woolen pants. He held them by the waist against him. Way too small. They'd never make it past his thick thighs.

He emptied another basket. Sticking out from the pile was something green that looked like a pant leg.

The women were entering the chamber now, chatting freely and laughing. He considered for a heartbeat trying to hide, but the women would see the mess he'd made as soon as they entered and surely investigate.

He shook the garments loose from the pile, positioned his thumbs inside the waistband, and without checking the size, stepped into them. He slipped them over his thighs and ass with ease.

He was tying the drawstring into a bow when the two circled around a pillar and froze. Their conversation ended midsentence and, mouths ajar, they dropped the loaded baskets they carried.

"Hey…," he said, then snapped his mouth closed again. His accent would certainly flag him as an intruder. Or at least a foreigner. "Ho there," he exclaimed, mimicking Dax's inflection, the only voice he knew well enough to emulate. "Well met and good morrow."

The two laundresses continued to blink at him. Did he get the accent wrong? Or was a man down here rare enough to stun them into silence? They might have been sisters—they had the same laugh lines around their mouths and both had their graying hair pulled back into identical buns.

"What…?" the left one began. Her gaze lowered to the clothes strewn about the stone floor, then lifted again to meet Hunter's wide eyes. She swallowed and flattened the wrinkles on the front of her apron. "What can we do for you, good sir?" Her eyes dropped to his bare feet for a fraction of a second, and then back up again to his face.

His heart thumped. Ten minutes into the castle and he

was already drawing the wrong kind of attention.

"Nothing. My coin purse. I think it might may have been picked up with the linens."

"Needn't have troubled yourself with that. We'd have searched for you."

"It's no trouble," he said quickly. "This sort of thing happens all the time. Was only worried someone would swipe it before it was found." He winced the moment he said that. Fuck. Now he was accusing them of being dishonest.

The women exchanged glances. The unintended insult didn't seem to register but some silent exchange happened between them. "Is your hair wet, milord?" said the second laundress.

His hand lifted to the top of his head as if to confirm it. "Uh… I… came from the baths. That was when I realized the purse was missing."

"You'll catch your death walking around like that," one of them replied with a shake of her head.

The other nodded at her friend's wisdom. "And no boots? Milord, that is unwise, if it's not too bold for me to say. You never know what you're apt to step in down here beneath the castle."

Hunter didn't want to think about it.

"Milord," the first continued, "far be it from me to tell an esteemed member of the king's guard their business, but I'd take more care with your hard-earned coin, sir. Too many owls loiter around those barracks ready to prey on the careless."

He had to fight to keep the surprise from his face. They assumed he was a guardsman.

"We'll keep an eye out for it, but…," the first replied with a sad shrug and a glance at her friend. They both clearly believed his fictitious purse was already stolen and would not be recovered.

Didn't matter. He had to get out of there. "You are certainly right. I'll leave you ladies to your work." He glided in the direction the women had come, and with a cheerful wave, hurried out of the chamber and into the underbelly of the castle.

Barefoot and underdressed, he scurried about the dark corridors like an oversized mouse. He hugged the walls and avoided people when he could, tried to look nonchalant when he couldn't. He gained some curious looks, but no one stopped him, or seemed even mildly alarmed that he was there. Certainly, no one yelled out "intruder" and went racing off to find a guard with their arms flailing about.

Zinnuvial had been right. Everyone trusted the guardsmen had the castle securely locked down, and people seemed too occupied with their duties to pay much attention to him. No one had time to consider the half-dressed man aimlessly bumbling about.

Here, in the grimy underpinnings, he skulked through the convoluted labyrinth of rooms, tunnels, and strange little nooks. He tried to make sense of the layout, but there was no logic to it, and there was too much ground to cover. Storage rooms, soapmaking, distilleries, stone cutters, and a large butchery—all the hidden dregs of the castle system that kept everything functioning up above, but no indication that access to the dungeon was anywhere down there. No guard presence. No cries of anguish. No smell of rot and despair.

Which meant prisoners had to be kept someplace else.

Of course it couldn't be that easy. He had no choice but to explore other parts of the castle grounds—but he was reluctant to head up to the surface. No one seemed to care down here how he was dressed, but up above his lack of attire might draw more unwanted scrutiny. And as Dax always liked to remind him, he wasn't exactly inconspicuous.

The first access to the surface he came upon was a large dumbwaiter at the back of a storage room. As he leaned around the doorway, three men were securing a stack of kegs on the wooden structure with ropes. He considered briefly creeping in, maybe slipping behind the stack of kegs to get hauled up with them, but it seemed too risky. No telling where he'd end up.

He found a stairwell, wide and well-lit, and ventured up it slowly. But as he rounded the second landing, he caught the sounds of a large group laughing farther up, and he doubled back down again.

This was taking too much time.

After searching further, he happened upon a flight of rugged circular stairs tucked inside an alcove. He ascended the unlit and twisting stairwell at a cautious speed, hand to the wall to guide him through the dark. It turned about dizzyingly for a long time—he was deeper underground than he'd thought. At last, light filtered down from above. Around the final turn, he arrived at a heavy door, banded with strips of iron, sunlight squeezing under the bottom edge.

He checked the latch. Unlocked, which surprised him. He held his breath and listened with his ear turned toward the door. Some distant banging and the wind was all he heard. So he gingerly eased the door open and stepped out.

The narrow yard beyond was wedged between the castle itself and the towering outer wall. The ground, shaded by the castle, was a lifeless strip of hard packed soil and gravel with only a few patches of stringy weeds making a go of it at the base of the wall. Little was around. A staircase made of logs and roughly hewed planks led to the top of the wall. He spotted movement up there, patrols pacing the ramparts, but the attention seemed outward and not down in his direction. At the base of the stairs was a stubby stone building not much bigger than a garden shed. It seemed quiet and he couldn't tell if anyone was inside it.

To the right, past the corner tower of the castle, the area opened and was basked in warm morning sunlight. A long building hugged the rampart wall. When the wind shifted, the smell of manure and hay was undeniable. The stables.

The northern door that Zinnuvial mentioned was nearby. Finding Dax was foremost on his mind, but if it was here….

He stayed close to the castle and headed west.

Two men, dressed casually in tunics and leather aprons, sat with their backs to the wall just past the small stone outbuilding. They shared a pipe and mumbled softly to each other. Their eyes shot up when Hunter marched by, but then they relaxed again and went back to their pipe. The two were clearly hiding out to take an unscheduled break from their duties.

Farther ahead, Hunter spotted a black tunnel in the wall. It was wide enough for maybe a small cart to get through but not much more.

Hunter glanced behind him. The two idlers still paid him no attention. Hunter strolled closer and peered inside the dark opening. There was a heavy iron door at the far end, with a guard seated on the ground, his back and head against it. His helm was placed next to him and his hands loose in his lap.

Asleep on the job.

Why wouldn't he be, Hunter thought. Assigned to this dark hole all day to guard an unused door was likely the most mind-numbingly boring post there was. This job was likely a punishment for something. But his day was about to get a whole lot more exciting.

Hunter had to make this quick and make sure he didn't alert the two idlers enjoying their pipe. Any cry from the guard would be easily heard.

On the balls of his bare feet, he slunk into the dark tunnel. The guard didn't move, and Hunter could hear him gently snoring. Hunter held his breath and lowered to one knee next to him; then he thrust his forearm under his chin and pressed his palm against the guard's mouth.

The man's eyes bolted open. He stared up at Hunter in alarm, and he thrashed about to break loose. But he was no match for Hunter's strength. He tried to cry out, but only managed to make a muffled gurgle against Hunter's hand.

Hunter increased the pressure against the side of his neck. The man tried to twist free, but Hunter shifted more of his weight against him. The flailing intensified as true panic took hold, and the guard's eyes bulged. It was gruesome to watch and made Hunter's stomach wedge into his throat.

The writhing subsided, and then after a few final kicks, stopped altogether. The guard fell limp. Hunter released the forearm from his neck but kept his hand over the mouth just in case this was a ruse.

"Please don't be dead. Please don't be dead," he mumbled to himself.

He pulled his hand away and he heard the whoosh of air entering the guard's mouth. But he remained unmoving. Out cold.

Hunter allowed himself a long exhale that puffed out his cheeks. His hands were shaking as he doubled back to the tunnel opening and leaned out. The smokers were on their feet. Hunter's heart thumped, afraid they'd heard something. But one tucked his pipe into a pouch on his belt, and the two strolled back the other way.

Hunter stripped the man of his uniform. He pulled the stained tunic off over his head, and gripping the top of it in two fists, tore it in half. Hunter used one half of the fabric to tie the unfortunate guard's wrists behind his back. He stuffed as much of the other as he could into the guard's mouth.

The uniform fit better than he expected. The tunic was a one size fits all variety, and the leather armor had adjustable lacings at the flanks. Even with the girth of his chest, he was able to buckle the front.

The armored door was heavily secured with both several bolts and a thick beam across the width of it. Hunter lifted the beam out of the brackets, then gently guided it between the guard's back and his tied wrists. If the man woke, the beam would prevent him from running off to get help. If all went well, he'd be here a while.

Each bolt on the door was fixed with a padlock of comical size. Hunter rummaged through the satchel the guard had with him and found a ring of keys at the bottom. In short order, he located the key that popped each lock open, and he slid each bolt aside.

He caught himself breathing a little easier. A bit of luck had landed him a passable disguise to get him around the castle grounds.

He checked the knots on the guard's wrists one more time and made sure the fabric shoved in his mouth was still secure. The man was still out cold but still breathing. He'd probably wake up with a terrible headache, but hopefully nothing more than that. Hunter returned the keys to the satchel and slung it over his shoulder. With a bit more luck, the keys would open more than padlocks. He tucked the helm under his arm, stiffened his spine, and marched out of the tunnel like he belonged there.

31

A RUSH came over him. The same kind he felt when jogging out on the pitch before a match. Both apprehension and determination were fused in an adrenaline-fueled cocktail that pumped through his bloodstream. His heart punched him from the inside. He kept his face locked in a stern scowl, like someone annoyed and on a mission, hoping it would keep people away.

The eastern yard of the castle was a hive of restrained commotion. It felt part village, part farm—but wholly industrious. Gray plaster buildings with thatched roofs were packed in, some pressed right up against the outer wall. Hunter ventured in, shoulders back, his eyes on everything while trying to seem like he belonged. He felt obvious and out of place. But no one paid him any mind. Everyone went about their business, parading about, heads low, some dragging small carts or with packs hoisted on their shoulders. Few bothered to glance his way.

At first, it seemed peaceful here. Tiny herds of sheep and

goats wandered about, nibbling any grasses that sprouted up in corners and along the foundation. A queue of women waited by a well. As the first in line hauled up the bucket to fill vessels, the others looked grateful for the opportunity to chat and do nothing for the moment. Hunter could hear a doleful twinging of a stringed instrument floating on the air.

Yet no one smiled. He heard no laughing or the sound of kids playing. The looming bulk of the castle seemed imposing and watchful. The air around him was taut—like a locker room after a humiliating defeat.

He had no idea what he was looking for or where he was going. His only hope was that he'd stumble upon something useful, some clue that might lead him somewhere, give him a direction.

"Guardsman," someone barked to his left.

Hunter's stomach clenched, and he came to a stiff halt.

"Off on a stroll?" a voice purred. The man who rounded Hunter's flank into view was nearly equal in height. He wore a three-quarter-length coat, the same deep red color as the leather Hunter wore, but it was embellished with gold to highlight his superior status. Hunter shifted his eyes enough to get a glimpse of the grizzled beard and cold eyes before he shot his gaze forward again, military style—the effect of obedience and discipline that was likely ubiquitous, regardless of the world.

"On an errand, s—milord." Hunter's mouth had dried up and his stomach was in his throat. He found it hard to form the words. But he was careful to keep the sound of Dax's accent in his head as he spoke. And the less he said the better.

"Here? In the bailey village?" the officer scoffed. He leaned in and Hunter could feel his hot breath on his cheek "Looking for a whore, more like."

"Yes, milord," Hunter replied. "A whore. But not for me. A visiting emissary has requested one, and he has particular tastes." Risky, he knew. He had no idea if such a thing existed here, but he had to say something—something that would give him license to search the area, and this was the first thing that came to his head. "I was instructed to keep it in strictest confidence."

He could feel the heat of the officer's eyes on him, considering him closely. Trying to gauge if he was lying. Hunter kept his eyes forward, staring at nothing in the distance. His heart seemed to go hollow in his chest while he waited. The crowd around him went about its business without taking any notice of him.

It must have held enough of a ring of truth to it, for he heard the man grunt low in the back of his throat. "Errand or not," the officer growled, "maintain a complete uniform." He snatched the leather-studded helm from under Hunter's arm and slammed against his breastbone.

Hunter grabbed it and flung it onto his head, shoving it down over his ears. A careless mistake—he wanted to kick himself. The helm was too small, and it pressed tight against his head. But if he could survive the skull-breaking pressure within a scrum, he could tolerate a snug helmet.

"Resume," the officer said.

Hunter heard the crunch of boots behind him as the officer marched off. He exhaled and waited for his head to stop swimming. Then he hurried off through the yard.

Up ahead, two men gripped the bridles of a pair of horses pulling a large enclosed wagon. They led the team between the buildings. Newly arrived and heading to the stables, Hunter guessed. He moved against a building as it wheeled past with squeaks and groans. The side of the wagon had small windows with iron bars. It was a paddy wagon. Bringing in prisoners.

Hunter hurried onward. Just beyond the bailey village, as Hunter suspected, was the main gatehouse, flanked on either side by stout towers that rose up above the walls. The sound of grinding gears rose above all other sounds, and as Hunter drew closer, he could see the lowering of the portcullis. With a crunch and a thump, it dropped into the trench that crossed the cobbled road.

His eye was drawn to activity closer to the castle. A dense cluster of guards stood at the base of the broad staircase that swooped upward toward a pair of massive gothic doors—the official and primary entrance into the castle. The guards loitered about as if waiting for direction, talking casually among themselves.

Hunter positioned himself in the shadow of a porch overhang to watch. Among the guards, a man and a woman were on their knees, arms bound behind them. The man's face was covered in crimson. He'd been beaten, and the gash over his eyes had bled down his face and neck. Hunter didn't recognize either of them, but they certainly didn't look like dangerous criminals. They were resistance members. Or suspected ones anyway. After the raid, the city guard was rounding up anyone they could find.

The queen was going to make a very public show that the resistance was crushed beneath her heel. And the crowning moment would be the execution of Dax.

Time was running out. Already midday and he was no closer to finding the dungeon where Dax was being held. But those two were the first solid chance of finding it. He closed his eyes a moment to ward off the flaring urgency in his gut. He had to keep his head, not rush this and make matters worse by getting himself captured too.

The two prisoners were dragged to their feet and shoved into motion. They shared a quick doleful look as they staggered forward. The man looked defeated, crestfallen. Yet Hunter saw strength and resilience in the woman's gaze as she glared at the two guards pushing them along. The rest of the troop fell into marching order and paraded behind them with stiff backs and weapons drawn. For two people who looked like nothing more than modest shopkeepers, the show of force was over the top, like putting a choke collar on a bunny.

Hunter understood what was happening. The guardsmen were sending a message to everyone in the bailey village: members of the resistance would be severely punished.

Hunter quickened his step to edge in closer to the procession. He followed in their wake, matching their pace, careful not to drift too close. The prisoners were herded southward, across the yard and past the gatehouse, toward a stone building that seemed to have grown right out of the curtain wall itself, like a distended tumor. Drab and utilitarian, it had a cold functionality about it. A group of men and women sparred within a wooden pen while others cheered them on from the perimeter.

Guard station. Barracks. Training ground.

Hunter bit the inside of his cheek in thought. Too many movies placed dungeons in the dark bowels of the castle itself, but it made pragmatic sense for criminals to be caged in the same location as the guards. The procession herding the prisoners dissolved as they reached the door of the station. Most of the guards peeled off to watch the skirmishes in the pen, while the two in front roughly hustled the prisoners inside.

A raised wooden platform beyond the training yard snagged his eye. The wood was blonde, unweathered—this was recently built. Stairs led up the side, and a conspicuous wooden block was positioned in the center. Hunter's insides hollowed like a dank cave at the sight of it. It was quiet and empty now, but Hunter felt like it was waiting. An image of Dax kneeling on that grim stage sprang into his mind, his head positioned over the block. A stark reminder of the outcome if he failed.

He had no time to be tentative. In for a penny, as they say. He pulled in a long breath, clenched his hands into fists, and marched toward the building.

The heavy door leading inside was stiff on its hinges, and he looked clumsy as he heaved it open. He couldn't see anything, but a wave of hot air assaulted him as he stepped past the threshold, a sticky mix that was part postgame locker room and part sleazy bar bathroom. He pulled the door shut behind him with a thud. His eyes were slow to adjust, but he moved in regardless, not wanting to look as if the place was unfamiliar. Even without seeing, the place felt grim and oppressive. He shouldered his way past the crowd that loitered by the entrance and pushed his way into the thick of it.

Half-blind, he caught his hip on the edge of a table. The man behind it, an open book splayed out in front of him, cursed at Hunter as he righted an inkwell that had spilled its contents across the table, traveling between the planks.

Hunter mumbled an apology and kept moving. He skirted around two guards and caught a fragment of their mumbled conversation.

"Main hall," said one as Hunter shouldered past. "Third day in a row."

The other made a sympathetic sound in his throat. "You piss off Venzura?"

"Who knows. All fucking day too. Stuck listening to those whining crofters makes my skin itch. Fucking ingrates."

"Don't know how the queen stands it, to be honest."

The crowd thinned beyond the vestibule, and Hunter's eyes finally adjusted to the dark. He goose-necked into a few rooms. Some were occupied; some were not. They looked administrative—nothing useful to him. He pushed onward and entered a long hallway.

From there, he took a moment to take stock. Most of the movement around him seemed relaxed. Routine. It appeared he'd stumbled in around the time of a shift change. To the left was a staircase to the second floor. A female guard tottered down, latching up the buckles on her leather armor. To the right, a wide double door had steady traffic in and out, and Hunter could smell cooked meat. The mess hall.

His heart pounded in his ears, and he tried to avoid eye contact with anyone. Someone of his size didn't blend in well. A few glanced his way. Hunter waited to be called out as someone who didn't belong, but each time, the gaze turned away, and they went about their business.

At the far end of the corridor, at the point the corridor

took a ninety-degree turn, a guardsman stood stiff against the wall. He held a long pike in his gauntleted hand that was firmly planted on the floor next to him.

A very formal stance. An on-duty stance.

Hunter attempted an official gait down the corridor. He marched forward, his boots making a conspicuous clomp on the wood-plank floor. The on-duty guardsman made no notice of his approach. He kept his eyes forward and unblinking. As Hunter reached the corner, the man's eyes shifted briefly his way. Hunter's heart jumped, but he locked the air in his lungs and made a tiny drop of his chin and kept moving. He fully expected the guard to order him to halt.

But nothing happened.

He quietly let the air from his lungs and kept moving.

This wing of the building carried a different energy. It was quieter, certainly, and had the timbre of seriousness, something more administrative. He slunk past rooms occupied by grunts hunched over desks, scribbling away in massive tomes. The corridor ended at a heavily armored door. The kind of door that would lead down into a prison.

He reached for the latch—then hesitated. If it was locked, it would look suspicious that he didn't know that. Someone authorized to be down there would know if it was kept locked or not. His hand moved to his waist. He still had the ring of keys from the guard he'd knocked out.

Was there one master key for all the important locks?

He took hold of one of the three clunky skeleton keys between his finger and thumb and inserted it into the keyhole. It was loose inside. He fiddled with it, trying to get it to catch the mechanism. Nothing. It wouldn't turn.

Voices provoked him to look over his shoulder. Someone was talking with the guardsman posted in the corridor.

"Fuck," he moaned under his breath. He could only see the profile of the man, but it was his voice that gave him away. Hunter recognized the sharp staccato punch he made with his words. It was the same officer who had confronted him in the bailey village.

He was trapped. He thought about doubling back, maybe ducking into one of the other rooms. But that seemed even riskier. The scribes wouldn't know him and would question why he was there. And while Hunter walked back down the corridor to get to one of the rooms, all the officer had to do was glance up and he would have a clear shot of Hunter's face.

Hands shaking, he fumbled with the second key. He jiggled that one around inside the lock too, but no angle or position would allow the key to catch and turn.

The officer broke off the conversation with the guardsman with a sharp "Carry on," and Hunter heard his heavy footfalls on the wood floor. Getting louder. The officer was heading straight for him. With each clap of the bootheel, blood roared louder in Hunter's ears.

One final key. He gripped it with white knuckles and tried to insert it into the hole, but his hand was shaking so violently he couldn't slip it in.

He used his other hand to stabilize it and help guide the end. His chest was tight and wouldn't allow air in, so he locked his breathing. He turned it. He felt the ends catch on the mechanism inside, and the key turned. The lock snapped, and Hunter almost passed out in relief.

He let out a breath. The officer must have been right at his neck, but he was too afraid to look. He depressed the latch with his thumb and pushed.

Nothing. The door wouldn't move.

Fuck!

The realization struck him like a punch in the gut. The fucking door had already been unlocked. He'd just locked it. He inserted the key again and turned it back around the other way. He felt the mechanism snap again.

He thumbed the latch and pushed. The hinges moaned as the door swung inward.

Trying to act casual while sweat cascaded down his

temple from underneath the too tight helmet, he stepped through the threshold into the poorly lit corridor beyond. As he swung the door closed, he saw the officer turn into one of the side rooms. Hunter hadn't been recognized.

The door slammed shut too hard. The sound of it reverberated like thunder through the corridor. That would get someone's attention. He locked the door again—if anyone came to investigate, the locked door would slow them down.

Hunter fell against the stone wall and tried to bring his breathing under control. His entire body quaked; his knees barely managed to keep him erect as adrenaline continued to flood his system. He had to keep going. His only option was to plunge even deeper into guard territory with no plan other than finding Dax. He'd figured out what to do once he found him—but he was going on blind faith that Dax was even here. Hand on the wall to steady himself, he shuffled down the corridor as fast as his wobbly legs would take him.

32

THE DANK stench of death and decay told Hunter he was heading in the right direction. It was exactly what he would have expected in a dungeon, and the fetid air constricted his throat and clung to his skin.

He didn't want to spend five minutes in here. He couldn't imagine being locked in a cage down here.

A single tallow candle burned in a carved-out niche in the rock. Years of yellow-brown wax formed slimy tendrils down the stone. It offered only enough light for him to shuffle his way along. The passageway was cramped and dreary, and the ceiling mere inches above Hunter's head. Hunter was stricken with a wave of hopelessness—as if he would never see the sun again.

The floor morphed into roughly carved steps that twisted downward. With a hand to the wall to steady him, he lowered each foot carefully. The staircase circled, taking him deeper.

And deeper.

He didn't think it possible, but the smell worsened as he

descended. His mouth salivated as his stomach spasmed, threatening to empty. When he was beginning to believe he would never reach the bottom, the stairwell opened into a small antechamber with a cluster of small rooms squeezing in around it. Weapons storage on one side. Swords, maces, and a variety of other sadistic implements of death hung from wooden racks on the wall. On the other side, two guards sat on crates at a round table. One male and one female. A lantern between them, they leaned in and shuffled small bone-white tiles back and forth on the surface.

Ahead, almost hidden behind a precarious stack of wooden crates, was an arched doorway.

He ducked in the weapons room and helped himself to a longsword and bandolier. In case things turned south, he told himself. And he would look more the part of a guardsman on duty. He slipped the leather strap of the bandolier over his head to let it rest on his shoulder. The weight of the sword on his hip felt oddly reassuring. Even though he knew that if this dissolved into having to use it, he'd likely end up dead.

A sound cut the grim silence of the place, a low and wretched moan that echoed off the stone. An iron clang followed. Then voices. Low at first but growing louder.

Hunter remained in the weapons room, back to the wall and out of sight.

"I'll report to Venzura. Secure the stools at Bull's."

"Not buying your mead," one grumbled.

"Gods, you spring me a coin one time, and it's all I hear about."

"Thrice, more like."

Hunter leaned around the doorframe and caught a glimpse of their backs as they entered the stairwell. Before they disappeared, one reached over and hooked a ring of keys on a spike driven into the stone wall. Hunter stepped from the weapons room. The two at the table hadn't moved or even lifted their heads from their game. Hunter wrapped his fingers around the keys to keep them from jingling and lifted the ring from the spike.

As Hunter started toward the archway, keys clenched in his white fist, something snagged the female guard's attention away from the game. Her eyes lifted and narrowed a fraction as if some vague question piqued her. Hunter resisted the compulsion to reach for the hilt.

"Quit your stallin'," the other guard grumbled at her. "Make your move already."

With her lip curling in a snarl, she returned her gaze to the game, Hunter forgotten.

Hunter tried to keep a natural pace as he delved into the corridor. A short flight of stairs and through a heavy door banded with iron, and he was in the thick of the dungeon. A guard was stationed at the bottom, his shoulders to the wall. He straightened when he heard Hunter's approach.

"Venzura has questions for one of the prisoners," Hunter grumbled to him as he marched past.

The guardsmen nodded and relaxed, and he let his shoulders fall back against the wall.

Hunter's blood was vibrating under his skin. His mouth was dry. He was close now. Or so he hoped. There was no guarantee Dax was even here, though it felt exactly like the place they would take him. Yet, a valuable trophy like him might be kept in a more secure location and with a heavier guard presence.

The corridor was lined with iron-banded doors. Each had small barred windows. He leaned over to peer through each as he worked his way down the corridors. The cells were cubes carved from solid stone. Some were empty. Some were filled with pathetic lumps curled into corners on the floor. None he recognized.

Filth was everywhere, at a level that was sickening. Inhumane. Bile scalded the back of Hunter's throat. He pressed his hand to his mouth, but it did little to ward off the stench that seemed to coat his tongue and teeth. He might never get the taste out his mouth.

He could feel the guard's eyes on his back. Trying to seem casual, he glanced back. The man was watching him with renewed interest, surely wondering why Hunter didn't know what cell to go to.

He hurried to the end of the corridor and rounded a corner. Another row of cells.

Without the guard eyeing him, he could spend more time inspecting each cell. He found the new prisoners who had just been brought in. They had been separated but were in adjacent cells. They both pressed their bodies against opposite sides of the same rock wall.

Halfway down the corridor, Hunter found Dax.

He was huddled in a corner, naked, shoulder and head to the wall, rigid as the stone around him. Hunter's insides twisted. It was too dark inside the cell for Hunter to see if his eyes were open, but his pale skin was a patchwork of bruising and his eye was puffy and swollen. He was almost unrecognizable. He'd been beaten. Tortured.

Clashing emotions rippled through him as if a stone had been dropped in the center of his soul. Relief flooded his brain in a euphoric wave like a drug hitting his system. His lungs cleared in one gush, and his brain felt like it had turned to vapor. He could pass out if he gave in to it. But seeing Dax so broken sent hot rage coursing through him. His heart felt cleaved at the sight of him. And the fear that he was too late, that Dax was already dead, formed a cold vacuum in his gut.

All of this came within the span of a single breath.

He looked down the corridor again, concerned that the suspicious guardsman might follow him. But the corridor was quiet except for indiscriminate moaning from a nearby cell. He fumbled with the keys and inserted the black iron teeth into the hole. It turned around one compete time and the mechanism inside the door opened with a sharp clank.

The sound seemed to ricochet around him, and Hunter cringed. He waited, air locked in his chest. But nothing happened. He pushed open the cell door, and it groaned on rusty hinges like some Halloween cliché.

He stepped into the cell, lowered himself down to next to Dax, and put two fingers under his chin against his neck.

A slow rhythm pushed against his finger.

"Hands off me, you ugly fucker," Dax groaned.

Hunter wanted to cheer, wanted to swoop Dax up into his arms and squeeze him until his eyes bulged. He wanted to lift him into his arms and carry him right out of the hideous place. But instead he pulled his fingers away and crossed his arms "Ugly? That's the thanks I get?"

Dax opened one eye. He looked up at Hunter with a brow knotted in confusion.

Hunter tore off his helm and tossed it aside with a clang. "If I had a mirror, I'd show you, in fact, who the ugly one is right now. You have had better days." Heart near bursting, Hunter couldn't contain his smile any longer. His face broke into a goofy grin born of relief and joy.

Dax swallowed as recognition dawned in his eyes, which widened into uncharacteristic astonishment. Hunter couldn't help but revel for a moment in for once surprising him with what he could do. "How...?"

"Long story, not important now." Driven by impulse, Hunter cupped Dax's face in his hands and pressed lips against his. Dax's lips were dry and cracked, but still warm and full against his own. Surprise gave way to release, and Dax pushed in to accept Hunter's lips, albeit weakly. The taste of Dax pushed away the ghastly smells around him and hijacked his brain like a heady cologne.

The metallic bite of Dax's blood was on his tongue. Reluctantly, he broke the connection between them. "I have to get you out of here."

"You shouldn't have come."

"I wasn't going to let you die here."

"Too dangerous. They knew I was coming. They were waiting for me."

"We know. Can you walk?"

Dax closed his eyes, his mouth twisted into an expression that Hunter couldn't read. "Give me a moment." He shifted and pushed himself up higher on the wall.

"A lot has happened," Hunter said. "We'll talk on the way."

"Do you have a plan?"

"Getting in here was the plan."

Dax shook his head. "I said you were going to get me killed one day."

"Such confidence. I got in, didn't I? We'll get out." He just needed to get to the northern wall again and get Dax through that door. With any luck, no one had discovered the bound guard yet. "We just need to figure out the small detail of how to get you past the guards and through the barracks without being seen."

Dax rolled his head back and forth. "There's another way. Through the dungeon. The other way. When I was dragged off to be interrogated, I saw them come through. Servants. From the kitchens."

"From the castle?"

Dax nodded.

"Are you sure?" Then there was a way into the dungeons from inside. He'd only missed it. Probably wasn't well marked for obvious reasons. Traipsing through the castle with Dax was only a moderately better option. He wouldn't be easy to pass off as anything but a tortured prisoner.

But then, Hunter was dressed as a guard.

Dax seemed to stall about halfway to his feet, his shoulder dropping to the grimy stone wall. Hunter put a hand under Dax's arm to lift him the rest of the way. Dax kept his hand against the stone, and he dropped his head as if he might be sick.

"I can carry you," he asked.

Dax gave him a side-eyed glance. "That's certainly won't look suspicious. Drag me out, like you're taking me to get interrogated."

Hunter winced. He didn't think he could do that and make it look convincing enough.

Dax, surveying Hunter's face, must have come to same conclusion. "Or find me a sword," he added.

"Fight our way out?" Hunter shook his head. "There's a hundred or more guards up there."

Dax fell quiet as he stared at the floor. "There's been a steady flow of prisoners brought in. Something's happened."

"Not important right now."

"Tell me."

The tone in Dax's voice didn't give Hunter much opportunity to resist. He sighed. "The hideout's been raided. Someone betrayed its location." Hunter turned his head away, afraid his eyes would somehow reveal what he knew. From the corner of his vision, he saw Dax's expression turn dark and dangerous.

"Who made it out?"

"A lot, I think. They were still assessing when I left."

"Quinnar?"

Hunter's stomach dropped. The concern in Dax's voice was obvious. "Yes," he said in a voice quieter than he intended. "And Zinnuvial and Corrad." He was tempted to tell Dax that Quinnar had no intention of organizing a rescue, that he was willing to let Dax die down here, but he held his tongue.

Dax didn't seem to notice Hunter's shift in tone. "Zefora's hammer, that's a relief. He's too important and knows too much to fall into their hands." His eyes lifted to the ceiling. "He'd not sustain their interrogation well."

Did he just imply that Quinnar was weak-willed?

Dax's eyes narrowed, lips tightening. "We have to get the others out too."

"My job is to get you out."

"They come with us or leave me behind."

Hunter puffed out his cheeks. They didn't have time for this. "And if I knock you out and drag you out of here?" The look in Dax's eyes gave him the answer. Dax would never forgive him. He would never willingly leave anyone behind.

He hadn't left Hunter behind, even when he'd had the opportunity.

Hunter covered his eyes with his palm. "You and your high-minded virtue and honor. Fine. All right. We rescue them too. But it probably means we'll all get caught and I'll die in this dungeon too."

How the fuck was he going to get all the prisoners to that unlocked door unseen?

Dax seemed more stable on his feet, and he stood with his back straighter. His face had hardened into a look of raw fortitude and purpose. The notion of getting everyone out of here had given him renewed strength.

"We need a distraction," Hunter said. He stepped out of the cell and looked up and down the corridor between the rows of cell doors. He had an idea. A terrible idea. And it was likely to get them all killed as surely as the executioner's ax. But every minute they delayed narrowed their chances of getting out.

It was time to act and hope for the best.

33

HUNTER MADE his way down the row of cells. He peeked in each window and unlocked the ones that were occupied—which was most of them. He couldn't do the ones down the first aisle because surely the guard was still there watching. He would have to wait to do those.

He pushed his way into each cell, cringing as each hinge groaned and resisted. Pale torchlight spilled into each tiny room, and each pathetic mass stirred nervously on the ground. He put a finger to his lips. "Quiet now." He swung each door as wide as it would go and stepped back into the corridor. Each prisoner stared back at him, wide white eyes set in faces covered in grime. He understood their reluctance—he was dressed as a guard.

"Trust me," he urged.

Some had clearly only been in here a short time—they looked scared but resilient, fight still in their eyes. Others had been forgotten in here for much longer. They were weak and malnourished. Broken. Seeing their cell door left open, life replaced the hopelessness and fear in their eyes, and with help from Hunter, they lifted from the straw-covered floor.

Dax limped out of his own cell to join him.

"Get them moving," Hunter whispered to him. The stone sitting in his gut seemed to grow. The plan was feeling more ridiculous by the moment. It wasn't going to work and would likely kill them all.

He moved into an empty cell and used the side of his boot to scrape all the filthy straw into the pile in the corner. Out in the hall, he lifted a tallow candle from its recess in the wall and carried it into the cell. He took several long breaths to build up the nerve.

Dax moved in behind him. The freed prisoners were already shuffling out of their cells and working their way down the corridor. He looked down at the pile and then nodded to Hunter. "Do it."

Hunter dropped the candle into the straw and stepped back.

The fire took immediately. Red and orange ate at the straw in a crackling wave. Noxious black smoke rushed to the low ceiling and spread like rolling storm clouds, the first tendrils clawing out into the corridor. Hunter fed the flames with more straw from other cells and in moments, the tiny cell felt like a kiln.

Hunter handed the keys over to Dax. "In case there's more."

"Stay low," Dax told the others as he shuffled them along.

The roiling black ceiling billowed farther down the corridor, sinking lower. It stung his eyes and coated his throat like acid. Hunter crouched to stay beneath it. This could all go terribly, terribly wrong.

He shuffled back to the entrance, and as he staggered out of the wall of smoke, he exaggerated a fit of coughs and fell against the wall in a dramatic show.

The guard rushed toward him. He threw himself under Hunter's arm and tried to support him.

"What happened?" the guard asked.

"Don't know. A candle must have fallen." He interrupted himself with more choking. "The whole area is in flames."

The guard dragged him toward the exit, but Hunter resisted and pushed him away. "No. I need to go back."

"The prisoners?" the guard said. "Forget them, man! They'd be facing the executioner in a day or two anyway."

"I need to warn the guards on the other side," Hunter said, breaking loose of the man's grip. "Get everyone out."

He shoved the guard into action. The man hesitated at first, staring back at Hunter with wide-eyed indecision, but then staggered into a run, shouting "Fire!" Hunter waited until he was up the short flight of stairs and out of sight before he started unlocking the cell doors in this corridor. One by one, he started grabbing prisoners and dragging them out. There was no time to be gentle.

Huddled in the corner of one of the cells was a figure in rags. She didn't react when the door opened or to Hunter's call. She was sprawled limply across the floor, eyes closed. Even in the dim haze, Hunter could see that beneath the dirt and grime that covered every inch of her, the skin was blue.

He scooped her into his arms. She weighed nothing. There was little left of her other than bones and skin. He had no idea if she was still alive—there wasn't time to check for a pulse. But he was going to get her out regardless. For Uri. Hunter knew instinctively that this was his mother.

Confused and frightened, the prisoners were huddled in the corridor, waiting for direction. "Follow me," he told them.

The amount of smoke was staggering. He took in as full a breath as he could and dived back into the wall of smoke. When he came back to the corridor with the others, he'd discovered the reason the smoke was much worse than he anticipated. The floor itself was on fire—the years of filth that caked the stone was apparently fuel enough to spread it. It was already out of the cell and lapping up the walls. Some floating ember had set alight the hay that covered the floor in another cell.

It was quickly getting out of control.

With the unconscious woman draped over his shoulder, he hurried everyone past the spreading inferno and followed them. They caught up to Dax, who was leading everyone down the corridor on their hands and knees. Everything was a gray haze, like looking through tinted glass. The black churning ceiling was already halfway down the wall and descending at an alarming rate. They'd all die of smoke inhalation if they didn't act quickly. He moved to the front, set the woman to the ground beside Dax, then rushed off down the corridor. He had to get the guards first.

His lungs burned like acid. And his head was swimming, his vision closing in around at the edges. He couldn't black out. He wouldn't let himself.

He followed the zigzag of tunnels as far as they would take him. Two guards were stationed at the end of it. They both covered their mouths as they peered through the haze.

"Fire," Hunter called as he approached. "Fire!"

"How did this happen?" one of them asked.

"No idea. But it's bad. Sound the alarm. We need water down here."

"The prisoners?"

"No hope for them. Go. I'm going to make one more sweep to make sure all the guardsmen are out."

The two looked at each other.

"Go!" Hunter bellowed at them again.

They flinched, then scrambled out of the tunnel. The way was clear.

Hunter doubled back. "Hurry," he called to them as he lifted the Mazentian woman from the floor and repositioned her over his shoulder. "We don't have much time."

They emerged from the gray haze like specters. One after another. Hunter guessed maybe twenty in all. How in the hell was he going to get this many people safely out of the castle?

Stairs twisted upward and fed into a corridor. Even here, the smoke was present—less thick but clinging to the ceiling in a roiling charcoal wave. It was finding its way upward. But it was now easier to breathe. Hunter's lungs gulped in the fresher air, which sent him into a real coughing fit. Everyone in the chain behind him did the same. Some were sobbing.

They scurried down the corridor. Hunter led the way. He could hear shouts bouncing off the walls in the distance. The alarm had been raised. Soon a parade of soldiers would be spilling down at them to contain the blaze. He had to get them all somewhere out of the traffic flow.

The tunnel was different here. Less grim and forbidding. Hunter could feel they were under the castle proper now. He could almost feel the weight of it over him. A new smell cut through the acrid smell of smoke.

Cooking. He could smell roasted meat.

He followed his nose through a tangle of passageways and the smell grew stronger. More shouting chased them. The barking of orders. Military style. And he heard the rapid pounding of boots on stone.

He pressed onward, his heart punching him from inside. How long would it take for those guards to douse the flames and realize the cells were empty?

One of the prisoners cried out and collapsed. An elderly man. He grazed the wall and landed hard. Others scrambled to lift him from the floor, while he groaned piteously and clutched at his upper arm. The incident seemed to choke off their momentum. Everyone seemed to wait to see if the man was okay.

"Keep moving," Hunter barked. He was going to find a way out of this.

Someone put the old man's arm around his neck and dragged him into motion again. Hunter kept a hard pace, and they stuck with him. He glanced back, looking for Dax, but he had taken the rear to keep people moving. He was too far back in the crowd for Hunter to see him.

He rounded a lazy corner, and firelight painted the tunnel wall up ahead. The smell of cooking was stronger yet, along with other savory smells. Holding out his palm behind him, he slowed his pace and crept closer. The corridor ended at a door left ajar, and warm light and kitchen heat pushed through the opening. He sensed nothing through the opening—no movement, no sounds—so he gently swung his arm outward to push the door open farther.

No one anywhere. Produce was abandoned on the table in midpreparation, and something steamed and bubbled over the sides of a mammoth kettle hanging from a hook over the stove.

Dax appeared behind him.

"They've cleared out," Hunter whispered.

"No one would want to be trapped down here if it somehow spread," Dax replied. "It's our chance to get everyone to ground level. While everyone is occupied with the fire."

Hunter glanced back at the pathetic band behind them. Soot-covered and dressed in rags. They were huddled together, silent and morose. "We can't take them through the castle like this, Dax."

"And we can't stay here. This will be the first place they sweep."

"The door in the wall to the north. You know it?"

"The postern door," Dax replied with a nod. "It is rarely used and always guarded."

"Well, I took out the guard and unlocked it. We just need to get everyone there. And it's a short distance from a stairwell."

Dax's lips pressed into a line. "Still risky. We'd likely be seen."

Hunter snapped his fingers. "The laundry. Where I climbed up."

Dax stared at Hunter incredulously. "*That's* how you got in?"

"Not important. Listen, if word of the fire has sent everyone to the surface, then the laundry area is likely

316

abandoned too. They can all clean up quick and change into clothes that are a little less dungeon couture."

"Then flee the castle with everyone else." Dax nodded his endorsement of the plan.

Yet, Hunter didn't recognize where he was. In his search of the bowels of the castle, he'd somehow missed this area. "I don't know how to get to the laundry from here."

"Follow me," Dax said.

Of course. In his days of being a scout, he would have spent time here in the castle, reporting what he'd learned. He would know his way around.

First signaling the others that it was time to move, Hunter and Dax skirted along the wall of the kitchens. Their ears strained the silence for any sign that someone had lingered behind to keep their soup from burning. The kitchen was a vast complex of interconnected rooms like the inside of a hive. Hunter wove through the tables and stacks of laden bushels at a crouch to find his way back to the corridor he remembered from earlier.

Dax held out his arm to bring him to a stop, then broke off and slipped into a side storage room lined with rows of barrels. Dax stood one of the barrels up and pried out the wooden stopper. He stuck his nose in and whiffed—and his whole body flinched.

He looked up at Hunter and grinned. "Spirits. Good spirits."

"A little early to toast to our success," Hunter replied dryly.

Dax ignored him and dashed off around the corner out of sight. He returned a few moments later with a shovel full of hot coals. "We could use an added distraction," he said and poured the hot coals on top of the barrel.

Hunter stepped back. "Whoa. What the fuck? Are you trying kill us?"

"It'll take time for the coals to burn through the wood."

"How long?"

Dax made a casual shrug. "Not sure. But we won't want to be around."

That was an understatement. He passed his eye over all the barrels in storage. This was going to cause one hell of a distraction.

Hunter fell in at Dax's heels, the others hobbling behind him, as he led them down several corridors. The bowels of the castle were abandoned, but the eerie sounds of distant chaos echoed around them, and the biting smell of ash and smoke was everywhere. Dax pushed through a door—Hunter followed, and immediately recognized where they were. How'd he missed this door before? He knew the way from here. When they arrived at the laundry room, Dax poked his head in. "Seems clear."

They shooed everyone inside. Staggering weakly and still coughing, the group shuffled in and began digging through the piles of garments for something to wear.

Hunter gently placed the Mazentian woman on a soft pile. In the better light, he could see her injuries. The skin of her back was covered in half-healed lacerations that were clearly infected. Yellow pus seeped from the sores. He pressed two fingers against her neck. He thought he felt something push weakly against his fingertips but couldn't tell for certain. If she was alive, it was only barely.

He could feel Dax's eyes him. His gaze shifted back and forth from Hunter to the woman.

With a sigh, Hunter straightened again, hands on his hips. He looked at the others preparing to leave, then out into the corridor. When he glanced over at Dax, he was staring back up at him with a knotted brow.

"You're an idiot for coming after me," Dax said.

"You're welcome."

"How'd you do it?"

"Still not important," Hunter replied. "Look, I can't believe I'm actually going to say this. We should do more. Since we're here."

A strange look entered Dax's eyes. "What are you saying?"

"I'm saying I have this sweet uniform on. We should put it to good use."

"Hunter—"

"We can put a stop to it. Right now."

Dax scoffed. "You've done enough." There was a thread of sadness in his voice. The sound of guilt or regret. "Like you said, this isn't your fight."

Hunter looked down at his feet. "Somehow, I think it became mine. Not only because of what they did her. That's part of it. But also for what they did to her reputation. Her character. She was a good person, Dax, and had a fierce integrity, and it kills me that people think she became some kind of monster. I can't allow them to continue to destroy what was best about her. That's why I need to do this."

And for Dax. He didn't want to admit it out loud, but that was also why he needed to do it. Because this was his fight.

Dax shook his head. "No. Someone has to lead them to the postern door."

"I can do it," came a voice. They both turned to see the woman Hunter had witnessed earlier being dragged to the guard house. She'd found a simple tan shift and blue headband, and had already quickly and efficiently outfitted herself.

Hunter and Dax stared back at her.

"Think I'm not capable?" she asked with a raised brow. "I know where the door is. I can lead us all there easy enough. Whatever you two have planned to stop this madness, do it."

Dax's brow was tight above the bridge of his nose while he considered her. "Don't move as one group," he told her. "Spread out. And head to the door only a few at a time."

She gave him a curt nod.

"If anyone runs into trouble, keep going," he added. "Get out as many as you can. Understand?"

Hunter gestured to the Mazentian woman. "And make

sure she makes it out too. Whatever it takes."

The woman made a single sharp nod to show she understood. "Of course." She rejoined the others to help them find garments and get them dressed. As Hunter and Dax moved back out into the corridor, Hunter could hear her voice coaxing the others to move.

"So, you have a plan?" Dax asked.

Hunter shrugged. "First, get me to where the queen lives."

"The royal apartments?" Dax lifted a single brow. "I thought you opposed Quinnar's plan."

"That? God, no! I have a different idea. Equally reckless, but it doesn't involve murder—at least I hope it doesn't. And I'd hate to see this guard's uniform go waste."

Dax narrowed his eyes at him. "You're certain about this?"

"In for a penny… as they say," Hunter replied with a shrug.

"Very well," Dax replied in a soft voice. His eyes caught Hunter's just as he turned away, and Hunter saw something behind them he couldn't quite read. Sorrow? Regret? Or was it something else? "Let's go."

Dax probably thought Hunter had lost his mind. He was probably right.

34

THEY FOUND a pair of tattered trousers for Dax to wear. It wouldn't do to have him running around the palace naked—although Hunter wouldn't have minded. Even bruised and filthy, he was a vision of perfection. It was absolutely the wrong time.

Outside the laundry, in the quiet of the corridor, Hunter pulled Dax close and slipped his hand behind him. His skin tingled against the bare flesh of Dax's lower back. Hunter pressed his lips to his gently. He nibbled on his lower lip and rested his forehead atop Dax's head. His hair smelled of sweat and smoke, but Hunter didn't care.

"When this is over," he said, looking into Dax's eyes, "we are going to have a long conversation about you leaving in the middle the night."

The corner of Dax's mouth lifted a fraction. "Fair enough." He held his gaze for a moment longer before he pulled away. "We have to survive this plan of yours first."

They began their trek up into the castle, up to the royal apartments. Dax led the way, playing the role of a prisoner.

The corridors of the upper floors were largely

unpopulated. Word of a fire had sent most scrabbling to the outside and to safety. Guard presence was certainly low. They were likely pulled to help fight off the fire in the dungeon and prevent it from spreading. Servants were about all that remained. Most of them had been charged with collecting and packing the valuables of the nobles they served—should the fire get out of control, their masters wouldn't want to lose their wealth, of course.

As Hunter and Dax rounded a corner, a group of near-panicked servants were hauling travel crates and tapestry bags out into the corridor. They froze upon sight of Dax.

"Step aside," Hunter barked at them. He gave Dax a superficial shove, who made a better show of it by stumbling forward and grunting in pain. Hunter believed it was only partially an act.

The servants scurried back into the room and slammed the door closed. Dax turned about and grabbed Hunter's sleeve.

"This will not work if you don't make it look genuine," Dax grumbled.

"They seemed to buy it."

"It won't convince any guards. Do better."

Hunter had never been all that concerned about causing injury to someone on the pitch. Everyone was trained to take a hit, and any injuries sustained were rarely more than bruising or the odd broken finger or nose. Hunter knew he was holding back now. Dax looked like shit, and Hunter could tell he was struggling to keep the pace they made through the castle's corridors. He was battered and in more pain than he was willing to let on.

"How can you be sure the royal apartments are empty?" Dax asked.

"I heard guards talking. They said the king and queen would be hearing petitions in the main hall all day."

The sound of boots on the stone floor ahead heralded someone's approach. A nobleman rounded the corner, a small wooden box clutched to his chest. Hunter forced himself to forget it was Dax in front of him and shoved him against the wall, his forearm pressed against his neck. He bowed to the nobleman as he scuttled cautiously by, hugging the opposite wall.

"My sincere apologies, my lord. Forgive me for exposing you to this filth."

The noble, dressed in a rust-colored doublet, hose, and very shiny little black shoes, curled his lip up in disgust. "Ugh. How dreadful." He pulled out a lace kerchief and pressed it to his mouth as if Dax was breathing out horrific diseases. "What is this scoundrel doing by my residence?"

"Escaped custody, my lord. You needn't worry. He'll be in irons again directly."

"I should hope so." The noble hurried off.

Hunter released Dax from the wall, who winced as he rolled his shoulder and massaged his neck. "That... was better," he said. Through clenched teeth.

They took another narrow and winding flight of stairs to the next floor. Halfway up the stairwell, the ground beneath their feet shook, and a deep booming reverberation rumbled through the stone like an earthquake. Followed immediately by another. And another. A long series of explosions that seemed to go on and on. The sound was like a rolling beat on a bass drum. The coals had finally burned through the wooden lid and set off a chain reaction, barrel after barrel. Hunter put his hand to the wall, worried everything would collapse and bury them where they stood. When it was over, dust and stone chips shook loose and drifted down around them like snowfall and the castle fell into silence.

"That should stir up the hive for a while," Dax said.

"Won't it also be enough to pull the king and queen from the main hall? They'll be returned to their chambers if their safety is considered at risk."

Dax nodded as he proceeded to limp up the stairs. "We'd better be quick, then."

Out of the stairwell, they heard shouting from the windows. The castle grounds were in chaos. A group of servants and what looked like a young family sprinted past them in panic. A woman dragged two young children along as a man shouted at them to keep up. They all plunged into the stairwell heedlessly, giving Hunter and Dax no notice.

They rounded a corner into a wider corridor lined with white marble. Stairs led up to a grand wooden door, flanked by two guardsmen in the king's livery. As Hunter and Dax came into view, the two stiffened into attention, the halberds at their side shifting to perfectly vertical orientation.

Hunter grabbed Dax under the arm and forcibly drove him forward. Dax made a low grunt and winced. Hunter wasn't sure how much was acting and how much was real.

"Halt," one of them spat as Hunter approached the steps. The knuckles of the hand gripping the halberd were white, and his voice was jittery. He was clearly rattled by the explosions. "State your business."

Hunter gave Dax a rough shove forward and made the salute he'd seen other guards make—a fist to the chest followed by a curt bow. The pretentiousness of their uniform was enough to signal these two outranked a standard guard, so he took the more subservient approach. "The queen wishes to personally speak to this prisoner."

Their reaction was muted—a sign that this sort of thing was not outside of the norm.

"Still won't talk, eh?"

"She intends to change that," Hunter replied.

The guard smirked in approval.

"What is happening out there?" the other guard asked. "Those insurgent dogs getting desperate enough to attempt a direct attack?"

"No idea," Hunter replied. "But I was told to bring this one, so that's what I did."

"The queen is not yet available," said the first. "Return the prisoner to his cell and you will be called for when she is—

"

The guardsman never finished. Dax was a sudden blur of motion that surprised even Hunter. Dax lunged up the remaining steps for the man and thrust the heel of his hand into the man's windpipe. The guard gasped, stumbled forward, and clutched at his throat. The second guard started, but as his body tightened to respond, Hunter was already moving against him.

Hunter made a quick jab at his face, stunning him and knocking him backward. He could feel the bones of the nose shatter beneath his knuckles. The man reeled and tried to recover, but Hunter slipped his arm around him from behind and pressed the crook of his elbow against his throat. He kicked the door open and dragged the man inside while he squeezed. He squirmed and clawed at Hunter's arm, but was no match for Hunter's raw strength. He stomped down on Hunter's foot, but the thick military boots protected him from the impact.

Dax took a more direct approach. He smashed the other guard's head against the wall three times until he lost consciousness and dropped to the floor.

The struggling of the guard against Hunter's chest eventually subsided, and he fell limp. Hunter lowered him to the floor as Dax dragged in the other body. The one man's helm was dented in, and blood oozed down the side of his face. Crimson streaks ran down the white marble wall.

The two were dumped unceremoniously next to each other.

"All that blood will be a tipoff that something's amiss," he said.

"No guards outside the chamber will do more to alert them," Dax replied. He kicked one booted foot clear of the door's path as he swung it closed.

Fair point.

Dax put his back against the door. His chin lowered, and his breathing looked labored. The short fight had taken much out of him.

"You all right?" Hunter asked.

"Let's just get to your plan. We don't have much time. What are you thinking?"

"Well," he said as he marched down the short hallway, "at first I thought we should hunt down the power source."

He entered the main room of the king and queen's residence, a vast circular chamber. In the center was an ornate sitting area with settees and several high-back chairs arranged in a comfortable circle. The cozy arrangement rested on an elaborate medallion of inlaid stone. Along the wall, surrounding the central seating area, were large tables, bookcases, various desks, and the largest fireplace Hunter had ever seen. A hearty blaze was happily eating up a small mountain of logs.

The far wall, opposite where Hunter stood, was a series of open archways that led to a wide balcony. Beyond that, Hunter could see the sprawl of the city.

Dax followed to stand at his side. He gave him a dubious sidelong look. "You think the witchstone is here?"

"Stands to reason, right? It's their private chambers. The most secure location in the castle."

Dax said with an approving nod, "But the illusion would require more witchstone than we could hope to run off with."

"I wondered the same thing. Which is why I have a different idea. Quinnar said something about how the imposter would need something of my mother in order to create such a convincing illusion."

"And you know what that is?"

"My mother's hand. In my world, she was missing half of her hand. I think they cut it off to use for the illusion before they sent her through the portal. Which means it has to be here. Near the source of power. In one of these rooms."

Dax nodded approvingly. "We find it and destroy it."

"Yes. And that should put an end to the illusion."

Dax's face scrunched up in thought. "A good plan.

Assuming you're right. But she will not have it simply sitting out on the mantel."

"Which is why I brought this." Hunter pulled the amulet from under his tunic. "This is supposed to glow in her presence, right? We use it to track her down."

Dax's mouth pursed. He looked up to the ceiling, forefingers hooked on his exposed hipbone. "Zefora's hammer," he murmured, and without warning, he grabbed Hunter's leather breastplate at the armholes and pulled Hunter in close with surprising strength. His warm full lips pressed against Hunter's with sudden fiery intensity. When he eventually pulled back, he had a rare glint in his eye. "I'll secure the guards, you search."

Hunter moved into the chamber. He had no idea where to even start and there was a lot of real estate to cover. Where did you hide a rotting piece of hand? And did the witchstone need to be close to the source of the illusion, or could the two be strategically separated? He undid the chain around his neck and gripped the amulet. It was cold against the skin of his palm.

Shouts and cries from outside continued to drift in over the balcony. From the sounds, the explosion had set off real panic down below.

First, he looped around the perimeter of the chamber. He looked in urns and opened boxes, not expecting to find anything. It wouldn't be that easy. He dug deeper. He pulled the thick leather-bound books from the shelves, tossing them aside, then pulled the stacks themselves from the wall to make certain they didn't hide a false back, or that there were no secret passages concealed behind them. He rummaged through desks, emptying out each drawer onto the intricately tiled floor.

All the while, he held the amulet out in front of him like a Geiger counter, looking for any change in the red stone, any sign of glowing from within.

Dax finished securing the guards with curtain ties and

dashed off down one of the hallways.

They were losing time. The sounds outside were tempering. They were less frenetic now, more orderly. Shouts of command were getting people in line. Hunter couldn't help but wonder if the other prisoners had made it out. Or had they been recaptured? Or worse. He continued to ravage the room at a fevered pace. He tore tapestries and paintings from the walls, hoping to uncover a hidden compartment. He overturned the chairs and the settees, ripped open the fabric underneath with his dagger, and pulled out the stuffing.

Nothing.

He stood in the center of the chamber, elbows bent, sweeping his gaze over the mess. He was missing something. There had to be some place that he hadn't thought to check. But he didn't know where else there was to look.

Maybe he was wrong about the amulet. Maybe for it to work, his mother had to be alive.

He looked down at the elaborate medallion at center of the room.

The floor. It was the only place he hadn't thought to look.

The medallion was constructed of at least five different types of stone. Red onyx and olive-colored jade formed a feathered designed that traced the perimeter. The inside was a pattern of swirling overlapping circles. The seams between the stone inlay were flawless—it didn't seem possible that it could be hiding secret compartment. It was more likely to be under one of the larger tiles around the edge of the chamber. But it would take forever to try and pry up every stone tile around the room. Time they didn't have.

But he had to try. Perhaps there was some telltale sign on the edge of the stone that indicated it had been pried up before. He began to step from the middle of the chamber, but then stopped. Something about the stones in the medallion triggered something in his head. He crouched and touched a piece of the lighter-colored stone. It was similar to mother of pearl but had an unusual translucence about it, and radiated hints of different colors.

"Holy fuck," he mumbled.

Dax wandered back into the chamber, shaking his head. "Nothing. There's nothing in any of the bedchambers." He glanced over at Hunter standing frozen in the middle of the chamber. He must have seen something in Hunter's expression, for he stepped closer, his chin lifting. "You found something."

Hunter nodded. "The floor."

Dax dashed over and lowered down onto one knee next to Hunter. He took in a sharp breath. "Hidden right under our nose."

"Witchstone?"

"Yes." His eye traced the entire circumference of the medallion. "I've never imagined so much."

"Enough to sustain her illusion?"

"For a century," Dax said.

"Then the hand must be nearby."

"Hunter," Dax said, grabbing him by the wrist. "The amulet."

It wasn't until that moment that Hunter realized he felt a warmth against his palm. He opened his hand. The stone glowed faintly red from the inside. He lowered the amulet closer to the floor and the stone glowed brighter.

His heart lurched.

Dax looked at him. Then at the amulet. "We need to find something that can break up this floor."

As Hunter and Dax lifted to their feet, the door to the chamber burst open and several guards rushed in. Hunter was looking down the shafts of five crossbows pointing directly at him.

35

HUNTER'S BLOOD went cold.

Dax took a step forward. "Hunter," he said low and deep in his throat, "when I make my move, sprint for the balcony. Fast."

"Forget it, Dax. I'm not leaving you behind." Besides, they were at least three floors above the ground. He wouldn't be able to simply jump down. And if he did survive it, what then?

"Do it," he growled.

"No."

A woman stepped forward from behind the line of guards. Hunter's heart twisted as she came into view. The queen. Her likeness to his mother was so flawless he wanted to run to her and throw his arms around her. Her dark hair was longer than he'd seen it, and she wore an extravagant red gown that his mother would have laughed at and called over the top. But the bright green eyes and smile lines around her mouth flooded Hunter's mind with memories he'd long tried to suppress.

But not everything was like his mother. She moved with

a sultry sway of her hips. And the smug smile stretched across her lips carried no warmth.

"Well, now," she said. "Appears we have visitors." Her voice sent ice racing over Hunter's arms and shoulders. It wasn't his mother's warm voice at all. The imposter could mimic his mom's appearance, but apparently couldn't disguise her own true voice. "You've had a busy day. Looking for something, are you?"

Hunter made a quick scan beyond the row of guards. The king was there, too, loitering in the background and inching his way along the wall. He was a large man, matching Hunter's own height, and his face bore a proud and robust beard. But the man visibly quaked. His hands were pulled up to just below his chin, and his eyes darted from the imposter, to him, and then Dax.

"Nice little trick getting the other prisoners out," she said. "Like to know how you managed it, but I know you won't say anything, so I'll make peace with the mystery." She took a step closer and shook her head. "You really should have made off when you had the chance. But it hardly matters anyway. We will round up your friends again soon enough."

"We will stop you," Dax told her.

"It's charming that you think that." Her hand drifted across the bulge around her middle. "You see, I've already won."

The guards brought the crossbows up a little higher.

"I wanted to make your death a beautiful public spectacle, but I'll not risk putting you in a dungeon again. Your head on a pike will have to do. Kill them."

Hunter involuntarily took a step back as he watched the guardsmen curl their fingers around the triggers of the crossbows. Her narrowed eyes bore down on him with hate. Hunter could feel a bead of sweat trailing down the small of his back. How sad would it be that that was the last sensation he felt before a bolt entered his heart?

The guard to the far right of their firing squad made a

sudden grunt and spasmed, arching his back. The crossbow fired, and the bolt shot up to the ceiling. It took out a chunk of stone as it ricocheted and flew out over the balcony.

The guard made a pathetic gurgling sound as he stumbled forward. An arrowhead protruded out from the base of his neck above the collarbone.

Other guards fired their bolts as well, but the unexpected distraction threw their aim. One bolt sailed wide of Hunter. Another hit the floor at Hunter's feet and left a sizable divot. Dax twisted to avoid a third, but it grazed his upper arm, leaving an angry gash that immediately started to spill bright crimson down his arm.

A battle cry exploded from the corridor. The guards spun about to meet the charge of resistance fighters flooding into the chamber. The first that broke the threshold was Zinnuvial. She abandoned her bow for a long sword and threw herself into the fray.

The postern door. She had followed him in like she promised she would and brought with her what appeared to be a small army. Corrad sprang in behind her.

Dax lunged for the fallen guard and stripped the corpse of his short sword. He looked back at Hunter. "I fear your wish of no bloodshed may have expired."

"Fuck them. Those assholes were actually going to shoot me." Hunter rushed to his side and grabbed his arm. "Dax, you're in no shape to fight."

"Dig up that hand." And he broke the grip Hunter had on him, and he launched into the fight.

A new cry rang out. More of the castle's soldiers were spilling into the room. Swords clashing and men shouting brought the volume to a deafening pitch. For Hunter, the sudden and frenzied turmoil had an unexpected familiarity to it. Like being on the pitch in the middle of a match. The commotion made sense to him—the way guards and rebels squared off like they would at a line of scrimmage. Only this was bloodier. Many would not walk away from this.

332

He spun about to scan for something heavy enough to break the stone. A black iron candleholder stood on a side table. A winged fairylike creature posed seductively on a wide square base and held up a flat platform. Hunter tossed aside the wide yellow candle on the top and hoisted up the big ugly thing. It was solid and even heavier than it looked. He turned it in his hand to position the corner of the base and gave it a mighty swing downward.

The corner struck the stone floor with a gunshot-like crack. Hunter expected it to jar everyone to a stop, but no one even seemed to notice. Except the queen. She'd retreated near her massive fireplace and was pressed against the wall, protected by several guards, but she glared at Hunter with fire behind her eyes.

"Stop him!" she cried. But guards had formed a protective circle around her and were too busy fighting back the hard press of resistance fighters.

Hunter gave it another swing. And another. The blows had little effect. The candlestick's corner chipped the stone at the impact point. A crack materialized down the center of one of the stone pieces. But the mosaic was largely undamaged.

He shifted his weight to one foot and brought it around in a wide circle over his head. The end picked up speed and momentum. At the apex of its flight, he put the strength of his arms behind it and brought it down.

His hands vibrated and stung with the impact. Stone fragments shot off in all directions like bomb shrapnel. Reflexively, he closed his eyes and turned his head away and felt the sting as shards struck his face and arms. He looked down. The floor had a divot the size of a golf ball.

Now he was getting somewhere. As he leaned back to give it another pounding, he heard Dax shout his name.

A guardsman had peeled away from the melee to confront him, his sword high. Hunter swung the iron statue like a bat. The base struck the man's forearm and Hunter heard the distinctive crack of breaking bone. The blow sent the sword spiraling through the air like a missile out of control, and the guard cried out and tried to turn and pull in his arm.

Hunter followed up with a backswing. The iron base struck the shoulder of the same arm as he attempted to pull himself away. Hunter heard a sickening crunch that sounded like thick ice breaking underfoot.

The guard spiraled about one full turn and collapsed.

For a brief moment, Zinnuvial was in his line of sight. She faced two attackers, both pressing her hard. Her face was rigid, but calm. Corrad was visible too. A guardsman had moved in too close—Corrad bashed his head into the man's forehead. Corrad laughed as the guard went down.

As always, this was just a game to him.

Hunter didn't see Dax anywhere. Bodies littered the ground, and a gruesome tide of crimson spread across the stone. His stomach dropped. No—he wouldn't have gone down that easily. Even as injured as he was. Hunter wanted nothing more than to find him among the chaos—confirm that he was all right—but he fought the impulse and returned his attention to the task at hand. He got two more swings into the floor before another guard came at him.

The new opponent was more cautious, easing in slow and deliberate. Hunter dropped into his defensive stance. He brandished the candlestick in front of him, feeling slightly ridiculous. The guardsman made a slow grapevine left, then right, a smirk lifting the corner of his mouth. Even with his size, Hunter couldn't have looked all that threatening with an ugly and cumbersome *objet d'art* as his weapon. The guard burst in with a curt downward cut aimed for Hunter's neck. The heavy candlestick was too unwieldy for quick defense, so Hunter pivoted backward instead. The sword's edge sliced past Hunter's shoulder with only inches to spare.

The guard stepped in, closing the distance between them, and spun the sword around over his head, this time bringing the blade straight down. Hunter grabbed the loose end of the candlestick with his other hand and held it aloft in front of him.

Sparks flying, the blade sheered sideways and wedged under the wings of the fairy creature hugging the central post. The blade snagged. A moment of panic sparked in the guard's eyes. He leapt back to slip the sword free again.

It was the opportunity Hunter needed. He pushed in and made a hard thrust with one side of the candlestick while the guard was still within range. The corner of the base smashed into the man's temple.

The guard staggered backward, arms turning boneless and eyes rolling back. He made a drunken stagger as if trying to recover, then dropped to the floor.

The fake queen continued to screech for someone to stop him while Hunter resumed the task of pounding on the floor. He tried to block out the roar of the battle around him, like he would on the pitch, but it was hard to ignore the number of bodies strewing the floor. The blood oozing out from beneath them. Too many people were dying. Too many of them resistance members. Their numbers were dwindling.

Between swings he searched for Dax, his heart bracing itself for the sight of him on the floor with the others. But he couldn't find him.

This was the bloodshed he'd hoped to avoid. This was his fault. And he had to put a stop to it.

He had to keep going.

The hole was growing, but too slowly. He threw all his strength behind it. Again and again. Pounding away at the stone. His hands were blistering. Bleeding. The candlestick was slipping in his grip. Each new swing brought more sharp stinging in his palm, and the metal edges cut into his skin.

He glanced up again. The queen had snatched a sword from one of the fallen and attempted to push past her protective wall of guards. She was going to go after Hunter herself. But the guards would not let her pass. With arms extended, they implored her to stay back.

The king, in his strange disconnected state, seemed almost unaware of the carnage. He'd fallen to the floor, crawled past the fireplace, and took refuge behind a padded stool.

Hunter again put the full strength of his arms and shoulders into a downward chop. Something felt different. The impact reverberated through the mosaic pieces. The grout fractured into dust and the stones shattered. The force shot outward in a wave. Fragments launched into the air.

Hunter discarded the candleholder, which clanged like a bell clapper as it hit the floor, and he fell to his knees. With his bare hands, he raked out the fragments, forced his fingertips under the broken pieces surrounding the hole, and pried them up one at a time. Shards cut into his already bloody hands, but he ignored the stinging pain and tossed the pieces aside. His fingernail caught something—fabric. He dug harder with frenzied desperation. He swept away the rocks and dust that were beneath the wreckage of the tiles.

A sack.

He pinched strands of the loose-weave fabric between his forefinger and thumb of both hands and pulled. The fabric ripped. It was still wedged in too tight.

He had to clear more away. Still on his knees, he took hold of the candleholder once more and used the corner of the base to break the stone around it. He tried again, but the sack was still too tightly packed into the hole. The fabric only ripped and wouldn't slip out.

Hunter dug into it. What he'd thought was more stone inside was instead dull white crystals. Rock salt.

Is heart lunged into his throat. With two fingers, he prodded into the bag with greater fervor.

A fierce cry of rage behind him announced that the imposter queen had broken loose from her protectors. He rolled onto his side just as the sword descended. It struck the fragments of stone not inches from his head. Spitting shrapnel from the impact pelted his face.

The image stabbed at his heart. His mother was trying to kill him with a sword. He knew it wasn't her—but his brain still couldn't process it.

She made another chop down at him. Hunter rolled, sharp edges of broken tiles cutting into his back. Again, the blade edge slammed against the floor, barely missing him.

He swung his leg in a desperate lateral kick. His shin caught her midcalf, and it sent her tumbling backward. She hit the floor on her shoulder and upper back. An angry and pained yelp burst from her mouth.

Hunter winced, and his stomach clenched. He didn't want to hurt her. She was pregnant, for fuck's sake. But what was he to do? She was trying to chop off his head.

For the moment, she was out of action. Her face was contorted as she squirmed in pain, and she retracted her sword arm against her side. Hunter lunged across the floor and snatched the hand that gripped the hilt before she had time to recover. With a bend of his own wrist, he twisted her hand back. She cried out and her fingers released the hilt. Hunter snatched it the moment it was released, and he tossed it across the room. It hit he floor twenty feet away with a clangor.

Her face red with unabashed rage, the imposter queen lashed at him. Her hand transformed into a twisted bestial shape with long vicious claws. She swiped at his head. He turned, but one claw caught him across the cheek and he immediately felt the flow of warm blood spill from the gash. Hatred shot from her eyes like venom as she tried to rise. Eyes that Hunter had never seen with anything but compassion, patience, and love. It was an ugliness so foreign, it made his throat constrict.

His hand contracted into a fist. All it would take was a solid punch to that imposter's face and it would be over, but he couldn't bring himself to do it. Even though it was tainted with malice, the face was still too much like one he loved.

He shoved her back and launched himself away from her, back toward the hole in the floor.

Frantic, he scooped more rock salt out of the hole. His fingers reached in deeper. With a shrill screech, she was on his back, clawing and pounding on him. The claws raked down his back and sudden pain erupted on his ear.

She was biting him.

He twisted and jabbed his elbow up at her. He hit something hard, likely her forehead. She was knocked back, but she held tight to him.

His fingers unearthed something. Something dry and leathery. He had a second, maybe two, before the queen recovered from the blow. He prodded deeper, his skin scraped from the sharp edges of the crystals. The knuckle of his forefinger curled around the buried object and as gently as he could, he slipped it out of the salt.

It came out as one piece. The gnarled, mummified remains of half a hand.

His mother's hand.

It was exactly the part that was missing from her. The part they had chopped off to use for their illusion before she was banished into his world.

"No!" the fake queen screamed in his ear. She pounced for it from her perch on his back, but he shrugged her off and rose to his feet. He turned to face her as she stared up at him with loathing.

"Give that back," she hissed.

He held the hand in his palm. It weighed nothing. It was shriveled and dried, but it was her. He could tell somehow. It was his mother. Tears stung his eyes.

"I will destroy you," the woman screeched at him. "You will perish a thousand deaths by the time I'm through with you. We will not fail."

He his gaze swept the room. The fighting had tapered to a stop. The palace guardsmen, the resistance, everyone stood in a loose half circle, watching. "You already have," he whispered. He stood very still, the shriveled fragment resting in his palm.

The fake queen sneered back at him. "We shall see." She rose to her feet. Blue sparks erupted from her fingers.

"All you'll do is expose yourself as the fraud you are."

"Not if I kill every witness here. These men are nothing."

Hunter could feel the confusion sweeping the room. The guards who only moments before were defending her were now beginning to realize they'd been duped.

"Even the king?"

"He sees only what I let him see. You cannot win." The sparks shot out farther. Hunter could feel the energy lift the hair on his arms. She was standing on a wealth of power to draw from. Who knew how much destruction she could unleash?

The sparks grew to small bolts of blue lightning that raced across the floor, across the pieces of witchstone embedded in the medallion. Everyone stumbled back away from her and pressed themselves against the wall.

One soldier made a run for it. He dashed for the exit, but the door slammed shut as he approached it. He heaved on the handle, but the door wouldn't budge. She'd trapped them all inside.

"Hand it over," she said.

Hunter didn't move.

She snarled at him. "I won't ask again."

A sharp clack and whoosh came from somewhere behind her. Hunter looked over to see Dax with a crossbow pressed against his shoulder. Almost distractedly, she lifted her hand, and the bolt exploded to ash just before it struck her.

If she wanted him dead, he would be. There was nothing stopping her. Except the fragment of hand he was holding. She was afraid of destroying it with her power. The strange blue lightning would incinerate it.

"Come and take it from me," he said.

Her face contorted with fury, her lips pressed into a hard, white line. Then her narrow eyes lit up and widened. A sinister grin lifted the corner of her mouth. "I don't think I'll need to. I think you'll hand it right over to me." She turned and scanned the crowd of survivors. Then she lifted her finger and pointed directly at Dax.

"I think I'll start with him. Give me her hand or I will make you watch as I cook him to a blackened husk." The lightning shot out in a sudden flare.

Hunter locked his gaze on Dax, who with wide eyes shook his head, silently imploring him not to give it to her. Hunter knew he wouldn't be able to stand there and watch her kill him. But he also knew that the moment she had it back into her possession, they were all dead anyway. She'd already admitted she'd eliminate every witness if she had to.

His heart splitting, Hunter knew what he had to do. He had to destroy the hand. And fast.

He could crush it to dust in his hand, but he had no idea if that would be enough. He couldn't take the chance. The flesh had to be destroyed.

He swung his gaze about the room in a wild search. There had to be something close enough that he could use to destroy it. He needed fire. But no torches or lit candles were anywhere around him. The only fire source was the fireplace across the room.

He'd never make it there in time. Dax would be dead before he made it halfway across the room.

The fake queen was lifting her hands, ready to unleash the blue storm on Dax. Others around him were backing away.

On the floor, not far from his feet, Hunter spotted a ceramic vase.

It was nearly the same size as a rugby ball.

He dove for it. The fake queen spun about at his sudden movement, but it was too late. He had already snatched it from the floor and shoved the hand inside. Holding it in two hands at the sides, he cocked his arms back. Then, he lunged forward, spinning the vase as it was released from his hands.

Hunter had never been the greatest ball handler. He was a forward, built for defense. He could run, tackle, carry the ball if he had to, but his main job was to put himself in the way of people trying get to the ball. But when it came to the passing the ball around, it was never his strength. His spin pass was always wobbly and tended to veer left.

And the fireplace was across the entire chamber. If it missed, all she would have to do was walk over and pick it up from the floor among broken shards of pottery.

But the vase flew straight. Like a cannonball.

It sailed level for about half the room before it began to arc toward the floor. The vase was heavier than a standard rugby ball. He'd misjudged the throw. He hadn't thrown it hard enough and it wasn't going to make it to the fireplace.

Hunter held his breath. The fake queen, too, watched with horror in her eyes as the vase cut across the room.

The vase hit the floor ten feet from the opening.

And bounced.

Hunter heard a crack. But somehow, miraculously, the vase didn't shatter. A piece of it shot off at a tangential angle, but the integrity of the vase remained intact. It tumbled, flipping over several times, and Hunter waited for the hand to fly out of the opening. But nothing came out.

The vase hit the stone back of the fireplace and exploded in a shower of ceramic chips. The fire flared briefly—the small dry hand incinerating in an instant—and returned to normal as if nothing happened.

The fake queen stumbled back in disbelief. Her eyes were fixed on the fireplace, the blue energy fading from her fingertips. The transformation began immediately. The countenance of his beautiful mother contorted into features that were hard and stern. Deep lines cut around thin lips and narrow eyes. The skin fell ashen. His mother's auburn hair turned black as coal, and horns twisted out of her temples.

"Now it's over," Hunter growled, stepping closer. A strange sense of relief washed over him. His mother's image and memory were no longer being defiled by this wretched creature. She was gone, as it should be. "Even if you kill us, your con game is over."

The Heneran sorceress glared at Hunter with seething

hate. She said nothing in return. Her chest rose and fell as her fingers flexed. Hunter could tell she was considering doing that—killing them all. Or at least him. He could see her need for retaliation burning behind her gaze.

She sprang unexpectedly. Hunter flinched back, readying himself for an attack. But instead of coming for him, she reached for the floor and grabbed a sizable chuck of loose witchstone. Screeching an incantation in a language Hunter didn't understand, she held the iridescent stone aloft. The witchstone burst with dazzling blue light. A clap of thunder reverberated through the chamber. A wave of air pushed Hunter backward. On impulse, he shielded his eyes.

When Hunter lowered his arm again, she was gone.

36

THE ROOM was silent. For a moment only. Then it erupted into chaos.

Some ran over to the king. Others ran over to Hunter. A few more lowered around those injured on the floor, checking to see if they lived. The enmity and strife that soaked the chamber only moments ago was gone.

Hunter felt hands on him. Someone slapped him on the back while someone else tugged on his shirt. Everyone seemed to be talking to him at once. But Hunter couldn't process it. His vision was a blurry turmoil, and the world had slowed down.

There was movement in the crowd around him. His vision focused enough to spot Zinnuvial and Dax as they pushed others aside to reach him. Dax grabbed Hunter's forearms and stared up at him, his eyes glossy and wide.

"Are you all right? Are you injured?"

"Me?"

Dax had been moments away from being incinerated, and he was worried about him? Hunter allowed himself a long exhale. With Dax near him again, his senses seemed to clear.

"I'm good," he told him. And the energy he was using to stand abandoned him all at once, and he dropped to one knee. After everything he had been through in a single day—starting with the swim through the water intake, ending with a showdown with a sorceress—he was officially on empty. Spent.

Dax dropped next to him, arm around him to keep from falling over. "It's over," he said. A hand slipped behind Hunter's neck and fingers wove through his hair. "You did it." He didn't seem to believe it himself.

Hunter looked up at the carnage around him. "At what cost," he replied.

"There is always cost in war," Zinnuvial said from behind Dax. "But it is now paid, and we can return to the life we knew."

"But… but she got away," Hunter sputtered.

"It no longer matters," Dax said. "She can do no harm now." He brought his forehead to rest against Hunter's. He dropped his voice to a whisper. "Hunter, you saved us all."

Hunter tried to smile but couldn't muster the strength. "I did it for you."

"I know."

The crowd around them shifted, and Hunter felt the change. People parted, clearing the way for someone. He lifted his head to see the king limping toward him, assisted by his guards. He was a large man, and would be nearly equal in height to Hunter if not for how he crouched forward weakly. Through a tight brow, he kept his eyes on Hunter as he approached.

Dax noticed the king's approach, too, and peeled himself away from Hunter. "Your Majesty."

"Move aside," one of the guards barked at the crowd around Hunter. Everyone leapt to obey, and a pathway opened for King Ruzad to advance.

Hunter and Dax exchanged a look, and the two of them rose to their feet.

Ruzad shuffled forward. He paused a few steps away and raked his eyes over Hunter. His mouth opened but it was several moments before he formed any words. "You'll forgive me," he said. "The effects of her sorcery still linger in my mind."

Guardsman and members of the resistance alike stood in charged silence, shock and bewilderment etched across every face. Everyone looked as if they'd been awakened from the same dream as they tried to process the events they'd witnessed. Some shook. Some stared at the blood on their hands. Some had quiet tears streaming down their faces. All eyes were on their king.

Ruzad made an unbalanced step forward. The guards flinched, seemingly confused as to what to do, but it was a resistance fighter who hurried in to offer support by sliding under Ruzad's arm and taking his weight upon his shoulder. Ruzad glanced at the man and nodded before he returned his attention to Hunter. "Who are you?"

"Hunter. My name is Hunter. Your Majesty."

"Hunter." King Ruzad repeated his name as if that meant something to him. His eyes scanned the silent crowd as if only becoming aware of them. "It is as if a fog has been lifted from my eyes. I know not how long I've been under her heel, but the effects are fading. There is much unknown to me. But I know that because of you, I am liberated."

Hunter didn't know what to say. He squirmed a little. "Err… it was a team effort, really."

Each moment that passed, Hunter could see the light behind Ruzad's eyes brightening. The frailty of before, the timidity, evaporated away, and Ruzad looked stronger. And he stood a bit taller.

"If that was not my queen, where is my Jenora?"

Hunter didn't think the room could sink any quieter, but all the air was sucked from the room with his words. No one dared breathe.

"Speak," Ruzad said in a low voice that declared he

would not suffer delay. "And speak true."

"She is gone, Your Majesty," Dax said, straightforward and direct, and without fear.

Ruzad turned his glare to Dax and something hard flashed in his eyes, but in a moment, it was gone. Hunter didn't know what reaction to expect. He would have thought it would be something more. But Ruzad's response instead was to fall very still.

Ruzad gently removed the hand of the resistance fighter who supported his arm, and he pushed his shoulders back. He already knew, Hunter thought. Somehow in his heart he knew. He was only waiting for the confirmation. And even in his current state, still rising out from whatever spell the imposter had him under, he had the uncanny poise to not show his grief here.

But Hunter, standing so near him, could see it nonetheless—pain that cut deep. He could see the shift in his energy, and in the way his eyes darkened. And in the way his lower lip, tucked inside beard, tightened and quivered.

Dax's words sent a ripple through the surrounding crowd as well. Guardsmen, believing they were simply following the orders of the queen, were now grappling with the reality that they'd been deceived all this time. That their queen was dead and they'd been doing dirty work for the imposter, and assisting in the subjugation of their own kingdom. The betrayal and loss began to register on their faces in expressions of horror and guilt.

"I will speak with the three of you," he said to Hunter, Dax, and Zinnuvial. "And you," he said to the nearest guard. "I will know what damage was done to my kingdom while my faculties were stolen from me. The rest, leave my chambers." For a moment no one moved, so Ruzad swept his eyes across them and raised his voice. "Now."

And the whole assemblage moved at once. In short order, the room was cleared. With the exception of the five of them and the numerous dead strewn about the floor. The carnage that remained made Hunter's insides sink.

"From your speech, you are not from Andreya." Ruzad walked about the center of his chamber, his eyes scanning the remains of the battle. His face was stone, showing nothing. He kicked aside one of the broken tiles that Hunter had pulled up from the floor.

"I am not," Hunter replied.

"From where do you hail?"

"Far away. From a place called Chicago."

Ruzad nodded as he righted a small table. "Strange that a man from so distant a land would find himself here, in my chamber, saving my kingdom from a Heneran plot."

"I kinda fell into it," Hunter replied. "Not by choice."

"All the same," Ruzad said as he turned about to face Hunter. "We owe you our gratitude. We will speak of reward another time. But rest assured your contributions today will be well remembered."

"That is not why I came here, Your Majesty."

"Regardless," Ruzad said. "I would like to learn what has transpired—" He stopped, eyes widening. "Where did you get that?" he growled. His lips tightened as he closed the distance between them in a span of a heartbeat. He reached out and snatched the amulet that hung around Hunter's neck. "Answer me now." The words dropped from his mouth like a slow beat of a drum.

Hunter felt the chain bite into the back of his neck. He seized Ruzad's wrist to keep him from breaking it free. Ruzad fought him, but Hunter's grip was too strong. Their eyes were locked.

"It belonged to my mother," Hunter replied.

Ruzad's nostrils flared. "Don't lie to me."

Dax stepped forward. He glanced up at Hunter, and then to Ruzad. "He speaks the truth, Your Majesty. I stole it from his chamber myself."

Something made Ruzad take in a sudden breath. He opened his fist to gaze upon the amulet, and color left his face.

The gem in the center glowed red.

"This isn't possible," he whispered. "You said she was dead."

"She is," Hunter replied. "I was with her when she passed."

"I… I don't understand. She must be here. The gem… it only glows when we are united."

United? Then Quinnar was wrong all along. It didn't just glow when she wore it.

"Zefora's hammer," Dax breathed.

"Where is she?" Ruzad said louder.

Hunter's eyes shifted involuntarily to the fireplace. Tiny shards from the shattered vase were strewn around the hearth. He'd destroyed what remained of her. He was certain of it. She wasn't anywhere anymore.

He felt Dax's eyes on him.

"She *is* still with us," Dax said. He put a hand on Hunter's arm. "She's in you."

"What are you talking about?" Ruzad demanded.

"Your Majesty, Hunter is son of Queen Jenora. There is your proof."

Ruzad released the gem and looked at Hunter from his feet on up. His confusion was understandable—he was likely only ten years or so older than Hunter. "Preposterous. This is some form of trickery."

"I realize this is hard to take in right now, Your Majesty. The Henerans sent Queen Jenora to another plane. One with a different timeline than here. During the time the imposter had taken her place, Queen Jenora lived a life in another world. Had a son, grew older, and died. Your Majesty, this is her son. He followed me back from their world when I stole the amulet from him."

Ruzad shook his head and stepped back from him. "Her son?"

As the distance increased, the amulet faded.

"Your Majesty," Dax continued, "there is more." His

eyes shifted hesitantly toward Hunter, and he took in a long, deliberate breath. "Hunter, the amulet glowed when you were close to Queen Jenora's hand."

Hunter was confused where he was going with this. "Right. That was how I found it."

"That's because there is a part of your father *in you*. Your father and mother were reunited then, and it made it glow."

Both Hunter and Ruzad stared at Dax, mouths open.

"My father?" Hunter said finally.

Dax's eyes shifted from Hunter's face to Ruzad's. "I can't believe I had not noticed it until now."

"Noticed what?" Ruzad commanded.

"The resemblance."

Zinnuvial stepped forward. "Yes. I see it too. The eyes. The jawline. Seeing you side by side, it is very clear…."

"Dax? What are you saying?" Hunter's insides were turning to jelly.

"Your mother was already with child when she was sent to your world."

Hunter's head was spinning. "No. I had a father. He left when I was young, but he was there."

Ruzad ran his fingers through the hair along the side of his head, and his eyes looked distant. "Jenora was with child once before. But the child was lost."

"Could it have been the imposter that told you of the miscarriage, Your Majesty? Not Queen Jenora?" Dax asked.

"I… I'm not certain. The haze of her spell was slow to take me. But yes, it is possible."

A wave of cold raced down Hunter's spine. The floor beneath him seemed to tilt, and his legs felt weak.

Dax closed his eyes and shook his head with wonder and incredulity. "Hunter, King Ruzad is your true father."

37

THE KNOCK on the door came gently, but it still jarred Hunter from his thoughts like a battering ram. He flinched, his chin launching off his knuckles, and he straightened in his chair. His thoughts of his mother evaporated as he was pulled back to the present.

His memories of her seemed different now. Occupying the sitting room that had once been her favorite brought a fresh closeness to her. This was the side of her that she'd hidden from him. His entire life he'd assumed it was a dark past that she was attempting to protect him from. But it was this. Loss, regret, homesickness. He understood her so much more now. Maybe now it would be easier to accept that she was gone.

He set the mug of honeyed beer on the table beside him and fought the urge to get up and open the door himself. It made guards outside flustered and uncomfortable, he learned. They were programmed to follow a certain protocol, and it wigged them out when Hunter colored outside the lines of accepted decorum. "Come in."

A click from the latch and Uri stepped in, stiff-backed and official. He was dressed in a formal doublet and hose, resplendent in the palace livery, his face clean and hair slicked back. The warm colors of the uniform brought out the blue in his skin. His expression was all business as he swung the door wide and stood with a lifted chin to the side.

"Master Dax, my lord," he announced.

Dax strolled in and he winked at Uri, who tried to maintain his stoicism, but the corner of his mouth broke and lifted. Dax whispered something to him that Hunter couldn't hear.

"She is recovering well," Uri replied. "Thank you for inquiring." Then Uri slipped out and shut the door behind him.

Dax made a cool scrutiny of the room. "Reaping the benefits already, I see."

"Don't," Hunter replied. "This wasn't my idea."

"I'm certain you fought valiantly against it." Dax circled around the room like it was a museum gallery. He fingered the drapes and pulled a leather-bound book from a shelf to inspect it, then slid it back into place. "An improvement from your tenement back in your own world, if I remember."

The comment stabbed at his homesickness. He missed his apartment. "And the hole I spent a week in."

Dax ignored that. "Your garments are also much improved, milord."

Hunter sighed. Why was he being a dickhead right now? He was acting distant. Aloof. "Again, not my idea. Took your sweet time in returning."

Dax looped around the table in the center of the room. "Much to do. The prisoners we rescued had to be reunited with families that were in hiding. Each safe house had to be informed of what happened and convinced the danger had passed. Took time."

Of course there was no one else to do that, Hunter thought. Not Quinnar. Not Zinnuvial.

Dax eyed the piles of delicate pastries, cheeses, and sliced meats displayed on ornate platters. "Help yourself," Hunter told him.

"Not hungry," he said, and he popped a grape into his mouth anyway. "So, you've taken Uri on as your valet. Certain you can trust him?"

Hunter bit the inside of his cheek and drummed his fingers on the arm of the chair. "How did you find out?"

"When we rescued his mother from the cell, her resemblance to Uri was undeniable. It was an easy leap to make."

"Anyone else know?"

"I've not told anyone. Why is he here?"

"Community service," Hunter replied. The guilt and shame the kid had to bear was enough punishment in his view. No one needed to know the truth, and Uri needed to be around to nurse his mother back to health.

Dax accepted the answer with the lift of an eyebrow. He loitered to a side table where a wine service was waiting. Dax poured himself a glass and lifted it Hunter's way. "To happy reunions," he said.

Hunter lifted his beer in return and took a sip, while inwardly sighing, begging for patience.

Dax seemed like a cat that could smell the dog nearby. It was exactly what Hunter had feared, that his newly acquired and uninvited aristocracy would be a wedge between them. Somehow, he knew Dax would hate that and be unable to see past it.

Hunter certainly didn't feel *noble*. He didn't ask for it and didn't want it. His whole life he'd had to fight to be included, fight for acceptance. Now he was the epicenter of everything—and the default was not only acceptance, but unearned deference. He hated it that he didn't have to work for anyone's approval anymore.

He couldn't imagine growing up like this. Had his mother never been sent away, this would have been the only life he'd ever have known. He hated the thought of that too.

But he hated even more that all of this had built a new wall between him and Dax. Hunter had to now decipher how high it was. And what it was made of.

"And how did things go with the king?" Dax asked.

The word made Hunter wince. "Strange," Hunter replied. It was the truth. Neither of them really knew how to navigate this. "Complicated." At least they had something in common. The loss of someone they loved.

A bit of Dax's guard came down as his eyes lowered to the chalice in his hand. "I'm not surprised. Has he accepted you as his son?"

"Mostly, I think. It must be hard to go from no children to discovering you have one that is an adult. The imposter queen has made him wary. I can understand that."

"You were instrumental in saving his kingdom. And his throne. That has to help."

"As were you."

Dax shrugged as if that detail was inconsequential. "Now that her spell on him is broken, and his faculties have returned, does he remember more?"

"Some," Hunter replied. "We compared details. He believes it was not the intent of the Heneran to send her to my world. That may have been a last-ditch effort by the court sorcerer to save her, perhaps hide her for a time. Apparently, the sorcerer has been missing in action for a while. And the timeline matches up with the imposter's arrival on the scene. Either he'd been killed, which meant no one was around to bring her back, or the sorcerer went with her. That seems more likely to me. She often spoke of a dear friend who lived with her and died before I was born. She was trapped there with no way to return home." Hunter leaned back in his chair. "Dax, you're pacing. Sit down over here."

Dax regarded him coolly and came no closer. "Have you spoken to him about political prisoners, and possible retaliation against any members of the resistance?"

"All being reviewed. That's what he said. Give him some time to wrap his head around all this. The man's been in a coma for year."

"We were trying to protect his kingdom," Dax replied, his voice hardening.

"He knows that. And appreciates it, I think."

"Yet no parades for those who fought her… or died."

"Dax, stop it. It's been one day."

Hunter had already pushed for Zinnuvial and Quinnar. She was quickly offered a command in the royal guard, and Quinnar a position in the court. Even Corrad was poised to land something respectable after the dust settled—even if Hunter wasn't convinced he deserved it.

Hunter could tell something was on Dax's tongue, ready to spill out. He was probably pissed that Hunter was defending Ruzad. Thinking that Hunter had already become one of them. Dax tightened his lips and didn't respond. Was he so accustomed to fighting that he was already picking a new fight? This time with the king? And him?

Hunter drummed his fingers on the arm of the chair for a time. The silence was painful, but he wanted to rein in his own trepidation first before he continued. There would be no turning back. "I want to talk to you about something."

Dax stiffened. He set the chalice onto the table and lowered his eyes to his boots. He wouldn't look at Hunter. "No need. I know what you have to say. He's offered to send you back. To your own world."

Hunter lifted an eyebrow. How was he always one step ahead of him? "Yes."

"And… with the amount of witchstone that was recovered from the royal chambers, the court sorcerers can effectively not only send you back but figure out how place you back at the time you left."

Hunter nodded. "That is what I am being told."

Dax distractedly swooped up the chalice again and drained it. "So, back to your old life. Picking up the threads right where you left off as if none of this had ever happened."

So… that's what this was about. Hunter forced himself not to respond.

"I appreciate you letting me know in person," Dax continued. He started toward the door. "I wish you well, milord."

Hunter stood from the chair. "Dax. Wait."

To Hunter's surprise, Dax came to a halt. Hunter wondered what compelled him to remain. Was it that Dax wanted to hear what he had to say? Or was he following a command from the king's son? "I need to know something. And I need you to be honest with me."

Dax lifted his chin before turning around to face Hunter.

"The night we spent together. What did it mean to you?"

Dax's face clouded with anger. "How can you ask that?"

"I need to hear you say it."

Dax looked at his feet. "Very well. Not that it matters now." His chin lowered, and he took in several long breaths. "Entering into something like that, it isn't easy for me. I am accustomed to being alone. Prefer it actually. But you have a power about you...." He stopped and closed his eyes. "That night was a mistake."

Hunter's heart constricted. "I see."

"It was a mistake," Dax continued, "because I allowed my own heart to open to you. I gave in to feelings that I knew I shouldn't have. And there is a price to be paid for that. But I do not regret it. That night meant everything to me and I will hold its memory forever."

Hunter's insides lifted as filled with helium, and he tried to restrain a smile.

"Do you love me?" he asked.

Dax's lips disappeared into a thin white line. "That isn't fair, Hunter."

"Answer the question."

He took a step forward. "It doesn't matter. I... I can't—won't—return with you to your world, Hunter. I am tied here, just as you are tied to your own world. I have agreed to help rebuild what was lost. I cannot turn my back on that."

"I'm not asking you to give any of that up," Hunter said

quietly.

Dax stared at Hunter several heartbeats, pain evident behind his eyes. Dax made a respectful bow. "I see. I misunderstood. Then, I wish you a safe journey home." Dax turned on his heels and headed back toward the door.

"Strange, isn't it," Hunter said to his retreating back. "You've always thrived on being the one who fights alone. As a part of the resistance, you've been forced to be part of a team, fighting against tyranny, but in a way you've never really wanted to belong, have you? Not really. It's why you took the mission to come to my world. Why you took on Quinnar's doomed mission to sneak in here. And me? I've always felt more comfortable as part of a pack, a grunt in the trenches with everyone else. But now here I am. Surrounded by powerful people who all want a nugget of my time. But I've never felt more alone."

Dax froze, and turned about slowly.

"The great irony, right?" Hunter continued. "I have to always find acceptance, and you need to be alone. What bothers you, I think…. No, what scares you, is that when you're with me, you don't want to be alone."

Dax eyes hardened as he stared back at him. "Nothing scares me."

Hunter chuckled inwardly. "For years, I never understood why I've never been able to make relationships work. The people I dated always seemed to want to segregate me from what I loved—a team. A pack. I needed the sense of belonging, the safe comfort. And everyone seemed to be threatened by that. But with you… it is different. You provide something for me that I need. That feeling of belonging. I can belong to something bigger, but still belong to you. And you challenge me. Like no one else has done before. And I like that."

"What are you saying?"

"I turned him down, Dax. I declined the offer."

Dax's head tilted to the side as if he hadn't understood.

"You're not returning?"

"I am choosing to remain here."

Dax's face shifted from hurt and frustration to confusion, which almost made Hunter laugh.

"Ruzad himself asked if I would consider staying." Hunter couldn't call him father. Not yet. That felt too strange. "Not as his son. His council is trying to come up with a way to explain me that the public can understand. A brother maybe. Or a nephew. Heir to the throne if something were to happen, but should Ruzad have another child someday, the new child would take my place. But more importantly, Ruzad wants me to head a delegation to begin peace negotiations with the Henerans."

Dax's mouth hung open, and he looked as if he'd been slapped. "After everything that has happened?"

"Precisely because of what had happened, Dax. This war between Andreya and the Henerans has lasted for a century and shows no signs of ending. How long before they try something like this again? And what if they succeed next time? I agree with Ruzad—the time has come for both sides to sit at the table."

"They are ruthless killers, Hunter. No peace will come."

"You are not alone in believing that. His own council is afraid that the imposter's influence is still affecting him in this decision. Which is why he wants me. I am a neutral party here, with no history or baggage to cloud my point of view." Hunter stood and walked closer to Dax. "I told him I would do this. On one condition."

Dax lifted one eyebrow.

"That you move in here. Into the castle. And be with me."

"Here," Dax repeated.

"I told him it is a package deal. You and me."

Dax took a step closer, his head tilted to the side. "And he agreed to that?"

"He did. Without hesitation."

Dax drifted a few steps, his legs seeming unsteady. "I was welcome here once before."

"You are again."

"You're willing to give up your home?"

"I suppose, technically, I am *from* here. I would miss certain things. Playing rugby. Thai food. The internet. But, honestly, there's plenty I wouldn't miss either. But if I went back, I would always miss you."

Dax's eyes took on a pained and troubled look. "Hunter, I don't think I'm suited as a courtier."

"And I am? Look, if I'm going to take on the role of diplomat and heir, I'm going to need someone in my corner I can trust. And there's no one in two universes that I trust more than you."

Dax still looked troubled. Unsure.

"At this time, while Ruzad tries to build a new relationship with the Henerans, he doesn't believe that your old post as scout would be the best idea. I'm inclined to agree. But your knowledge of them and their way of life would be invaluable to any effort during negotiations. Ruzad thinks that a role as my advisor would be better suited. If that's what you wanted. You can even have your own apartments here in the castle if you prefer—"

"You don't want me living with you?"

"Of course I do, you idiot. But if you're not ready to rush into this—"

Before Hunter could finish the sentence, Dax had crossed the room. His warm full lips were pressed against his, and strong hands reached around to grip Hunter at the center of his back. Hunter pulled Dax in tighter. He inhaled Dax's scent like a drag on a cigarette and relished in the taste of him on his tongue. He raked his hand into Dax's hair and gripped it tight, while the other slipped under Dax's tunic and caressed the silk-like skin of his back.

"Does this mean you accept the terms?" Hunter whispered against Dax's lips.

He felt Dax smile, and a little puff of laughter burst into his mouth. "I need some time to think about it."

Hunter gently bit down on Dax's lower lip, while his hand followed the shape of Dax's perfectly round ass. The curve of it felt like he was palming a well-inflated rugby ball.

"All right," Dax said. "I've thought it over. I agree."

"I'm not certain I believe you. You may need to work harder to convince me."

"My afternoon is free. I can spend the rest of the day assuaging your doubts if need be."

"It may require that. I can be hard to convince."

Dax's hand drifted to Hunter's groin and his fingers traced the line of his expanding cock. "Well, you're hard anyway."

Hunter bent forward and scooped Dax up over his shoulder. Dax yelled out in protest, but he really didn't put up any sustainable fight. Hunter carried him into the next chamber and threw him roughly onto the bed. Dax bounced on the mattress, arms flailing—then propped himself up on his elbows.

Hunter grabbed the heel of Dax's boot and held it firm while Dax pulled himself free of it. He tossed the boot to the floor and ran a thumb up the arch of Dax's naked foot. Even the shape of his foot was strong and beautiful. He bent down and kissed the ball of it, and ran his tongue up the arch. Dax's entire body shuddered. "You don't have any intention of sneaking off again while I'm asleep, do you?"

"Your Highness," Dax said, as Hunter removed his other boot, "if the prince were to order it, I would remain naked in his bed until the end of days."

"Consider it so ordered," Hunter said with a laugh, and lowered himself over Dax.

Acknowledgments

VERY SPECIAL thanks to Kimberly Gabriel, who relentlessly kicks my ass, tells me the honest-to-God truth even when it stings, and never lets me settle. I trust you more than anyone and my work is only good when you say it's good.

Also, this novel would never have made it off the ground were it not for the stalwart readers that suffered gladly through early drafts and offered such amazing and vital feedback. Thank you, Jessica Trent, Tye Radcliff, and Suzy Austin for your wisdom, insight, and fearless honesty. Your input is beyond invaluable.

I must also thank all those that are the veritable whetstone of my creativity, the ones that stretch my storytelling muscles week after week and never let me forget that the truth is in the tension. Thank you, TJ Austin, Robert Black, Jimmy Brown, Kimberly Dwan-Collins, Wallace Fajardo, Wesley Kinkaid, Rachel Loos, Tyler Ullrich, for sitting at my table and challenging me to be an ever-better crafter of characters and weaver of adventures. May your dice never fail you.

MASON THOMAS is the author of three other novels of speculative fiction that center on gay protagonists. He lives in Chicago with two extremely spoiled cats. He enjoys anything nerdy and his list of fandom is too long to include here.

Website:
masonthomasbooks.com
Social Media:
Facebook: www.facebook.com/MasonThomas999
Twitter: @MasonThomas999
E-mail: masonthomas999@gmail.com

More from Mason Thomas

A Lords of Davenia Novel

Auraq Greystone, once a military officer with a promising future, exists on the fringe of society. Accused of murder, Auraq is on the run from the ax—until two fugitives crash into his solitary life. One is a young man named Kane. The glowing marks on his arm pulse with an otherworldly power, and they have made him the target of a sinister organization called the Order of the Jackal. When the old man protecting Kane dies in an ambush, Auraq swears an oath to take his place.

But the runes are far more significant than they realize. They are a message from the shadow realm, a dark memory of the past—one holding evidence of a bloody massacre and its savage architect; one that will shake the kingdom to its foundation. Risking arrest and execution, Auraq fights to get Kane to the capital city where the cryptic marking can be unlocked. And with assassins close on their trail, Auraq might never get the chance to show Kane what's in his heart—or the way their journey together has changed him.

The Shadow Mark is an epic tale of magic, murder, conspiracy, betrayal, and—for the two men tasked with unraveling the mystery—love and redemption.

A Lords of Davenia Novel

Scoundrel by nature and master thief by trade, Mouse is the best there is. Sure, his methods may not make him many friends, but he works best alone anyway. And he has never failed a job.

But that could change.

When a stranger with a hefty bag of gold seduces him to take on a task, Mouse knows he'll regret it. The job? Free Lord Garron, the son of a powerful duke arrested on trumped up charges in a rival duchy. Mouse doesn't do rescue missions. He's no altruistic hero, and something about the job reeks. But he cannot turn his back on that much coin—enough to buy a king's pardon for the murder charge hanging over his head.

Getting Garron out of his tower prison is the easy part. Now, they must escape an army of guardsmen, a walled keep and a city on lockdown, and a ruthless mage using her power to track them. Making matters worse, Mouse is distracted by Garron's charm and unyielding integrity. Falling for a client can lead to mistakes. Falling for a nobleman can lead to disaster. But Mouse is unprepared for the dangers behind the plot to make Lord Garron disappear.

www.ingramcontent.com/pod-product-compliance
Lightning Source LLC
Chambersburg PA
CBHW071218300726
48975CB00002B/270